Berkley Sensation titles by Erin Quinn

HAUNTING BEAUTY

HAUNTING WARRIOR

HAUNTING DESIRE

HAUNTING EMBRACE

Haunting Desire

"Erin Quinn weaves pure enchantment in *Haunting Desire*."
—Kathryne Kennedy, author of the Elven Lords series

"Ms. Quinn's writing is the crowning glory of these books. It's chilling. It's intense. It's haunting. It's perfect for this alternate realm she's given us in this book as much as it is for the entire series. She weaves her story in and around and through you as you read. You become part of every emotion and feeling, every touch and look, every fight and betrayal. You feel it clear to the bone just as each character does."
—*The Good, the Bad and the Unread*

"Quinn impresses again with a time travel masterpiece. *Haunting Desire* has action, romance, and magic aplenty." —*Fresh Fiction*

"The relationship between Shealy, a modern woman, and Tiarnan, a warrior of the past, will melt your heart." —*RT Book Reviews*

"*Haunting Desire* is fast-paced and unique. Shealy and Tiarnan created a sexual tension to die for . . . I highly recommend."
—*Night Owl Romance*

"The plot is a delicious mixture of intrigue and suspense that left me flying through the pages to see the outcome. The ending is a stunning climactic finish." —*Smexy Books*

Haunting Warrior

"Erin Quinn has a notable talent for the complex and mysterious."
—Diana Gabaldon, *New York Times* bestselling author

"A highly recommended must-read!"
—Jennifer Ashley, *USA Today* bestselling author

continued . . .

"Edge-of-my-seat thriller." —*All About Romance*

"Ms. Quinn brilliantly weaves the past and present into a dazzling display of sword fights, honor, and a love that crosses time and touches your heart. This is an excellent time-traveling paranormal romance that is sure to please." —*Night Owl Romance*

"Lyrical writing, breathless passion, and mystical intrigue makes *Haunting Warrior* a must-read. It will literally blow you away."

—*CK^{2}S Kwips and Kritiques*

"I am just in total awe of Ms. Quinn's Haunting books. These first two books are some of the best I've read in the last year."

—*The Good, the Bad and the Unread*

"*Haunting Warrior* has it all—magic, mystery, and lots of beautiful, sweet loving." —*TwoLips Reviews*

"Brimming with magic, mystery, an originally creative plot, wonderfully complex and compelling characters, plot twists, nail-biting suspense, time travel, seductive passion, and true love, this novel will haunt you long after the last page is read and the book is closed."

—*Romance Junkies*

"A hauntingly beautiful series." —*Fresh Fiction*

"An enthralling read. Quinn's mélange of paranormal, time travel, and romance is outstanding!" —*The Romance Readers Connection*

"A powerful story of magic, betrayal, and redemption set in the luscious Emerald Isle." —*Smexy Books*

"A must-have, must-read author." —*Lovin' Me Some Romance*

"Rory [of *Haunting Warrior*] is one of my favorite types of heroes: alpha to the core, tortured, sexy, and honorable and loving when it comes to his heroine." —*The Romance Dish*

"Bewitching . . . Jaw-dropping, hard-hitting, and an exceptionally compulsive read from the word *go*." —*Over the Edge Book Reviews*

Haunting Beauty

"Erin Quinn writes with passion, power, and heart."

—Nalini Singh, *New York Times* bestselling author

"A complex, mysterious, and very satisfying story!"

—Diana Gabaldon

"An intriguing, highly absorbing book . . . I was completely swept away by the mystery, the magical ambience, the vivid setting, and the chilling and original plot." —Jennifer Ashley

"Erin Quinn weaves a mystical tale of intrigue and seduction . . . The imagery is breathtaking and the prose is beautiful and authentic . . . You live the story, not just read it."

—Calista Fox, author of *The Pleasure Principle*

"A dark and passionate romance with the literary brilliance of *The Time Traveler's Wife*." —Kathryne Kennedy

"A unique new paranormal series." —*The Romance Readers Connection*

"I love it when an author gives me something so different than what I've ever read before, and Ms. Quinn definitely does that. This is one of the best books that I have read lately."

—*The Good, the Bad and the Unread*

continued . . .

"I savored every page and still wanted to reread it when I reached the end." —*CK²S Kwips and Kritiques*

"Ms. Quinn has woven together a complex story with lifelike characters, seductive passion, and she's added a wonderful dash of magical mystery . . . *Haunting Beauty* is a book that you won't want to put down and leaves you breathless for more." —*Night Owl Romance*

"Fans of paranormal romance will relish this tale so rich with magic and mystery, especially those with a passion for Ireland."

—*Fresh Fiction*

"A superb debut . . . written against a backdrop of Ireland in all its lushness and myths. If you read one book this summer, don't miss this one! Fantastic!" —*Romance Junkies*

"Enthralled, entranced, rapt, take your pick. That's the effect *Haunting Beauty* had on me. I was completely ensnared in the web of magic so masterfully woven by Erin Quinn." —*Manic Readers*

"[It] enthralled and captured me . . . A mysterious and haunting story that absorbed and swept me away." —*Mom Musings*

"Celtic fans will enjoy this trip into the Irish mists, which had plenty of legends and mystical visions." —*RT Book Reviews*

"Filled with fascinating characters, wonderful detail, and the beautiful scenery of Ireland. Readers will be drawn in right from the start. I would recommend this book to fans of paranormal romance that enjoy mystical elements and edge-of-your-seat suspense."

—*Darque Reviews*

Haunting Embrace

Erin Quinn

BERKLEY SENSATION, NEW YORK

THE BERKLEY PUBLISHING GROUP
Published by the Penguin Group
Penguin Group (USA) Inc.
375 Hudson Street, New York, New York 10014, USA
Penguin Group (Canada), 90 Eglinton Avenue East, Suite 700, Toronto, Ontario M4P 2Y3, Canada
(a division of Pearson Penguin Canada Inc.)
Penguin Books Ltd., 80 Strand, London WC2R 0RL, England
Penguin Group Ireland, 25 St. Stephen's Green, Dublin 2, Ireland (a division of Penguin Books Ltd.)
Penguin Group (Australia), 250 Camberwell Road, Camberwell, Victoria 3124, Australia
(a division of Pearson Australia Group Pty. Ltd.)
Penguin Books India Pvt. Ltd., 11 Community Centre, Panchsheel Park, New Delhi—110 017, India
Penguin Group (NZ), 67 Apollo Drive, Rosedale, Auckland 0632, New Zealand
(a division of Pearson New Zealand Ltd.)
Penguin Books (South Africa) (Pty.) Ltd., 24 Sturdee Avenue, Rosebank, Johannesburg 2196,
South Africa

Penguin Books Ltd., Registered Offices: 80 Strand, London WC2R 0RL, England

This book is an original publication of The Berkley Publishing Group.

Cover illustration by Tony Mauro.
Cover design by George Long.
Interior text design by Tiffany Estreicher.

PRINTING HISTORY
Berkley Sensation trade paperback edition / October 2011

Library of Congress Cataloging-in-Publication Data

Quinn, Erin, 1963–
Haunting embrace / Erin Quinn.—Berkley Sensation trade paperback ed.
p. cm.
ISBN 978-0-425-24313-8
I. Title.
PS3617.U5635H386 2011
813'.6—dc23 2011023838

PRINTED IN THE UNITED STATES OF AMERICA

10 9 8 7 6 5 4 3 2 1

This book is dedicated to my dad,
the most honorable man I've ever known.
Though I'm sure the angels are rejoicing to have you with them,
I miss you each and every day, Daddy.

Charles Edward Grady, 1938–2011

Acknowledgments

My sincerest gratitude goes out to Kate Seaver of Berkley Sensation along with the fabulous Katherine Pelz, editorial assistant, and wonderful Kayleigh Clark, publicist. A special thanks to the amazing art department at Berkley Sensation, especially Tony Mauro, George Long, and Jim Griffin, for the fabulous covers on the Mists of Ireland series.

My deepest appreciation to Paige Wheeler, agent extraordinaire. So glad to be working with you.

Lynn Coulter, as always, I doubt there'd be a book without you. Kathryne Kennedy, I am so grateful to you and your magic wand. You both make me better than I am. Thank you. And of course I must thank my family and friends for all of their support, hugs, encouragement, and special delivery coffee. I am one lucky woman and I couldn't make it a day without you all.

Chapter One

STANDING on the deck of the small fishing vessel, Áedán watched the dark opening of the sea cavern at the base of the jagged shoreline. From here, it looked smaller than he knew it to be, but it called to him, a black hole that was at once ancient, threatening, and expectant. So many turning points of his life had played out in that cavern. In his mind, it had become a great, yawning beast waiting to devour what was left of him.

Even at this distance, he felt the dark power of it. In the short time since he'd come to this place, it had gnawed at him, taunting him to face it. So far, he had resisted, but now he sensed that something had changed within that hollow abscess. He could feel it in his bones, though he couldn't identify it.

High above the cavern, castle ruins teetered in crumbled disgrace, the desolate remains adding another layer to the menace that shrouded the cliffs. Slowly, he scanned their stark solitude before his gaze returned unerringly to the arched opening at sea level, where the icy tide surged in and out, in and out. Each suck and pull begged Áedán to come closer and impelled him to flee until he felt mad from the conflicting urges.

He'd been too long without emotions, without the trappings of humanity. Now the influx of so many disagreeing reactions left him feeling bound and burdened.

He forced himself to look away and focus on the fishing net in his hands. Since they'd docked in the bay an hour ago, he'd been cutting away the rotted sections and replacing them. It was a tedious, loathsome task—something he'd never imagined one such as he would be reduced to. He refused to consider that his present circumstances might be anything but temporary, though.

"Sure and isn't it like a woman," Mickey said, stepping out of the cabin and joining Áedán on the deck.

Confused, Áedán looked up at him.

"The cavern," Mickey went on pointing with his chin. "The way it hovers there just above the tide line, like a whore raising her skirts, teasing a fellow with little peeks of what's inside. Making him thinking there's a treasure there for the taking."

The bitterness in Mickey's tone hung as thick as the sea air. Mickey had no respect for women, especially his own pretty wife.

"Have you been inside the cavern?" Áedán asked.

"Aye. Couldn't resist it, could I now? Hadn't been on the island for a week before it had me slipping and sliding down to its mouth."

Áedán scrutinized the sharp features of Mickey's face and the flinty gleam in his eyes. "And? What did you find?"

"Not a fecking thing. Like a woman," he repeated cryptically and spat over the railing into the murky waters. "Lures you into a black nothing that pretends to be more. I couldn't wait to get out of there."

Áedán caught his bottom lip with his teeth, watching Mickey mask something that looked suspiciously like fear despite the dispassion of his words. He wanted to probe, to pry the tight lid off and see what lurked beneath his indifference. Had he sensed the inherent enmity of the place? The dark history that made it more than simply a sea cavern carved by time and nature?

"You're looking peaked, Mr. Brady," Mickey interrupted his thoughts. He eyed Áedán critically. "Are you under the weather, then?"

Mr. Brady. Áedán hadn't known where he was and—at first—couldn't remember how he'd come to be there when Mickey Ballagh had found him five days ago, washed up on the rocky beach. Mickey had asked his name and Áedán answered without thought. For too long he'd been known only as Brandubh, the Black Raven, the Druid, and he'd nearly announced to this stranger that he was the powerful entity of the ancient Book of Fennore—the being that had been feared by humans for thousands of years.

"Bra—I mean, Áedán," he'd amended quickly, using the name given to him at birth instead of Brandubh, his Druid name. "My name is Áedán."

Mickey had stared at him with narrowed eyes. "And would that be Brady, you were about to say?" he asked, knowing he hadn't gotten it right but inadvertently offering Áedán the cover he needed.

Áedán nodded. "Yes. Brady."

"You're a tad south, aren't you?"

Áedán shrugged, not sure what was meant by that.

"Ah, well. What's it matter? You speak a bit odd, but I won't be hiring you for your elocution, will I now?"

To that, Áedán said nothing. Mickey had put him to work on *The Angel* and questioned him no more. From that point on, he became Áedán Brady, and every day since then, he'd toiled like a slave for the privilege of sleeping in the surprisingly tidy berth below deck and taking meals with Mickey, his lovely, pregnant wife, Colleen, and his infant son, Niall.

It was incomprehensible that this had become his reality. That he, *Brandubh*, had come to this miserable existence.

"I am fine, Mr. Ballagh," Áedán answered Mickey's question now, looking into the big fisherman's ruddy face. "Just a bit seasick, I suppose."

"Aye?" Mickey frowned. Mickey was more at home at sea than on land.

The choppy tide roiled and then surged suddenly, tilting the boat to a dangerous angle, halting any other comments as Mickey hurried to check the lines securing her. "I can't say I've ever seen the bay like this," he said, eyeing it distrustfully before cutting his gaze to the man-made barricade—which usually subdued the fierce waves enough to create a safe harbor—and then back to the cavern for a drawn moment.

At last Mickey tilted his head back and studied the sky. "Would you look at how fast that storm is moving in? Best batten the hatches, else it will be on us before we've a hint of what's in store."

It was much more than a storm approaching, but Áedán didn't say it. He didn't know what came under its guise, even though it rasped against his senses like the scales of a serpent slithering through the night.

He picked up the knife he'd been using, intending to sheath it so he could help Mickey, just as a more violent surge slammed the boat. The knife jerked across his other hand, cutting it deeply. Immediately blood began to spill from a long slice on his palm and drip to the deck beneath his feet. It caught him by surprise, the sight of his own blood. He could not recall the last time he'd seen it.

His involuntary curse had Mickey hurrying to his side. "Ach, looks bad, lad," Mickey said, whipping a soiled handkerchief from his pocket. He gave it a dubious glance and then wrapped it around Áedán's hand anyway. "You best go on to the house and tell the missus to patch you up. She's not worth much, that woman, but she can stitch as well as any doctor."

Áedán shook his head. The ship still needed to be readied before the storm.

"Don't worry on that," Mickey said, following his thoughts. "I'll finish it up and you'll have your meal and your bed just as if I'd had a full day's labor from you. It will all come out right in the end."

Áedán held to that thought. Yes, it would all come out right in the end. When he was restored, when he was once again as powerful as he'd been, Áedán would remember Mickey's act of kindness.

Gratitude. He frowned in disgust. *Another* emotion.

With a nod, Áedán stepped onto the weathered dock and strode away in the direction of Mickey's small house. With each step, the lure of the cavern intensified until he found himself turning toward it.

No, a voice of reason spoke sharply in his mind. *Do not go there. . . .*

But denying the cavern's silent summons seemed pointless and too cowardly—*too human*—to tolerate.

No matter that he answered to the name of Áedán Brady now, inside he was still Brandubh. The Black Raven. The most powerful Druid to ever draw breath.

As soon as he crested the first hill and was out of Mickey's sight, he veered off, his feet moving faster of their own accord as he headed to the ruins that landmarked the place to descend. The sky darkened and lightning split it into a thousand gray white pieces as rain began to pelt him with fury.

Filled with urgency, he fought down the pervasive dread that battered him like the sea against the cliffs. He did not know what waited in the cavern, what new turning point it had in store. But he refused to let fear control him. Never again would he allow anything—*anyone*—to rule him.

By the time he reached the point where he could see the ruined castle, he was drenched and out of breath. For a moment, he stilled, quaking inside as thunder exploded above. Emotions he couldn't begin to comprehend churned into foam and flotsam, miring any logic that might have surfaced.

Pausing at the top of the stairs, he gazed at the deteriorated slope of steps down to the rocky beach below. He knew it had been millennia since he'd hacked them out of the granite cliff, but seeing the eroded decay somehow made the sense of an eternity come and gone more real than ever. Yet he could remember clearly the feeling of dangling over that abyss, of laughing at the danger, the peril of a fall as he'd carved each descending tier. The stone had sparkled with hidden crystals, and the sun had favored them, favored *him*. He'd been Brandubh, the bold Druid. Powerful. Feared.

Betrayed.

The steps were nearly worn away and caked with moss and slime.

Treacherous in this storm, and yet he made his way down, trying to convince himself that his actions were his own. That he came because he was ready, not because he was compelled. The throbbing pain in his wounded hand kept him alert, kept him here and now when it felt like a thousand hooks had embedded in his skin with the lines attaching them stretched taut and towing him forward.

The storm had arrived with all the stealth and vehemence of his perdition. It whipped the sea into a tempest, and huge waves slammed against the beach, trying to shuck him out from between the rocks. They did not dissuade him. He was set now—determined to reach the cavern and face whatever it was that made a Druid fear.

He breached the point where giant boulders made rebellious sentries to the entrance, withstanding the rage of the tides. Then at last he stood in the small passageway that led into the cavern.

A shudder shook him from inside out, like the thunderous storm unleashed. Power crackled around him as he stood on the threshold and peered into the blackness.

By degrees, his eyes adjusted and he saw the shadows inside heaving and lulling with the fearsome waves, splashing a black tide pool up against the guard stones that surrounded it. For a moment, he took it all in, comparing every detail to his memory of them—the rough walls, the uneven floor, the oily pool that glittered like a thousand mirrors reflecting and refracting the waning light from outside. But it was the runes on the walls—endless spiral symbols that had burned into the stone—that struck him to the core.

Those symbols covered the Book of Fennore, had flowed over each of its cursed pages. Those symbols were embedded in his soul like scars upon scars.

It was here, in this cavern, that Áedán had breathed life into the Book of Fennore. Here, that it became a sentient being. Here, that the first, greedy, grasping human had sought it out in hopes of wielding its terrible power.

And here, that Áedán became its slave. . . .

He took a deep breath, wary now as he surveyed the cavern without crossing from the passageway into the interior. Eons had passed since he'd last stood on this brink. Time so endless that he'd forgotten the reason he'd been so determined to stay away. Now, as if under the beam of a spotlight, Áedán faced the truth.

This cavern wasn't merely a place to him. It was a cage, a prison, where memories of the hell he'd survived for millennia still lived, still breathed . . . still sought to bring him back into the fold.

What pierced him now was not a pervasive dread that might be shaken off by turning away. It was terror, bone deep and sharp as splintered glass.

The shock of it held him hostage for a moment. Terror. From the mighty *Brandubh.*

Sickened by the realization, he allowed his self-disgust to propel him forward when self-preservation fought to hold him back. Breathing deep of the wet salty spray, he advanced into the cavern.

Chapter Two

On guard, Áedán paused just inside and waited. A feeling like a soft breeze trembled around him, brushing his skin. For a moment, it seemed to leach the life from him. His legs wobbled, his vision blurred, and his head felt light and fuzzy. But just as quickly everything snapped back into focus, and he thought his imagination—his hated *fear*—had caused it.

Uneasy, he turned and surveyed the dark cocoon. Nothing moved. No slicing pain or debilitating pressure bore down on him. No vulnerability weakened his limbs. Only the steady beat of the tide and the rage of the ferocious storm broke the cloying silence. Carefully he opened his senses, testing the air, tasting the dark, seeking the danger he felt sure he would find.

Nothing. Only a vague sense of incompleteness that he couldn't define.

Relieved to the point of stupidity, he squared his shoulders and charged forward, wanting to laugh in the face of his enemy now that he had invaded its fortress. His triumphant laughter caught in his throat as he stumbled over something on the ground and nearly fell on top of it. On his knees, arms braced over the motionless form, Áedán stared in shock as recognition kicked him in his gut. A woman lay still as death on the cavern floor, her skin so pale it looked translucent, her arms and legs askew—as if she'd been dropped from above.

Meaghan.

She was so still that he thought she must be dead, and a startling sense of remorse tangled with his utter shock at seeing her again. But then she took a deep breath and her chest rose and fell.

Alive.

He did not like the relief that flooded him. He didn't care for the woman. He cared for only himself and his need to regain his power and take control of the bizarre circumstances that had brought him here. But he could not keep his fingers from brushing the soft skin of her cheek.

Meaghan.

He'd met her only days ago in the night world that belonged solely to the Book of Fennore. They'd been prisoners and allies of sorts. The world of Fennore existed in a realm most humans could not even conceive. Like heaven and hell, it was more a state of being than an actual place. But everything that had happened there felt horribly real . . . was, in fact, as real as the cold that seeped into his skin now. The world of Fennore was a nightmare that had the power to follow the dreamer into the light.

Áedán knew this better than anyone.

He narrowed his eyes at the female on the cavern floor. Could she be the reason he'd felt compelled to come here today? A mere human? Had she lured him here to trap him?

She looked frail and defenseless, yet he knew better than to forget that beneath that pallor lurked a feisty woman who'd almost broken his nose the first time he'd met her.

His gaze shifted to the full curves, the soft slope of her belly, bared where her T-shirt rucked up around her ribs. Dark, greenish bruises covered her arms, and a particularly nasty one spread upward from her hip bone, black and purple above the waist of her jeans. For a moment, the sight of her battered flesh touched off something inside of him. Sympathy? Compassion? Concern?

The alien emotions mocked him. He did not care about others, especially those who weren't of some use to him. For *eons* he'd been an entity, a thing that did not experience, did not rejoice, did not mourn. He'd lived to siphon the emotions of others, to drain them dry, make them so empty that they'd choose death over their hollow existence. But he'd *felt* nothing for them, for their plight, for their demise.

And he felt nothing for this woman either.

He cupped her cheek and let his thumb trace the soft bow of her lips. She stirred and he jerked his hand away. Her pale blue eyes opened in the darkness. She looked frightened, and with a groan, she tried to lift her head. It seemed the effort would take more than she had, but after a moment's struggle, she sat. She hadn't seen him yet, but her hands moved to tug her T-shirt back in place and smooth her hair in a self-conscious manner so unguarded that it made him pause.

She was not aware. Not of him. Not of the cavern. Not of the danger.

Leave, a voice inside him urged.

As if hearing his thoughts, she turned that clear, bewildered gaze to his face.

"Áedán," she breathed, and in the moment it took for the sound to whisper over his skin, he saw her expression change from puzzlement to recognition and then to something darker, sweeter. It surprised him even as it shocked a response from him. Her eyes widened and took on a shade of lavender that teased something in his ancient memories.

How long had it been since he'd known a woman as a man was meant to?

The stark answer filled his head. An eternity without end.

"What are you doing here?" he demanded, his confusion making his voice harsh, his infuriating fear still riding him.

Her eyes widened, wounded, and like a fool, he felt another wave of compassion. *Feck,* he thought, using one of Mickey Ballagh's words.

He leaned closer and she flinched, the small reaction like a flame held to his bare skin. "I'm not going to hurt you," he snapped. "How did you get here?"

She shook her head, and Áedán noted that her eyes seemed glazed and unfocused as she searched his features. Instead of answering his question, she placed one palm against the roughened stubble on his cheek and the other over his pounding heart. He found his own hands against the soft, rounded curves of her shoulders and told himself he meant to push her away.

He didn't, though. Instead he stood, gently pulling her to her feet with him.

When he would have stepped back, Meaghan held on to him and rose to her tiptoes, leaning into his body and brushing her lips against his in a caress as fleeting as it was riveting. Áedán froze, unprepared for the heat that licked his nerves and burned with his blood. A beast within him lifted its head and growled with satisfaction at the hot thoughts that filled him. Perhaps this woman did have use.

But he didn't understand what motivated her to touch him, kiss him, any more than he understood how she'd come to be here in the first place. When they'd met before, she'd been combative, berating him with little care for what he might do in retaliation. She'd had a wicked tongue that she'd used to lash out at her enemies. He'd expected that behavior from her now, but instead, her mouth moved over his again in a silken heat.

What game did she play?

He wanted to ask, but his brain had locked down, refusing any distraction from the sensuous slide of her skin against his. The hand on his cheek trailed to the base of his skull, and she pulled his head down, teasing his lips with her tongue—which was velvety soft, not wicked, not cruel—until he gave in and opened for her, pulling her body against the hard planes of his in the same simultaneous act of conquest and surrender. Her taste hit his senses like a whisper of hallowed memories, evoking the sultry languor of summer nights, the fragrant spice of misted fields, the perfume of female, aroused under a pale moon. . . .

Her soft curves molded perfectly against him, vanquishing any thought but keeping her there, yielding, responding, filling some hollow he hadn't known existed. She made a sound in her throat that set him on fire, made his hands hungry, his lips needy, his body parched.

It was his total capitulation that pierced the fog of want and made him hesitate.

This was not right. *She* was not right.

The Meaghan he'd known so briefly had been fire and hellion. She hadn't yielded to anyone, for anyone.

She opened her eyes slowly, confused by his hesitancy as she tried to pull him back into her embrace. Her gaze was unfocused, her pupils so huge they'd swallowed all but a thin strip of that beguiling lavender blue at the edge. None of that fierce spirit he'd come to grudgingly respect glowed within them.

Entranced, he thought. *Bespelled.*

She fought his efforts to set her away from him, her movements sluggish, not quick and able. This woman had brought him to his knees with two quick blows within minutes of meeting him, but now she seemed barely capable of standing.

"Meaghan," he said sharply, holding her at arm's length as she struggled to reach him. *"Meaghan!"*

He gave her a hard shake and then withdrew, needing space from her heat, from her soft scent, from her closeness. His body disagreed with his decision and urged him to take her—no matter what the terms. Have her, use her. She was only human, after all.

He scowled at his own surprising reluctance, but before he could decide what he meant to do about her, she stumbled over an uneven stone and lost her balance. He lurched toward her, trying to halt her momentum, but he couldn't reach her in time. Her shriek joined the echoes of his inner turmoil as she plunged into the icy tide pool.

She burst back to the surface and stared at him in shock. Her eyes were blue again, wide and snapping with anger.

"What the feck is wrong with you?" she shouted in a shaking voice. "You fecking pushed me!"

That was the Meaghan he knew. Quick on the defense, showing anger when fear might reveal a weakness.

"I did *not* push you, Meaghan. You fell all on your own." He quickly moved to the side and reached out to her. "Here. Take my hand," he ordered.

She flashed him a furious glare and swam to the side, ignoring his outstretched hand. "I don't need your fecking help," she said, the damp and cold framing her words in a vaporous cloud that hovered at her lips.

The injustice of the moment hit his fury and perplexity like oil-soaked kindling. To think, he'd thought of *her* feelings instead of simply taking what he wanted and leaving her to deal with her own circumstances.

"I didn't push you in and you know it," he said, still reaching for her, still confounded by the fact that he hadn't already stormed from the cavern.

Her eyes held defiance and fear. Her body shook with the cold. "Don't be stupid," he said. "You'll freeze to death if you don't get out."

"I-I k-know."

Meaghan, back to her familiar stubborn and irritable self, tried to haul her body from the pool, but the freezing temperature had already made her muscles stiff and her reactions slow. She hefted herself halfway and then slipped again.

Ignoring her feeble protest, Áedán gripped Meaghan by her arms and heaved her out of the icy waters. Cursing beneath his breath, he looked at the pathetic and bedraggled female and again he felt that alien tug of compassion swiping the feet out from under him.

She didn't want his help. He should leave her and call it a good riddance.

He sat her on one of the big flat boulders and hunkered down beside her, shrugging out of his coat and wrapping it around her as he began to rub her cold hands.

"How did you get here?" he asked as he worked.

"Wh-wh-whe?" she answered.

"Where? We are on the Isle of Fennore."

At the panicked look in her eyes, he shook his head. "No, not in the world of Fennore." Not the place where they'd met, where nightmares had been the only reality available. "I believe we have arrived in the year of nineteen hundred and fifty-six. I got here five days ago."

She absorbed this in silence, still shaking from head to toes. "Oth-oth—"

"No, I haven't seen any of the others." He searched her face, looking for hints of what had come to pass since those last, terrifying moments when they were together. "What happened to you, Meaghan? Where have you been since—"

The sound of a rock scuttling into the cavern behind him drew his attention and silenced the rest of his question. He stood and faced the passageway just as Colleen Ballagh—Mickey's young wife—stepped from the shadows into the cavern, a satchel in one hand, her baby in another.

He could not have been more shocked.

She wore a shapeless brown dress with a black shawl over her shoulders and serviceable shoes on her feet. Her hair and clothing dripped damply from the storm outside, which seemed to have abated, unlike his own storming rage. She paused as she crossed the threshold to let her eyes adjust to the dark.

"What are you doing here?" he demanded, too shocked by the sight of her to temper his tone or words. *With the baby in her arms, at that?*

Colleen ignored him as she peered through the gloom, anxiously hefting her son up on her hip, making a soothing noise in her throat. Then her eyes fixed on Meaghan, and she let out a gasp.

"Jesus in heaven," she exclaimed, staring at the shivering woman. "Were you in the water? But why? It's nigh on winter, girl. You'll freeze to death!"

As if the two of them couldn't have discerned that without her help, Áedán thought. Not even a brash woman like Meaghan would have chosen to dip into the frigid tide pool fully clothed.

"She slipped," Áedán said. "We need to get her warm."

Colleen didn't even glance his way. Instead she gaped at Meaghan as if she'd never seen a wet female before. Granted, Meaghan was a sight. The jeans she wore clung to her legs and the T-shirt had become a second skin, outlining something lacy over her breasts, communicating just how cold she really was, reminding him how hot she'd felt just moments before in his arms. That traitorous feeling inside him protested at the sight of her body wracked with cold, but he steeled himself against his own baffling reactions.

Bending—for Colleen's benefit, he told himself—he took Meaghan's hands between his again and continued to rub. The gash in his palm had soaked through Mickey's handkerchief and throbbed, but the bleeding had stopped and he ignored the pain. Meaghan's breath plumed in front of her. Outside their shelter, distant thunder boomed ominously, and all three of them startled. Colleen tucked the infant closer to her body, adjusting the blanket over his head to keep him warm.

What could have possessed her to come to this cavern?

"What are you doing here, Mrs. Ballagh?" he asked again.

"Sure and didn't she tell me I'd find you here and to bring clothes, but I didn't know why, did I now?" Colleen said, still staring at Meaghan.

And with a trickle of unease, Áedán realized that she had yet to answer him, had yet to even glance his way. Was it deliberate? Was she angry about something? Colleen had never been anything but kind and thoughtful to Áedán since her husband had brought him to their door and commanded that she feed him.

"Who told you she'd be here?" Áedán asked warily. When Colleen still didn't respond to his question, he looked at Meaghan, glad to see that spark still glinting in her eyes instead of the vacant look she'd awakened with. "What is she talking about?"

Teeth chattering, Meaghan shook her head.

"It's the truth," Colleen went on, as if Meaghan had denied her claim. "She told me that I'm to go to the cavern this afternoon. 'Bring clothes,' she says. 'They might be needed.' She said I would find a girl and she might be as naked as Eve in the garden. Instead I find one near turned to ice, but I've no doubt it was you she meant."

"Who?" Áedán barked again. "Who told you?"

He stood and stalked to Colleen's side, feeling, once again, that dread coiling tight and fear tripping over his skin. But with each step, a new kind of horror overtook him. Colleen's gaze never flickered from Meaghan. Even the baby in her arms looked right through him as he stopped in front of them both.

"I don't suppose I even need to ask if your name would be Meaghan, do I?" Colleen went on, shaking her head even as she confirmed her suspicions. "What other young miss would be down here in the cold, shivering like an ice maiden?"

"Mrs. Ballagh," Áedán said, reaching out to take her arms in his hands and demand her attention. He watched a shiver go through her body at his touch, but she didn't look his way, didn't acknowledge that he was even there. Instead she moved toward Meaghan with an air of purpose, brushing him out of the way without a glance.

"I don't know how you got here, missy, or who you might be, but I mean to help you. Let's get you out of those wet clothes and into the dry ones I brought."

In that moment, Áedán realized that he'd been right to fear this cavern.

After five days of taking meals across the table from Colleen, of working with her husband from dawn to dusk, of doing whatever menial task would help her, suddenly she couldn't see him. Suddenly she looked right through him as if he were invisible . . . as if he didn't even exist at all. . . .

He jerked his gaze away from Colleen to Meaghan, where she sat on the boulder shivering. She stared back with wide, uncomprehending eyes. So he wasn't invisible to her. The realization both comforted and terrified him. Why could *she* see him and not Colleen?

That dark and insidious feeling that had greeted him at the gaping mouth of the cavern surged triumphantly around him now. It mocked the ego that had cloaked him as he'd crossed into this den, and now he felt again that strange wobbling weakness in his limbs. The air reeked of the Book of Fennore, of the world that had been his prison for longer than he could remember.

And it whispered that Áedán would never be free. . . .

Chapter Three

MEAGHAN felt frozen from the inside out. Shivers wracked her body, clenching muscles, churning her insides, pounding in her brain. But none of that compared to the eviscerating shock that sliced through her as she grappled with the three unbelievable truths that met her eyes.

One, she was back in the cavern, back where her nightmare had begun on the Isle of Fennore. Only, if Áedán could be believed, decades had passed—or been lost. If it was 1956, then Meaghan had regained consciousness over thirty years before she'd even been born.

Impossible. And yet, impossible had become her new normal, hadn't it?

She shook her head, moving to the second in her list of unbelievables. In the chaos of their escape from the nightmare world where they'd met, somehow Áedán and Meaghan had landed here together. How, she didn't know. Why, she couldn't guess. But it felt preordained in a way that filled her with foreboding. Áedán was six feet plus of muscle and man, but Meaghan wasn't foolish enough to think him *just* a man. There was something otherworldly about Áedán.

Something that pinged against her instincts and warned her not to underestimate him.

When they'd been trapped together in that nightmare world that belonged to the Book of Fennore—a world that defied description or explanation—Áedán had been invisible to everyone but Meaghan. She hadn't known if that made him a ghost, an illusion, or a twisted figment of her imagination. She'd eliminated the last from the line of options; his touch had been too real to be fabricated by her mind. Out of necessity, they'd become uneasy allies with a common foe, if vastly different goals. But she didn't trust him.

Even now she didn't know who or *what* Áedán really was, other than dangerously attractive and masculine in a way that made every feminine cell in her body vibrate. She'd been dreaming of him when she'd awakened. Crazy, carnal dreams, filled with scent, taste, texture, and desire that burned hot enough to incinerate her. When she'd seen him leaning over her, she hadn't thought twice about wrapping her arms around him and losing herself in the arousal that had followed her out of the dream. She still fought the urge to go to him, to finish what she'd started.

And he knew it. She could see it there in that hot gaze that took in every detail, from her heaving breasts to her swollen lips. It might have been humiliating, being so open, so easily read by a man she wasn't sure she liked and knew she certainly didn't trust.

But Áedán wasn't immune to her either.

Meaghan didn't need her empathic skills to feel Áedán's lust coming at her like the tide, rolling in waves that shushed over her and then retreated, leaving in their wake a hollow, achy yearning and the mystifying taste of fear. The longing she understood, but the fear confused her. She didn't sense danger around them and couldn't begin to guess what he might be afraid of here, in this deserted cavern with only two women and a child.

Her gaze moved at last to the tiny figure holding her baby—the third and most unbelievable truth she had to face.

The young woman who stood an arm's length away, wearing an

expectant expression that Meaghan knew all too well, was none other than Colleen Ballagh.

Colleen Ballagh.

She couldn't mistake the familiar features. The dark eyes, the cheekbones that Meaghan had always wished for, the full lips. No more than five foot three, Colleen Ballagh still managed to have a presence about her, a bearing that spoke of strength and pride. Meaghan had always thought that wisdom and age had given her that regal air, but now she saw that it must be innate, because in this crazy reality Colleen looked years younger than Meaghan. She hardly seemed old enough to be a mother, let alone have one child in her arms and another on the way.

Meaghan closed her eyes for a moment, besieged by her own realizations. Oh yes, she knew Colleen Ballagh. But the last time she'd seen this woman had been at a funeral. *Colleen's* funeral. She'd died a feisty old woman, leaving her family bereft and mourning her loss.

"Who is she?" Áedán demanded, cutting his eyes between them.

"Colleen Ballagh," Meaghan managed to say.

Colleen. Ballagh.

Here. Now. Alive. But how?

"I know her name. But *who* is she? Who is she to *you*?"

My grandmother. And I think the child in her arms will one day be my dad.

She didn't say that part, though. It was too crazy, too fundamentally wrong to voice.

"That's right," Colleen said, and for a moment Meaghan thought she'd heard her thoughts. "I am Colleen Ballagh. And you would be Meaghan, isn't that the way of it?"

"How does she know who you are?" Áedán asked, his voice thick with suspicion. Evidently he didn't remember that Meaghan's last name was also Ballagh. "Why can't she see me?"

Meaghan wanted to answer him, to tell him she didn't have a clue how Colleen knew who she was. She wanted to ask him why Colleen's inability to see him came as a surprise when no one else but her had been able to see him before. Then she remembered . . . when Colleen had first entered, Áedán had expected her to recognize him. He'd spoken to her familiarly. He'd been shocked when she looked right through him.

"Ask her," he insisted.

Don't tell me what to do, she wanted to bark back, bristling at his commanding tone. But she couldn't say that, not unless she wanted Colleen to think her crazy—crazier than she probably already did.

"How do you know who I am?" Meaghan asked calmly, shooting Áedán a speaking glance to back off. He might be the sexiest man to grace the earth, but he got under her skin—and not in a good way. He'd had that effect on her since the first moment she'd met him.

"Now isn't that a question," Colleen answered with a tight smile. "The two of us, we've a tale to share, have we not? But you'll freeze to death if you don't get changed into dry clothes, and I've not the time nor the energy to nurse you back to health, so I suggest you get to it and then we'll have our chat. I'm not sure how the clothes will be fitting you—they're mine and you're a bit bigger than I am, but dry is dry. The shoes belonged to my husband's first wife and are too big for me. They should be fine for you."

Colleen dropped her satchel to the ground and knelt down, balancing the baby in her arms as she began to work the knot that held it closed. Over her bent head, Áedán captured Meaghan's gaze in the deep forest green of his own, trapped her between the shifting shades. He was angry—she saw it in the hard glitter of gold that flecked the greens, sensed it in the chilled air between them. But the other emotions spewing and frothing within him held her under. He felt she'd betrayed him in some way, but she couldn't fathom why.

"What have you done, beauty?" he said, using the absurd pet name he'd given her when they'd been trapped together. "Why did you lure me here?"

She hadn't, but even if she could argue the point with him, she could see it would do no good. His mind was made up. He cloaked the churn of bitterness he felt behind a placid expression of arrogance and boredom she knew too well. When they'd met for the first time, her ability to sense emotions had been suppressed by the eerie energy of the world of Fennore, and that mask had fooled her. Now she could see behind it. She only wished her empathic gift came with subtitles.

"What have you done?" he repeated, moving closer, invading her personal space with his size and sheer presence. He made the cavern seem suddenly too small.

"Nothing," she whispered.

Colleen paused and looked up from the bag. "Nothing? Well, I'd hardly call this nothing, would I now? It's more like a miracle. Or maybe an omen. Time will tell the truth, I suppose."

"What do you mean?" Meaghan asked before Áedán could tell her to do it.

"You, being here where you don't belong." When Meaghan would have fired another question, Colleen held up her hand. "Don't bother to ask, I won't answer another. Not here. I don't like this place. Never have."

No, Meaghan had never liked it either. The cavern held an air of malignant blackness that went deeper than the inky pool at their feet. She'd seen the underbelly of what caused that rotted, malevolent feeling. It was the Book of Fennore—an ancient tome that predated even the Bible. It housed more than the archaic runes, which covered its pages from edge to edge, symbols of an extinct language that told a terrible tale. The same symbols that marked the walls here. The Book held a curse, the curse imprisoned an entity—a powerful being bent on destruction.

Áedán made a sound of irritation and turned his back, frustration etching every fine line of muscle trailing from broad shoulders to lean hips and long legs.

"How did she know to bring you clothes?" he muttered.

It was a good question, though she was loath to act as his parrot and ask it.

"How did you know I'd need clothes, Co—Mrs. . . ." Meaghan

trailed off, looking uncertain about what to call the other woman. She'd been Nana to Meaghan since she'd learned to speak. All of Colleen's grandchildren called her Nana.

"Colleen will do just fine," she said. "And I swear to tell you everything once we get you changed and away from this place. We can only hope the storm keeps moving. We won't make it up the stairs if it starts to rain again. I had to wait it out in the castle ruins before I could come down. Now, can you dress yourself or do you need help?"

Meaghan gave a jerky nod. "I can manage it on my own. My fingers are just a little numb, but they work." Reluctantly, Meaghan shrugged out of the coat Áedán had draped over her shoulders, shivering violently as his warmth went with it. Colleen caught the jacket up, staring at it with consternation.

"Where did you get this coat, missy? 'Tis a borrowed one from my Mickey. He gave it to Mr. Brady, his deckhand."

Mr. Brady? Deckhand? Meaghan shot a glance at Áedán and then looked away from his piercing eyes. He seemed to thrum with emotion—violence, bewilderment . . . *pain.* The pain went so deep that it dominated everything else. She didn't understand the complexity of what he felt, but she couldn't miss the power of his feelings.

"Tell her you found the coat here," he said when the silence stretched.

"I found the coat on the rocks," she mumbled, mesmerized by the shock waves of his feelings. Gaze narrowed on hers, he stepped closer, invading her space again, stealing all the air in the cavern. When she would have looked away, he took her chin in his hand and held her steady, searching her face, trying to pry her thoughts from inside her.

Colleen made a small tsking noise. "That's not like Mr. Brady to be so careless."

"I've been working for her husband since I got here," Áedán said.

She jerked her chin from his long, warm fingers, noticing for the first time that he had a handkerchief wrapped around his palm and it was soaked in blood. He'd been working for her grandfather? It was hard to imagine Áedán doing any type of labor.

"He can see me," Áedán went on. He pointed to Colleen. "*She* can see me. Everyone on this forsaken island can see me—or could until now. Until *you* appeared."

Stunned by this news, she tried another silent question. *Why?*

"I've no fecking idea," he said. "Get dressed so I can get some bloody answers."

All too aware of Áedán's hot eyes following her every movement, Meaghan reached in the bag Colleen had brought and pulled out a shapeless bundle of brown wool. It was a dress, apparently. The twin to the unflattering sack Colleen herself wore, by the looks of it.

Nearly blue with cold, Meaghan pulled her sodden T-shirt over her head. She heard Áedán suck in a soft breath, and glanced up to find him standing very close, the heat of his body scorching the air, his attention fixed on her breasts, puckered against her wet, nearly transparent bra. The look he gave her burned her icy skin as he lifted a hand and softly traced the scalloped lace with a finger.

Had Colleen not been there, she would have told him to take his fecking hand off her, but her grandmother stood quietly by, her cheeks pink as she caught sight of Meaghan's sheer bra.

And Áedán's touch had momentarily immobilized her. No, it was more than his touch. For one unguarded moment, emotions flashed across his face. She saw vulnerability; she saw grief. She saw hopeless longing that touched her more deeply than his hands. She felt his hunger in the air—had tasted it in his kiss when she'd first opened her eyes. There was more to Áedán than the cynical and disdainful front he showed the world, and it was all there in his gaze for that fleeting instant.

While Meaghan stood like a statue, he trailed his fingers down to her cleavage and then suddenly glanced up, catching her by surprise before she could conceal the knowledge of what she'd surmised. Immediately that window into his soul slammed shut, and there was nothing but challenge in his face now. He cupped her breast, daring her to do something, to say something when he knew that she could do neither. She raised her brows, trying to appear tough, insulted, and unaffected. His quick flash of teeth told her she'd failed.

With a glare, she tugged the brown dress over her head, forcing him to step back. She didn't reach for the fastening on her jeans until it covered her. Fighting the wool, she had to twist and turn to peel the wet denim off her legs, too aware of the green eyes tracking her every move, but finally she was free of her dripping garments and immediately warmer for it. Colleen had brought thick black stockings and the promised shoes. Scowling, Meaghan put them on, fighting the desire to look up to see what lurked in his gaze now. She was afraid he'd see how much he'd disarmed her with that brief caress, with those knowing eyes. She tasted lust in the air between them. His or hers? She couldn't tell and didn't want to pursue it for fear of the answer.

Blasted man.

But she couldn't banish the memory of that stark longing she glimpsed on his face.

"Well," Colleen said brightly. "You certainly fill that out better than I do."

"Indeed," Áedán agreed in a silky, dangerous voice.

As Colleen had said, Meaghan was bigger boned and taller than her grandmother, and the dress didn't hang like a sack on her. Instead, it hugged her hips and thighs, and she had to pull the fabric together in order to button up the front—which she did as quickly as her frozen fingers would allow.

Holding the baby with practiced ease, Colleen began stuffing Meaghan's discarded clothes into her satchel, but a deep boom of thunder warned them that the storm had not moved on as they'd hoped. An instant later, the downpour erupted, sealing them inside with its fury. Meaghan shuddered. She wanted to get away from this cavern and all that it represented.

"What's the matter, beauty?" Áedán murmured, standing too close.

"Don't call me that," she muttered under her breath so that Colleen, who had moved to the mouth of the cavern and stood staring at the rain with a frown, would not hear.

"I had no idea you wore such interesting trimmings beneath your garments," he baited in that velvet voice, the light tone a sign of danger if she'd ever heard one.

"Well, I hope you got a good look, because you won't be seeing my *trimmings* ever again," she snapped back in a low undertone.

He smiled darkly at that, but she could still feel his touch tracing the lace of her bra, warming her skin, seducing her senses despite her desire to resist him.

Colleen sighed and turned back to face Meaghan, her eyes anxious. "It looks like we'll be stuck for a while more, like it or not. Best have a seat and wait it out."

Nodding, Meaghan sat on one of the boulders and Colleen perched on another, shifting her baby to a comfortable position. Áedán stood nearby, watching, waiting . . . a dark and dangerous shadow with lust in his eyes and who knew what in his heart.

Meaghan pried her gaze from him and nervously glanced at Colleen, wanting to pepper her with questions but knowing better than to do it. The Colleen that Meaghan had known all her life was a woman who liked things on her own terms. She couldn't say if, like her regal bearing, it was an innate inclination or one she'd grown into.

Besides, tension knotted Meaghan's stomach and she didn't know how to begin. If this was her grandmother, then Meaghan had somehow awoken in the past. What if she did or said something that might impact her future? What if she changed history? She'd seen *The Butterfly Effect.* She'd read *A Wrinkle in Time.* She knew she walked a dangerous path—but how did she get off it? How did she get back to her own time?

The gray-green light from the stormy sky outside trickled in and gave the cavern an eerie cast. The echo of rain coming down in great sluicing sheets combined with the surging tide and made Meaghan feel as if she sat in the belly of a great beast. She eyed the markings on the ceiling anxiously, knowing just how true that might be. The Book of Fennore was a monster of another kind, and this was its lair. She felt it to her bones.

"I knew to come to the cavern because I had a visitor who told me to do it," Colleen said abruptly, slicing through Meaghan's fearful thoughts and answering the question she hadn't known how to form.

"Who?" Meaghan and Áedán asked at the same time.

"She said her name was Saraid."

Áedán gave a muttered curse, and she felt the blast of his shock but couldn't ask him why or how he knew this *Saraid*.

"Saraid?" she repeated, watching Áedán pace from the corner of her eye. "She's a friend?"

"Ach, no. I'd never seen the likes of her before. She just appeared at my house without warning. She was dressed in the queerest clothes, and I'll tell you, she seemed a bit delighted to catch me by surprise."

"Delighted?"

"Aye. There was no mistaking it."

"But she was a stranger? You didn't know her? Why—"

"Well, sure and don't I wish I knew why. I was doing me wash, as always, and suddenly I turned and there she was, standing just behind me, dressed in costume, would you believe?"

Meaghan shook her head. But really, at this point, what wouldn't she believe?

"I swear it. She says to me, 'Colleen of the Ballagh, I've come to give you a message.' Just like that."

The baby in her arms—Niall, Meaghan's *father*—fussed, interrupting them. Colleen took a moment to soothe him. When she looked up again, her eyes gleamed blacker than midnight.

Áedán said, "Ask her—"

"What kind of message?" Meaghan interrupted him impatiently.

"She says to me that she's come from the past, she did. The past. She says, 'You are of my blood.' Then she says her name is Saraid of the Favored Lands, if you can imagine such a thing. Like it were a title she'd been given. I'll tell you now, I was more than a bit afraid of her. I didn't know if she was a spirit or something worse." Colleen paused to let the significance of that sink in. *Something worse* could mean many things to the Irish. "But she weren't of this world, that much was clear."

"Tell her to get to the point," Áedán snapped. "What did Saraid want? What did she say?"

Meaghan scowled at him. As an old woman, Nana Colleen had been able to silence the birds with a mere look. One did not simply demand that Colleen Ballagh *get to the point.*

"The woman, Saraid, she says to me that she was sent by Ruairi. Not just any Ruairi, mind. She says it's Ruairi of Fennore who sent her."

Áedán gave a bark of bitter laughter and shook his head. Meaghan was too stunned to do more than gape. Ruairi of Fennore was a mythological Irish hero who had lived over a thousand years ago.

He was also, Meaghan suspected, her lost half brother who'd vanished during Nana Colleen's funeral. Her brother's name, though not pronounced in the ancient Irish way, was also Rory. Meaghan had been searching for him when she herself had been swept away from the real world and into another, twisted realm that she still could not comprehend.

In the days before it had happened, she'd chanced upon a picture in a book about the great hero, Ruairi of Fennore. She could still remember the shock she'd felt as she stared at it, as she took in the familiar features, the blue eyes so like her own. Her half brother, Rory, and Ruairi of Fennore did not merely resemble one another. They were identical in every way, right down to the scar on his chest that she'd glimpsed when he'd come home for Nana's funeral.

She had a good idea of just how much power the Book of Fennore wielded, and she suspected that somehow Rory had been caught in it, as she had. And like her, he'd been sent to another time, another place, where he'd become the stuff of legends. . . .

And now here was her grandmother telling her that Ruairi of Fennore had sent a woman to deliver a message to Meaghan. . . .

"Oh, I know what you're thinking," Colleen interrupted her thoughts. "And I won't deny that I've had a drop or two in my time, but I swear to you now, I'd not a thing to drink but tea. Not that I believe she was *really* sent by Ruairi of Fennore. Ach, no. Could have been anyone. Show me a man who doesn't think he's Ruairi of Fennore once he gets a pint or two in him, is what I say to that."

Colleen finally glanced into Meaghan's face and then she paused. "Now tell me why you're looking like that, missy?"

"You won't believe me," Meaghan said, shaking her head.

Colleen snorted. "Didn't I just tell you I had a visitor from the past? The woman sent by a myth, for the love of Mary. And what she had to say . . . Well, no sane person would believe it."

Colleen shook her head in complete bewilderment and went on. "I thought her simple, I did, but now I don't know, for she said I'd find you in this cavern, that I must go and help you, and isn't that just what I did? Tell me what it is you think I won't believe, missy. I'm finding meself as gullible as a child at Christmas."

But Meaghan didn't dare put into words even one of the crazy thoughts in her head. As if sensing the conflict within her, Áedán moved to her side and gently touched her shoulder in a brief but comforting way. Surprised, it took all of her self-control not to look at him, not to give in and search his face for clues to his thoughts. She could feel the heat of him burning through the chill and wanted to lean closer.

Instead, she focused on her grandmother and asked, "Was that it? Was that all she said? Go to the cavern and you'd find me?"

Still eyeing Meaghan with those piercing black eyes, Colleen asked, "Would you be wanting a prediction or something? It's not enough that she told me to come here? She made some comment about a chicken and an egg and which came first. I don't see the relevance of it, but she thought it quite amusing." She paused for a moment, and then, "Now it's your turn. Why don't you tell me what you're doing in this cavern, Meaghan Ballagh?"

"Ballagh?" Áedán repeated slowly, moving around so he could see her face. "Meaghan *Ballagh*?"

The second time it sounded like a condemnation. With a muffled curse, he shook his head and withdrew another step. Immediately, she missed the warmth and comfort of having him at her side and called herself a fool for it. She didn't understand the accusation she heard in his tone, though. She'd told him her full name when they'd met. It wasn't her fault he'd forgotten it, but he looked at her as if she'd pulled an elaborate scam on him.

Frowning, she eyed her grandmother. What did *she* think of their shared last name? Had Saraid told Colleen that Meaghan was her granddaughter? Or did Colleen think they were merely distant relatives, if even that? Ballagh was common enough in Meaghan's time, especially on the Isle of Fennore.

"Well?" Colleen said with raised brows and a pointed look, waiting for Meaghan to answer her question. "How did you get here?"

Meaghan swallowed hard. How could she explain *that* to Colleen when she didn't understand it herself? She looked at Áedán with a helpless expression.

"When I was found, I told Mickey I'd been lost at sea," he said.

Well, that wouldn't work twice. No one would believe two strangers had washed up on these shores in the same week. But she couldn't tell her grandmother the truth. It was too unbelievable.

"I don't know how I got here, Colleen. I think I must have hit my head. My memory is fuzzy."

Colleen clicked her tongue at that and narrowed her eyes. She stiffened her back and her lips became a thin line of displeasure. Meaghan realized her lie had offended her. *Shit.*

"Colleen—"

"I've told you the truth," she said sharply. "I risked your ridicule, but it's truth I told. I deserve the same."

"No, she doesn't," Áedán said softly. "No good can come of it."

"You're right," Meaghan answered. Áedán looked stunned at her agreement until she spoke her next words. "You deserve an honest answer."

Colleen shot her a wary glance.

"I am . . ." Meaghan took a deep breath and—feeling foolish though it was the truth—said in a rush, "I'm from the future."

As the echo of her words died away, Meaghan braced for Colleen's guffaw, which never came. Instead her young grandmother gave her a considering once-over and then nodded.

"That would be what Saraid had to say about you."

"She did? So you knew?"

"How could she know that?" Áedán said.

Colleen shrugged, her eyes sparkling with interest. "Why else would I have risked going to the cavern in a storm? With a baby in my arms and a change of clothes in my bag, no less. Of course I knew."

"Did she tell you anything else about . . . about who I am?" Meaghan asked, hearing something else in Colleen's tone.

Áedán stepped closer again, then bent down so that his face was level with hers. "And just who are you, beauty?" he asked in that deep, smoky voice of his. For a moment, he held her captive with his gaze, and it seemed that everything else faded away.

"Oh, she had quite a bit of information, she did," Colleen said, her voice pulling Meaghan back when she felt like she might fall into the endless green of Áedán's eyes.

With effort, Meaghan looked past him to where her grandmother sat. Colleen wore a smug expression. Heart pounding, she waited for Colleen to finish, for it was obvious the other woman was taking pleasure in drawing out the drama of her next words.

"Quite a bit of information," she continued. "She told me you were my granddaughter. What do you say to that?"

"Her granddaughter?" Áedán muttered, "Colleen Ballagh is your *grandmother*?"

"I say it's unbelievable," Meaghan murmured softly. "It couldn't possibly be true."

Colleen nodded. "Aye, those would be my words, too. And yet, here you are."

Áedán cursed beneath his breath. "I thought it was chance that brought us both here," he said. "But I should have seen the truth. It was you, wasn't it? You did this."

Did what? she wanted to snap back at him. What did he think she'd done? How could he imagine that she'd had any control over where the two of them had landed after their narrow escape from the nightmare they'd shared? But she couldn't say any of that, didn't dare look at him when Colleen watched her expectantly, waiting for her response.

"Yes," Meaghan said. "Yes. Here I am."

"One big happy family," Áedán murmured darkly before he stalked to the mouth of the cavern and stared out at the storm.

Chapter Four

AT last the rain slacked and then ceased altogether. Colleen wasted no time leading the way through the small passageway out into the fresh air. Meaghan slung the satchel with her clothes in it over her shoulder and followed, noting that the baby had fallen asleep inside the warm cocoon Colleen had made of her blanket and Áedán's coat. Now her grandmother carried him without his waking.

With a deep breath, Meaghan emerged from the cavern, feeling as if she'd been within its gaping maw for years. Áedán hesitated before he crossed the threshold, and again she felt that bite of fear in his tangled emotions. When he stepped out, relief washed over her like the brisk air. Had he been afraid that the black abyss would hold him captive, just like the nightmare world they'd barely escaped had? Troubled by the thought, she turned to the familiar sea, surging against the rocks and the crude stairs leading up the side of the cliffs and tried to tamp down her own alarm at such a possibility.

Colleen had already started her ascent, setting a brisk pace, climbing the stairs like a sure-footed goat, baby balanced with what appeared to be little effort. Meaghan followed more slowly. She wasn't a fan of heights and so took care with each step.

"Why didn't you tell me Colleen Ballagh was your grandmother?" Áedán asked, following close behind her. His lips brushed her ear when he spoke and his hand settled steady and warm at the curve of her hip as she moved up the next uneven tier.

"When was I to do that?" she whispered back. Colleen had moved ahead and seemed intent only on reaching the top. She hadn't once glanced back to be sure Meaghan followed, but things were crazy enough without her grandmother hearing and thinking Meaghan talked to herself.

"Do not lie to me again," he said.

The unfairness of it combined with all of her uncertainty and fear and made her furious. She whipped her head around and glared at him. The action, though childishly satisfying, made her stumble, and if not for his quick reflexes, she'd have careened over the edge.

Stupid. What was it about this man that made her react without thinking?

For a moment, she was caught up in his arms, held tight against the hard muscles of his chest, wrapped in the seductive scent of him—soap and salty air and something dark and woodsy that was all his own. Time seemed to freeze, and she had the inexplicable feeling that they'd been here before—dangling above an unknown doom, reliant on only the whims of fate and the strength of Áedán's arms.

Shaken by the disconcerting thought, Meaghan pushed on his chest, but he didn't back off. She was beginning to realize that Áedán *Brady* was not a man who ever backed off. Up ahead, Colleen continued to climb the stairs with the focused attention Meaghan should have been exerting.

Finally, with a knowing smile, he released her and she stepped away. But it was not so easy to distance him in her mind.

"Back off, Áedán," she snarled.

He laughed softly, tauntingly. "I don't think so, beauty."

Finally, they reached the top of the crumbling stairs, and with a dry mouth, Meaghan gazed at the castle ruins perched at the apex of the island's craggy edge. On the day she'd gone to the cavern beneath it to look for her brother, the castle had been wholly restored. A home with warm hearths and tapestries.

In the distance rose an ancient dolmen. Comprised of three standing stones with a fourth perched table-like on their shoulders, historians believed dolmens may have been used by the earliest people of Ireland as burial chambers, but no one knew for certain why they'd been constructed thousands of years ago or for what purpose. Folklore painted the formations as portals to the world of the fae, doorways from which the unsuspecting human might be snatched by the fairies, never to be seen again.

Ballyfionúir had its own ghostly figure who walked the valley where this dolmen stood against the elements and time. The people called her spirit the White Ghost or the White Fennore, depending on who told the story. As a child, Meaghan had glimpsed the ethereal woman gliding from the dolmen and for a petrifying moment, it seemed that their eyes had met and locked. Time had stretched unending as the spirit's emotions bombarded Meaghan, more conflicted and complex than anything her child's mind could understand. Terrified, she'd fled and had never gone near it again. Even as an adult, Meaghan avoided the tall formation completely.

Colleen stood with her back to Meaghan, staring at the castle ruins eroding down the plummeting cliffs to the sea.

"It's a sad sight, isn't it?" Colleen asked without turning around.

Meaghan nodded. "Maybe one day it can be restored."

"Maybe," Colleen agreed. "But who would want to do that?"

Her sister's husband, for one, but Meaghan didn't say it.

With a sigh, Colleen turned to face her, and then let out a small yelp of surprise. "Mr. Brady. You gave me quite a fright. Where did you come from?"

Surprised speechless, Meaghan spun to face him. Áedán quickly masked his shock at Colleen's sudden ability to see him and casually turned to give the stairs they'd just come up a fleeting glance, reminding Meaghan of the emotions she'd sensed from him when he'd exited the cavern. He'd said that he'd been on this island for five days, during which time he'd been seen by all. Was it the cavern that made him insubstantial? Or, more likely, the cavern's innate connection to the Book of Fennore?

The thoughts went through her head in a split second but she was certain she'd stumbled on the reason. From the look in his eye, she guessed Áedán had drawn the same conclusions. Whatever he thought of it, though, he concealed and without missing a beat, turned a heartbreaker's smile on Colleen.

"You found it," he said. "My coat. I've been looking for it. I went down on the beach exploring last night and realized only this morning that I'd left it on the rocks."

Colleen stared stupidly at him and then the coat bundled around her baby. "Oh," she said, a bit breathless, no doubt from his killer smile. Meaghan felt her own pulse speed up at it and he hadn't even directed it at her.

Blushing, Colleen said, "Yes, we found it in the cavern. I thought it odd that you'd been so careless."

"I'm afraid I went to the Pier House with Mr. Ballagh and had a few pints," he said, looking suitably chagrined. "'Tis lucky I didn't fall down the stairs and break my neck."

The explanation appeared to be good enough for Colleen. She nodded and moved to unwrap the coat from her sleeping son.

"Don't disturb him," Áedán said, stopping her. "I'll see you back at the house and get it then."

"I'll be along shortly," Colleen said.

Áedán gave her a polite nod and then strode away without another word. Meaghan watched him go, feeling both relieved and afraid. He'd become, once again, her ally in this strangely shifting world, and the thought of him disappearing terrified her. If he could be invisible one moment and seen the next, his very presence could not be relied on. What if he vanished and left her here alone?

Meaghan liked to show the world a face of strength, of confident defiance, of unshakable self-reliance, but inside, she never felt that way, and the last few days had tested her inner strength and made her feel painfully inadequate. Meaghan would forever be the last child, the lost child. Her half brother and half sister had a different father—their mother's first husband, Cathán MacGrath—and they were twins, connected in ways Meaghan could never be. Meaghan was not a MacGrath. She was a Ballagh and yet, she never quite fit in either genetic pool. Her family loved her, but there had always been something a little odd about Meaghan, not that any of them would say it.

And being unusual in a family where odd was a relative term—well, that had never been a thing to brag about. Deep down, Meaghan had always feared that her abnormalities went far beyond anything her family might have imagined. It was a secret she kept very close.

Drawing in a shaky breath, she forced herself to glance away from Áedán's retreating back. Down below, the sea looked like an undulating storm, surging with power against the porous stones of the Fennore cliffs. They were jagged and blackened, glistening like rotted teeth against the onslaught of winds, tide, and time. The entire island was surrounded by such barriers, which had kept the Isle of Fennore from habitation for centuries. Invaders had found inhospitable waters and impossible landings when they'd tried to come ashore. Fierce waves had slammed them into rocks while riptides had sucked any survivors down into the cold depths. While the rest of Ireland was pillaged and plundered, the Isle of Fennore remained pristine. The Vikings had called it cursed. The English had called it worthless. The people who finally managed to settle on this island called it a blessing.

Legend said that Ruairi of Fennore had been the first to navigate the vicious seas surrounding the isle, and he'd done it with mystical powers. He hadn't walked on water, but the stories told of him sailing his small round *curraghs* over the tops of the waves, like hovercrafts over flat terrain. When Meaghan was a child, it had been one of her favorite stories. Ironic, if she was right and Ruairi of Fennore really was her half brother . . . a time traveler just like Meaghan.

Colleen began to walk again, but Meaghan knew in her gut that the woman who would become her grandmother had more to say than what she'd revealed in the cavern, and whatever it was, it wouldn't be good. Both fascination and fear filled the glance she cast at Meaghan—a look she'd been on the receiving end of many times before from others, but never from her grandmother. Nana Colleen had understood Meaghan like no one else.

Meaghan braced herself for the worst even as she acknowledged that, at this point, she couldn't even guess what the worst could be.

"It wasn't just Saraid who told me you were coming," Colleen said. "I saw it myself, though I didn't know just what I was seeing."

Meaghan swallowed a lump in her throat. Her grandmother had visions—sometimes of the future, sometimes of the past. When Meaghan had been a child, Colleen had always known when she'd been up to mischief. She'd always known when her granddaughter was in trouble, too. Often Colleen's visions came out of sequence and context, but they were rarely wrong.

"What did you see?" Meaghan asked softly.

Colleen's eyes narrowed and Meaghan watched the swift calculations going on behind them. Meaghan hadn't asked what she'd meant by "I saw it myself" and now Colleen worked through the implications of that and came to the inevitable conclusion. Meaghan hadn't asked because she already knew.

"I've not had many visions," she said. "My first came only last year."

Surprised, Meaghan blurted, "You didn't have them as a child?"

Colleen shook her head. "My mother had them and her mother before her so I knew it was only a matter of time before they started for me. I'm not sure if coming here spurred them to start or if it was just my time, though."

Meaghan suspected that the Isle of Fennore had a role in it but she didn't say it. Instead she waited impatiently for her grandmother to reveal just what had happened in this vision.

"I saw you with two others," Colleen said at last. "A big, strapping blonde man with the bluest eyes I've ever seen."

That would be Rory. Her half brother.

"Beautiful eyes like yours," she went on, surprising Meaghan. "There was another woman with you. A lovely lass. She had eyes like a stormy sky."

Danni. Her half sister.

"What were we doing, the three of us?"

"You were in the cavern."

"Alone?" she asked.

Colleen shook her head. "I don't think so. I heard other voices, but all I could see was you three. That and a book."

Meaghan's mouth went dry. "What book?"

"Now isn't that a strange question. Does it matter what book?"

Yes, it could matter a great deal. Especially if the book had been the Book of Fennore.

"That's it? That's all you saw? Did we say anything?"

"Nothing that made sense. I thought I heard *what will be, must be* or something of the like, but I'm not certain of it."

Meaghan pondered that, as perplexed as Colleen seemed to be by the vision and its message.

"How long ago did this happen, Colleen?"

"A few days."

"And why do you think . . . what does it mean?"

Colleen was silent for a long moment and then she said, "Saraid, she told me that the Book of Fennore had been found—found and opened. I didn't believe her. The Book of Fennore is a legend. A myth."

A myth like Ruairi of Fennore, Meaghan thought, swallowing a bubble of hysteria. Once Meaghan had considered the Book of Fennore a myth as well. The half-known bits and pieces of its history had drawn Meaghan's curiosity for as long as she could remember. Like a dark fairy tale, the legend told of an evil Book that imprisoned a powerful entity, a twisted genie in the bottle who promised dreams and delivered doom.

Her mother's first husband, Cathán, had been obsessed with

finding it, convinced he could bend the entity inside it to his will. Instead—like Meaghan's half brother—he'd vanished from the cavern beneath the castle ruins never to be seen by the good folk of Ballyfionúir again.

But Meaghan *had* seen Cathán again—when she'd found the Book of Fennore, he'd been there. She'd felt the terrible power of the Book and cowered before the entity that controlled it, wondering how anyone could be foolish enough to think they could manipulate such a great and terrible thing. Then she'd realized that Cathán had become one with that twisted power, an integral part of the evil that oozed from the Book's ancient covers and blew in the breeze created by its fanning pages.

"The Book exists," Meaghan said, remembering the cold light that had glittered in Cathán MacGrath's eyes. "I've seen it. It is everything the legend claims it to be, only worse."

"You've seen it?" she said with a wry smile. "And do you have visions as well?"

Meaghan shook her head and Colleen's eyes widened at the implication of that. If Meaghan hadn't seen it in a vision, then she'd seen it in reality.

"You've seen the Book of Fennore," she repeated. "And where, might I ask, were you when this happened—No, never mind, don't answer that. I don't want to know. But I suppose next you'll say there's an evil Druid afoot, too?"

Meaghan shook her head. "Did Saraid tell you there was . . . an evil Druid?"

"Well, I wouldn't have made it up, would I? She said this Druid was the Book's master and now he's free. So tell me. Is it true?"

A shudder went through Meaghan at the idea that it might be true. "I don't think so, but I only just got here. I don't know. Perhaps."

"Perhaps?" With a snort of disgust, Colleen thrust Niall in Meaghan's arms. "Hold the wee lad, will you now?"

As the weight of the baby who would one day grow up and become her father settled against Meaghan, she felt as if she'd splintered into a thousand pieces. She'd begun to hope that she might be able to deal with the shifting planes that had become her life, but all it took was this—the cooing infant in her arms—to send her into a wild tailspin. There was only so much one person could take, and Meaghan feared her threshold had been reached about the time she'd awakened in the cavern and seen Áedán staring at her with that complex and frightening look in his eyes. Holding her infant father in her arms breached it completely.

Unaware of Meaghan's distress, Colleen dug into the pocket of her ugly brown dress and pulled something out. She held it in her closed fist for a long moment, as if unsure whether or not she meant to show it. Meaghan felt dread fill her in a chilled wash. Whatever it was that Colleen held, Meaghan didn't want it. She didn't even want to see it.

But she couldn't bring herself to turn away. It was as if she'd been nailed to that spot and then turned to stone.

Colleen opened her fingers, and there, against the faint pink lines of her palm, was a soft pouch with a drawstring top. She made short work of opening it, then let the contents spill into her open hand. Strung with a leather cord was the most incredible pendant Meaghan had ever seen. And coming off it in steady, thrumming waves was menace.

She tried to take a step back but couldn't move.

The pendant wasn't beautiful for all its bling. It glittered with an array of jewels that radiated from an emerald set like an island at its center. Diamonds, dazzling stars in a midnight sky, and opals, mysteriously opaque and alive with colors, made a rich web around it. Rubies like drops of blood woven with silver and gold twisted into spirals that seemed to go on without beginning or end.

The markings of the Book of Fennore. The same symbols that were etched on the walls of the cavern she'd just come from.

This was not the first time she'd seen the pendant. The night before Colleen's funeral, Rory had been carrying it in his pocket, and she'd glimpsed it when he'd pulled it out during Colleen's wake. She remembered the churning turmoil of his emotions as he'd fingered it. The next day, he'd gone to the cavern and never returned.

"Saraid gave that to you?" Meaghan breathed, staring at it now, knowing the unique amulet was the same one.

"Aye," Colleen answered. "But she said it was yours. She was adamant that I deliver it to you. Would you know why?"

"No," Meaghan said numbly.

But there could be no mistaking that the pendant was connected to the Book of Fennore.

Colleen reached for her son and shifted him into her arms before she held out the pendant to Meaghan, as if sensing that something momentous might occur the instant Meaghan touched it. Who knew if she was right?

Swallowing a lump that lodged in her throat, Meaghan gingerly took the amulet, careful to keep the small satchel between the silver and her palm. The thought of touching it with her bare skin repulsed her. Had Rory felt this way?

Her hand shook, and Colleen's eyes darkened as she watched her. The pouch she held around it was very soft, the pendant surprisingly light. And yet, the weight of it was ominous. She lifted the leather cord and let it dangle for a moment, mesmerizing as it glinted in the clouded daylight.

"Are you going to put it on?" Colleen asked with interest.

"No."

"And why not?"

Because it scared the piss out of her, Meaghan wanted to say, but didn't. After all she'd been through, it seemed ridiculous to fear a piece of jewelry.

"I wouldn't be telling you what to do," Colleen said with an ingenuous gaze. "But I got the sense that you'd have to put it on to know."

"To know what?"

"Whether or not it will take you home."

Blankly, Meaghan stared at her grandmother.

"It can do that?" she asked. "Saraid said it would take me home?"

"Not exactly. But why else would she have come all that way to deliver it?"

Meaghan stared at the pendant with frustration and a sick fascination. It seemed to taunt her as it dangled in front of her, teasing her blasted curiosity. What would it do? What *could* it do?

Meaghan was a lot of things, but she'd never been one to bow to her own fear. Without giving herself time to doubt, she put the cord over her head and let it drop to her chest, glittering against the backdrop of brown wool. She wasn't foolish enough to let the silver or gems touch her skin. For an empath, metal was a great conduit of the emotions its last owners had felt. Something this old would have a thousand memories—a million emotions—embedded in it, all of which might pull her down and never let her surface again.

"Is that it, then?" Colleen demanded when nothing happened.

Meaghan clenched her fist around the pouch she still held. She felt nothing, not even the humming power that had rushed at her when Colleen unveiled the pendant. Was this really her ticket back home? And if so, was she supposed to do something to activate it? The amulet was quiet and serene now, and she no longer felt that air of threat around it.

Colleen sighed. "Well then, it looks like you'll have to find the Book of Fennore and see if that gets you home."

"Find the Book of Fennore?" Meaghan repeated, her voice shaking with anger and resentment.

"Aye, she mentioned that, too."

"Did she happen to give you a hint about where it might be or what the feck I'm supposed to do with it once I find it?"

"Don't be using that tone with me, missy."

"I'm sorry. But really? Find the bleeding Book of Fennore. I just escaped it, for the love of Jesus."

Colleen raised her brows at that, but she didn't comment. Meaghan supposed she should feel grateful. How in the world could she possibly explain being *inside* a world created by the Book of Fennore?

"She didn't tell me where it was, only that this Druid is free and now there's another evil, a more terrifying evil, within the pages of the Book."

"Evil is evil," Meaghan said testily.

"Well, I wouldn't be arguing that point. All I'm about is telling you what she said."

"I know. I'm sorry. Please, go on."

"She said the Book has always had a master, and that master was the Druid."

"Who is now free."

"That's right. And so someone else is in there now."

"And he's more evil than the Druid was," Meaghan said with a desire to laugh at her own deadpan tone and casual acceptance of the ridiculous.

Colleen nodded. "Some*one*, some*thing*. Who knows what it is that can climb between the covers of a book?"

Meaghan did smile then, albeit grimly. "You'd be amazed what that Book holds."

"Aye, and aren't I wondering how you know. But I'll save my questions until my message is delivered. She said it was important. This evil inside the Book now, he knows the future, she told me. Just as you do. He will be trying to change it."

"Change the future? Well, that's fecking fantastic, isn't it? Why does he want to change the future?"

But even as the words left her mouth, Meaghan knew. In those final moments when she'd been trapped with Áedán in the world of the Book of Fennore, there'd been a battle between none other than her mother's first husband, Cathán, and a small army of men who fought against him.

Cathán, the father of her beloved half brother and half sister, Rory and Danni. Cathán, who'd vanished from the cavern beneath the castle and been presumed dead before Meaghan was even born.

But Cathán was very much alive when last she'd seen him. Alive, but imprisoned by the power of the Book, just as the rest of them had been.

She recalled the cold ice of Cathán's blue eyes. The cruel twist of his mouth. If ever Cathán had been human, if ever there'd been compassion or kindness inside him, it no longer resided in the man he'd become. She had no trouble at all believing he'd turned to the dark side—no problem accepting that somehow he'd become this *new evil. The more terrifying evil.*

And he already knew the future. Like Meaghan, he'd come from it. If he could move freely through time, he could change whatever he wanted. The question was . . . what would Cathán want to change? Meaghan knew her mother had still been married to Cathán and been pregnant with her when Cathán had disappeared. She also knew that Cathán was not her biological father—and Meaghan had stupidly blurted out that fact when she'd met the awful man.

She remembered the fury in those frigid eyes when he'd learned who she was. Áedán had warned her not to taunt him, but she'd been victim to her own anger, and she hadn't been able to stop herself from throwing in his face that her father was Niall Ballagh, a good man. *The better man.*

Horrified by her own idiocy, she looked at the baby in her grandmother's arms, the child who would grow up to be her father, and her heart was cold with fear.

What would Cathán do if he had the power to change anything?

Would he begin by wiping out the man who would steal his wife and children?

And then . . . another thought. She didn't know the year of Cathán's birth. He'd meant nothing to her until she'd become his prisoner. But if the child Colleen held was Niall, then most likely a baby Cathán existed somewhere in this time and place, and perhaps even now cried for a bottle or a nappy change?

"Sure and I don't know what is going on in that head of yours, but I can see it's taking you to someplace dark and unwanted."

Silently, Meaghan nodded.

"I don't know why this Saraid told me the things she did, but I'm thinking there are reasons. I'm not after knowing what they are. A person shouldn't know too much about what awaits them in the future, should they now?"

"No." Especially if that future was at risk of changing for the worst.

"You best keep that pendant where it's safe," Colleen said. "Who knows what it will do."

Wishing she could fling it over the cliffs of Fennore and into the churning sea below, Meaghan pulled it from around her neck, ever so careful not to touch the pendant. As soon as it was off, that insidious drone began again. A jolt of electricity went through her as it dangled in front of her eyes, turning, glinting, multifaceted and inconceivable. For a moment, Meaghan felt as if it were alive—living, breathing, *yearning* . . .

Colleen said something, but Meaghan couldn't hear it. The world around her began to blur and dim in a crazy kaleidoscope of color. It looked like an inked sketch, immersed in water. The colors ran together, making new shades, different shapes. She saw a picture trying to emerge from within the swirl, but she couldn't bring it into focus, couldn't comprehend what the blots and blurs could be.

The sky remained overhead, the earth beneath her feet, and yet it felt as if the globe encasing them had been shaken and now a new vista lay ahead of her. One with a dark blight at its center. That air of malevolence engulfed her, and for a moment, she felt as if invisible eyes had turned her way and made note of her presence.

And she hadn't even touched it yet. What would happen if she dared let it press against her flesh?

From the numbing silence, a voice tried to answer, but it whispered words she could not hear, did not *want* to hear.

She squeezed her eyes shut and sucked in a deep breath. And then another. Her heart pounded painfully, laboriously, and her head felt light. It took will she didn't know she possessed to slow down her pulse, to stay grounded.

"What in the name of Mary was that?" Colleen breathed.

Slowly, cautiously, Meaghan opened her eyes again, and Ballyfionúir snapped back into focus.

She didn't ask Colleen what she'd felt. The pale face and frightened eyes that looked into her own were answer enough.

Quickly Meaghan stuffed the pendant back into its pouch and pulled tight the drawstring before shoving it into the dress's deep pocket. Still she could feel the pendant heavy against her thigh where the pocket rested. It felt hot. Sly. Intent.

Intent on what?

"Well then," Colleen said, eyeing her warily. "Let's get on with ourselves."

Meaghan's mouth was too dry to answer. All she could do was nod. And, sick with dread, she followed her grandmother home.

Chapter Five

COLLEEN seemed engrossed in her own thoughts as they trudged up the winding rocky path, and Meaghan was glad for it. Her own mind was too jumbled, her fear too close to the surface to manage any semblance of a conversation. So much had happened in such a short amount of time, could she really trust herself to understand any of it?

She couldn't begin to guess why she'd fallen through time—why she'd gone backward to her grandmother's youth. And who in bleeding hell was Saraid, and why had she given Meaghan this pendant that had been her brother's and was undoubtedly linked to the Book of Fennore? Until those dark days when she'd been imprisoned in the world created by it, Meaghan had never been near the Book, though she'd been obsessed with finding the Book for years.

And yet, she'd recognized it the very instant she'd seen it.

It was too much. Her head hurt. Her emotions felt bruised. She needed a few moments alone to recharge, regroup. But some internal ticking clock told her she didn't have time for any of that.

She looked at the landscape spread out around her, trying to find solace in the familiarity of the view. It was not much different today than it would be in Meaghan's time, more than fifty years from now. Sure, a few more houses would dot the countryside, the roads would be better paved, and the shops more plentiful. But Ballyfionúir had not undergone massive changes with the progression of years. As a teenager, Meaghan remembered wanting nothing more than to escape the provincial life here. And yet the place where she'd grown up held her heart in ways she couldn't describe, and she'd never been able to distance herself from it for long.

She'd always felt she belonged on this island. Now she wondered if her ties were deeper even than family, than home.

She and Colleen came around the last bend, and Meaghan caught a glimpse of Áedán turning at the gravel walk that led to Colleen's front door. He glanced back before he started up, and for a moment, their eyes met. The distance was too great to read his expression, and yet something in the manner, in the solemn tilt of his head, the square of his shoulders, in his looming presence, shot through her like an arrow.

And damn it all if her thoughts didn't turn immediately to that kiss, to how it felt to be held in his arms—connected in a way that made no sense at all. But like her presence here, in a past that she shouldn't be part of, sense had little to do with anything.

"Mickey will be home by now," Colleen said in a low voice. She shot Meaghan a worried glance. "My husband is not likely to be happy at my bringing you home with me."

And then she hurried forward, her shoulders hunched and her eyes anxious. Meaghan followed, too confused to form words into questions. Numb, she trailed Colleen into her cottage, bracing herself for the rush of nostalgia that nearly swamped her.

The house looked very different and somehow exactly the same as it had the last time Meaghan walked through the door. In the small front room, two chairs and a settee grouped around a rag rug and a coffee table. The cluster of furniture was crude and seemed about as comfortable as church pews. The last time Meaghan had been there,

Colleen had two big, plush recliners with a table between them in their place. One for herself and one for a guest, should she choose to have one. She didn't encourage company and didn't want to make the stray guest feel so comfortable that they lingered or came with a crowd. Her son, his wife, and her grandchildren were the only exception to that rule, and none of them minded sitting on the floor if the chairs were occupied.

Eventually Colleen would have a tiny television in the corner, but now there was only a small bookshelf with a neat row of books and a few knickknacks that Meaghan had never seen before. They didn't look like anything her grandmother would appreciate, and Meaghan wondered if they were her grandfather's contributions to the decor. As they stepped over the threshold, the air was thick with smoke, and with it, the taint of anger rushing at them.

Meaghan braced herself as a man came from the kitchen, a cigarette in one hand and a glass in the other. If the black waves of fury he gave off weren't enough to frighten her, the look on his face would have done it. She'd never known her grandfather; he'd been dead long before she was born. She'd heard once that he and Colleen had been distant cousins—both Ballaghs even before they'd wed, but no one talked of her grandfather much. Not Nana Colleen and not her dad, and she'd never really asked.

He was just one of many dead ancestors whose pictures she'd glimpsed over the years. He'd been a big man, with broad shoulders and the heavy build of a seaman. The life of a fisherman was rarely an easy one, and Michael—Mickey—Ballagh looked like every year he'd spent afloat had left a mark on him.

"Where the hell have you been?" he demanded, looking past Áedán to Colleen, who stood like a fear-frozen rabbit in the talons of a hawk.

Meaghan didn't know what shocked her more—the vehemence of her grandfather or the timidity of her grandmother. In all her life, she'd never seen Nana Colleen cower to anyone.

"I just went out for a wee bit, Mickey. I—my cousin, Meaghan, is here."

Mickey's gaze flicked from Colleen to Meaghan and back. "Cousin? Here? From where?"

"Well, from the mainland, of course. She tells me her mam has died."

Colleen was not the best liar and Mickey looked to be better than most at smelling deceit. He cast his cold scrutiny between them with restless ire. "So what if her mam's dead?" he said. "What does she want here? Do you think I'm the fecking king that can feed all your sniveling relatives?"

Meaghan felt her face flush with heat. Colleen took in quick and shallow breaths, and a vein throbbed at her throat. She seemed too fearful to be embarrassed by her husband's rudeness. Fear was something else Meaghan was not accustomed to seeing on her grandmother's face, and it caught her as much by surprise as anything else that she'd seen since opening her eyes in the cavern.

"Of course not, Mickey," Colleen said in a rush. "But it would be nice if we could offer the poor girl a meal and a bed for the night. She's all alone in the world. She's got nothing."

Mickey took a deep drink from his glass and swayed slightly. He was drunk, Meaghan realized. And mean with it.

"Where did *you* go?" Mickey demanded, shifting that cold hostility to Áedán, who'd been watching with the kind of still attention a cat gave something it stalked.

Meaghan noted that he could see Áedán, too, and her theory that the cavern caused his earlier invisibility grew more solid. The cavern was the lair of the Book of Fennore. She'd felt it to her bones. Meaghan had been in the cavern when she was sucked into that nebulous, terrifying world of Fennore where she'd met Áedán. He'd been invisible to everyone but her there, too. Now piecing it together, Meaghan thought the connection was obvious, if twisted. Close proximity to the Book's power must have some impact on him. But why? Why did it affect Áedán and not Meaghan? If there was an answer to that question, it eluded her. She would have to wait until she could speak to Áedán alone to learn more.

"I didn't go anywhere. I slipped in the mud and hit my head," Áedán answered Mickey's question, his voice smooth and unconcerned. "Knocked myself out, evidently."

Mickey scowled. "You're all right now?"

"I am."

"But your hand still needs stitching, I see."

Colleen jumped as if prodded. "Have you hurt your hand, Mr. Brady? Well, let me tend to it right away."

"I want you here when I get home," Mickey snarled at her as she hurried by. "Not off gallivanting with your beggar relatives. I work all day, and when I walk through that door, I bloody well expect to find my wife waiting with me tea."

He pronounced it *tay* like Meaghan's father did. But his snide wrath made it sound offensive instead of endearing.

"I'm sorry. I didn't think you'd be so early," Colleen said.

She hunched her shoulders and tucked her chin, like a puppy caught peeing on the floor. Meaghan wanted to say something, to step in and defend her Nana, but there was peril in the antagonism wafting off Mickey Ballagh, and it kept her mouth shut for a change. She wasn't known for her restraint, and she could tell by the sharp look Áedán gave her that it surprised him. He'd watched her mouth off to guards twice her size when they'd been imprisoned. But this was different, and some deep sense of self-preservation guided her.

Colleen spoke in an unnaturally high voice. "I'll be on the tea this instant. Sit down, Mickey, and I'll bring it out to you."

"I don't want it no more. And I don't want fish for supper. Are you hearing what I say, wife?"

Wife. Slave. Imbecile. Meaghan could see the meaning he gave the word with his hard, derogatory tone.

Colleen nodded meekly, pulling Meaghan into the kitchen with her.

"Take care of Mr. Brady's hand right away or else your cousin will find herself doing his share in the morn," Mickey barked after them.

With that, he slammed out of the house, leaving a vacuous silence in his wake.

Meaghan let out a shaky breath. "Where is he going?" she whispered, though he was long gone and couldn't hear her.

She thought Colleen mumbled, "To hell," but she couldn't be sure. Tight-lipped, her grandmother shook her head and moved away. Áedán followed the women into the kitchen and went to the sink to rinse the nasty cut on his hand. He didn't look at Meaghan or Colleen as he held the wound under the water, wincing as he applied soap.

"There's nappies in the bag just there," Colleen said to Meaghan, handing over Niall as she pointed to the bag on the ground next to a crude shelf of jars, cans, pots, and pans. "Give him a change, will you, while I get his porridge ready. Would you mind too much if I asked you to feed the wee lad as well?"

"Not at all, Colleen."

Colleen hurried to the stove, lifting the lid on a pot at the back burner, pulling it forward, and stirring it as she adjusted the flame.

"Mr. Brady, use plenty of soap and then sit down over at the table please."

With skill borne of practice, Colleen heated the porridge, set water to boil, and pulled a jug of cream from the small refrigerator in the corner. As Meaghan finished with the diaper, Colleen scooped the porridge into a bowl, added cream and sugar, and set it aside to cool.

Meaghan waited for Áedán to finish at the sink before she washed her own hands, painfully aware of his size and physique as she moved around him. He seemed to fill every vacant space in the room, and he looked as out of place in the tiny kitchen as a knight in an apron.

As if feeling her attention on him, he turned and gave her a dark look, searching her face for something that he seemed very interested in finding. She stared back, trying to pretend his steady perusal didn't unnerve her, but the truth was, it did. Face hot, Meaghan dropped her gaze.

He brushed against her as he passed, and a starburst of images exploded in her head. Áedán's mouth on her body, his tongue a soft whisper against her skin, his hands—she put brakes on the slide show and took a few quick breaths, but still her pulse raced and her temperature spiked. His glance turned knowing as he stepped away, and that only made it worse. She felt like the words *Do me* must be spelled across her forehead in the shades of her blush.

Glad she'd been tasked with feeding the baby and not stitching the silent man who watched her with those unflinching green eyes, Meaghan put Niall into his high chair, then took the bowl of porridge Colleen gave her. Niall ate with delighted gusto, and she might have enjoyed watching him had she not been so aware of Áedán.

The intensity of him was like a hot flash that incinerated her from the inside out and made her pulse erratic, her breath shaky. He sat next to her on the bench that ran the length of the table, close enough that she could smell the soap he'd used to wash with, and beneath that the deeply masculine scent of his skin, unique, utterly enticing, undeniably Áedán. It was forest leaves and fresh air, sweat and passion, seduction and strength.

He lounged carelessly back against the edge of the table, his long legs stretched out, but she knew he was alert and watching her. She glanced at his unwounded hand, where it lay lightly on his muscled thigh, long fingers brown and somehow elegant despite the many cuts and scars covering them. She had the crazy impulse to touch him as she stared into those enigmatic eyes.

"Mr. Brady," Colleen said, pulling a thin line through her needle and then dropping it into a cup and pouring alcohol over it. "Are you ready?"

He nodded, settling his wounded hand on the table, fingers up. With a towel to catch the spill, Colleen splashed alcohol on his palm, making sure she'd thoroughly flushed the gash, then fished the line and needle from the alcohol, pinched the nasty cut shut, and began to sew with skilled precision. Meaghan saw Áedán's jaw tighten, but he gave no other sign of pain. In moments, Colleen finished and tied off the knot.

"Should have done this a bit ago," she said. "It's not good to wait so long before closing a wound, but there you have it."

She took a salve from a cupboard beneath the sink and slathered it on the red and swollen skin around the stitches before wrapping it with clean strips of cloth. Áedán said nothing through it all, but when she finished, he covered her hand with a gentle touch.

"Thank you, Mrs. Ballagh," he said softly.

Colleen flushed. "You're welcome."

Áedán looked like he might say more, but instead, he cast Meaghan one last glance and then he stood. In that look, she'd felt him weighing options, piecing together the jagged edges of his thoughts, and working out a way to make them fit nicely. The look became considering, and she guessed he'd reached a solution.

His mouth quirked in a small but satisfied smile that sent a shiver down her spine. Then, without a word, he lifted his coat from the hook where Colleen had hung it, and strode from the kitchen. A moment later, she heard the front door opening and closing on the silence he left behind. Colleen stayed where she was, frozen for a moment, and then she hung her head, looking very young and lost.

"I suppose he's off to find Mickey," Colleen said on an exhalation. "He'll be at the pub, is my guess. The drink will either mellow Mickey or it will turn him into a bear. There's no way to know which it's to be until the deed's done."

Meaghan didn't know what to say to that. She felt angry and helpless. This was her Nana, a woman who'd sheltered Meaghan her entire life. Someone she'd shared her tears and joys with when they could be trusted to no one else. Now she wanted to console her grandmother but knew Colleen's pride would not allow any show of sympathy.

"Niall's finished eating," Meaghan said softly.

Colleen turned and let her gaze rest on the chubby baby, who looked like he wore more of the porridge than he'd eaten, no matter how careful Meaghan had been in feeding him. He gave Colleen an elated smile, clenching his sticky fists and opening his fat fingers as he squealed with pleasure.

"Would you like me to bathe him?" Meaghan asked.

"Ah, that would be good of you. The tub's right there, tucked up beneath the shelves."

Meaghan pulled the large metal tub from its place and set it on the table, and she and Colleen filled it with water, adding some from the pot simmering on the stove to make it warm. Niall watched with squirming curiosity.

Colleen gave him an indulgent smile. "He does love his baths," she said.

Indeed, it was all Meaghan could do to get the wriggling, porridge-covered bundle out of his chair and nappy and into the tub, where he splashed with unabashed glee. Her father had been a butterball, she thought with a silent sense of hysteria. She supposed when things got so strange they could no longer be processed or viewed with any type of objectivity, they were simply accepted, perhaps earmarked for later consideration, and then filed away.

"How long have you and Mickey been married?" Meaghan asked as she held the baby with one hand and gently poured water over him with a cup Colleen had given her.

A wave of guilt came from Colleen before the words followed, startling Meaghan.

"Four and a half months," Colleen answered without meeting Meaghan's eyes.

Confused, Meaghan glanced at the baby, who had to be close to a year, and then back at Colleen.

"He's not mine. Did you not know that?"

"No. I didn't."

Her world tilted in a crazy way. She'd always assumed she and Colleen were blood, but if her father had not been Colleen's biological son, that wasn't true. It hurt her to learn this painful fact, though really, it had no bearing on her feelings for the woman she called Nana.

"Mickey's first wife died in childbirth and left him with a son he could scarce care for. He mourns her still."

"But he married you anyway?"

Another wash of emotion, this one tart with resentment.

She nodded. "Out of necessity. Nothing more. There's no love lost between us."

It shouldn't have shocked her, given the cold disgust in Mickey's voice when he spoke to Colleen, but somehow it did. Meaghan glanced over her shoulder, where Colleen bustled between the counter and the stove as she chopped chunks of lamb and dropped them into a pot with hot oil and bacon to brown.

"Okay, so I get why *he* needed a wife, but why on earth would *you* marry him?" Meaghan asked, incredulous. "I mean, what compelled you? He's hardly civil to you."

And the bastard had knocked up her grandma within the first week of marrying her, by the looks of it. She shuddered, thinking of what she was certain had been a cruel conception of the child Colleen carried. No way had Mickey been tender, not when he looked at his wife with such contempt.

The emotion spicing the air now was shame. Colleen swallowed hard and looked away, her chin rising with that stubborn pride that made Colleen who she was, who she would one day be. "I best get dinner on the table. No telling when they'll be back."

Meaghan wanted to apologize for the insult she'd obviously—thoughtlessly—given, but Colleen's expression was shut tight, and Meaghan knew she'd do more damage than good if she tried to say she was sorry. Instead, she finished with bathing Niall and put him in a clean diaper.

"He'll be ready for a lie down," Colleen said. "Upstairs, there's a cradle near the bed. Could you put him in with a bottle?"

"It's not good to leave him with a bottle, not of milk or formula anyway. Bad for his teeth. And you should always wipe his gums and teeth with a cloth to clean them before he sleeps."

As she spoke, Meaghan took a clean towel from the folded stack on the shelves, dampened it, and demonstrated.

"Where did you learn that? Have you children of your own, then?"

"Oh, no. None of my own. But my sister and I run a care center for children," she said.

Colleen cocked her head, her look quizzical. "Is that a fact?"

"Yes. It's the sugars that rot the teeth," Meaghan went on, thinking of the brilliant white teeth in her father's smile. She stilled and a dark laugh bubbled up inside her. "Chicken or the egg," she muttered.

"What's that?" Colleen asked, wooden-handled fork held over her skillet.

"You said Saraid made that comment. Well, my father—Niall here—will grow up to have a radiant smile. I was just wondering, is it because I told you to care for his teeth just now? And did I tell you because I know what they'll look like in fifty years, or would they have looked like that whether or not I was here to tell you at all? It's what Saraid was asking. Which came first, the chicken or the egg?"

Colleen blinked at her, but her face went pale. She nodded tensely, and turned back to the sizzling meat with a pensive expression. Without another word, Meaghan went upstairs to lay Niall down for his nap.

The room where Colleen and Mickey slept was small, with a narrow bed that was probably a tight fit for them both. Meaghan stared at it, thought of Colleen swollen with child, and felt overwhelmed with sadness.

She'd been close to Nana Colleen, and if anyone had asked her before today if she'd known her grandmother well, Meaghan would have answered, absolutely. But now she saw that Colleen had hidden many secrets behind those sparkling dark eyes, and Meaghan wondered if she was ready to know them all.

Chapter Six

DOWNSTAIRS again, Meaghan decided she'd better get busy and find the fecking Book of Fennore, if that was what she needed to do to get back to her own time. Colleen chopped vegetables with a vengeance that made Meaghan think she imagined something other than carrots and potatoes beneath her blade.

"Colleen," Meaghan began hesitantly. "I've been thinking about what you told me."

She caught herself reaching for the pendant in her pocket and stopped, surprised. She still felt repelled by the thing, and yet, something about it baited her, lured her to touch it. She realized it had insinuated itself into her thoughts without her being aware. She could still sense the hum of it, muted but insistent, and if she tried, she thought that voice might still be there, whispering, waiting for her to hear.

And with it, temptation. A part of her *wanted* to hear its horrible message.

She longed to go home, but after being near the Book of Fennore, after seeing it firsthand, she knew better than to trust anything linked to it. If the pendant had a connection to the Book, then she would wait until she had them both before she touched either one—and even then, she'd do it only if she saw no other choices.

Colleen glanced up at her, knife poised over her cutting board, head cocked at a curious angle. The mannerism and expression was so like the Colleen that Meaghan had known in her own time, it made her want to smile.

"And what did I tell you that has you thinking, missy?" Colleen prompted.

"Well, you said I'd have to find the Book of Fennore to get home. Have you heard rumors about it? About anyone seeing it?"

"Aye, there are always rumors. We've, I mean to say, Br—Mr. MacGrath—he's our landlord, and, well, you probably know already that he owns pretty much the whole island. Anyway, he's had a bit of luck lately—not that he hasn't always been lucky, that one. But people talk, you know, and they wonder if there's more to it than just luck. It is *good* luck, though," she said hastily, as if concerned that Meaghan might get the wrong impression. "Good enough that it's trickled down to his tenants."

"What do you mean?"

"Only that his cattle are going for top price. His herds are breeding. His pockets are lined, and we all benefit. He's dropped rents—unheard of in other places."

Meaghan frowned, trying to figure out what that had to do with anything. And then she remembered one of the legends that surrounded the Book. It was said to hold the power of the universe. It could grant any wish. Of course the most asked for would be wealth.

Cautiously, she asked, "And people attribute Mr. MacGrath's good luck to the Book of Fennore?"

"Some."

"Why?"

Colleen fixed her attention on her cutting board again, and Meaghan knew instinctively it had more to do with wanting to hide her thoughts than dice the bleeding vegetables. A curious mixture of pride and anger hovered around her grandmother.

"People talk," Colleen said again, her voice husky. "You know how they are. They say Mr. MacGrath has been behaving strangely. They say he's a queer look in his eye."

"Has he?"

"His eyes sparkle like sunlight on blue waters," she said casually.

But Meaghan was watching her grandmother and saw a flush creep up her throat, felt a rush of longing waft off her that seemed at odds with her grandmother's stiff back and pinched expression.

Like Ballagh, the name MacGrath was an old name on this island, part of its history. If she'd been right in her earlier guess, she suspected that *this* MacGrath would have to be Cathán's father.

"You know him well, Mr. MacGrath?" Meaghan asked.

Colleen gave a soft laugh. "We're speaking of the lord and king of Ballyfionúir. He's a wealthy, important man. What would he know of a fisherman's wife?"

Yet the stiffness in Colleen's shoulders, the bitterness in her voice and emotions all contradicted her words. Meaghan wanted to probe deeper. She wanted to understand the mixed signals, but at that moment, Colleen looked very small, very vulnerable, and Meaghan knew she was poking around in something painful for her grandmother. It piqued her interest, but she had too much respect and love for this woman to give in to it.

Meaghan waited, hoping the silence would urge Colleen to fill it. After a moment, she did.

"A year or so ago, a few strangers came around and settled here," she said. "They asked a lot of questions about the Book. Thought they'd find it on our island. Not surprising, an island and a Book that share a name would seem to go hand in hand, wouldn't they? We've had other treasure hunters seeking it from time to time. These men were foreigners and no one had much to tell them. One was a black man."

This in a tone that implied a black man on the Isle of Fennore was rarer than a sighting of the Book itself. Meaghan wasn't surprised. Not until the Celtic Tiger—the "economic miracle" that took Ireland from one of the poorer European countries to one of its wealthiest—was Ireland attractive enough to immigrants to draw them from other countries. Ballyfionúir, being on an isolated island, was inhabited mainly by people who'd been born there or were related, one way or another, to a native of the island. Even in Meaghan's natural time, the island was only sparsely integrated with cultures and races other than Irish.

"Have you ever met these strangers yourself, Colleen?" Meaghan asked.

"Me? Heavens, no. They keep to themselves, more or less. And well, it's said that they're quite a bit on the odd side of things. Most people here just stay out of their way."

Meaghan mulled that for a moment, trying to draw the correlation between the foreigners and Mr. MacGrath's rash of good luck. Obviously, the Book of Fennore formed some type of connection between them, but she couldn't see how.

"Did the lucky turn of events begin for Mr. MacGrath around the same time the strangers came?"

"That's right. About a year ago it started."

Meaghan frowned. A year ago? Her thoughts had been creeping to a conclusion that somehow she or Áedán had brought the Book with them when they'd traveled through time. But this new revelation blasted the weak theory.

"Where are they now? Those men? The strangers?"

Colleen looked up from her chopping, confused by the jump from MacGrath back to the foreigners. "Why would you want to know that?"

"Well, I think I'll go talk to them."

"Are you crazy, missy? You can't just go off talking to strange men."

"Sure I can."

"But it's just not done. Not here anyway."

The scandalized look on Colleen's face masked the last of the mysterious regret, which had pulled her features into a frown when she spoke of Mr. MacGrath. In Meaghan's time, Colleen was fearless. She thought nothing of convention and cared less about what *was done* than she did about what *she wanted to do*. To see her so outraged by Meaghan's suggested visit was almost funny.

"Nana—I mean, Colleen, I've got to get back home. I don't belong here. You know that."

"Aye, I suppose I do." She looked down, a sad little smile on her lips. "Is that what you call me? Nana?"

"We all do."

At the questioning look in Colleen's eyes, Meaghan explained. "My sister and brother, Danni and Rory, they call you that, too. Danni has babies now, and her daughter, she calls you Ninnie. She's very cute."

Colleen's eyes looked like black pits in her pale face. "And are all my grandchildren like you, missy?"

"What do you mean?"

"Well, there's something off about you, isn't there now? Something I can't quite put my finger on, but it's there. I feel it. You're different, aren't you?"

Meaghan felt whipped by the casual observation. Swallowing hard, she looked away. "Yes. I guess I am."

"Sure and wouldn't you have to be, time traveler that you are? Well, I've been called strange myself, so I'm not one to point fingers. What would be the sense of it? For all I know, people will think I'm crazy by the time I'm an old woman."

Meaghan forced herself to smile to hide how much Nana's words had hurt her.

You're different, aren't you?

"Perhaps a few people think you have a screw loose or two, but only because you want them to think it. Life is never boring where you're concerned, Nana. You are loved more than anyone in the world."

That ghost of a smile tilted Colleen's lips more, and her eyes took on a misty gleam that she quickly hid. She cleared her throat. "Loved by all, am I? Well, then, I suppose I must do a lot of changing."

Because Colleen wasn't loved so very much now.

The words didn't need to be spoken for Meaghan to hear them. She gave her grandmother a fierce hug, finding the woman was more solid, less frail, taller even than she remembered—but her scent had not altered. She still smelled of baked bread, summer mornings, and faintly of something Meaghan thought now might be grief. She'd always known there was sadness in her grandmother; she'd just never realized it had been there for so long.

"You don't change that much, Colleen Ballagh. And it's glad I am of it."

Colleen gave Meaghan a bemused glance, and then said, "The lighthouse is to the north of the island. It's where the men who talked of the Book live, or so I've heard. They keep to themselves. Might have moved on, for all I know. If you take the road out, it curves along the cliffs—"

"I know where to find it," Meaghan said. In the future, the lighthouse still stood and was still inhabited, not by foreigners but an old man missing one eye and nearly blind in the other. He claimed he didn't need to see the sea to know her, and no one had ever challenged him on it. So far, no ships had crashed into the island, so she supposed he knew what he was about.

Meaghan gave Colleen a reassuring smile. "I won't be long."

"It's a good walk, missy. You won't have much time before you'll need to return. Mickey will be . . . unpleasant if you're not back before we sit for supper."

Meaghan heard the fear in her grandmother's voice, and it made her want to smack Mickey Ballagh across his sour puss.

"Don't worry," she said with a small smile. "I'll be quick about it."

Colleen nodded, but her expression remained anxious. "There's a jacket on the hook by the front door. You best take it. And be careful. No one knows much about those men. They've never given us a reason to worry over them, but you never know. You're a looker and men tend to lose what little sense God has given them around a pretty girl."

Chapter Seven

ÁEDÁN leaned nonchalantly against the side of the house, watching the back door. The stove kept the kitchen overheated, and Colleen always left the door cracked. He'd heard Meaghan and her *grandmother* talking, and he knew Meaghan would be coming through that door soon, heading for the lighthouse. Seeking the Book of Fennore.

His stomach tightened at the thought of it, and a dark emotion washed over him. *Fear.* He knew it by scent, by taste. Every human that had ever begged him for salvation had smelled of the intoxicating emotion, had been infused with its flavor. But coiled within him, it felt rank and unsavory. Áedán had not feared for millennia. He did not like it that he did now.

The door opened and Meaghan stepped out. She wore a coat of Colleen's and the sleeves came up short, leaving her wrists bare, her pale hands exposed to the raw wind. The chilled air put a flush on her cheeks and added a sparkle to her blue eyes. She was not a small woman, and yet there was something fragile about her, a vulnerability that she tried so hard to hide behind her tough talk and belligerence.

More than that, he found a femininity about her that roused forgotten instincts in him. Gazing at her awoke an ancient need to protect and possess her. An unfamiliar hunger that consumed him as he studied the curves that her ill-fitting coat pronounced, her breasts pressed against the heavy wool, her hips offsetting the line of its drop.

Fear of a different kind twisted inside him. This woman drew him, like *he* had drawn so many humans before. She offered temptation, relief, escape. But as with the many promises Áedán had pledged over the eons of his reign, he knew the offering would come with a very high price.

"Where are you off to, beauty?" he asked, pushing away from the wall.

She startled, spinning to face him with a small gasp. He glimpsed relief when she saw him and then another emotion that turned the bright blue of her gaze into a swirling mix of lavender and cobalt, a color so unique that it stole his breath. Once in his ancient past, he'd seen eyes that color and they'd made him feel what Meaghan's did now. Hot. Hungry. In those eyes, he saw *desire.* He recognized it. Felt it to his bones. That primitive male inside him howled with satisfaction at the knowledge that she yearned as he did.

But, why? Why did *this* woman make him feel as if his blood burned in his veins?

She lowered her lashes, hiding the heat of her gaze from him. He wanted to growl, to take her by the shoulders and force her to give him that look again. He wanted . . .

"What are you doing lurking around in the shadows?" she demanded.

"Waiting for you," he answered calmly.

"What do you want?"

Áedán paused, giving her straightforward question an air of innuendo he knew she hadn't intended. Slowly, he smiled, taunting her, letting her see his thoughts in the hot gaze he ran over her features, down the curve of her throat, to linger on the buttons that threatened to spring from the pressure of her breasts.

Eyes narrowed, she lifted her chin with defiance. She did not fear him. He could not fathom why.

When she did not rise to the bait he dangled, he said curtly, "You will tell me everything Colleen told you."

Meaghan's brows shot up and the corners of her mouth tightened with displeasure. Curiously, he watched her, noting that her eyes changed colors yet again, now more gray than blue.

"Listen, Áedán," she said, seeming to choose her words with great care. Her tone was steady, and yet he sensed the clang and churn of her temper just beneath it. She stepped off the porch and moved toward him. He found her anger amusing, but with each step closer, she brought a jolt of disquiet that shocked him.

Something was different. He felt it in the air around her. Something had changed.

She had changed.

"You and I need to get a few things clear," she said, fearlessly pointing a finger at his chest, stopping just short of jabbing him with it.

Her head did not reach his chin, her weight was a fraction of the full nets he hauled each day. Before the Book of Fennore, he'd been a stone worker and had carved the pillars of his tribe's temple with anvil and chisel. Without even exerting himself, he could crush her. Yet suddenly it was Áedán who felt the chill of dread tripping down his spine, as he had that morning when he'd been drawn to the cavern. Drawn to this woman who'd ensnared him with the sweet taste of her mouth and the yielding curves of her body.

He'd thought her bespelled when she'd wrapped her arms around him, but now he wondered if it was *he* who'd fallen prey to sorcery.

Something had changed in Meaghan.

He felt it, a vibration that seeped beneath his skin, though he couldn't identify it. But he'd borne the curse of the Book of Fennore for too long not to recognize its signature in the air around her. Had she found it already? Had Cathán, ensconced in his new throne as the power of the Book, corrupted her?

She went on, unaware of his turmoil. Unaware of the emotions building in him. *Human* emotions. A tangle of feelings he no longer knew how to unravel.

"I don't like orders," she said in clipped tones. "I don't *take orders*. So if you want something from me, you had better learn how to ask and how to say please."

He might have laughed had he not been so shaken.

Meaghan paused to take a breath, and he sensed that she drew her defenses close, fortifying them in preparation of his retaliation. Through the translucence of her skin, he saw that a vein at her throat pulsed quickly, revealing nerves she didn't show. As if aware of what he saw and what it revealed, she lifted her hand and settled it at her collarbone, fingers nervously plucking at the woolen coat. That small, telling gesture gave Áedán some much-needed strength.

She'd not been despoiled by Cathán, not yet anyway. If she had come in contact with the power of the Book, it had not touched her.

The skin between her brows puckered as she studied him, and he stared back placidly, hoping that he hadn't shown her any signs of weakness.

"What's going on with you, Áedán?" she said. "First no one can see you, now everyone can. What's up with that?"

He felt certain that the cavern had caused him to be unseeable. He remembered the weakness that had made his legs wobble when he'd first crossed the threshold, as if his very essence had been sapped from him. He'd thought his fear had fabricated the sensation until the moment Colleen had looked through him and he'd realized . . . But he didn't want to give Meaghan the power of that knowledge.

Instead, he said, "From the moment I came to this island, I have been a man like any other. Until you lured me to the cavern."

Could she tell that speaking those words made him want to choke? *A man like any other.* Even before the Book of Fennore, he'd never been like other men.

"I didn't lure you," she said, surprised. "I wasn't even conscious when you got there."

"And yet I felt compelled to come, though I knew the dangers."

"Did it occur to you that it was the Book of Fennore compelling you and not me? I felt its power there."

Yes, of course he had felt it, too. And yet, he was still convinced that Meaghan had been the draw.

Between them, a silence filled the air, grainy and hot. It pushed them apart while pulling them closer with its barely perceptible tremor. Did it come from Meaghan? It must. And yet he hadn't noticed it when he'd held her, kissed her.

What had changed?

"Tell me what you and Colleen talked about when you walked from the ruins to the house. I looked back, and you seemed engrossed in whatever she was telling you. I want to know what she said." He remembered belatedly to curve the command into a question with his tone. At her sharp glance, he tacked on a harsh, "Please."

It seemed she knew just how much that cost him, and she grudgingly nodded. "Come with me, then," she said.

"To the lighthouse?"

"You were listening?"

"It seemed prudent to find out what you and your *grandmother* are about."

"And?"

"Only a fool would escape the Book of Fennore and then turn around and seek it out again."

"Yeah, well, I've been called worse than that."

He fell into step beside her, painfully aware of the soft scent of her skin. Colleen made soaps to supplement their meager income. Her most coveted creation blended honeysuckle and oatmeal, ground fine. The soft aroma clung to Meaghan's skin and mixed with her own seductive scent to cloud his brain, making him want to press closer, to breathe her in.

"Why were you angry when you found out Colleen was my grandmother?"

Her question snapped him from his thoughts and cleared the haze from his mind. "I wasn't angry. I was . . . disconcerted by the revelation. First you appear and render me invisible, and then she revealed who she was to you. It felt . . . conspired."

"I was just as stunned as you were, Áedán. I don't know why I'm here, *now*, in my grandmother's time."

"But you do know why you were sucked into the world of Fennore. You know why Cathán took you captive."

"Do I? Well that's news to me."

He couldn't tell if she lied or spoke the truth. He said, "Your family has been linked to the Book of Fennore for many years."

"How do you know that?"

"How is not important. What you should be asking is why? Why are you linked?"

"You know Cathán MacGrath was my mother's first husband."

He nodded. She'd revealed this when Cathán held them prisoners. Cathán had thought her someone of use to him, and Áedán was certain his interest in her went beyond a familial relationship. Countless prophesies and myths entwined with the tales of the Book of Fennore—so many that even Áedán did not know which were truth and which were fable. At first he'd suspected that Cathán thought Meaghan was the woman who could open the Book and release all who were trapped in the unnatural world of Fennore. He'd been wrong. But who was she? What gift did Cathán think she had?

"Cathán was your mother's husband, but he is not your father," Áedán said. "Correct?"

"Exactly."

As if that explained everything.

"That is not reason enough for you to have been pulled in by the Book of Fennore. Cathán had another motive for keeping you captive."

"Fecking revenge was his motive," she said with a haughty arch of her brows. "He's a tosser that my mother couldn't get away from fast enough. It pissed him off that she married my dad and had me. She was pregnant before Cathán was even out of the picture. You heard him when he figured out who I was. He called my dad a filthy fisherman, like that was the worst thing imaginable. I hope he's trapped in there forever. I hope he rots and dies in that hellish world."

"He won't die."

"Of course he will. Everyone dies."

"Not where he is. But he will grow more powerful. He will do whatever he can to escape."

"And what are you? A fecking Book of Fennore-ologist?"

Yes, he supposed he was. "I know people," he said. "A man cornered with no options will do anything to survive. Use anyone."

"I won't say you don't have a point. But for all we know, he's out already. He could have followed us. He could be here, now. Just waiting to make his move."

"No," Áedán said. "I would know."

"Is that a fact? You're also a psychic now, are you? Seeing the future?"

"I don't need to see it to know it's there, do I?"

She made a dismissive sound, but that telltale pulse beat furiously at her throat. After a moment, she said, "The Book of Fennore is evil."

Her glance was lightning fast, but in it he glimpsed the terror that her defiance worked so hard to hide. He wondered what she saw in his eyes before he looked away.

For a thousand years or more, humans had rumbled about the evil inside the Book of Fennore. Blind fools, they didn't understand that the evil came not only from the Book, but from the greed and lust for power that they brought with each wish. Yes, there had been some who came innocent and needing, but they had been as rare as red diamonds, and they had sold their souls as readily as the twisted monsters who thought to use his gifts for their own selfish needs.

Wealth. Power. Women. He'd grown so weary of their pathetic pleas.

"Few would dispute the claim of evil within the Book of Fennore," he said when it appeared she waited for his response.

"Saraid told Colleen that the Book's master is a Druid. An evil Druid."

He might have laughed but for the seriousness of her tone. He'd never been the *master* of the Book of Fennore. Yes, he'd wielded its power. Yes, he'd been its voice. But the Book of Fennore was a sentient being with a will of its own. It had no master, only slaves that it branded as its own. And each time a wretched soul solicited its help, the Book grew stronger. It drank in their wishes, their entreaties, their prayers and it became more twisted and more powerful each time.

Meaghan went on, watching him closely, making him fear she could somehow hear the tumultuous thoughts racing through his mind.

"Colleen said this evil Druid is now free."

"Free? In what way is the Druid free?"

The question obviously baffled her. Meaghan looked at him with those big blue eyes, once again the color of a summer sky, and shook her head. "Out, I guess."

"Out and free are not necessarily the same thing."

She caught her bottom lip between her teeth and worried it, pondering this.

"What else did Colleen have to say?" he asked before she worked out an answer.

"Nothing. It's just that . . . well, when we were trapped in the world of Fennore, I felt Cathán's presence. His *power*. If there's a master, I don't think it's this Druid. I think it's Cathán who's in control."

Her perception surprised him. She'd stated nothing more or less than he'd already surmised himself, but he hadn't expected her to be so astute and hearing the truth spoken aloud on this crisp Irish day made Áedán's blood run cold. Had Cathán truly managed what Áedán had considered impossible? Had he somehow leashed the beast? Had he become more powerful than the Book itself? If so, how? After millennia, Áedán had been no closer to usurping the Book's supremacy than he'd been in the beginning.

"What is your point, Meaghan?" he asked, as if her calm revelations hadn't shaken him to the core.

"That Cathán is more evil than the Druid ever was," she said softly, still studying him from the corners of her eyes.

She stopped walking and faced him, head tilted to one side, gaze intent on his. That strange and disturbing hum that seemed to ruffle the air intensified—a flare of interest that made him want to step back. Her expression was somber and anxious. She brushed an errant wisp of hair away from her eyes with one hand, and he saw that it shook. She was afraid, he realized with surprise. But she hid it behind a mask of courage.

"Are you . . ." she began, her voice low and uncertain. She squared her shoulders and lifted her chin. "Are you the Druid, Áedán?"

"Áedán!"

The man calling his name startled them both and saved him from answering. They turned to see someone huffing and puffing as he lumbered up the road behind them. Áedán recognized the man. He docked his ship near *The Angel* and could usually be found at the pub as drunk as Mickey.

"Who is that?" Meaghan asked.

"Hoyt O'Shea," Áedán answered, wondering what the man wanted with him.

Two other men who'd been accompanying Hoyt waited at the bottom of the hill as Hoyt came to stop beside them.

"Áedán," he said breathlessly. "It's lucky for me I saw you walking. I've been wanting to have a chat with you, now, haven't I?"

He beamed at Áedán and gave Meaghan a curious but dismissive glance. She was a stranger in his town, but she was not his goal, that look said. He had bloodshot eyes and fumes of alcohol wafted off him.

"I know Mickey's got you working like a slave, he does," Hoyt said eagerly. "And I come to tell you that I can offer you better. You can board on the *High Tide*, take your meals with me and me wife—she's as fine a cook as there is in all of Ballyfionúir. *And* I'll pay you a wage, I will. A fair one. Ten percent of me taking."

Áedán tried to look suitably impressed by the offer. "Thank you, Mr. O'Shea—"

"Hoyt. Call me Hoyt. I'm not like Mickey that way."

"Thank you, Hoyt, but Mr. Ballagh has been good to me, and it wouldn't be fair—"

"Oh, he's got you fooled, doesn't he? He's made you think he's done you a favor, taking you in. Truth is, he's a user, that man. He's not done right by you. You do the work of five men. Sure, and haven't I seen it with my own eyes. His catch is more than double—nay triple—what he brought before you come. Bet he didn't tell you that, did he?"

No, he had not. It wouldn't have mattered, though, even if he had. Áedán did not plan to be on this island much longer. He'd taken Mickey's offer of labor for food and board only to hold him over until he could determine what exactly had happened and what, exactly, he'd become.

He'd once been the powerful Druid that Meaghan spoke of. But now . . . he'd thought himself a mere man until Meaghan had appeared. Now he didn't know if he was even that.

Hoyt's excitement was nearly as overwhelming as his odor. Seeing what he thought to be indecision on Áedán's face, he pushed. "He's got you thinking you owe him, and it's the other way around, isn't that a fact? He's done you a disservice, Áedán. That's the truth. Jump ship, lad. Come to the *High Tide*."

Áedán glanced at Meaghan and quickly away. He had no intention of jumping ship, not now. He needed to stay as close to Meaghan as he could, and the easiest way to do that was to keep toiling for the disagreeable man, Mickey.

"I'm afraid I can't do that, Hoyt, though I do appreciate your offer. I'm where I should be for the time being. If circumstances change, I will let you know."

For a moment, Hoyt stared at him blankly, as if it went beyond belief that Áedán would—could—turn him down. Then his expression became sour and his eyes hard. "You think I'll just hold the offer for you until you decide it's good enough, then? Well, I won't. It's now or never."

"Then it's never," Áedán said without apology.

Hoyt's mouth opened and closed before he spat, "That Mickey gets all the luck, doesn't he now? Well, you have it your way."

And with that, he stomped back down the hill. Silently they watched him join his friends and give what appeared to be an animated rendition of their conversation, arms waving, fingers pointing.

"He seems quite upset," Áedán commented, hoping the interruption had derailed Meaghan's questions. When he looked back at her, though, he knew he would not be so fortunate. Meaghan watched him with the attention of a scientist studying a rare anomaly that she planned to categorize and document.

He started walking again, forcing her to fall into step. The sky had cleared and now the clouds made a patchwork of the gray and blue, casting soft shadows that whispered over the sloping hills and hulking boulders, diluting the sunshine into a buttermilk haze. It was late afternoon. The pubs would be swelling with fishermen done for the day. Mickey would be in the thick of it, swigging brew and talking out of both sides of his mouth.

"I'm still waiting for you to answer my question, Áedán," Meaghan said, as he'd known she would. "Are you the Druid that Saraid warned about?"

"The evil Druid? The one who could destroy the world if he so wanted?" Áedán mocked.

"Yes."

"Well, of course I am. And can't you tell by looking at me that I'm all-powerful? That's why I'm working on a fecking boat the size of a shoe, just for the privilege of eating and sleeping somewhere dry. You heard Hoyt O'Shea. I'm slave labor, beauty. If I had a choice, if I had the power to change things, I'd be living under better circumstances, wouldn't I?"

She narrowed her eyes and he knew she'd seen through his sarcasm. She was not some brainless child who'd accept the attempt to deflect her questions. Not this woman.

"What were you doing in the world of Fennore, Áedán?" she asked softly, and yet, in her voice, he heard steel and anguish. As if it was *she* who'd been betrayed.

"I was a prisoner, just like you," he said. "You know that."

"Really? Then why was I the only one who could see you?"

"Perhaps you are the Druid."

She spun at that and stopped him with a hand on his wrist, her fingers cold against his heat. That simple contact seemed to draw all of his energy, all of his attention until the rest of the world faded and there was only this moment, this woman. He felt that unnerving vibration rattling his teeth and stretching his nerves, but overpowering it was something more primal and fierce.

"Stop it," she said. "This isn't some fecking game. I want answers from you. Why were you a prisoner?"

Her demand sparked against his sudden—maddening—arousal. "You think I'm playing games? What about you, Meaghan? What secrets do you hide? Your own grandmother said there was something *off* about you. That you are *different*. Let us explore that instead."

He took a step forward, forcing her to step back, and then he kept going until he had her pinned between his body and one of the many boulders that littered the side of the road. The primitive male within him roared, but his voice, when he spoke, was soft and deep, the voice he'd used a million times or more to seduce the unwary.

"How are you different, beauty?"

"I told you to quit calling me that."

"But you *are* very beautiful."

The eyes she turned on him were wide and wounded, as angry as they were injured. He'd poked at something hidden and now she would come out snarling. "Tell me," he said, leaning closer still, his body pressed against every lush curve of hers. A part of him wanted her to fight, to resist, and another part desired only that she yield.

"How are you different?"

"Well, I'm a fecking time traveler, aren't I?" she said, using his own tactic to deflect him. But her sarcasm worked no better on him than his had on her. "I'm her granddaughter, come from the future. I'd say that's different enough."

He smiled, admiring her defiance even as he worked to tame it. "That's not what she meant," he said, lips against her ear.

She tried to evade his mouth, but he kept her pinned, one hand at her waist the other at the base of her skull. She was too proud to openly fight him, too stubborn to show him that his nearness disconcerted her.

"You seem to be an expert on the subject," she said, her voice wavering. "You tell me what she meant."

"I feel something around you. A vibration—a disorder to the natural flow of things. It's disturbing. *You* are disturbing."

She jerked away, surprising him with the sudden violence of her movements. Before he knew it, she'd escaped his hold and stood a few paces away. Her chest heaved and her blue eyes snapped.

"There's nothing wrong with me," she choked.

Ah. A reaction she hadn't wanted to reveal, it was there in every line of her stance. "I never said there was. I only said you were different."

"Disturbed."

"Disturb*ing*. Not the same thing."

He realized then that the shine in her eyes had less to do with rage than it did with pain—not physical pain, but something deeper, rawer.

"I've hurt you," he murmured, his tone a dark brew of fascination, shock, and revelation.

"Feck off."

She turned and began walking again, her steps tight and fierce, her arms stiff at her sides, fists balled in the pockets of her borrowed jacket. Intrigued, he followed, catching up easily enough. The indignant silence that hung around her felt as cold and abject as a blustering storm. It spurred something inside Áedán that he didn't recognize at first.

Remorse.

He was sorry for baiting her. The emotion staggered and dismayed him.

"Meaghan," he said. "Meaghan, wait."

She turned on him like a predator. "Wait for what, Áedán? Do you want to tell me lies? Or do you want to insult me? Tell me that I'm not normal? Well, I fecking know that already. I've never been *normal.* But I'm not some freak—no matter what has happened or why I'm here, I know that."

"I never implied that you were."

"No? Then why did you bring it up?"

"To distract you," he stunned himself by saying.

The taut silence that followed toyed with the myriad of exposed emotions twisting tight inside him. Cautiously, he stepped closer to her, stopping less than an arm's length away. Too close, he knew, but he could not bring himself to retreat.

The flesh between her brows puckered again, and without thinking, he brushed his thumb over the silky flesh, smoothing the furrow away. And once the frown vanished, he found his hands cupping her chilled face, wanting nothing more than to heat her flesh with his, wanting nothing more than to hold her. It confounded him, the need to comfort her, but it seemed that where this woman was concerned, his actions came with a will of their own. He pulled her to him, her body stiff and unbending.

"I am sorry," he said, meaning it. Astonished by it.

Her rigidness ceded just a bit, just enough to give him a measure of hope.

Hope? He shoved that away, refusing to analyze it.

"You came from the future, Meaghan," he said, reluctantly giving her the explanation she deserved. His lips hovered once again over the fragile shell of her ear. "I came from the past."

"When?" she asked, her voice muffled by his jacket. But the hands that had been pushing against his chest eased, neither taking nor rejecting.

"Longer than you can imagine."

"I can imagine a lot after what I've been through."

Yes, he supposed she could. "Millennia," he said, and the word hurt as it emerged. "I was condemned to the Book of Fennore an eternity ago. That is why I was imprisoned there."

He swallowed painfully, confused by his own need to confess to her. A voice in his head urged him to be quiet, to reveal nothing more.

"Why?" she asked.

"I've never known. In all the years, I've never known. I was condemned without explanation or justification. Condemned with the suddenness of a lightning strike."

She tilted her head back and scrutinized his face. He fought to keep his expression bland, to hide the crippling panic he felt at being so exposed. "Who condemned you?"

She asked too much. He could not reveal the depth of the betrayal. But the answer, when it came, shook with honesty.

"The woman I loved," he said simply, but there was nothing simple in the wash of emotions that went through him. Dark and complex, they tried to tow him under, reminding him why for centuries on end, he'd chosen not to feel.

Meaghan caught her lip between her teeth as he'd seen her do before, saying nothing as she waited for him to go on. Her silence somehow soothed him even as the vibration around her flared and his own pathetic words emerged.

"When you met me, I told you that I was called Brandubh."

"Brawn-doov," she repeated, her voice giving the old title a melodic sound. "The Black Raven. Yes, I remember."

"And to that you scoffed and demanded to know my *real* name. The name my mother gave me." He almost smiled, remembering her feisty jeer, but he felt too hollow for that. "Brandubh was the name given to me when I joined the order of Druids."

She stilled in his arms, and then her fingers clenched the fabric of his coat, and she looked up into his face, wary but not yet afraid. Her eyes grew wider, the color so clear he thought he might drown in the depths of blue.

"Druids?"

"My family was slaughtered by marauders when I was a boy. My mother lived just long enough to take me to the place she'd thought I'd be safest. To the Druids. I was raised among them. I learned their ways from the time I could walk."

"Were they evil?" she asked innocently.

Áedán shook his head and he did laugh, though the sound had more sorrow than joy. "No. It was not an order of evil. They taught me to nurture the land, the people, the gods that governed us. They taught me to be one with nature."

She waited, her hands still bunching the wool of his coat, her knuckles red and chapped from the cold. He kept one arm around her, holding her against his body, needing her softness, her strength as he bared his soul. With his other hand, he pried her fingers free and tucked her balled fists beneath his open jacket where they settled like small, frozen birds against his chest. He felt a shiver go through her, felt its echo in himself.

"I was an apt pupil. I learned their ways, embraced their rituals. I was the most gifted of all their students. And when I grew to a man, it was to me the leader of my new tribe came for counsel. He granted me favors. The people worshiped me like a god. I began to think I was kin to the gods. That I was above the laws of mankind. I grew drunk on my own sense of power and I turned my back on my teachings to be my own teacher. I learned the dark ways and thought myself justified because I was Brandubh and I had the right to do whatever I wanted."

Her fingers spread against the rough cotton of his shirt and pressed against his thumping heart, forcing the confession from his lips.

"I am Áedán, son of Áedán," he said. "I am Brandubh, son of no one. I am the Druid of the Book of Fennore. I am everything and I am nothing. And I am that which you call evil."

Chapter Eight

MEAGHAN stared at Áedán, certain for a moment that she'd misheard him. Surely he hadn't said *he* was the Druid? She'd asked him the question point-blank, but she hadn't really expected him to say yes. If anything, she'd been braced for a jeering denial, more sarcasm to make her feel like a fecking idiot.

I am that which you call evil.

Evil? Really? How did she begin to put the parameters of its definition around the tall man standing in front of her with his forest green eyes and sculpted features? Even when they'd been prisoners and she hadn't known if he should be feared or trusted, Meaghan had never sensed *evil* about him. She didn't now, despite his admission.

He watched her, his eyes guarded, his expression giving nothing away of what he might be thinking. How did he expect her to respond, for the tension in his stance told her he anticipated a reaction. Screams? Condemnation? Terror?

She thought it might be all of the above. Though he worked hard not to expose his thoughts, she felt him mounting his defenses, girding his vulnerable underbelly against whatever she might do or say next. His confession had left him open and exposed. But how would she use this information? Who would believe her if she ran into the streets crying out, "Áedán is evil"?

Perhaps that was the point. Perhaps he was merely manipulating her. Giving her a reason to fear him without the ability to do anything about it.

As if agitated by her thoughts, the pendant in the pocket of her ugly dress grew suddenly hot against her thigh and a faint hum began to drone from it in low, jerky pulses. She realized that the pendant seemed to be reacting to her emotions, becoming somehow disturbed as the tension rose within her. Unnerved, she withdrew her hand from where it pressed against his. Using the padding around the pocket to insulate her fingers, she pulled the pendant away from where it rested against her leg and clenched it tight, but the almost-sound it made vibrated down into her bones.

She wanted to take it out and see what had caused the strange flare, but she didn't. Not in front of Áedán. Not until she knew more.

"Why tell me the truth?" she asked, staring into his unsettling eyes, searching for answers. For something that would justify the feeling lodged deep in her chest, urging her to believe in him, regardless of the fact that he'd just called himself a devil by another name.

"Your enemy is Cathán," he said. "You were correct. He controls the power of the Book now. It is in my best interest that you know that."

True, but not the entire truth. Not the answer to her question either. Why he'd told her was hidden in the knotted emotions he'd camouflaged behind the greens and golds of his wary gaze.

Meaghan took another step back. The corners of Áedán's mouth tightened in response. Trying to appear calm and unruffled, she asked, "But Cathán is trapped inside the Book of Fennore. He can't get out, can he?"

Áedán nodded cautiously. "His physical form is locked away, but do not think that makes you safe from him. He can summon you—

enthrall you—merely by his voice. He can entice others to do his bidding."

"How?" she asked.

His brows lowered as he thought through his response. She had the sense that it was important to him that she understand completely.

"Cathán is no longer corporeal, but his essence is very real. He can see what is happening in the world around him. More than that, he can sense it. He can discern grief from joy. The Book anchors him to a place and time, but within that realm, he can reach out and speak to the hearts of those in need. The more desperate the soul, the louder their voice and the more able he is to hone in and deceive them. Use them."

"But can he force them? Can they say no?"

Áedán's smile held no humor, and the chilled flatness of it made her shiver.

"Yes. And some will. But humans are wretched beings. They need, constantly. They crave more. They yearn for that which they think has been denied them. They feel mistreated. They want their due."

"Humans? You speak as if you aren't one," she said.

He shrugged, neither confirming nor denying her observation. Since they'd left Colleen's, she'd felt the complex and confusing swirl of his emotions brushing against her own like mink against naked skin. Her subconscious had used it as a barometer to gauge the hidden undertones of his words. Now she felt only the absence of any feeling from him at all. A cold nothingness that undermined her determination to remain composed.

"Okay," she said. "So Cathán can lure some unsuspecting person into his web and use them. What about you? What can *you* do, Áedán?"

His gaze snapped to hers, and she saw bitterness layering the glittering green. It ran deep as the ocean and quick as the tides.

"I can do nothing," he said. "All the power I had when I spoke for the Book of Fennore is gone. It belongs to Cathán now."

"But before Cathán, before you were condemned to the Book of Fennore, you said you were a powerful Druid."

"That was centuries ago."

Centuries. She fought to keep her mind from stumbling on that and falling into a spiral of lunacy.

"So you don't know how to . . . do it anymore? Whatever you did as a Druid that made you so powerful?"

He narrowed his eyes, anger and something that looked a lot like panic gleaming with them. "I told you. I was cursed to spend all of eternity in the Book of Fennore."

"I understand," she said and then shook her head. "Forget I said that. I don't understand at all. What I mean to ask, though . . . well, if you were once a mighty Druid, then how could escaping a curse change that?"

"It changed me," he said reluctantly. "The curse changed me. But even before that . . ." He swallowed and looked away. "I broke my covenant and betrayed my calling."

What he'd done pained him. *Shamed* him. She didn't have to be empathic to feel the wash of his disgrace or the steel door slam on that line of questioning.

Carefully, she chose her next words. "For years—centuries, you said—the Book of Fennore has been destroying people."

"People destroy people. Greed and corruption destroy people. Hatred and vengeance destroy them. I was just the vehicle that took them there."

"Evil."

"Yes."

And still she felt no evil in him. Nothing to support that simple affirmation. "Did you want to hurt them?"

"Yes."

"Why?"

"They disgusted me with their sniveling pleas and their petty grievances. They came to me knowing the cost, and still they begged for my gifts, then cried when I took what they owed."

"Why?" she said again.

"Why what, Meaghan? Why did I take or why did they come?"

Meaghan shook her head, uncertain of the exact question she meant to ask. "Why were you so cruel?"

His lashes came down over the jewel brightness of his eyes, hiding what he thought, but the blast of his emotions bit at her skin like a shower of frost. "Cruel?" he repeated disbelievingly. "Cruel is being condemned for all of eternity. *Cursed* to live millennia in a solitary existence."

"But that wasn't their fault."

"I cared not. Does that shock you, beauty? Does that offend your sensitivities? I do not care about my *fellow man*. I do not consider them worthy."

"I don't believe you. You helped me when Cathán wanted to hurt me."

"Cathán thought you were useful. My guess is that he still does. And if you are of use to him, you might be of use to me. That is why I helped you."

The words were meant to cut, and they did. But like salve, she felt the wave of remorse that followed them. The man was a conundrum, but he was not as unfeeling as he would like her to believe.

"I think you're lying," she said. "You've made friends here. My grandmother obviously thinks a good deal of you. I could tell by the way she treated you."

"Delude yourself if you must, but only a fool would try to paint a pretty picture of me. Are you a fool, Meaghan?"

He cocked a brow, looking down his fine straight nose at her. Maybe he was right and she was a fool. Or maybe it was the dull throb of uncertainty that she felt in him, but still she didn't believe what he said.

He stepped closer, crowding her with his big body, reminding her that he had pinned her earlier without exerting any effort at all. "For a thousand years and more," he breathed into her ear, his voice husky and deep, his breath hot and intimate against her skin. "My only contact with the outside came from the greedy dredges who wanted nothing but to take from me. To possess what little was left of me. They wanted my power. They wanted to control me. To *use* me. Yet *I* was cruel for giving them what they wanted."

"What did you do to them?" she asked, her voice small.

"I gave them exactly what they asked for. This one wanted wealth. I made him rich beyond belief. That one wanted power. I made him king. Another wanted her deformed children to be whole and unflawed. I made them beautiful."

"But in all the legends . . . they say each person who used the Book of Fennore suffered unbearable consequences. Most of them died for it. Is that a lie?"

"No."

She turned her head, risking peril as she looked into his eyes. His face was very close, and she could see each facet, each shade, each alluring shift in color. His scent surrounded her, elusive and male, seducing her to breathe deeply and take him in. How could she think of him as *evil*? Dangerous, yes. Arrogant, absolutely. But evil?

"What would you crave more than anything if you'd spent eternity alone in a world without texture, without touch?" he asked softly.

"I don't know. Company?"

"Emotion. *Feeling*. A reminder of what it is to be human. That is what I asked in return for each gift I gave."

"You wanted to feel? That was your price? Not their souls? Not their lives? But . . . why . . . how did that kill them?"

"They killed themselves," he said bluntly, and in his words, she felt satisfaction. Not pleasure, but a sense of justice.

She frowned, trying to merge the sparse pieces he'd scattered in front of her into a picture that made sense. In her pocket, the pendant flared with heat and that almost-hum that she felt even if she did not hear. She clenched it in the fabric of the coat, unable to do more than contain it.

Áedán went on, his voice mesmerizing, his words disturbing.

"They could not bear what they became without the ability to *feel.* They could not bear a year of what I withstood for eons."

"You took their ability to feel *anything*?"

"Anything good," he said.

Meaghan's eyes widened as she thought that through. Anything *good.* Joy, love, compassion? He'd taken their ability to experience the things that made life worth living.

"I left them their greed and anger. Their hatred."

Oh God.

She swallowed hard, her heart aching for the poor fools who'd come to the Book of Fennore for help and in return had been stripped of life but not of living.

"And you enjoyed it?" she said. "Hurting them like that."

"Yes."

"You want me to think you're a monster, don't you?"

"I am a monster, beauty. What I want matters not."

"But now you're free."

"Am I?"

"Well, you aren't trapped in this curse anymore, are you?"

"And yet, from moment to moment, I might find myself invisible to anyone but you."

Meaghan heard the barely suppressed violence in his words, saw the tightness in his features, felt the burst of hot breath as he exhaled.

"Do you still want to hurt people, Áedán?"

"I told you. It's never been about what I wanted."

"What about me?"

"You, I definitely want."

Her face burned hot at the carnal wave of emotions that hit her, so tangible that they formed pictures in her head, yearning deep in her body.

"I meant, do you want to hurt me?"

He stared at her long and hard, his gaze steady and probing. "No."

It seemed the word had come from someplace deep within, emerging with harsh unwillingness.

"Do you still think you're some kind of a god?"

He broke his stare and looked off into the distance, his lips quirking in a grimace. "I think I am less than a man. Even my substance is lacking."

Without meaning to, she reached out, settling her hand beneath his jacket again. His heart thudded strong against her palm, his gaze intent once more on her face. "You feel pretty substantial to me," she said, her voice as soft as the silence that whispered around them.

He said nothing, but his hungry gaze devoured her, demanding that she keep talking. That she heal the open wound she felt aching within him.

"I know something about people, too," she said. "And I don't think you're evil."

"Then you are wrong."

"I think that's what you'd like me to believe."

"You do not know me, beauty."

At that, she met his gaze and spoke from her heart, surprising herself with the words that came without hesitation. "I feel like I do. I feel like I have history with you, Áedán. For the life of me, I can't explain it. But ever since I woke up in the cavern . . ."

He waited for her to continue with a stillness that disconcerted her. She wanted to backpedal. To pretend her words had not been spoken.

But something fragile had formed in the touch of her hand over his heart. Something that drove her to say the things she'd not even admitted to herself. In truth, they seemed to blossom in her mind, forming and insisting on words before she'd even considered their veracity.

"I feel like there is unfinished business between us, Áedán."

Something between them that begged for closure, though she couldn't fathom what it might be. But the thought of not discovering what it was, of leaving it incomplete, made her feel inexplicably bereft.

"What business?" he asked, moving closer, bringing his big,

scarred hands to her waist, sliding them beneath her coat so they settled against the curve of her hips. Hot. Possessive. Needing.

In her pocket, the pendant hushed, as if it, too, waited for her answer.

"You. Me. Us," she murmured.

His eyes widened in surprise and then suddenly narrowed, as if an answer he'd been seeking had unexpectedly revealed itself.

"Yes," he agreed, his voice deep and dark, making her think of clandestine meetings and unmentionable secrets.

He stood so close she could feel the heat of his body searing the length of hers, the warmth of his breath against her temple. And mixed in it all was the silken honey of his emotions. They weren't conflicted now. They embraced her, coaxed her, beguiled her completely.

"Let me help you, beauty. Together we will find the Book, if that's what you want."

"Why?" she breathed.

"Because you are no match for Cathán."

"So?" she said. "I thought you were Mr. Evil. What do you care about me?"

He leaned in, pressing his forehead against hers. His lashes made a silky screen, hiding his thoughts from her, but the bite and burn of desire and denial tore at her ragged nerve endings, unraveling her will to understand. Did it really matter why he helped her?

The thought stunned her and almost snapped her from the spell she seemed to have fallen under. She needed to breathe, and Áedán seemed to take more than his share of the oxygen, but she couldn't force herself to push him away.

"What happened to the woman you loved?" she whispered without meaning to. "The one who cursed you?"

Trapped in the storm of his emotions, Meaghan stilled, waiting. For one unguarded instant, he lifted solemn and endless eyes to meet hers, eyes filled with the bitter regret she tasted in the air. The anguish she saw in them compelled her to look away, telling her she'd stumbled, stumbled onto something too painfully personal to witness. At the same time, his gaze drew her in. She found herself lost in the color of trees, of leaves dappled with sunshine, of dark forest shadows dancing in a misted breeze.

"She left me," he said at last. "She left me to rot in my misery and never looked back."

In his words, she felt love and hate bound into links of a chain that tightened around his heart and squeezed. Emotion blazed bright, blisteringly hot and anchored as deep as his soul. She swayed with the power of it, leaning forward, entranced.

"Why?" she asked.

She watched his throat muscles flex as he swallowed, knew that his feelings had clogged his passageways.

"Love is often a violent and doomed thing," he murmured. "It acts without reason."

And everything that made that simple statement more than just words hit her like a blow.

Violent. Doomed.

He released her and stepped back, letting the cold race in where his heat had kept her warm. As she watched, his expression smoothed into the placid mask he wore so well. He offered no explanation when he began to walk again, and Meaghan found that she could not bring herself to ask him more questions.

"We should hurry," he said over his shoulder. "Colleen was right—Mickey will be enraged if you hold up his supper."

His reminder snapped the last sticky tendrils of his spell. Alarmed at how she'd lost track of time, Meaghan nodded and hurried to catch up, then set a brisk pace, keeping her thoughts to herself. Effortlessly, Áedán matched her strides.

"The Book of Fennore is nothing but a trap waiting to be sprung," he said.

"And my ticket home," she answered.

"I do not think so, but you are the kind of woman who must see things with her own eyes before you believe them."

She shrugged defensively. It was true and she didn't waste her breath denying it. From beneath her lashes, she cast him an uneasy glance. In her whole life, Meaghan had never met a man so complex and mystifying.

But he wasn't just a man, was he?

Feeling lost and unsure, Meaghan crested the top of a hill. Down below, the sea churned restlessly, the surging tide a match for the waves of confusion that threatened to pull Meaghan out to the middle of the vast waters and strand her.

Entrenched in the cliffs of Fennore was the lighthouse that had stood unchallenged for ages on end. Stark and towering, it warned the unwary ship to veer away. Keep away. A pale spire in the shale and shake, the lighthouse looked somehow otherworldly. A passageway into the realm of fairies and fantasy.

Steps had been cut into the cliffs leading down to the lighthouse, and a rusted rail gave her a handhold as she descended, aware with every cell in her body of the big man following her. She hated admitting that she was glad he'd come with her. Hated acknowledging that having him there made her feel safe.

Hated the voice in her head that said *safe* was the last thing she should feel around him.

The lighthouse door had been bright red at one time, but had faded to a shade that hovered somewhere between pink and maroon. The white paint that coated the pointed round tower had dulled to a stained gray, moldy and chipping at the base.

She slowed her steps as they approached, glad Colleen had told her to bring the jacket, because here the chill had a cruel bite. The wind whipped without restraint, burning her cheeks and making her nose numb. She wrapped the coat tight around her against the damp and cold as she stepped up to the stoop, at last allowing herself to glance at Áedán. He stood an arm's length away, watching her with a considering look in those beautiful green eyes.

Neither of them spoke, and Meaghan felt the borders of the wary silence growing between them, creating a boundary that dared no crossing. She didn't like it. Her fist clenched around the thick padding of the coat, feeling the pendant held in the middle of her pocket, once more hot and humming. She caught herself rubbing it.

What *was* this pendant that flared and ebbed with her emotions, as if it, too, were empathic? What purpose did it have? If all of her wild assumptions were right, her brother had sent a messenger from the *past* to deliver it to Meaghan because he thought it would help her. But she had no idea how to make it work. Áedán might know—chances were he *did* know. But what if the pendant was a gateway of some sort, as Saraid had hinted?

If this pendant had been responsible for transporting her brother through time, what else could it do? What if it opened the door to the Book of Fennore? Could she trust Áedán not to take it from her? Not to use it for . . . evil. There was that word again—the one she couldn't bring herself to apply to Áedán. So why hadn't she told him about the pendant? He'd been honest with her; she should be honest with him. For all she knew, he was aware of it already. He'd said he felt something different about her. He'd *sensed* it.

Of all people, Áedán would know what it was, and if she really believed even one of her mixed emotions that urged her to heed her instincts about him, then she should turn to him now and *trust* him.

"Áedán—" she began, just as he reached up and pulled the rope of an old sea bell that dangled outside the faded door. It clanged loudly, echoing with an ominous tone that felt daunting. From within she heard a voice shout, "Hang on."

"What is it?" Áedán asked.

The door opened before she could answer, and they both turned to face the man on the other side. All thoughts of the pendant fled in her surprise.

She'd expected a gnarled and wizened old fisherman who'd been forced to give up the life on a boat in exchange for one of the solitary lighthouse keeper—someone like the old man who lived there in her time. Instead, she found herself face-to-face with someone she knew—or at least recognized. The man standing before her was no more than forty, tall and muscled, with the look of someone who'd spent years in the military and liked it. His skin was the color of aged bourbon and his eyes were so dark she could not tell where the pupil ended and the iris began. The whites looked very clear and bright. Meaghan didn't even know his name, wasn't sure what his relationship to the Book of Fennore was, but he'd been trapped in the netherworld of Fennore, too.

He stared at her with an open mouth, eyes widened with shock.

"And I thought I'd seen it all," he said, cutting that dark stare from Meaghan to Áedán and back. Then he shouted over his shoulder, "Kyle, get your ass down here. We got company."

Áedán took a step closer to her until his shoulder brushed against hers. She glanced up and caught a brooding expression on his face before he hid it.

A moment later, another man appeared in the doorway. Meaghan recognized him as well. He'd been dressed as a priest when he'd been captured by Cathán. He wasn't wearing his clergy collar anymore, though, and with his overlong hair and shadowed jaw, he looked anything but holy. She remembered the first time she'd seen him, she'd thought him too sexy to be a priest. She'd wondered how many of his flock had sat through his Mass thinking of sinning with the good Father.

Now he wore faded blue jeans and a tattered gray sweatshirt that brought out silvery flecks in his hazel eyes. He caught sight of her and stopped, foot suspended over the last step down.

None of them seemed able to speak when a third man came around the bend of the lighthouse, climbing up from the rocky shore. A scar at his right temple cut three parallel lines through his short hair. Chain links made of black tattoos circled his throat and his wrists, binding him to some figurative ball and chain that it seemed he carried wherever he went. At his feet stood a wolf the size of a small pony.

He, too, froze as his gaze landed on Meaghan.

Though they acknowledged her with wary nods, none of them

seemed to even recognize Áedán. Meaghan wasn't surprised. She'd been the only one able to see Áedán when they'd all been trapped in the world of Fennore, after all. He'd been invisible to all of these men.

The man who'd opened the door held it wider. "You might as well come in. Looks like the gang's all here."

Chapter Nine

ÁEDÁN stood beside Meaghan while every instinct shouted at him to get as far away from this place, this woman, as he possibly could. He felt threatened just by her presence. Endangered by the waves emanating from her, grating against his skin. At the same time, he couldn't bear to distance himself from her. She weakened him with the emotions she stirred, and at the same time, she entranced him with her scent, her voice, her unfathomable blue eyes.

She didn't think he was evil. Of course, she was wrong, but he could not shake the way her implacable faith had made him feel. *Feel,* he thought disparagingly. What was becoming of him that he pondered on *feelings*?

She'd said they had history.

Yes, he knew it to be true, but he couldn't begin to understand why. From the start, he'd felt drawn to her, and each moment in her presence only increased his undeniable fascination. In his mind, he pictured the way she'd looked when he'd found her in the cavern and she'd wrapped her arms around him, pulling him closer. He'd noted her unfocused gaze, suspected that she'd been bespelled. Even knowing that, he'd had to force himself to push her away.

With that indiscernible hum enveloping her now, the notion that her actions were being influenced by something outside of herself became more grounded, but the *how* and *why* of it confounded him. He didn't believe the Book had corrupted her yet, but he had nothing to base that belief on. Insidious and treacherous, the answers he sought hovered just out of reach, like the whispering drone that Meaghan seemed blithely unaware of.

Cathán was trapped in the Book now, had been even before Áedán had escaped. He'd grown strong there, feeding on the power of the Book, taking to the symbiotic relationship like a fish to water. He hadn't fought it, like Áedán had in the beginning. No, Cathán had embraced it, and in return, the creation that was the Book of Fennore empowered Cathán.

Áedán could scarcely fathom how it had happened. First Cathán's children—Danni and Rory MacGrath—had injured Áedán by damaging the Book, and then Cathán had moved in for the kill. And now here was their sister, stirring emotions inside him. Radiating an energy that had to be linked to the Book of Fennore.

But *how* did Meaghan fit into this twisted, shattered puzzle?

Cathán had the power of the Book in his grasp, and even though he didn't fully understand all that he could do with it, he was a fierce opponent. Though Áedán hated to admit it, he feared Cathán. Feared what he might do next. Feared what he *could* do. Already he could be more powerful than Áedán had ever been, though once again, the how of it eluded him.

How had Cathán gained so much in so little time?

Áedán shook his head. No matter his strength, Cathán still lacked the knowledge that Áedán had spent eternity amassing. Knowledge Cathán would come after, Áedán was certain.

And once he'd learned everything he needed to know, Cathán would destroy Áedán, and with him, the only enemy with a chance of defeating him.

It was what Áedán would do in his shoes.

Now more than ever, Áedán needed his sharp mind and keen, ruthless instincts. He needed them ready, honed, and poised for attack. He knew there was danger every way he turned. He couldn't outrun the Book of Fennore. He'd seen others try when he'd been the hunter. It was futile.

Besides, Áedán didn't want to simply outrun it. And he refused to become a prisoner again—not Cathán's, not the Book's. He'd been the genie trapped in the bottle for too long.

"I'm Jamie," the black man who'd opened the lighthouse door interrupted Áedán's ominous thoughts. He gestured over his shoulder at the other men as he led them inside. "That's Kyle. He's Eamonn."

Áedán knew who they were. He recognized all three men even if they didn't know his identity.

The scarred one who had chained himself to his shame with the black tattoos was Eamonn. At one time, Áedán had considered him a foe. Now he simply thought of Eamonn as a miserable landmark to a past he'd fled but, it appeared, could not escape.

Jamie, the dark-skinned man, and the one called Kyle were among the last of a line of Keepers—men who'd been tasked with preventing the Book of Fennore from finding its way into human hands and from anyone who might be corrupted by its lure of power, its bribes and promises. There'd been another Keeper with Jamie and Kyle when they'd been trapped in the world of Fennore—an old man with knowledge of the old ways. He'd been the most dangerous of them. Had he not escaped with the others?

Áedán needed to be wary of the Keepers. Even if only Jamie and Kyle remained and the old man had not survived, these two were still his enemies. True, the Keepers had failed dismally in their job over the centuries. For a time, they'd ceased to believe the Book was real. Certainly, they'd forgotten its threat. When he'd been the voice inside the Book of Fennore, Áedán had been able to call his victims from afar, the Keepers no more than an ineffective barrier he'd been forced to circumvent on the rare occasion.

Then Áedán had discovered Cathán. Pathetic, needy Cathán, who'd been willing to sell his soul, sell his own children for a taste of the power Áedán had offered. Who could have guessed that such an unworthy prey could wreak so much havoc on the predator?

Brooding, he followed Jamie and Meaghan up the winding stairs, with Kyle and Eamonn behind them. He didn't like having them at his back, but he didn't want to reveal his discomfort at being here, in his rival's keep.

As if hearing his thoughts, Meaghan glanced back at him, and what he saw in her eyes almost made him stumble. For an instant, the flare of that strange hum that he sensed hovering around her surged, and it seemed that behind the sparkling blues in her gaze, something else looked out. No, that wasn't right. Not something, but some*one.*

Breathing heavy, he followed, waging a silent battle with himself over what he'd seen. Memories bombarded him. Meaghan, waking in the cavern, looking at him with those lust-filled eyes. He'd felt it even then, that flicker of recognition as the blue had taken on the color of amethyst, but he'd been too stunned by the soft heat of her mouth to dwell on it. And today, as they'd set out from the Ballagh house to here, he'd been entranced with the shifting shades as her eyes had gone from blue to gray to *lavender.*

In all his endless years, he'd known only one other woman who had eyes like that. Eyes the color of *fuath dubh*, the delicate, violet, *poisonous* flower that grew tenaciously among the hedgerows and scrub. With just one look, she'd been able to twist him to her own desires just as it seemed Meaghan could.

Her name was Elan—known to the people of their tribe as the White Fennore—and he'd foolishly thought himself in love with her right up to the moment when she'd betrayed him. . . .

Alarms jangled inside him, completely unraveling his composure. Suddenly the rounded staircase felt like a cage, trapping him. Fury, confusion, terror—the conflicting swamp of hated emotions kept him climbing, kept him calmly following when he wanted to bolt.

She'd said they had history.

He shook his head in silent denial, but deep inside, he feared its truth. They did have history. A long, bloodied, vengeful one.

Jamie exited the narrow stairs into a circular room nearly filled by a lone table and six chairs, abruptly halting Áedán's agitated thoughts. A compact kitchen fanned out from the awkward space beneath the column of stairs that continued to rise up, presumably to the top of the spire. Three long narrow windows peered out at the stormy skies and the violent sea, dragging in the reluctant glow of the waning sunlight. A bench ran the circumference of the room, hammered to the wall and supported by thick legs. It looked uncomfortable and invited the casual guest to move on to somewhere else.

"Áedán?" Meaghan asked softly, moving to his side. He glanced down into her upturned face and saw eyes as blue as a summer sky. No tint of lavender, no hint of another behind them.

Had he imagined it?

Kyle came up behind him and gestured for Áedán and Meaghan to take a seat at the table. He touched Meaghan's arm casually, spurring Áedán to put a proprietary hand at the curve of her spine as he led her to the far side of the table, where he could face the open stairwell. He held out the chair beside the one he chose for himself. Meaghan searched his face as she sat, and he forced a placid mask over his features, lowering his eyes so she could not see the stark panic that he feared lurked within them. Eamonn perched on the bench, away from the others. His strangely tame wolf flopped at his feet, watchful and fierce.

The wolf came from the world of Fennore, where ravenous beasts abounded, and it mystified Áedán that the animal obeyed Eamonn. He wondered if it had drawn blood before it submitted. Whatever had clawed Eamonn's face had left a deep scour in his flesh. Eamonn gave him a dark and soulless stare, his eyes disturbingly vacant, as if the man behind them had moved on to better vistas.

"When did you get here?" Jamie asked, cutting through Áedán's thoughts. He addressed Meaghan and Áedán bristled at the abrupt tone.

"This morning," she answered with a nervous smile. "When did you get here?"

"Last year."

"Last . . . But how?" Meaghan asked. "We were all together before. . . ."

"Beats the fuck out of me," Jamie said.

The man called Kyle reached across the table and touched Meaghan's wrist. "You're Meaghan, isn't that right?"

She nodded. "And this is Áedán."

She gave him a quick smile and encouraging nod. He saw only Meaghan within her blue gaze, but the doubt had been seeded.

The three men in the room evaluated him with suspicion, and Áedán thrust his thoughts away from Meaghan and onto the events unfolding at the table. He needed to be alert and wary. Focusing on the men, he returned their hostile assessment without flinching. They did not know who he was. If they'd had even a clue, he would not be sitting at their kitchen table.

"I remember seeing you there," Kyle went on, still speaking to Meaghan, referring to the realm of Fennore, where he, too, had been imprisoned. His fingers now rested on the fine bones of her hand. Áedán had to fight the urge to push him away. He didn't like how Meaghan looked at him, and he certainly didn't like the way Kyle gazed back at her.

Kyle said, "Were you hurt when you . . . came through?"

Áedán understood the man's hesitation. There seemed no right way to describe the journey between the realm of Fennore and the real world.

"No, I wasn't hurt," Meaghan said. "Just confused."

"It was the same for us."

Still standing, Jamie leaned forward and braced his knuckles on the table in front of Áedán. "Why are *you* here?" he demanded rudely.

"Áedán was trapped there with me," Meaghan answered for him.

It was probably best. Áedán didn't like Jamie's aggressive tone and wouldn't have responded with civility to his hostile query.

Kyle glanced at Áedán with curious eyes. "You were there? In the world of Fennore?"

Ironic that he would ask. For centuries, Áedán was one with the world of Fennore. The power, the drive, the vengeance.

"I was there," he said calmly.

"Funny, I didn't see you," Jamie said, easing back so he could swing a chair around, his hard expression saying he found nothing funny about it at all. He straddled the chair with his arms resting across the back in a deceptively casual manner. He didn't fool Áedán. The man was as tight as a trigger. "Everyone else in this room, I saw," he went on. "But not you."

He raised his brows in blatant challenge.

Áedán could feel Meaghan tensing beside him, knew she was outspoken enough to blurt the truth—that no one but she had been able to see him. He leaned closer to her, settling his arm around her and giving her shoulder a gentle squeeze. The action distracted her as he'd hoped it would.

"There was a lot going on, as I recall," he said in a bored tone. "What with the monsters and the bloodshed."

Jamie's eyes narrowed, but Áedán's reference to the chaos, the incredible battle that had been waged, seemed to make him consider the possibility that he'd somehow missed seeing Áedán during that bloody encounter. He leaned back, but not for a moment did Áedán think the other man had let down his guard.

"Meaghan."

Kyle again, trying to get her attention.

Áedán let his hand drift up to Meaghan's nape and the silky skin beneath the heavy warmth of her hair. He rubbed in a gentle, possessive way that every man in the room noted. She shot him a startled glance, and he thought she might push him away. Instead, she looked back at Kyle and nodded.

"Tiarnan—the big warrior who was with us there—he said that

he'd damaged the Book of Fennore somehow and left it open and gaping like a giant Devil's Triangle, just waiting to suck people in. That's how we all ended up in the belly of that nightmare. We were trying to seal the Book up in the end."

Áedán went very still, intent as he watched Kyle speak.

"We trapped Cathán—I still don't know how we did it. But there was another—someone who was supposed to be even more powerful. A Druid, if you can believe. He escaped."

Meaghan glanced at Áedán and quickly away. Would she tell the truth? Would she reveal his identity to his enemies? Betray him?

Was the history she thought they shared about to be repeated?

He forced himself to remain relaxed, composed, when inside his turmoil raged.

"Where is this Druid now?" she asked, looking for all the world like this was the first she'd heard of him.

Áedán felt something knotted in his chest begin to loosen.

"We don't know," Kyle answered. "If he's walking around, we haven't seen him."

Meaghan cocked her head. "How would you recognize him if you saw him?"

Kyle blew out a breath of air. "We're hoping instinct will guide us."

There was irony there that should have struck Áedán as funny, but in the taut silence that followed, Áedán felt like he'd been stretched across a huge divide, and each moment thinned him until he might split down the middle, two halves forever incomplete.

"*I'll* know," Jamie said, still glaring at Áedán. But he didn't accuse, he didn't attack. He might have some suspicion, but not enough to spur action. The man had too much confidence to believe his enemy would dare stroll into his den.

Meaghan cleared her throat. "So you three are the only ones who made it here?" Meaghan said after a moment.

"Until you," Kyle answered.

Áedán felt a moment of relief at the confirmation that only these two Keepers and Eamonn had made it to this world. The old Keeper who'd known the ancient words had been separated from them. Áedán felt sure *he* would have known what Áedán was.

"We haven't seen anyone but you three either," Meaghan said in a calm, earnest voice.

"You two came through together?" That was Jamie. He arrowed that glowering scowl on Áedán.

Coldly, Áedán gazed back. "No," he answered. "I came five days ago. Alone."

"No rhyme or reason," Kyle said with a sad shake of his head, and Áedán had to assume that none of them had arrived together. Like petals thrown into the wind, they'd landed at different times, wherever chance had taken them, some here and some who-knew-where else? This affirmation of what they'd all experienced seemed to subdue the aggression he felt from Jamie.

"The old man and the others are gone," Eamonn said from his seat on the ledge. "There's no purpose in asking what happened to them or to my brothers. Let us hope they are in a better place than we are."

"It could be worse," Áedán said. "You could still be there, trapped inside."

Eamonn did not respond. Sullen, he looked down at his wolf.

"Have you heard anything about the Book of Fennore since you came here?" Meaghan asked. "Any rumors? Do you know where it is?"

"We looked for it—still do—but we've yet to hear even a hint at where it could be. Lately though . . . I could swear I feel it," Kyle admitted.

Áedán forced himself not to react to that. If Kyle was aware of the Book, then the Book was aware of Kyle. Was that what Áedán had sensed as he and Meaghan approached the lighthouse? Was it connected to these men and not to Meaghan at all?

"Yeah," Jamie said with a deep breath. "I feel it, too. Stronger today than ever before."

As one they all looked at Eamonn. He said nothing, but a gleam of panic prowled deep in his eyes.

"What do you mean, you feel it?" Meaghan asked.

Kyle cut his eyes to Jamie before he answered. At first, Áedán thought Kyle was asking for permission to share. Obviously Jamie led this small pack. But then he saw the weight of that exchanged glance. It wasn't about permission, it was about trust. These men had survived a year in this place with only themselves—and Eamonn with his wolf, he supposed—to rely on. They did not risk without consensus.

Áedán made note of it for later.

Kyle shook his head. "I can't explain it. It's just a sense that the Book is out there. And today it seems closer."

"It's searching," Áedán said. "It's what it does."

"And how the fuck would you know what it does?" Jamie demanded.

"I, too, was its prisoner. For far longer than you."

"That's what you said. I still don't remember seeing you."

"Do not blame me for your own blindness."

Jamie looked every inch the warrior he'd once been, bristling with aggression as he glared at Áedán from across the table. The fierce black man was not the biggest monster Áedán had ever faced, though. It would take more than his wrath to intimidate Áedán.

"What's it searching for?" Meaghan cut in before the antagonism ratcheted up another notch.

Me, Áedán didn't say.

"Who the fuck knows?" Jamie muttered.

"I'm told I must find it," Meaghan admitted with a note of desperation in her voice.

"Told?" Jamie leaned forward against the back of his chair, gripping the ladder railing tightly. "*Who* told you?"

"No one you'd know," she said quickly.

"Try us," Jamie said in a silky, dark voice that dripped threat.

"I grew up on this island. My family has lived here for generations. My grandmother lives here now."

Under other circumstances, their shock might have been humorous. As it was, Áedán could find nothing to laugh at in the situation.

Meaghan said, "She has a gift, my grandmother. She sometimes knows things before they happen."

"And she told you?" Kyle asked gently.

Meaghan nodded.

Kyle covered her hand with his once more, holding it as he stared deeply into Meaghan's eyes. "Why? Why must you find it? It's an evil thing. You've seen the other side of it. You of all people should know what horrors it holds."

Áedán tensed beside her. He hated that she looked at Kyle with such unabashed trust, wished that she'd look at him that way. He tightened his hold around her shoulder without meaning to, squeezing hard enough that she glanced at him with surprise. He knew he should ease up and release her, but he didn't.

"I have to find the Book because it's the way out," Meaghan said softly. "The way back to where I belong. Perhaps where we all belong."

Kyle caught his breath and Jamie sat back for a silent moment. Áedán felt his skin go icy. He was the only one who didn't want a way back. He would never return to the world of Fennore.

"It's not a way to where I belong," Eamonn said, his voice shaking with anger. He stood suddenly, startling the wolf, which bounded to its feet, fur on end and teeth bared. "There is no such place for me."

With a low growl, the wolf followed Eamonn as he stalked from the room. Its huge paws padded against the worn wooden floors as it passed. As he watched the other man leave, Áedán felt a strange kinship to him. There was no place where Áedán belonged either.

Jamie dismissed Eamonn with a soft snort of breath. "Fucking drama queen."

Kyle looked a bit more sympathetic. "His has not been an easy road," he said.

"And ours has been a walk in the park?" Jamie asked.

"They don't know anything that will help you, Meaghan," Áedán cut through, tired of the men already.

He felt confined in the strange round room, with its narrow view on the world outside. He wanted to quit this place, and he wished he could simply stomp out as Eamonn had. But he would not leave Meaghan, and he knew she was not inclined to go at the moment. She stared at Kyle like he was a work of art, something crafted from gold and meant to be revered. Áedán wanted to lunge across the table and wrap his fingers around the other man's throat.

"I think you're wrong, Áedán," Meaghan said. "There's a reason why we five ended up here and no one else did. We are meant to find the Book. I know it."

She paused, and Áedán floundered in the wary silence she left in her wake. Then slowly, she lowered her hand to her thigh, rubbed something that lay within the pocket of the ugly brown fabric of her dress. He'd noticed her doing it several times before but hadn't dwelled on it. Now he wondered what she had hidden there. With a look of determination, she pulled the button free of its hole and clenched something in her fist. As she raised her hand to the table, Áedán saw a fine tremble go through it.

She shot him a quick, apologetic look that he didn't understand, and then she set a small black pouch on the table. "I have this," she said.

Áedán's breath stopped completely. He stared at the tiny bag, feeling the waves of power emanating from within it, and at last he understood what he'd felt humming around Meaghan. He knew without having it unveiled what waited inside. Knew without yet seeing that *this* was what he'd been sensing all along, what spiked his dread into something darker, colder, more terrifying. Deep within him, the doubt that the brief glimpse of Elan staring out of Meaghan's eyes had planted began to take root.

No, a voice within him still tried to deny it. *No.*

With obvious reluctance, Meaghan reached for the drawstring.

"Don't," he said without meaning to.

Her startled blue gaze swung to meet his. For a moment, he held it, silently begging her not to open the pouch. For a moment, it worked. For a moment, no one spoke. No one moved.

And then the color of amethyst filled in the hues of her gaze, and once again he saw Elan watching him. Filling him with icy dread. He could do nothing as Meaghan pulled the string and dumped the pendant out on the table. The drone of its power lashed out at Áedán, so strong, so sudden that it shoved him back. He lurched to his feet, his chair zinging across the floor.

Alarmed, Meaghan asked, "What's wrong, Áedán?"

He shook his head, unable to voice the warning as she reached for the leather cord and dangled the pendant from her fingers. It swayed in time with the laborious beat of his heart. His lungs felt shrunken, his need to breathe exponentially enlarged. Alternating waves of blazing heat and vicious cold seemed to wash over him as he followed the pendulous swing of the talisman she held.

He forced himself to look away and took in the entranced expressions of the two men at the table. Both watched with fascination and dismay, mixed so completely that one could not be discerned from the other.

"What is it?" Jamie asked, but he'd leaned back, as if instinct had guided him away from the thing she held.

"Where did you get it?" Kyle murmured, voicing the question Áedán could not form. The other man leaned forward, as if dared by some inner voice to hide his fear.

"Do you know what it is?" Meaghan asked.

"Looks old," Jamie said.

Áedán fought the urge to cover the damned thing, to hide it from their prying eyes. He knew exactly what it was. He knew, because he had made it with his own hands. He'd hammered the silver, set the gems, given the sacred amulet to Elan, the woman he'd loved, with his pledge, with his heart.

And Elan, who could see death, had used it to entomb him within the Book of Fennore.

As he stared, mesmerized by the ancient sparkle and dull shine, he had the sense of something huge moving beneath his feet, beneath the earth, like a rampant fire, devouring all that lived as it consumed the crust that divided the land from the lavas that flowed underneath. It shook the ground, it sent tremors through the air.

Meaghan held the key to the Book of Fennore. With it, she could open the Book.

And if he was right about what—about *who*—he'd glimpsed behind Meaghan's eyes, then she could lock it up with him inside once more.

No, he wanted to shout. But on that day when Elan had cursed him, she had promised to return one day and judge him again. *Judge. Him.* His fury flared at the memory. He'd waited in vain for that day to come. Could it be now? Had she chosen to use Meaghan as her vessel?

Meaghan turned suddenly and pinned him with her gaze, looked so deeply *into* him that he felt as if he fell through the tunnel her eyes had become. Down and down he plummeted until he saw his own soul laid bare by the beauty and treachery within her. And suddenly he understood the history that seemed to span their past. The history they shared was with the Book of Fennore.

And with a past that seemed destined to repeat itself.

Chapter Ten

KYLE stood as if mesmerized and moved around the table to her side. Meaghan forced her gaze from the endless green of Áedán's eyes to focus on him. She, too, pushed to her feet, unwilling to remain seated between the two towering men. A wave of vertigo unbalanced her when she stood, making her sway while black and white spots bloomed behind her eyes. She felt like she might topple into some great abyss, a darkness that held every fear she'd ever conceived.

Kyle reached out and caught her arm to steady her in the same instant that Áedán grabbed the other, and panic shot through her at the searing touch of both men. She twisted and tugged, staggering back once she was free. She didn't understand the terror that suddenly gripped her, but it vibrated in the air around her, pressed down like a fierce storm from above.

She still held the pendant in her hand. It dangled gleefully, swishing back and forth in the invisible currents that buffeted them all.

"What the fuck?" Jamie muttered. He was on his feet as well.

Meaghan couldn't answer. She looked back to Áedán, found him staring at her with shocked eyes and a pale face. His emotions ripped through her like hot razors, slicing deeply but so quick and clean that she was sure pieces of herself would fall free before she even registered the pain. For a moment, it seemed that only the two of them existed, trapped once again in a netherworld.

She snatched the pouch from the table, dropped the pendant inside it, and pulled the drawstring with a snap that commanded the silence encapsulating them all. She could still sense the drone of power buzzing from it, and she felt exposed, endangered . . . preyed upon in this bizarre circular room. She swallowed hard and moved to stuff the pendant back in her pocket, but Jamie reached across the table to stop her.

Beside her, Áedán moved so quickly it left her stunned. His big hand slammed Jamie's shoulder, knocking the other man back before he could reach her.

"Don't touch her," Áedán warned, his voice low and full of threat.

The two men faced off, every muscle tense, ready to rise to a challenge that Meaghan hadn't seen coming. Quickly Meaghan stuffed the pendant into her pocket and buttoned it. She could feel the burn through the fabric and wished for her coat to protect her skin, but it hung on the rack just inside the door downstairs, and she didn't dare turn her back on the fuse that hissed between the men.

"Where'd you get that pendant, Meaghan?" Jamie asked her, but he didn't look at her while he spoke. He and Áedán remained locked in a silent battle, and neither seemed inclined to disengage.

"My grandmother gave it to me. It's a family heirloom."

The words must have caught them both by surprise because, as one, they faced her. Jamie with confusion. Áedán with something more disturbing, as if she'd unwittingly offered a solution to a plaguing quandary.

"Why?" Jamie asked.

"When?" Áedán demanded.

"And you think it will help you find the Book of Fennore?" Kyle said calmly—yet she knew he focused on the tension between Jamie and Áedán as much as she did. The two men were like a rumbling storm in the strange room, with Meaghan and Kyle at the precarious eye waiting for the deadly shift.

She chose to answer Kyle and ignore the other two.

"I think it must be linked to the Book of Fennore," she said softly. "This pendant is embedded with the same symbols that mark the cover and pages of the Book."

That wasn't the only reason she knew the pendant and the Book of Fennore held a connection. Even if the pendant had looked nothing like the symbols of the Book, she'd have known they belonged together. When she held it, it made her feel like a channel to something deep and unknown. It was tantamount to balancing on a blade's edge above a gaping chasm.

Áedán's stare was fixed and penetrating. She had the uneasy feeling that he'd heard her omissions along with her words. There'd been a moment there when the room had seemed to vanish, when only Meaghan, the pendant, and the verdant stretch of Áedán's eyes had existed. She'd been galvanized by the sensations shooting through her.

Kyle said, "Why did your grandmother give the pendant to you, Meaghan? Did she know what it was?"

He touched her again and Meaghan looked warily at Áedán. He didn't like it. She'd have to be blind and dim-witted not to realize that. Áedán looked like a great beast guarding his territory, and somehow she'd fallen into his perceived boundaries. He made a sound deep in his throat, but he was more concerned with Jamie than Kyle at that moment.

Cautiously, she put some distance between her and Kyle; at the same time, she reached out with her senses to gauge the emotions churning around her. Either Kyle was as cool and calm as he looked or her sensors had been dulled by Áedán's wildly flaring aggression and the persistent buzz of the pendant burning into her leg.

"I don't think my grandmother knows anything about the pendant," she said in answer to Kyle's question.

She could feel the amulet thrumming, blazing now. Angry, wanting to be free. The reaction felt strong—stronger than before. Why had it become so agitated? Was it because of someone in this room? Because of the chaos and tension that bound them together?

"Are you all right, Meaghan?" Kyle asked gently.

Keeping her eyes lowered, she rubbed her forehead with her fingers and nodded. "I'm fine. Sorry, just a little overwhelmed, I guess."

"We all felt that way in the beginning," Kyle said.

His tone and his words held consolation. He used past tense. Did that mean he no longer felt beleaguered by what had happened to them? If she remained stuck here, would she come to look at it as something terrible that no longer affected her too much?

Don't even think about that. She refused to consider for an instant that she might be trapped here forever.

"What time is it?" Meaghan asked as the steady ticktock of the clock in the kitchen penetrated her confusion. She was suddenly fearful that she'd lost all track of time in the shifting currents that swirled around them.

"Almost five," Kyle said.

"I need to go." She moved abruptly toward the stairs, glancing at Áedán as she did. His expression was closed, his eyes reflecting nothing of what he thought. "I told Colleen I would be back before dinner."

"Colleen?" Jamie repeated.

"Colleen Ballagh," Meaghan answered. "My grandmother."

He muttered something that sounded like *Colleen of the Ballagh*, but didn't explain. Colleen's visitor, Saraid, had called her the same thing.

"Do you know Colleen?" she asked. In a small town like Ballyfionúir, most people knew each other, but Colleen had said they'd never met. Meaghan didn't see recognition in Jamie's expression, only caution. If she didn't find it so hard to believe, she might even think he looked afraid.

"Heard of her," Jamie said.

If possible, Áedán became more rigid.

"Can I come back?" she asked, directing her question to Kyle. "Will you help me find the Book of Fennore?"

"Yes," Kyle said without hesitation. "If you believe it can get us out of here, then yes, I will help you."

"You realize it could just pull us back to where we were?" Jamie said, his tone sharply edged. "I'd much rather live in a lighthouse than fight for my life every day there."

Jamie voiced nearly the same sentiments Áedán had earlier, but instead of agreeing with him, Áedán asked, "Are you such a coward, then?"

Jamie didn't even bat an eye or raise his voice, but then, he didn't need to.

"You want to find out what kind of man I am? I can give you a lesson right here, right now."

The smile that curled Áedán's lips was cold and fierce. He wanted to grasp that gauntlet. Meaghan could see it in his face. She didn't understand how or why the situation had spiraled so out of control, but clearly these two men wanted to take one another down.

Feck. "We don't have time, Áedán," she said quickly. "I have to get back. So do you. Mickey will wonder where you are."

Áedán had not looked away from Jamie.

"Áedán," she insisted. "You know he will punish Colleen if we arrive late."

The mention of Colleen facing Mickey's wicked temper did the trick. She saw the tension ebb from his shoulders, and he tore his gaze away from the black pits of Jamie's eyes. His fists, though, remained clenched tight.

"Perhaps later, you can give me your *lesson*," Áedán said to Jamie, the taunt insultingly clear.

"That'd be my pleasure."

Jamie took a step forward and so did Áedán, both men as graceful as cats. Very big cats, roped in muscle and ready to pounce.

"Do you think we could crank the testosterone down a wee bit? It's giving me a headache."

Meaghan put a restraining hand on Áedán's arm, mentally rolling her eyes as she did it. Like *that* would make a difference. Holding him back if he meant to attack would be like holding back a charging lion.

But these thoughts vanished as soon as her skin touched his because, at that moment, two things happened.

He snapped his gaze to where her fingers curled over his muscled forearm, Jamie forgotten.

And everything he thought, everything he felt rushed at her like a torrential storm.

Hatred and suspicion, anger and betrayal, pain that raged through each cell in his body, and fury that demanded blood to be satisfied flooded Meaghan. And holding it all together was the agonized bewilderment of a man who never saw the precipice until he'd plunged headfirst over it.

The churn and turn of each conflicted sentiment slaughtered her own thoughts and feelings, leaving her a shredded and bleeding mass of uncertainty.

Áedán's eyes narrowed and he shook her off, backing up a step. The horror in his expression slammed against her, making her suck in a breath.

Unaware of the turmoil and conflict, Jamie gave a bark of laughter, muttering something about the testosterone giving everyone a headache, and then he turned his back on Áedán and the rest of them.

Feeling like she walked a tightwire over disaster, Meaghan said good-bye and fled the lighthouse, a host of questions dogging her footsteps.

And a man she didn't trust but couldn't ignore, following too close for comfort behind her.

Chapter Eleven

MEAGHAN would never know how she'd managed to keep her face from showing her thoughts. Perhaps she failed, yet Áedán strode silently beside her, absorbed in his own ponderings. He might not have noticed if she'd sprouted multiple heads.

What had she seen when she'd touched him? For there'd been images in that dark mix of emotions, pictures blurred by the impact of his furor. Mysterious, dangerous, obsessive memories that had flashed with the speed of a shuffling deck of cards. She'd been unable to grasp any one image before the next toppled over it, before another took its place.

Where had that perplexing hatred she'd felt in him come from? And why had it seemed to be directed at *her*?

Áedán waited until they'd traveled along the twisted path and the lighthouse was no longer in sight before he spoke.

"When did Colleen give you the pendant, Meaghan?" he asked softly. His voice sounded deeper than usual, and the deep rumble of it made her shiver.

"After we left the cavern. She said her visitor, Saraid, told her to give it to me."

"Why didn't you tell me?"

"It frightened me." *You* frighten me.

"It should," he said but didn't bother to explain. "Did Colleen tell you why Saraid meant for you to have it?"

Meaghan shook her head. "She thought it might take me home. Obviously, it didn't. Do you know what it is?"

"A key."

Meaghan swallowed. She'd guessed it, but hearing his confirmation unsettled her even more. She nodded slowly, saying, "A key to the Book of Fennore. Does that mean it opens it or that it controls it in some way?"

"Both. And neither."

His eyes glimmered with a thousand shades, myriad emotions swirling in golds and greens, flecked with pain and grief, with rage and yearning.

Meaghan forced herself to look away from all she saw there. "I'm sick of your cryptic answers," she said. "Why can't you just tell me the truth?"

He turned on her suddenly, hostility burning in his eyes, but with it, something else. Something wounded. "What truth do you want to hear, little witch?"

"Little wit—? Why are you so angry? Let's start there."

His flare of rage singed her skin and made her stumble backward. He advanced on her intently. He looked big and scary and wild-eyed, and Meaghan was completely at his mercy on this isolated and deserted road.

"What do you mean to do with your key, Meaghan?" he demanded. "Trap me?"

"Trap you . . . ? No. Why would I do that? I'm trying to get us home."

"Home?" he repeated. "Get us *home*?"

He spoke softly, but the whip and lash of his outrage flayed her.

"It is because of *you* that I was trapped for all of *fecking eternity*," he said. "Because of you, I have no home."

She stared at him, uncomprehending. "What are you talking about? Do you know how crazy you sound? I wouldn't know how to trap you if I wanted to—and I don't. Are you listening? I don't even *want* the fecking pendant."

"No? Then give it to me."

"Why? What will you do with it?"

Instead of answering, he gave her a smile colder than the waters she'd plunged into that afternoon. She bumped against something hard and realized that once again he'd backed her into one of the huge balancing boulders at the cliff's edge. They were alone up here, just the two of them, with not another soul in sight. If he wanted to, he could take the pendant, push her over the side, and no one would be the wiser.

She licked her lips, tried to slow her shallow breaths. He watched her every move.

"I didn't trap you anywhere, Áedán. I was a prisoner just like you were."

"Oh yes, and why, I wonder, did Cathán want you there?"

He took another step, using his arms to cage her against the boulder. *Caught between a rock and a hard place,* she thought grimly. In her pocket, the pendant purred happily.

"Why did he want you, little witch?"

"Don't call me that. I'm not a witch."

He lowered his head and breathed in the scent of her, a huge predator ready to abrade her skin with its sandpaper tongue before it began to feast.

"You heard them," she said, gesturing back to the lighthouse, trying to keep her voice steady to hide the terror she felt. "The Book was like a Devil's Triangle. People were sucked in. I was one of them. It wasn't Cathán who wanted me. I was just in the wrong place at the wrong time."

"Bollocks," he said softly, using slang he must have learned from Mickey. "More than chance brought you. I see what's in your eyes."

His voice dropped an octave until it became something she felt rather than heard. He lifted a hand to her throat, let his fingers curl over the sensitive skin. He didn't squeeze; he didn't hurt her. In fact, the emotions pouring off him now were much sweeter than rage. They spilled like hot, spiced rum over her, coating her. Turning her into something perilously flammable.

"It was much more than chance," he breathed against her cheek. His tone was like the caress of his hands on her skin. Like the brush of his lips against her temple.

Meaghan's legs turned to rubber. She leaned against the stone to catch her balance, trying to calm the mated frenzy of fear and longing that he'd managed to set loose inside her. Her feelings knotted in a melee as confusing as this man.

"Let me go," she said.

"No."

He moved closer, his body heavy and hard, so hot that it melted her to the bone. He smelled of the woods, of fresh, salted air and deep shadows peppered with secret hollows and ancient mysteries. Elusive and seductive, his scent made something coil tight and low within her. Made her want to arch against him despite the fear and the certainty that this man would be her doom.

"You want the key to make you powerful again, don't you?" she forced herself to ask.

"Yes, I do. That is exactly what I want." He said it with a harsh bite in his tone, a gnashing of syllables and tearing of vowels.

"Why? All that power didn't do you much good before."

"I will not return to my prison. I will not be at your mercy ever again."

"I never asked you to be at my mercy, Áedán," she whispered. "That's not what I want either."

He stilled, his body hot against hers, her curves molding to the hard, muscled angles of his. "Then what do you want, beauty?" he asked, his lips brushing her temple again, his breath stirring the fine strands of hair there.

Mouth dry, she fought the urge to look into his eyes.

And lost.

Stunned, hurt, needing more than anything for the crazy tilting of her world to be righted, she gazed into those eyes of green, found herself surrounded and overwhelmed by what she saw. His big hands cupped her face. The white bandage still around his stitches was softer than his roughened palms. His thumbs brushed her jaw as his fingers curled around her neck to the vulnerable skin at her nape. Each touch, each sensation sparked along her nerve endings and made her feel like she'd been plugged into the sun and now it melted her down, restructuring her foundation, reshaping her into a new mold.

The shock of his lips on hers shuddered into her soul. He pressed her back, against the solid wall of stone behind her, using his body like a tool to cleave her to him. Her traitorous hands moved to his ribs, sliding over rippled layers of muscle, around to the hard slope of spine, up to the ridge of shoulders. She'd meant to push him away, but something deeper drove her now.

Meaghan flattened herself against him, feeling like a junkie sliding that needle into her vein, injecting herself with ecstasy that would eventually bring her to the gutters of existence.

He'd betrayed her once. He would do it again.

She didn't know where the thought had come from. Didn't understand the clarity of its voice.

He parted her lips with his, let the soft hot velvet of his tongue find hers, wiping all thought from her mind, altering her perceptions until she was only corporeal, incapable of thinking at all. Incapable of reason, of doubt, of fear.

He bent his knees, rocked his hips against hers in a deliberate, carnal motion that found a response in every cell of her body. That primitive movement beguiled and enticed, it made her blood roar in her ears, made her loins feel heavy, needy. She wanted to open herself to him, wanted to welcome him inside her, grip him with the same liquid yearning that filled her. The intoxicating mixture of his desire and his resistance raged through them both. He didn't want to want her. Well, she didn't want to want him either, but stopping now would be like denying her body air.

His hands were on her hips now, urging her up, lifting her, molding her to him. Christ, she was ready to shag him right here on the cliffs.

"Wait," she breathed into his mouth, and the intimacy of it nearly pushed her past the point of no return.

"I've waited forever," he said. "Too long."

Her dress bunched at her waist, her legs wrapped around his hips, the hot center of her hard against the length of him. He thrust against her, and her head bumped the rock behind her. It hurt but she didn't seem to care. He felt huge and ravenous, and she could think of nothing but assuaging his hunger, of satisfying her own. Her hands went to his fly before a cold drop of reason sizzled against the inferno burning out of control inside her.

Seduced . . . Consumed . . . Enthralled.

She saw herself as if from a distance, skirts rucked up, eyes glassy with passion, drunk for a man she barely knew and didn't trust. She'd asked him for the truth, and instead of giving it, he'd backed her into a sexual corner and conquered her with desire.

Her withdrawal caught him off guard, and she squirmed free before he knew what she'd intended. Chest heaving from the effort it had taken to break his thrall, she stood a few steps away. He was hard and flushed, his eyes glazed and heavy lidded. Her fingers had messed up his short black hair. He looked like sin itself, and oh, she wanted nothing more than to rip the ugly dress off her body and lay down, right here on the jagged shale, and give herself to him, mind and body.

The silence between them crackled and hissed. He searched her face for answers to questions that didn't need to be voiced. Then shutters came down over his bottomless eyes and all she saw was herself, disheveled and lost inside them.

The need to escape swamped her. Not caring that it made her a coward, she turned and she ran. Ran like the devil was on her heels. Ran like she might actually stand a chance of escaping him.

Áedán did not follow, but she felt him watching until she disappeared over the bend, and she knew her reprieve would not last.

Chapter Twelve

MEAGHAN was still shaking when she stepped through the back door of Colleen's tiny house. Colleen took in her disheveled appearance with curious and somehow knowing eyes, and Meaghan couldn't stop the blush that heated her cheeks nor could she meet that shrewd black gaze. She'd stopped running before she reached the small cottage, before she got close enough to be seen by any of the nosy neighbors who lived in Ballyfionúir. She'd used her fingers to comb out her hair and then braid it into a rope, but obviously, she couldn't fool Colleen Ballagh. Some things never changed.

"And did you get what you were after?" Colleen asked in a casual tone that made Meaghan's face flame hotter.

"I met the men who live in the lighthouse. They weren't strangers. I recognized them."

That wiped the smirk from Colleen's lips. "You what?" she asked in an astonished voice. "And how would you be recognizing the likes of them?"

Meaghan sighed and pushed back a strand of hair that refused to be confined. "I could tell you, but it wouldn't make sense. It's all part of the Book of Fennore, though. I feel like everything since my birth must have been wrapped up in that fecking Book."

Colleen scowled. "What did they tell you, these men?"

"That they'll help me find it."

"And it's certain you are that finding it is the thing to do?"

"It's what Saraid told you, isn't it? It's why she gave you the pendant to give to me. It's my way home, right?"

"Sure and isn't that what she said."

But Colleen's voice held doubt, and Meaghan couldn't blame her. As Jamie had told her, what if finding the Book only condemned them to returning to the world they'd just escaped?

She couldn't think of it, not now when she felt so torn and tormented by everything she'd learned, guessed . . . still didn't know.

"No matter," Colleen said cryptically. "It's glad I am to see you back before Mickey comes in."

Mickey and his sparkling personality. Another problem she wished she could forget.

Colleen had finished with the stew. The kitchen looked spotless and smelled heavenly. Meaghan's stomach gave a loud growl in appreciation, surprising her. It seemed that things like food shouldn't matter in the strange circumstances that had become her life.

"Is the baby sleeping?" she asked calmly, as if she wasn't a bundle of nerves, as if every inch of her didn't crave a touch that felt dangerous and forbidden. Where had Áedán gone after she'd run away? What was he doing? Did his skin burn for her hands as hers did for his?

"Still sleeping," Colleen said with a sharp glance. Meaghan would swear her Nana could read her mind. "He'll wake for a bit, but he's a good babe. He'll just want a little snack and a fresh nappy, then before long, he'll be off to sleep again until morning."

"And Mickey? You haven't seen him since I left?"

"Not hide nor hair," Colleen said, the warm note that had touched her voice when she spoke of Niall turning cold at the mention of his father. "You'd know if himself were about."

Yes, she supposed she would. Mickey was not a man who'd sit

quietly in the front room. She'd met him only once, and already she'd figured that out.

"Can I help you with anything?"

Colleen's expression held such surprise that, for a moment, Meaghan thought someone must have come in behind her and caught the other woman off guard. She glanced over her shoulder, but there was no one there.

Colleen cleared her throat. "Well, yes. If you'd want to set the table, that would be grand."

Meaghan took the cups and utensils from the cupboard and drawer and began to place them. For a moment, her mind settled and cleared as she performed the simple task of setting the table.

She felt it then.

At first it was only a whisper, a dark breeze blowing through her thoughts.

Come to me. . . .

She looked up quickly, but Colleen stood stirring the pot on the stove and no one else had come in.

I can help you. I am what you seek. . . .

She'd taken a step toward the door before she even realized it.

I am not to be feared. I want only what you want. Freedom. Life. Acceptance. . . .

The spoons she held clattered to the floor, making both women jump with surprise. Meaghan gave a sharp yelp and then a nervous laugh.

"We're both of us stretched tight as wire," Colleen said with a stiff smile.

Before Meaghan could answer, someone pounded on the front door. Not a tentative knock—the summons echoed loudly and demanded attention. Meaghan had a bizarre image in her head of the Book of Fennore hurling itself against the door until it opened. She almost laughed at the visual, but it wasn't funny. She was certain that the voice she'd heard had come from the Book, although how she knew was a mystery.

Jamie said it searched. Like a beacon. Áedán had concurred.

That's how that voice felt—like a signal broadcasting on an open frequency, seeking a listener.

Upstairs, the baby began to fret, and then the knock came again, loud and insistent. Niall let loose an outraged cry at being woken.

"I'll go see to him," Meaghan said, heading for the stairs, but as she passed, she met Colleen's eyes and paused. Her grandmother looked frightened. A shiver danced over her skin. Had she heard the voice, too? "What's wrong?" Meaghan asked.

"Nothing," Colleen said too quickly, too breezily. "Just late for visitors is all."

Twilight had settled outside, and still Mickey and Áedán had not returned. The kitchen didn't have a clock, and Meaghan didn't really know just how late it was, but it couldn't be much past six or six thirty. Yet Colleen's reaction made it seem like midnight.

She heard the door open behind her as she started upstairs. Niall fussed again, but now that the pounding had ceased, he sounded like he might settle easy enough. Pausing halfway up, Meaghan could see the open front door without being seen herself. A man stood just on the other side bathed by the dim and dirty light spilling from the fixture overhead.

He was heavy-set, with broad shoulders and a solid middle. She couldn't make out his features, but even in the shadows, she could tell his clothes were of a better make than Mickey's or Áedán's had been. He wore a coat that fit him well and looked warm, not like the threadbare woolen jacket Áedán had shared with her.

"Colleen," the man said, gazing at her grandmother. Reassured that her grandmother knew the visitor, Meaghan continued upstairs to check on the baby. Niall had found his thumb and sucked furiously as she checked his diaper, found it dry, and arranged his blankets while murmuring soothing nonsense to him. He was an easy baby, used to comforting himself when his parents were too busy to dote. Within a few minutes, he'd fallen back to sleep.

Quietly she made her way from the room, closing the door behind her all but a crack. Colleen's voice traveled up as she moved to the landing.

"... cousin Meaghan is upstairs with the baby."

Meaghan hesitated on the steps, eyeing the man below before making herself known. Colleen had kept him on the porch, and she couldn't get a good look at him. She could see Colleen clearly enough, though. Her entire body was rigid with tension.

"Is Mickey here?" he demanded, his tone gruff, his words hard.

"Lower your voice," she admonished the man. The hand that held the door open was white knuckled, but Colleen's voice remained calm as she answered him. "And the answer is no. He's gone to the pub, but I expec—"

The man didn't wait for her to say more. With one step, he barged over the threshold and pushed Colleen against the half wall that anchored the banister. He kicked the door shut behind him, but the rag rug slowed it and kept it from slamming. Meaghan clasped a hand over her mouth to smother her shout and looked around for something she could use as a weapon. An umbrella stand stood at the bottom of the stairs. As Meaghan calculated the distance in her mind, she had a ridiculous image of herself sliding down the railing, snatching up one of the black umbrellas, and bashing the stranger senseless with it.

His words stopped even her imagination.

"I've missed you so much, Colleen," the man said, his voice dropping, now husky and deep with emotion.

Frozen, Meaghan stared down at the top of his head as he loomed over Colleen. Now that he'd come indoors, she could see he was a fair man, with golden red hair, but from this angle, she couldn't make out his features. He stood pressed against her grandmother, one hand cupping her cheek, the other braced against the spindly rails of the banister where they met the rising wall. Though he had Colleen trapped between his thick body and the stairway, she did not try to get free. Her hands rested gently against his arms, and her face turned up to his.

"You must go home, Brion," she said softly. "You know you cannot be found here."

"And yet I cannot bring myself to walk back out the door. Why did you leave me, Colleen? Why? And for a stinking fisherman? I could give you a better life. You know it's true."

"We've been through this, Brion. I'll not be your whore."

"But you'll be his? He doesna love you. Everyone knows it."

Colleen lowered her eyes, and Meaghan saw the flush of shame creep up her throat.

Brion pressed his point. "And you don't love him either, do you? Look at me and tell me I'm a liar."

Colleen did not obey. Even Meaghan knew he spoke the truth, whoever he was. Why had her grandmother married Mickey, who looked at her as if the very sight of her made his stomach turn? Why hadn't she wed this man, if a wedding was what she'd craved? He wasn't unattractive. In fact, he had a magnetism about him that made him more than handsome, and he looked very strong and able. If his voice was anything to go by, he thought Colleen hung the moon.

He lowered his head and brushed a kiss against Colleen's forehead, the caress gentle and caring. "Come back to me," he whispered.

"And what of the baby I carry? Would you take him as your own?"

Brion stilled but only for a moment. "If the child is a part of you, then he is a part of me. Why do you not believe me? Why do you think me so shallow that I would forsake flesh of your flesh?"

Colleen took a shaking breath, and Meaghan felt a lump in her throat. There'd been sincerity in his tone, and his heart had been in every word. She didn't doubt for a moment that he meant what he said. He would take her child by Mickey and he would love it. But Colleen's next words shattered the benevolent feelings Meaghan had begun to form.

"And your wife, Brion MacGrath? What will you do with her? What about the child she bears you?"

He pulled away and stared into her face as if she'd slapped him. "It's not mine," he said gruffly. "The child cannot be mine."

"And yet it is your wife who carries it. Why do you deny such a blessing?"

Meaghan wished she could see his eyes, but the light shining down from the landing cast long shadows on his face. Still she couldn't miss the red flush that crept up from his neck. When he spoke, his words were like stones clattering into a concrete basin. "For years I've been her husband and I've lain with her in my bed. Never once did she take my seed. Not once."

"Until now," Colleen said, her voice unwavering. Determined.

"I tell you, it's not my child." He looked away as if he couldn't bear to see her reaction to what he said next. "It's me—not her—that makes me so certain. I cannot father a child. There have been other women, my love. Before you. It pains me to say it, but mine is a cold marriage as it has always been. I've strayed from it many times. Not once would I stray from you, though."

The last should have sounded tacked on, but it didn't. He meant it, but that didn't necessarily mean he could follow through. He didn't look shamed by what he'd told Colleen, but he didn't look proud either. His expression said this was his reality. He was a man forced to cheat on his wife. It was something beyond his control. Meaghan thought he'd fit right in if he lived in her time. How many famous men had she seen confess their sins on the evening news, taking full responsibility for their actions while at the same time, admitting they were not responsible at all?

"Not one of them ever got with my child. Not one," he went on. "Not even you, Colleen."

Her face was ablaze, but she kept her gaze lowered. "I took precautions, Brion."

"You lie, my love. You think to spare my feelings. But I am not a man to be deceived. It makes my heart heavy to know I cannot give a woman my baby, but that does not mean I should let another man cuckold me and place his changeling in my home."

"What other man would dare cuckold you, Brion MacGrath? Tell me that."

"I do not know who he is. But I will find him."

"Marga is a good Catholic, Brion. She would not stray from you."

His eyes narrowed and he slammed his open hand against the wall, making Colleen jump. Meaghan did as well.

"She has, I tell you. I know that baby is not mine, and I will not play daddy to the bastard."

"You are wrong," Colleen said, and her voice broke. "You are wrong. The child is innocent. Wait to see it before you judge, Brion. Wait."

He hung his head in defeat, his hands moving to cup Colleen's face in a gentle hold. "There will only be you in my heart. Why do you forsake me?"

"It is too late to change the course of our lives," she whispered, and her voice hitched with emotion she couldn't quite fight back. Even if she had, Meaghan still would have felt it hanging so thickly in the air.

"I have Mickey's child to care for, and I love him like my own." Her hand brushed her swollen belly. "And then this baby will come, and I will love it as well. They are my future now."

Brion pulled back, his face thunderous with rage and frustration. "He does not deserve you."

"Perhaps not. But who am I to deserve more than my lot? I have sinned in the most carnal of ways. If I burn in hell's fires now, it is my own fault."

Brion shook his head, refusing to hear her soft words. "This is not over between you and I," he said in a low and fierce voice.

"It is. I tell you it is. You must let it be over. Now go, before Mi— before my husband comes home."

"If I were that man, I'd not be at the pub when my lovely wife was here waiting for me."

"He'll be back soon. He's a good man and he puts food on the table as he should."

"A husband should be more than a steady meal."

Colleen raised her chin, pride prickling in the tilt of it, the square of her shoulders. Brion had gone too far.

"Perhaps you should take your own advice, Mr. MacGrath. For haven't you a wife at home awaiting more than her supper?"

Brion's jaw clenched and he looked like a man without control. But he said nothing. Instead he leaned in, gave Colleen a hard kiss, holding her face so she could not evade him, gentling his mouth over hers, coaxing until she made a small sound of defeat. Her fingers clenched around his arms and she returned the kiss with hunger that couldn't be hidden. Only then did Brion MacGrath pull away.

"Some things are meant to last forever. What I feel for you is just that, Colleen. Denying it will not change it. It will only hurt like a festering wound that will destroy me. Is that what you're after?" He took her hand, stroked her fingers, and then placed her palm over his heart. "Come back to me."

But Colleen turned her head and slipped from his grasp. Her sorrow was a tangible thing that blanketed the chasm between them. Slowly, she opened the front door and held it wide.

"Thank you for coming," she said, her gaze fixed to the buttons on his coat, her eyes glittering with tears. "I will let my husband know you came to pay him a visit. I know he'll be sorry he missed you."

Brion made a sound like a growl, but his aggression had died. Silently, he stepped into the cold Irish night.

"'Tis not the end, lass," he murmured before she shut the door. "Only a new chapter."

Chapter Thirteen

THE stew had been simmering for an hour or more, and still Mickey and Áedán had not returned home. Meaghan was both glad and angry. Glad because she couldn't face Áedán again, not yet. She'd kept busy helping Colleen, trying not to think of what had happened earlier, but she knew the time would come when she must deal with all of the questions and feelings that Áedán aroused. She was angry, though, for Colleen. Mickey had married her to take care of his child, but *he* treated *her* like he had done the favor.

After Brion MacGrath left, Meaghan had waited until Colleen went back to the kitchen before making her way down the stairs. Colleen gave her a searching look when she'd entered, and Meaghan knew she wondered what, if anything, Meaghan might have heard.

"Who was that at the door?" Meaghan had asked with studied nonchalance.

"I'll not be talking of that," Colleen had answered in no uncertain terms.

Meaghan was okay with that. She'd already had enough shocks

to her system. Discussing her grandmother's love life might have been the end of her.

It was almost eight and her stomach growled again. Meaghan put a hand over it. She couldn't remember the last time she'd eaten, and she was starving. Niall had awakened a short time ago, had a bottle and snack, and now sat on a spread blanket playing happily with his wooden blocks. Still no sign of Mickey.

Colleen stared at the back door as if willing it to open.

"Will he expect you to wait dinner on him this late?" Meaghan asked, knowing the answer and adding another black mark next to the others she'd tallied for her grandfather.

"I'm afraid so," Colleen said. "But if he doesn't come soon, we'll have just a bite to hold us over. He'll never know."

"All right," Meaghan said. Silence descended again, and in an effort to break it, Meaghan asked, "How long have you known Áedán?"

Colleen gave her a startled glance. "Áedán, is it? Not Mr. Brady?"

Blushing, Meaghan said, "In my time, we're not so formal."

"Ah, is that a fact. I've known *Áedán* a little less than a week."

Well, at least he'd told Jamie the truth earlier. She'd half expected Colleen to say he'd been there months.

"Poor lad was down on his luck when Mickey found him. Been in a boating accident or something, from the looks of things. He's not one to share and Mickey won't pry. As far as my husband is concerned, Áedán might have come from heaven, sent down in a time of need, which is surely now. I sometimes wonder if Mickey would recognize a fish if it was hanging off his nose. He wasn't born a fisherman by any call, but since Áedán started helping . . . Well, Mickey's got cause to be grateful."

It was what Hoyt O'Shea implied as well. Meaghan wasn't surprised. Áedán struck her as the kind of man who'd be skilled at whatever he turned his hand to.

"Mickey can't afford to pay him," Colleen went on, "so he works for meals and he sleeps onboard. I've done my best to make sure the berth is clean and tidy. Mickey gave him handoffs to wear, and I wash them when I do my laundry. He seems to appreciate what we give him even though it's not much."

Meaghan caught the corner of her lip with her teeth. "Where is he from?"

"Mickey thinks Kildare, but who knows for sure? Mr. Brady doesn't talk about himself much." Colleen pulled her attention from the door and gave Meaghan a suspicious glance. "Why do you ask?"

"It just seems to me that his coming—"

The back door slammed open, ending the conversation with a bang. Mickey staggered in, stinking of fish and drink. His shirt was stained down the front as if many a glass had spilled on the way to his mouth. He looked as mean as a cornered bully in a schoolyard brawl.

Meaghan stared at him in shock while the pendant, which had remained quiet and cool inside her pocket since she'd left Áedán, suddenly began its menacing drone. She'd suspected that it somehow fed on emotions—and the more aggressive those emotions were, the more agitated the pendant seemed to become.

She remembered something Áedán had said as they'd walked to the lighthouse today. He'd asked her what she'd want most if she'd spent an eternity in a world without texture, without touch. He'd told her it would be *to feel.* If the pendant was a part of the Book of Fennore, a part of that cold, flat world he referred to, perhaps it, too, sought emotion. Only instead of siphoning all feelings, it somehow amplified them. She remembered the hostility in the lighthouse and how it felt as if the pendant were somehow engaged in the conflict. . . .

Could that be the reason Áedán had looked at her with such shock and . . . dread? He'd been enraged when they'd left, and she hadn't understood why. Had the pendant churned some feeling in him that had flared out of control?

"Where's my fecking dinner?" Mickey slurred in a booming voice.

Colleen jumped to her feet and scurried to the stove. "It's ready and waiting, Mickey. Have a wash and it will be on the table—"

"I'll wash if and when I fecking feel like it," he snarled.

"Sure and I understand. If you'd just keep your voice down so as not to upset the baby—"

The sound of his hand slapping her face came like a sniper's bullet. Meaghan sucked in a gasp and stepped forward just as she saw Áedán, who must have been on the back porch, move quickly to grab Mickey's wrist before he could hit Colleen again.

In the stunned silence, Mickey glared at Áedán and jerked his hand free. "She's me wife. I'll beat her if I want," he said angrily. "Do you hear my words, Áedán Brady?"

The pendant's drone rose in pitch until it rattled Meaghan to the bone, growing hot as it had before. She no longer had the coat to use as wadding against it, and it burned her through the thin layer of her pocket. If she hadn't felt threatened by Mickey's antagonism, she might have flung it out of her pocket just to escape its heat.

Áedán stared at Mickey with steady eyes for a long, drawn minute. She felt the sharp spike of his shock and then a plunge of disbelief. Whatever he saw in the depths of Mickey's gaze disturbed him. More than that. It filled him with alarm. She could almost hear it tolling like the bells of doom.

The fingers of Mickey's other hand curled into a fist, and he raised it threateningly at Áedán.

"Will it make you feel better to strike me, Mr. Ballagh?" Áedán asked in the calmest of tones, but beneath it, Meaghan sensed the heavy mist of dread. "For I owe you much and will gladly take the blow if it will ease you some."

Meaghan didn't believe it for a moment. If Mickey moved to strike Áedán, she knew Áedán would knock him to the floor. The hard gleam in Áedán's eyes contradicted his deferential tone and the fear she felt whispering in the silence. He was no man's punching bag, and the fool who took him for one might not live to regret it. Meaghan watched with a dry mouth.

Mickey faltered, backing up without backing down. Obviously he'd drunk too much to realize the dangerous path he teetered across. Belligerence jutted out his jaw. "That's right, you owe me. You all owe me." He jabbed a finger at Colleen. "You especially."

Colleen's hand shook as she steadfastly ladled stew into shallow crockery and handed it to Meaghan to place on the table, but Meaghan felt her rage. Bubbling fiercely, it welled inside her grandmother like a volcano about to erupt. How she kept it all from spewing out, Meaghan couldn't begin to guess. Why she did was more obvious. Though Meaghan had no sense of what Mickey might be feeling inside—if, in fact, he experienced anything so complex as inner turmoil—no one could miss the violence radiating from him. Meaghan didn't like being anywhere near the radius of Mickey's fist, but she hurried to help her grandmother. Imitating Colleen, she kept her eyes down as she served the stew.

Mickey lurched across the kitchen, snatching a bottle of something golden brown off the shelves as he went. Whatever it was, it didn't have a label but looked potent. He nearly missed his chair at the head of the table and caught himself awkwardly before he stumbled into it.

Only then did he turn his eyes on Meaghan, and what she saw made her stomach clench and the pendant squeal with something that might have been delight and might have been dismay. The amulet's temperature spiked until she felt it must surely be melting her pocket. Mickey's eyes glittered flat and hard, the gray color lost in the cold gleam. Like a mirror, they reflected the bright lights and deep shadows, but no soul gleamed behind them.

She caught her breath and drew a warning glance from Áedán. His concern felt like a welcome wash of warmth, but it could not chase away her apprehension. On the blanket spread in the corner, Niall found his bottle amongst his toys and gurgled happily over it. He, at least, seemed immune to the tension in the room.

With a cautious look at Mickey, Áedán went to the sink, removed his bandage, and washed his hands and face. Silently Colleen handed him a towel, and he dried with deliberate movements. Meaghan caught herself staring at his hands, remembering how they felt against her skin, beneath her dress. . . .

He looked up, as if hearing her thoughts, and his gaze roamed possessively over her body.

"How is your hand, Mr. Brady?" Colleen asked, breaking the electric contact.

Áedán gave her a tight smile. "Almost as good as new, Mrs. Ballagh. Thank you for stitching it."

"Oh, she's good at that," Mickey said with a sneer. It seemed to have a double meaning for him, but Meaghan couldn't decipher it.

Colleen's temper flared and cut through the distance separating her from the man she called her husband. As if aware of the emotion she managed to keep from showing in her eyes, in her expression, Mickey smiled. His lips stretching across his yellowed teeth looked like a ghastly grimace, and the flat gleam in his eyes made it all the more sinister.

Meaghan wanted to jump to her feet, scoop up the baby, and drag her grandmother out of there as fast as she could. She forced herself to stay put.

Filth covered Mickey's hands, but he didn't wash. He pulled his cup of water to him, gave Colleen a deliberate look, and then dumped it on the linoleum floor before filling it with the liquor from the plain bottle. It had a sharp scent that Meaghan could smell from where she stood.

"You, Áedán?" Mickey said congenially, his hateful words from earlier evidently forgotten. "Would you care to try a drop of mother's milk?"

"No," Áedán said.

The entire room seemed to suck in a breath at that, and the baby made a skittish sound. Mickey's soulless gaze studied Áedán for what seemed an eternity before he muttered something under his breath and slopped another splash into his own cup.

"Where did you go tonight?" Áedán asked him.

Since they'd arrived together, Meaghan had assumed they'd been in each other's company, but now she took in the details. Mickey was obviously drunk, but not Áedán. His hands were steady, his eyes watchful. His threadbare clothes had stains that looked older than the cloth. They were clean, though. If he'd been drinking tonight, he'd made a neater job of it than Mickey had.

"I don't answer to you," Mickey said in a low, warning voice.

Colleen put a plate with warm soda bread in the center of the table, and Meaghan took her seat across from Áedán. Colleen sat stiffly at the opposite end from Mickey.

She folded her hands in prayer, and Meaghan quickly did the same. Áedán followed suit, although she caught the glimmer of irony in his eyes as he did it. Mickey ignored them. He held his spoon clasped in his dirty paw like a caveman as he shoveled food into his mouth. The stew had been simmering on the stove, and he sucked in air as he slurped, then let pieces drop from his lips back into the bowl.

"It's too fecking hot to eat," he said, ripping a hunk of bread from the loaf and dipping it into the broth.

The Colleen that Meaghan knew would never have permitted such foul manners or language at her table. She'd have grabbed Mickey by the ear and twisted until he fell to his knees begging for forgiveness and leniency. The Colleen that Meaghan knew would not have given it. She'd have booted his smelly arse into the street. In the silence, she could feel the toxic mix of Colleen's conflicting emotions as she fought the desire to do just that.

Instead, she sat stiffly at her end of the table, face pale, eyes downcast. Meaghan had been hungry for hours, but now her stomach felt knotted and sour. She wanted to push away from the table and escape. Niall began to fuss.

"Shut the brat up," Mickey barked.

Meaghan nearly flew out of her chair as she rushed to gather the baby and keep him off Mickey's radar. She bounced him on her hip as Colleen watched with mingled gratitude and anger. The anger,

Meaghan knew, was not for her, but for the vile man who sat at her table.

Mickey paused and glared at Meaghan for a moment. The inhuman eyes made her want to squirm just as they made her want to challenge him. Knowing that's what he wanted, what he craved, she settled back in her chair and cuddled the baby. The pendant's drone seeped beneath her skin until it felt like it came from inside rather than out. Áedán watched her, as if worried she might draw Mickey's vehemence to herself.

"I've not had a stew in a long time," Áedán said in an obvious ploy to defuse the ticking bomb. "You are a fine cook, Mrs. Ballagh."

Colleen smiled at him tensely and took a small bite. The whole scene wore the tint of the surreal. Nothing was right here. Not the strange man with his merciless eyes, not the stress and strain that warred with the polite façade that everyone but Mickey tried to maintain. Not her grandmother, who spoke with calm and felt with fury. Not Áedán, who seemed to be viewing the situation with a set of criteria that Meaghan couldn't grasp. He'd made some connection about Mickey's behavior that she hadn't, but she couldn't ask him to explain.

"I used the last of the lamb," Colleen said in a light voice, as if her rage wasn't as thick as the steam from her pot on the stove. "Not fish, just like you asked, Mickey."

Mickey looked up from his bowl. Grease and slop covered his chin, but he made no move to wipe it away. "The last of the lamb," he mocked. "You used the last of the lamb. Well, do you expect me to keep you in lamb unending, then? Do you think I can prevent it from ever running out? You spoiled slut. Next you'll be wanting *beef* on your table every night, isn't that the way of it?"

Colleen recoiled and Meaghan saw her shoulders square and her chin come up. A red abrasion stood out starkly on her face from where he'd slapped her, and her eyes sparkled with a hard light.

Meaghan wanted to jump up, jump in, and defend her grandmother, but Áedán caught her eye and gave a warning shake of his head.

The wrath Colleen had kept tapped down suddenly exploded.

"Beef every night?" Colleen repeated, and a harsh and disrespectful tone replaced her subservience. "I'd sooner expect golden plates to shoot out of your arse than for you to provide what any Irish woman would expect from a man."

For a moment, Mickey's mouth opened and closed like a fish as his face turned an alarming shade and those eyes became sharp blades of malevolence. Beyond control of her ire, Colleen glared back.

Mickey's chair went flying and he lunged across the table, spilling stew without care, burning himself, she was sure, but too enraged to feel it. She got out of the way as quickly as possible, holding Niall tightly as the baby let out a fearful cry.

"Are you going to kill me now?" Colleen taunted, dancing out of his reach. "Then who will care for your spawn, you miserable swine?"

The shade of Mickey's face bespoke apoplexy or aneurisms. He circled the table and grabbed Colleen's big butcher knife on the way. At the same time, Áedán caught Mickey from behind, locking Mickey's arms at the elbows with his own and holding them back. Mickey fought the wrestler's hold, could have escaped it if he'd let his body go limp, but he was too far gone to think it through, and he twisted and bucked like a caged animal. Áedán struggled to keep him captive.

"Get out of here," Áedán shouted to the women. "Take the baby and go."

He didn't have to tell Meaghan twice. She yanked Colleen away but couldn't keep her grandmother's rising taunts from coming. Colleen must have been swallowing them for a long time and now she couldn't stop. She flung them like acid, criticisms of his stench, his foul manners, his tiny prick. Mickey raged in Áedán's grip, nearly escaping. She knew that Áedán was made of solid muscle. She'd been held tight against all that brawn only a few hours ago. But Mickey was mindless with fury.

"Come on," Meaghan said, hauling Colleen out to the porch and the cold. Fear propelled them to the crude road, where they stopped and looked back, as if they might see through the walls to what went on inside. They could still hear the fight, dishes breaking, the thud of fists against flesh and the angry curses that accompanied them.

Doors began to open and buttery light spilled out from the cottages on either side of Colleen's. A large woman in a housedress and slippers hurried down her walk to where Colleen and Meaghan waited. On the other side, a man and woman watched from their porch. Meaghan realized she knew them—or at least she would in about fifty years. The couple sniffed, as if scenting danger, and then scurried back inside.

"Drunk again, is he?" the fat woman in the housedress said in a voice filled with sympathy. Her concerned gaze moved from the bundled baby in Meaghan's arms to Colleen's swollen belly and tight expression, and then back to Meaghan.

"You must be her cousin. I've heard you came to visit. I'm Enid Sullivan. Come now. Bring the baby inside where it's warm. Mr. Brady will take care of that man while I make us a cup of tea."

Meaghan recognized the other woman even before she'd introduced herself. Enid Sullivan had been her grandmother's best friend for many years. Meaghan had never met her, but she'd seen pictures of the two and heard stories about their friendship. She thought she would have known her anywhere.

The way Enid said *that man* left Meaghan in no doubt that she'd witnessed Mickey's drunken rages many times before. But instinctively, Meaghan knew *this* episode was different. For all the cruel incivility he'd shown Colleen earlier, there'd not been this violence. Nor had there been that cold flat glitter in his eyes.

"Colleen," Meaghan said, drawing her grandmother's attention from the open door. "Take the baby and go with Mrs. Sullivan. She'll take care of you."

Colleen gave a tight nod and reached for Niall, who went to her with a woeful sniffle. The poor child shivered with fear. Colleen held him tight and Meaghan felt a lump forming in her throat at the love she saw seeping in and replacing the anger in her grandmother's expression.

"What am I to do?" Colleen breathed against the downy cap of baby hair.

"There's nothing you can do, lass," Enid said kindly. "But come inside and sit at my table where it's warm and safe. Perhaps Jesus above is watching over you and that fool of a husband will get himself kilt."

A snort of reluctant mirth escaped Colleen. "I've never been that lucky, and I doubt the morrow will bring a change."

"Aye, well, we could hope."

Feeling relieved that her grandmother and father were in good hands, Meaghan took a step away.

"And where would you be off to?" Colleen asked, alarmed.

"I can't just leave Áedán. . . ." She realized how telling her words were but didn't care. "He might need help."

Both Enid and Colleen wore identical expressions of shock. "And just how would a slip of a girl like you be helping a great hulking man like Mr. Brady?" Enid asked.

"I'll brain Mickey with a frying pan if I must."

And with that, she hurried away before either of them could stop her. As she stepped through the front door, she heard Colleen saying, "Let her go. There's more to her than you or I can see."

Meaghan hoped that was true. She didn't let herself even consider that Áedán might come out the loser. She refused to examine the grinding concern that filled her as she followed the sounds of the fighting into the kitchen.

Chapter Fourteen

ÁEDÁN fought to keep Mickey locked in his hold while the women escaped. It should have been an easy feat, but his own fear worked against him and made his movements sluggish. He'd languished in the terror and desperation of others for eons unending, but to experience it himself, to fall victim to an emotion as unfamiliar and debilitating as *alarm* nearly shattered him. This was not the place to unravel his actions and reactions, though. Not the time to pretend that the feelings racing with his blood were not legitimate or worthy.

He'd seen the hard glitter of Mickey's eyes. He knew what it meant.

The Book of Fennore had found Mickey Ballagh—or Mickey had found the Book—and now its power moved within him, giving him strength beyond his own. It made him more dangerous than either of the women could have imagined.

Mickey had wanted to kill Colleen, and sure as the sun rose on this island, he'd meant to harm Meaghan as well. The thought of it twisted Áedán into knots and further stunned him with the savagery of his own response. He didn't bother to ask himself why he should be so desperately concerned about Meaghan and her fate.

He cared. No amount of denial would make it otherwise.

He manhandled Mickey to the back door, then down the porch step and into the yard. Only then did he spin and shove Mickey away. Mickey staggered across the dirt and then turned furiously to face Áedán. He still had the butcher knife clenched in one hand.

"I know who you are," Mickey said, but the voice that came from his lips was not his own.

Depraved and familiar, it belonged to the Book of Fennore. Once Áedán had used it to call, to coax and cajole his victims. Now another man controlled the seductive tones. *Cathán.*

Had Áedán only known what hell Cathán MacGrath would bring to his cursed world, he would have sought someone else all the years ago when he'd honed in on the pathetic man's pleas. Willing humans had been like weeds in a garden. It would have been so easy to pluck another.

But fate had matched them, and now it would exact its price.

"You know nothing about me," Áedán said coldly. "If you did, you would be running away. You think you are strong? You think you can frighten *me*? I was the first nightmare. I will be the last. I had thousands of years to twist humanity into my personal playground. You are nothing but a child in grown-up clothes. Run away, child. There's still time."

Mickey's dead eyes stared back without blinking. "I do not run from *humans*," he said in that voice that seemed to come from nowhere and everywhere.

"Nor do I."

"But that's what you are. That's what you've become. *Human*. Tell me. Is it the girl that owns you now, Brandubh? Is it she who makes you weak?"

Áedán clenched his jaw, circling the other man. The creature that was Mickey mirrored his stance and steps, turning with preternatural grace, never letting Áedán get behind him.

"I could call to her," Mickey said in Cathán's voice. "Would you like that? I could bring her to her knees, right here." He pointed to the ground in front of him, and then slowly mimed taking her head in his hands and thrusting his hips into the space between them.

Fury flamed inside Áedán's gut like a madness. "Stay away from her."

"Or what? You have nothing, *Druid*. You *are* nothing."

That he spoke the truth made it all the worse. Once the most powerful Druid known, he'd been reduced to just a man. But he still had a mind. He still had two hands and a body that obeyed his commands. He would fight this mutated version of Mickey to the death if that's what it took to protect what was his. Cathán would not touch Meaghan. Not with his hands, not with his voice, not with his monster.

"Oh but I will," Cathán answered his thoughts.

"Where did you find the Book, Mickey?" he asked, speaking to the person who no longer existed, knowing it would vex Cathán.

Áedán didn't need an answer to his question, though. He knew. From within the world of Fennore, Cathán had sensed Áedán and used Mickey to get to him. He needed Áedán—or at least he thought he did. He wanted to know how Áedán had escaped the Book. He wanted to follow Áedán into the real world and wreak havoc here.

"Do not play games, Brandubh."

"Why did you choose Mickey?" Áedán tried again. "Why him?"

"Mickey Ballagh is but a tool and I, a craftsman."

Áedán's mouth went dry, his palms grew damp. The reaction was so human that he couldn't even pretend otherwise.

"And what can you build with a tool like Mickey?" he asked calmly, forcing himself not to reveal the panic screeching through his nerves.

"A trap. The pendant is near. I feel it."

The words reverberated in Áedán's head and filled his belly with ice. *The pendant?* In that instant, Áedán realized what he should have seen all along. Cathán, and by proxy the Book of Fennore, didn't want Áedán.

They wanted the pendant. They wanted the key. With that, they'd have no need for Áedán and his knowledge. No need for Meaghan or anyone else. Cathán could open the door of his prison, free himself, and unleash the power of the Book of Fennore without help from anyone.

But there was something that Cathán had not considered. Áedán curled his fingers into his fists, thinking. He'd created the pendant to lock the Book of Fennore, to keep its secrets from the prying eyes of the other Druids who had, by then, turned against him. But like the Book, it had become a power in its own right, as Elan—the mystical White Fennore—had so elegantly demonstrated when she'd used it in her spell to condemn and banish him with her curse.

In the millennia since he'd been trapped in the Book of Fennore, he and the Book had morphed into something neither Áedán nor Elan could have envisioned. During that time, what had the pendant become? What powers had it bled from the universe, what transformations had *it* undergone?

The Book of Fennore had become a force beyond comprehension. And if Áedán had thought it through correctly, the Book and the pendant were connected by creation and evolution. The pendant had a power of its own that somehow Cathán had honed in on, and that power traveled in the airways between the Book and the pendant.

And Meaghan had been carrying it around in her *fecking pocket*.

He quickly smothered the thought and masked it from Cathán.

"If you give it to me, I will let you live," Cathán said again, inching Mickey's body closer.

Áedán knew that Cathán lied. Áedán had never shown mercy himself, and he was not so foolish as to think Cathán would either. But he couldn't know that Meaghan had the pendant, or he wouldn't have tried bargaining for it.

Relief nearly took the legs out from under him.

"What is it you think the pendant will do?" he asked, not expecting an answer. Surprised when he got one.

"Free me."

Áedán gave him a sardonic grin. "If it'd only taken the pendant to release me, do you think I would have remained a prisoner for millennia, Cathán? Are you so ignorant?"

The flat eyes narrowed and the soulless Mickey tightened his grip on the butcher knife he still held in his hand. Every day for nearly a week, Áedán had watched Mickey gut and clean his catch and then fillet it neatly. The man knew how to use a blade. But a knife that size required little finesse. He'd need only to plunge it into Áedán's body to do irreparable damage.

Áedán did not intend to give him the chance. Wary, he kept circling, hoping to keep the other man off balance. But something caught at the corner of his eye and distracted him.

Meaghan.

She stood on the porch outside the open kitchen doorway watching the two men with a look of horror on her face. For a moment, Áedán could not fathom that she was there. He'd *told* her to leave. He'd *ordered* her to get away. Damn the woman for being too stubborn to ever listen to what he said.

"Get out of here, Meaghan," he commanded, keeping his attention on his foe when he wanted to march over and shake some sense into the bloody female.

"I've called the authorities," she said boldly. "They'll be here soon."

Authorities? What was she talking about?

Mickey laughed. "How have you done that? Did you stand on the shores and shout across the channel?"

With a disconcerted frown, she spun and looked for something in the house before turning back with a stunned expression. "There's no telephone?" she said.

"Not on the whole bleeding island. You could ask Brion MacGrath to come to your rescue, but I doubt his wife would let him go. Things are not right in that household, are they now?"

Áedán wasn't sure what a telephone was and didn't know Brion MacGrath, but it didn't matter. This was between Cathán and Áedán. No *authorities* would be required.

"Meaghan, go away."

"What's wrong with your eyes?" she demanded, ignoring Áedán again as she stared at the man she knew only as Mickey Ballagh.

"Come closer and you'll see," Mickey answered.

"I don't think so. I don't like your voice either. It sounds different."

"Like Cathán," Áedán said pointedly.

As he'd hoped, Meaghan realized instantly what he meant. But the blasted woman still didn't leave.

"Sweet Jesus," she said. "You have the Book of Fennore?"

"I *am* the Book of Fennore," he said, and his voice echoed in the night. He rose from his crouch and spread his arms. "I am invincible."

"Fecking stupid is more like it," Meaghan said, goading him. She poked a tiger with a stick, but Áedán couldn't tell her that, and he doubted she'd heed his warning even if he could. "Don't you know anything? The Book of Fennore doesn't make you invincible. It makes you a slave."

Slave, Áedán thought. Yes, that's what he'd been. All the power in the world, and he'd been merely a slave.

Mickey's eyes narrowed until only the freezing gleam of malice showed.

Undaunted, Meaghan said, "Tell me. What did Mickey ask for when he found the Book?"

"He asked for power," Cathán answered. "He asked to leave the world of stink and fish behind. I granted his wish."

Meaghan turned her gaze to Áedán, and he knew she remembered his own words. *I gave them exactly what they asked for.* And in exchange, he'd taken their very humanity and left only a shell, just as Cathán had done.

"You don't look very powerful," she said. "You look like a walking corpse."

The cold eyes narrowed and the face contorted with a twisted expression—something far beyond human.

"As will you when I'm finished, Meaghan Ballagh."

Distracted, Áedán didn't see him move until it was too late. Cathán charged—not at Áedán, but at Meaghan.

"Meaghan, run!" Áedán shouted.

Everything slowed to an excruciating speed, throwing each particle of air into stark relief as Mickey attacked, wicked knife leading the way. Áedán saw the puff of dust that rose from his footsteps. The flash of his blade as he brandished it. The ice in his dark eyes.

Meaghan watched him come with fear so strong it fragranced the air. But she didn't flinch as he bore down, only a few feet away from reaching her. Instead she plunged her hand into her pocket and pulled out the pouch that held the pendant.

Áedán cried, *"NO!"* but it was too late.

She'd snagged the leather cord and jerked the pendant from the bag before the echo of his warning had begun. The dark kept him from seeing the color of her eyes, but in that instant he knew—*he knew*—what he would see if there had been light. . . .

Lavender swallowing the blue.

The pendant dropped to the end of its tether and then swung back and forth. With each pendulous motion, Meaghan seemed to transform. Her hair blew in a nonexistent wind until it cascaded around her face like a silvery veil. At once she seemed taller and more slender, her features morphing into those of another woman. A light seemed to glow from within her, illuminating her skin until she looked like an angel. An avenging angel.

The White Fennore. Elan.

He had no time to take it all in, not an instant to react to what he saw. The last vestiges of the man Mickey had once been vanished completely as Cathán's greed and desire became a frothing storm around him.

Áedán lunged at Mickey's body, knowing he couldn't stop the other man, but needing to *try*. While he fought to defy the laws of gravity and momentum, a snapping moment of clarity broke through the chaos in his mind.

The Book and the pendant were connected by creation and evolution—two pieces of a whole—a Book that could be locked and a pendant that was its key. The pendant had a power of its own that called to the Book. And if somehow that power traveled in the airways between the Book and the pendant, it could be used.

He'd felt the humming drone of it all along, but he hadn't understood. Now he felt the power surging and sparking like electricity all around him.

Instinct took over, and without knowing how he did it, Áedán drew on something within himself that he'd thought long dead. As his body hurled through the air, in his mind, he groped for that part of him that had once been *Druid* and turned it loose. He called to the power he felt around him, and he wielded it to his own purpose.

Mickey evaded his tackle and Áedán slammed to the ground. But just as the other man reached Meaghan, Áedán shoved him away. Not with his hands. Not with his body. But with his *mind.*

With a *Druid's power* he'd feared lost forever.

As far as he could see, every light went out, plunging them in a black velvet shroud, as if he'd pulled not only the power of the pendant, but tapped into the electric current that supplied them. Then the force of his thoughts propelled Mickey's body through the air like a leaf caught in an icy gale and flung him to the ground. He hit hard and bashed his head against a buried rock, then lay stiff and unmoving.

For a moment, neither Meaghan nor Áedán moved. One by one, the lights came back on as shock traveled through Áedán's nerves numbing his limbs and robbing him of speech. Back doors opened and neighbors stepped out onto their porches to find out what was going on.

Afraid of what he'd see, Áedán glanced quickly at Meaghan. She blinked blue eyes owlishly at him, her skin pale and creamy, her hair a sleek golden fall at her shoulder. The illusion of illumination had faded completely.

Áedán kicked Mickey's knife beneath a bush before approaching her. She'd stuffed the pendant back into its pouch, her fingers shaking uncontrollably as she shoved it into her pocket.

"It's all right now," he murmured, pulling her into his arms even as he called himself a fool. "You're all right."

She nodded, but her whole body trembled. "How did you do that?" she asked against his throat. The hot touch of her breath melted the frozen numbness inside him. He lowered his head and breathed in her scent, grounding himself in the soft familiarity of it.

She felt like Meaghan. She smelled like Meaghan. But the knot in his gut would not go away. He'd seen her *change*, though she seemed completely unaware of it.

She pulled away a bit and repeated her question. "How did you do it?"

How indeed? Whatever power he'd felt had been sapped by the effort. His return to normalcy had come with a crash and left him feeling hollow and somehow . . . used.

Behind them, Hoyt O'Shea appeared and knelt beside Mickey's unconscious body. As if some bell only fishermen could hear had been rung, others trickled in to join the small group. He wondered if they'd been watching all along. Had they seen Áedán fling Mickey into the air with his thoughts? If so, would they have attributed the unbelievable to their faulty eyesight or poor vantage point? Humans were always willing to explain away what they couldn't understand.

Regardless of what they thought, the fact remained that their coming eliminated any chance Áedán had to finish Mickey off. He dared not kill the man, not with so many witnesses.

"Drunk again, was he?" Hoyt asked with a scowl. "Maybe now you'll think better of my offer."

Mute, Áedán nodded. It seemed the thing to do, and he was in no shape to respond otherwise. Keeping one arm around Meaghan, he rubbed his thumb over the fingertips of his free hand.

He'd called the power of the Book. It had been right there, within his reach, and he'd used it. The pendant had created the bridge he'd needed. Even now he could feel it humming through Meaghan's pocket where her hip pressed against his thigh. Could he do it again if he tried? He'd thought his Druid powers long dead, but now he wondered. . . .

Mickey moaned and his eyes fluttered open. "What happened?" he asked as he squinted from one face to another. It sounded like his own voice, but Áedán saw that the eyes still gleamed flatly and sparkled with that soulless light.

"You picked a fight with our Áedán," Hoyt told him. "You're piss-faced, Ballagh. Again."

Mickey blinked his eyes guilelessly, but Áedán saw the sly gleam within them. "Of course I'm drunk, you fecking wanker. And don't I plan to get drunker?"

A man who docked his ship near *The Angel* let out a hoot of laughter. "Come on then, you mean old lunatic," he said. "I'll buy you the first round."

"And I'll let you," Mickey answered, grabbing the offered hand and rising to his feet. He cast a look over his shoulder at Áedán as he sauntered off toward the Pier House. In that look, Áedán saw the threat he didn't need to voice.

Mickey would be back. And when he came, he would leave a bloody trail in his wake.

Áedán didn't want to follow them. He wanted to get Meaghan alone and strip her of the pendant that had given him his power back, if only for a moment. He wanted to test his theory that the power he'd called could be summoned again. But Meaghan watched him warily now, and he needed to think things through first. He didn't understand why he'd never suspected the power it held. In all his time as the nameless entity trapped within the Book of Fennore, he'd never sensed the pendant. Never heard its call. So why did Cathán?

He eyed Meaghan as the answer formed in his thoughts. *Elan. She* had to be the conduit that connected them all. Elan had used the pendant to lock him away in the cursed Book. She'd made him her prisoner. She'd made him her slave.

Did Elan's spirit move inside Meaghan with a purpose? Were his worst fears about to come true? Elan returning to play out her role as history repeated itself and she condemned him once more to the Book of Fennore?

"What's wrong, Áedán?" Meaghan asked. "Why are you looking at me that way?"

"What way?"

"Like I'm a stranger."

"I'm not," he lied. "I'm just shaken." Admitting to the human reaction galled, but it did the trick on Meaghan. She nodded and he continued before she could question him further. "Go get Colleen and lock yourself inside. I need to see where Mickey goes next. Don't worry, I won't let him come back here."

He would kill Mickey before he let him hurt either of the women or the child.

Meaghan nodded again, but her brows had pulled in a frown and her blue eyes looked shadowed and concerned.

Even with all his suspicions, seeing her troubled pulled at something inside him. Áedán could not leave her so anxious. "I won't let him hurt you. I promise."

Áedán would not make the same promise for himself, though. Elan, the White Fennore, had betrayed him once before. No matter how complex and confusing his feelings were for Meaghan, he would not allow it again.

Chapter Fifteen

NUMB, Meaghan did as Áedán asked. She made her way through the messy kitchen and out the front door. Her legs moved automatically, but her mind remained locked in that moment when Mickey—Cathán—whoever it was that lived behind those cold eyes, had reached for her.

She didn't know why she'd pulled the pendant from her pocket, why she'd thought it could protect her. The action had been like an instinct—the automatic step back from a snarling dog or the flinch from a hand raised to strike. She hadn't even been aware of what she did until she saw it dangling before her, jewels glimmering, silver and gold flashing.

And then . . . And then she'd felt as if an invisible shield had surrounded her. No, not that. It was as if she'd stepped into someone else's skin. She felt the power crackling around them, and she'd pulled it to her and then amplified it, turning it into something that lit the horizon like a sunrise, made her squint and wince against the fierce glow. The feeling had grown, becoming brighter, hotter, deeper until it melted down to a mercurial substance. It covered her from head to toe, inside out.

She still felt it inside her now, flowing in her bloodstream and speeding her pulse.

Drawing in a deep breath, Meaghan tried to compose herself. Áedán had told her to get Colleen and return home, lock the doors, and wait. He'd promised to keep Mickey away, though he hadn't explained how he meant to do it. She'd have to trust him.

Enid answered at the first knock, and soon Colleen stepped outside with a sleeping baby in her arms. The time with Enid had done Colleen good, and the color had returned to her face, though she still looked shell-shocked and unsteady on her feet. Exhaustion painted dark circles beneath her eyes and made her appear much more fragile than Meaghan knew her to be.

"Áedán said we should go back to the house. He'll keep Mickey away."

Colleen nodded. "It won't matter. He's like a match—strikes hot and burns out. The drink wipes his memory. By now, he's forgotten it happened."

Colleen sounded very certain, but Meaghan couldn't bring herself to believe it.

As they made their way up the walk to Colleen's front door, a soft male voice calling her name stopped Meaghan. Instantly alert, she turned to the deserted road that trailed off in the opposite direction.

"Meaghan," the man repeated, and she saw a familiar shape standing in the shadows.

"Kyle?" she said. "Is that you?"

He stepped forward until the light from the porch illuminated him. "Is everything all right, Meaghan?"

All right? Was he serious? Things were about as far from all right as possible.

"Oh, everything is grand, Kyle. My cousin and I were about to go inside and have some stew. Will you join us?"

Colleen looked surprised by the invitation, but she didn't protest. Silent and stoic, she led the way into the cottage, and Meaghan wondered what went on behind her façade of calm. Her grandmother was like the misted Irish hills in the gloom—mysterious, unfathomable, and inconsolably bleak.

Kyle followed silently. He didn't need to be told that things in the Ballagh household were not right. He was a smart man, and after nodding when Meaghan introduced him, he took Meaghan's lead, exchanging meaningless chitchat as they cleaned the broken crockery and splattered mess. While he wiped the floor, Meaghan pulled the rubbish bin from beneath the sink and slipped out the back door.

"I'll take that for you," he called.

"No worries, Kyle. I've got it."

She wanted a moment alone. She still had the pendant in her pocket, and in light of what had happened earlier, it seemed foolish and dangerous to keep carrying it around.

When she'd come back from the lighthouse earlier, she'd seen a pile of discarded, rusty tackle leaning haphazardly against the side of the house. Now she hurried toward it. In the glow coming from the porch light, she found a tin can in the heap that held old hooks and pulled it free. A brief burst of images assaulted her as she pried the lid open and dumped the hooks out: Mickey, sitting in a dark room next to the still, gray body of a woman. He sobbed, crying silent, painful tears as, nearby, an infant squalled angrily. Startled, she almost dropped the can.

Quickly she stuffed the black pouch with the pendant inside it into the tin, feeling it scream in protest. It took a surprising strength of will to replace the lid and hide it beneath the mound of debris. Once it was done, the hum silenced and the sickness in her stomach eased.

Quickly, she dumped the garbage into the receptacle in back before returning to the kitchen. Colleen had put the baby to bed and now scooped three bowls of stew from her pot. They sat to eat like this was a normal meal, and Colleen bent her head in prayer. Kyle seemed faintly startled by the act, and Meaghan wondered if she'd been mistaken about the clergy attire she'd thought he'd been wearing the first time she'd seen him when they'd been trapped inside the world of Fennore. She wanted to ask but didn't know how.

Instead, she concentrated on the food Colleen had prepared. The stew smelled delicious, and her empty stomach thanked her for taking the time to feed it, but Meaghan doubted that any of them really tasted what they methodically chewed and swallowed.

Kyle brimmed with curiosity. Meaghan could see it in his warm, hazel eyes, but for some reason, she couldn't feel it in the air around her. She didn't know if her ability had been burned out by the intense emotions the pendant and Áedán had spurred or if sealing off the pendant had somehow affected her senses. It might be both or neither. If Kyle had once been a man of the church, perhaps he'd learned a calming of spirit in his studies that made him soothing to be around, the polar opposite of the tempestuous storm of emotions she felt when with Áedán. Whatever the cause, Kyle remained closed off.

She caught him watching her with a quizzical expression, but like Meaghan, he asked none of the questions she knew he wanted answered. When they finished eating, Meaghan stood.

"You go on upstairs and try to sleep, Colleen," she said softly. "I'll clean the kitchen."

Colleen started to protest but Meaghan cut her off. "I insist."

"All right then. Thank you. Before I go, let me show you where you'll sleep tonight. It's not much, be warned."

While Kyle pretended extreme interest in his last bite of stew, Meaghan followed Colleen through a door off the kitchen. Bigger than a pantry and smaller than a bedroom, it was about seven feet long and six feet across. In the future, it would become a combination of a mudroom and laundry room, with hooks above a bench for hanging rain jackets before sitting to take off muddy Wellies. A deep utility sink for washing up and counters for folding clothes would be added later. Now it was bare but for a set of crudely crafted shelves in a corner and an old cot shoved against the wall.

It seemed that Mickey and Colleen barely scratched out a living and had no surpluses to store. Among a few large pots on the shelves stood an ancient-looking washbasin with a wringer screwed to its top and scrub board sitting inside it. Colleen had neatly arranged her broom and mop, bucket and detergents beside the door. She cleared her throat as Meaghan took it all in.

"Tell me, granddaughter," she said with a tired smile. "Will I always be stuffing my company into the closets?"

Meaghan shook her head. "Someday you'll have two spare rooms and you'll grouse that they don't stay empty long enough. You are loved by everyone, Nana, and you have many visitors."

"Everyone, is it?"

Meaghan shook her head. "Well, I guess that would be an exaggeration. You do tend to piss people off, but it's one of the things *I* love about you."

"That I'm contrary?"

"Of course. Who wants to be fecking agreeable?"

Meaghan grinned at the astonished look on Colleen's face.

"I know that you feel trapped right now and that things with Mickey . . . they aren't right. But this will not be forever. Long after he's gone, you'll be around to greet the day."

"Drinks himself into an early grave, does he?"

"Hit by a tram, drunk."

"Are you serious?" Colleen asked with wide eyes.

"No—I've no idea how he goes. But it doesn't matter what happens to Mickey, Nana. Only what happens to you."

Colleen blinked rapidly and then looked away. Giving Meaghan a small, tight hug, she wearily made her way upstairs, where Niall once again slept safely in his cradle. In Meaghan's time, there would be three rooms up there, but now there was only one, built under the slope of the steepled ceiling. She hoped Mickey hit his head on it each time he staggered into bed, but that thought brought more angst over his possible return. Áedán had said he wouldn't let Mickey come back here, but what if he couldn't stop him?

Mickey had spoken in Cathán's voice. He'd meant to kill her to get the pendant. And those eyes . . . Mickey was not a kind man, not a good man. But his eyes had been human. What she'd seen in their dark depths tonight, had not.

Before Colleen reached the second floor, Meaghan called softly, "Don't worry about anything. I'll lock up before I go to sleep."

Colleen gave a low, grim laugh. "Sure and I wish you luck with that. The back door hasn't a lock that works. Mickey keeps saying he'll fix it, but he never has."

Meaghan shook her head at that dire news, but she supposed a mere lock wouldn't keep Mickey Ballagh out if he wanted in anyway.

"I still can't understand what happened," Colleen said, pausing at the top of the stairs to look down. "He's never acted so violent like he did tonight, and I've never let my temper loose like that either."

"No one could blame you, Colleen," Meaghan said. "Get a good night's sleep. We'll figure things out in the morning."

With a heavy heart, she rejoined Kyle in the kitchen. They heard Colleen's soft footsteps overhead and exchanged a glance, but neither of them spoke. He seemed different this evening than he had earlier, although she couldn't say just why. He still wore the same clothes, his hair was combed the same way, but there was something she couldn't quite put her finger on. . . .

He'd said he'd come to talk, and Meaghan was anxious to hear what he had to say. As she cleared the dishes from the table, he rose to help, grabbing a towel to dry when she filled the sink with soapy dishwater.

"What did you want to talk about Kyle?"

"You, Meaghan. I wanted to talk about you."

Surprised, she looked at him. "Why?"

"You seemed . . . unwell when you left earlier."

"I was overwhelmed. It's a lot to take in, traveling through time. Finding you three here."

"Talking about the Book of Fennore," he added gently.

"Yes, that, too."

He said, "It's a terrifying thing, the Book. I was only in its presence a short time, but it was long enough that I never want to be near it again."

She knew exactly what he meant. "Is it the Book itself, do you think, that makes it so horrifying or is it the . . . entity inside it?"

"They are one and the same, Meaghan."

"Are they? Are you certain about that?"

His eyes narrowed. "No. I'm not certain about anything. Not anymore."

"It's just that . . . you said earlier, when Áedán and I came to the lighthouse, that you'd sealed Cathán inside the Book, but not the Druid."

His eyes hardened for a moment. "No, not the Druid. He escaped."

"Well, if the Book and the Druid are linked . . . I mean, if they're one and the same, then how could that be?"

He inhaled, nodding as understanding filled him. "I see your point. Unfortunately, I think the answer is the worst scenario. The Druid did not separate from the Book when he left it. He simply brought all that is wrong with the Book of Fennore out into our world."

"All the evil? Is that what you mean?"

"How could it be less? We can't even comprehend the duration of his life. *Thousands of years* he was trapped in there, bound by body and soul in the corruption and curse. A devil in every definition of the word."

She swallowed hard. The same thoughts had filled her mind before. But now she had a hard time thinking of Áedán in such a light. Not since he'd touched her. Not since she'd felt the turmoil of his emotions battering him down into a darkness he tried so hard to escape.

"You're saying there is no way the Druid could ever walk away from that? No way he could change, overcome it?"

"You don't need me to answer that, Meaghan. You know the truth."

Yes, she supposed she did. And yet, she'd seen Áedán fight to protect her. She'd felt his fear, his passion. Even now she wanted him here, beside her.

"Temptation is any devil's most powerful weapon," Kyle said

softly, as if he'd heard her thoughts. "Destruction of innocence. Rejection of anything that is good or holy. From our earliest stories, those of Adam and Eve, there has been temptation."

And consequences to giving in to it. Yeah, she got it.

She took a deep breath and exhaled. "The first time I saw you, you had on a clergy collar. Like a priest . . ."

His glance held disquiet and a scowl. She hadn't brought it up with much finesse, but his talk of the devil had spurred the question.

"There was a time in my life when I thought I'd been called to serve God."

"But you changed your mind?" Meaghan asked.

"Let's say I had it changed for me. I learned that I was a member of a different order. Keepers of the Book of Fennore."

"Keepers?"

"We were intended to keep it safe from humanity. Obviously we failed."

Meaghan nodded. "I see."

But she didn't. Not really.

Kyle went on. "I couldn't pledge myself to God and still believe in something as sacrilegious as an evil entity and cursed Book that should not exist in the natural world."

"Ah," she said. "Bit of a conflict of interest."

He smiled sadly. "Exactly. If truth be told, though, I don't think I'm cut from the right cloth to have taken my vows. Even before I learned of the Keepers, I had doubts."

"People change," Meaghan said.

"Yes."

"What if—what if he has changed, too," she asked without meaning to, still dwelling on the idea of Áedán with a forked tail and horns. "What if he wants a second chance?"

"Who, Meaghan?" Kyle asked. "The evil that has plagued us for longer than we can remember?"

Put that way, she heard how naïve the question sounded. How pointless the hope she seemed to be harboring was.

"What about Cathán?" she asked. "What if he took all the evil when he took the power?"

"We were able to imprison Cathán. He is the least of our concerns now."

Meaghan didn't agree, but Kyle studied her face with an intensity that told her he found her questions disturbing. She didn't want to give him reasons to dig deeper and find out why she asked them. Carefully, she chose her words.

"Cathán has found a way to use others."

Kyle frowned. "What do you mean? What *others*?"

She told him about Mickey, omitting any reference to the pendant and its strange reactions or Áedán and his surge of power, which had ultimately saved her life. She glossed over as many details as she could, laying out only the bare facts. Mickey had spoken with Cathán's voice, had looked out of eyes flat and dark, and he'd attacked.

"Áedán managed to knock him out, but he meant to kill me."

"My God," Kyle murmured. "Why?"

"I don't know. But there's a reason why I'm here. Why all of us ended up here."

Silent, Kyle mulled this over as she handed him the plates and bowls she washed from their meal.

"Do you know how the Druid escaped when Cathán didn't?" she asked.

"How the Druid broke free of the Book?" He shook his head. "There was a prophecy that he would escape."

"What prophecy?"

"It had to do with the woman who saved us. She had a gift that allowed her into the world of Fennore and allowed her to get the rest of us out."

"And this prophecy said she'd set the Druid free?"

"Yes. I'd hoped it wouldn't come true. I'd hoped we'd be able to stop it. But I know now we failed. He is out. Isn't he, Meaghan?"

"How would I know?"

He considered her question as he methodically dried the dishes, and Meaghan felt her stomach plunging. If he asked if the Druid was Áedán, would she tell him yes? Or would she lie to protect a man she'd just met but felt like she'd known forever?

"Do *you* know where the Druid is?" she said before he could ask that question.

Kyle shook his head, lowering his lashes so she couldn't see his eyes. "I don't. But I would assume he's nearby."

"Why?"

"Because he'll be looking for the Book of Fennore. The Book is the heart of his power. Without the Book, he'd be just a man like any other."

I'm less than a man, Áedán had said. But that was before . . . now they both knew it wasn't true.

"What if he wants that? To be human again."

"He doesn't," Kyle said with gentle but firm certainty. "There can be no good left in him, Meaghan. Surely you can see that?"

She could, and yet that fecking hope wouldn't let her accept it.

"I can't see anything," she answered. "I don't know a fecking thing about Druids and Books of power. But I think you're wrong about Cathán. I know something about him, and he's never been good. Not even before he found the Book. We should be thinking about what he'll do next. What he might want."

"Perhaps."

Surprised, she glanced up at Kyle.

"The Druid is evil to the core, Meaghan. Cathán was victimized by the Druid. There might yet be something left of his humanity."

"You think he can be saved? If you'd seen what I did tonight, you wouldn't."

Kyle shrugged, hands out, palms up. "You might be right. I don't know what I think anymore. But my educated guess would be that there's a chance. Of the two—Cathán and the Druid—I'd put my money on Cathán."

Meaghan swallowed, seeing the reasoning behind his thoughts, knowing Kyle made sense, but what she'd seen in Mickey's eyes told a different story.

"Tell me about this Áedán," Kyle said softly.

The question sent a shaft of cold through her. It was one thing to know what Áedán was but another to speak of it—especially to Kyle, who had already judged and sentenced him. Áedán had just placed himself between a butcher knife and Meaghan without thought to his own well-being. He might disparage being human again, but Meaghan saw something deeper than his words. He had issues, but at the heart of him, the man still existed. And at the heart of *her*, she knew Áedán was a good man.

"What do you want to know about Áedán?" she asked, plunging her hands back into the hot soapy water and washing the last of the utensils they'd used.

"You said he was imprisoned with you before," Kyle answered in that calm and coaxing voice. When he leaned closer to take the spoons and knives from her fingers, she smelled soap on his skin and felt the comforting heat of his presence.

Logic urged her to trust Kyle. He'd once been a man of the church, for the love of Jesus. Who better to trust as an advisor against evil? And he'd come here to help her. For all the times she'd wanted to block out the emotions of others, she wished she could reach Kyle's feelings. Maybe then she'd feel right about voicing her suspicions.

"Yes, I met Áedán in the realm of the Book." And now she remembered that while they were there, Áedán had told her about a prophecy as well. Cathán had thought Meaghan someone of power and Áedán cautioned her to disabuse him of that theory. Even then, he'd steered her from danger. Why would he do that if he were evil?

Kyle took the washcloth from her hands and wiped down the table and counters as he spoke. "Áedán told us today he was there during the battle at the end."

She nodded as she drained her dishwater. "It's the truth. He was there."

"None of us saw him, Meaghan. Not me, not Jamie, and not Eamonn."

"There was a lot going on," she hedged.

"Yes, I do remember that," he said wryly. "But Áedán is the kind of man it would be hard not to notice."

Understatement of the century, she thought.

That protective instinct that wanted to keep secrets fought against her common sense. Kyle was not her enemy. Perhaps he could be trusted with the truth. "Only I could see him when we were inside the Book, Kyle."

Kyle froze, watching her with narrowed eyes. She stared back, thinking that it looked as if something had clicked into place in his mind.

"Only you? And you could see him just fine?"

"Yes. From the start."

"Why?"

"Not a clue. To others he was like a ghost. But to me, he appeared as real as you are."

"Interesting."

The word was benign enough, but Meaghan heard something beneath it that had claws and teeth. Frowning, she reached out with her senses, trying again to read what Kyle felt, but she found only calm blankness where, at the very least, confusion and curiosity should have been.

"What are you thinking, Kyle?" she asked.

"It's just that when you came to the lighthouse today, we all felt the Book. We all felt as if it hovered over us for a moment."

"I felt it, too. I thought . . ."

He waited, brows raised. "Yes? What did you think?"

"I think you felt the pendant. It's connected to the Book. It makes us feel its closeness."

"That very well might be but . . . I don't feel it now and you still have the pendant, I assume?"

"Yes," she lied, heeding a whisper of caution she didn't understand. The fewer who knew about the amulet and what Áedán had done with its power, the better.

Kyle waited a moment, as if giving her a chance to reconsider and tell him everything. She wondered if he'd learned that skill in the church. Be silent and the confessor will tell all. . . .

Finally, he said, "What do we know about this Áedán? Nothing but the fact that he was in the world of Fennore and now he is not."

"That's all we know about any of us."

"Perhaps. But . . . what if he's linked to it, Meaghan?"

What if he's the Druid? Kyle didn't ask it. He didn't have to. They both knew they'd been skirting the issue since he'd appeared out front, cloaked in the ominous veil of night.

Meaghan said nothing. Silently she waited for him to continue.

"Do you know the entire story of how the Druid came to be in the Book of Fennore? How the Book came to existence?"

"Bits and pieces, but nothing more."

Kyle searched her face, as if suspecting she lied. Curious, she tilted her head to the side and stared back.

"Let's have some tea and I'll tell you what I know of it. Perhaps between the two of us we can come up with some answers."

With that as motivation, Meaghan moved quickly to put the kettle on while she cleared away the dry dishes and the leftover stew. When she had everything clean and in its place, she and Kyle sat down to a hot cup of tea.

"You've heard of the White Fennore?" he began, his voice soft and deep.

"I'm from the Isle of Fennore, Kyle. Of course I've heard of her. I think I saw her once when I was little."

This made him lean forward. "What did you see?"

Meaghan shrugged, embarrassed. "Pretty much what you hear. I saw this . . . *ghost* come out of the dolmen—the one by the castle. She wore a white gown and it billowed in the wind. I remember her hair . . . it looked like tinsel in the moonlight. Scared the piss out of me."

"Did she carry anything?"

"I don't remember. I was only seven or eight."

But she did remember the stories about the White Fennore. Some said she came from the underworld by way of the dolmen to wreak vengeance on all mortals for an injustice done to her before she died. Others thought her one of the fairies that lived beneath the hills. A few thought her an angel. Some saw her with a book clutched in her hands and others with a silver comb. All accounts of sightings remarked on the mournful wail of her keening.

The words *Fionúir* and *Fennore*—as in the Isle of Fennore, as in the Book of Fennore—were a derivative of the same word. Ballyfionúir roughly translated into Town of the White Ghost and they called the place her spirit had most often been seen the Valley of the White Ghost.

Kyle went on. "Some legends claim she was a beautiful sorceress who bewitched the Druid. The Druid coveted her power and lusted for her beauty. He proclaimed his love, but in truth, he resented her. He was jealous. Jealous of the things she could do."

"What could she do?"

"She saw the dead, for one."

Meaghan shook her head. "What does that mean, she saw the dead?"

"She was a banshee. The dead appeared to her before they passed and begged her to save them."

Meaghan shivered, suddenly cold down into her bones. "Did she? Save them, I mean?"

"No. She did not have the power to change their fate. Only to see it."

"Well, that had to suck."

Kyle smiled. "I'm sure it did. The people of that time were pagan and very superstitious. They began to fear her. They suspected that she called death to them, not just saw it coming. They interpreted her warnings as a heralding. They thought she cursed them. At the same time, the Druid Brandubh—"

Brawn-doov, she repeated silently, hearing the deep tones of Áedán's voice as he'd told her how he'd gotten that name.

"—was the people's . . . connection to the gods. It was his job to keep sickness and death at bay, to make their fields fertile and the cattle reproductive. But he became so obsessed with the White Fennore that he shirked his duties. Their crops began to wither. Their livestock died while birthing. The people thought the gods were angry."

"And they blamed him?"

"No. People are what they are. They blamed *her* but wanted *him* to fix it."

"Fix it how?"

"When the White Fennore proclaimed that she'd seen the king's child stillborn and his wife dead on the birthing bed, the people rose against her. They demanded that Brandubh sacrifice the White Fennore to the angry gods."

"You mean kill her?"

Kyle nodded. "The Druid was a treacherous man who valued power over all else, and with the White Fennore, he became very powerful. Knowing who would die before their death came gave him an edge that he used without qualm. He knew that if he could keep her from telling everyone except for him about the death she saw, he would become even more formidable. He convinced her to write down what she saw, instead of speaking it."

"And he created the Book," she said numbly.

"Not alone. She helped with each step. All that went into the Book of Fennore was sacred, from the smelted silvers to the skins forged into the covers and the vellum of its pages. It was a thing of power before it had ever been used."

A shudder went through Meaghan, and Kyle covered her hand with his. The touch was gentle, comforting, but the colors in his eyes had darkened, becoming more golden brown than hazel. He gave her a look sharp with awareness, making her very conscious of the fact that the two of them sat alone in the kitchen in the intimacy of long shadows and muted light. Aware that any minute Áedán might return and he would not be pleased to find Kyle there.

"Brandubh told the White Fennore to use the language that only the two of them shared so that no one else would be able to decipher what she wrote."

"She trusted him."

"So the story goes. And for a time, the rumblings of the people stopped and they knew peace. The Druid focused on the fields and the cattle and everyone prospered. But then the king's son was born dead and his wife died as well, just as the White Fennore had predicted. In his grief and rage, the king once again demanded her sacrifice."

Another shiver went through her, and Kyle took both of her hands in his, cupping them in the warmth of his palms.

"But the White Fennore was a seer of death and that was Brandubh's downfall."

"Because she saw her own?" Meaghan guessed.

Kyle nodded, leaning closer. "She confronted him with it, but he told her that he meant to trick the king and people and what she'd seen was only his ruse. He convinced her to trust him, to go along with his plan."

Trust me, Meaghan. . . .

"And then he sacrificed her anyway."

Kyle nodded.

"And she knew it. She saw it coming?" Meaghan said, wishing he'd contradict her. Wishing he'd tell her what she wanted to hear. That, at the last moment, Áedán had proved his sincerity and saved the woman he'd claimed to love.

"She cursed him as her blood spilled over his hands. She condemned him to spend eternity in the Book of Fennore."

But Áedán had told her a different story. He'd said the woman he loved had betrayed *him*. He said she'd condemned him without reason and then blithely walked away and never looked back.

Kyle touched Meaghan's cheek, pulling her from the memory.

"What is it, Meaghan? You've gone pale and your hands are like ice."

A shudder went through her, and Kyle moved closer, gathering her to him, pressing her face to his shoulder as he rubbed her back and murmured soothing words.

Áedán's voice spoke in her head. *I will not return to my prison. I will not be at your mercy ever again. . . .*

"I've upset you," Kyle said, his tone bewildered.

She wasn't surprised. He had no way of knowing why the story of a woman dead for centuries unending would have such an impact on Meaghan. She didn't even understand herself.

Slowly she pulled away, but his arms remained around her, his eyes filled with concern. Meaghan felt as if she'd been impaled by the sharp blades of truth, and now her only hope was to wrench herself free of their piercing hold, take a chance by trusting when her instincts screamed she should trust no one.

"Kyle," she said. "Do you have any idea why I was sucked into the world of Fennore? Or why Cathán would want me?"

He shook his head. "I've wondered if there was a reason. For some of us, there was. But a few seemed to be collateral damage."

She nodded, absorbing this, wishing she could place herself in the same category.

"Meaghan, whatever it is you're not telling me . . ." He cupped her face in his warm hands and tilted her chin to look in her eyes. "I hope you know you can trust me. I will help you in any way I can. We want the same thing. To go home."

Meaghan nodded again, but his touch and his words disconcerted her. She cleared her throat and stood, stepping away from him.

"Will you promise me to be on your guard where Áedán is concerned? You don't know who he is."

Yes, she did. Áedán hadn't tried to hide it. Not from her. But did she really know him? Had he betrayed the woman he loved and murdered her? And then spent millennia blaming her for what had happened?

"When I touch him, I don't feel evil, Kyle."

Kyle stilled. "You don't *feel* evil. What do you mean?"

Her face grew hot as she explained her gift. "I'm empathic. I sense what others are feeling, and I swear to you, Áedán may be confused, but he's not evil."

Kyle moved to stand in front of her, watching her expression with wide eyes.

"What do you feel from me?"

It was the question everyone asked when they learned about her gift.

"I don't feel anything. You're closed off. Did you learn to find that inner calm from your training with the church?"

His brows shot up and he shrugged. "Not a clue. But if what you say is true, you should be sensing things from me. You should be feeling how worried I am for you. The fact you're not tells me that perhaps your gift is not an . . . exact science. It might be misleading you down a path of danger. I know we've only just met, but, Meaghan, I feel like I've known you much longer." His voice deepened and she heard a note of desire in it that made her uncomfortable. "I've felt this from the first moment I saw you, back when we were trapped in the world of Fennore."

Her face grew hotter and Kyle looked away, embarrassed by his declaration.

"I should go now," he said softly. "Do I have your permission to share what we've discussed with Jamie and Eamonn?"

Feeling like a traitor, Meaghan nodded. "Don't make assumptions and accusations about Áedán, though. He has a right to speak on his behalf before a judge and jury tries him without all the facts. Make sure Jamie gets that message, too. He strikes me as a hothead."

Kyle laughed beneath his breath. "He doesn't 'pull his punches,' as he phrases it."

Silently she walked Kyle to the front door. He turned on the porch and gave her a meaningful look. Then he leaned down, lowering his head until his mouth was only inches away from her own, catching her off guard.

"Be safe, Meaghan," he murmured, and he brushed his lips to hers in a fleeting caress.

And then he was gone, leaving Meaghan surprised and alone in a blanket of fog and confusion.

Chapter Sixteen

After Kyle left, Meaghan checked the back door and found that Colleen had not lied. The lock didn't work. She tried using one of the chairs to wedge beneath the doorknob, but their backs stood too tall to make it work. Moving the shelves in front of the door might slow him down, but it wouldn't stop him. Most likely it would only make Mickey mad. Besides, he could always go around to the front door. He lived here. He would have a key.

Áedán said he'd keep Mickey away, and she'd have to trust him. Still, she placed one of Colleen's kitchen knives under her pillow and climbed into her makeshift bed. Sleep came with swift stealth, snatching Meaghan's reluctant consciousness away and tumbling her into a deep and troubled slumber. Darkness coated her dreams—coal and soot walls that boxed her in and left her feeling filthy and bound. The only relief from the obsidian world glimmered always out of reach, taunting her to stumble further into its inky lair. Then suddenly she was no longer alone. A man stood in the ebony pit, and like a moon in a starless night, he brought light.

"Come," he said, reaching out to her.

Meaghan moved without thought, towed closer by the rich timbre of his voice, ensnared by the wild beauty of his eyes. They were a forest at night, the greens so deep they became a patchwork of branches and leaves shivering in the soft evening mist. His nearness filled her senses. He smelled of pine, of fresh spring breezes, of leather and clean sweat. The combined scent intoxicated her and made her want to press her face into his chest, to inhale him, to taste him. Something deep inside her grew hot and liquid, burning and spreading until every inch of her skin felt alive with the sensation.

Forbidden.

Why, she didn't know.

"Elan," he said. *"You have made me your slave."*

The dream twisted and suddenly she and Áedán stood in the midst of an endless valley that shimmered in the crystal-clear air. She stared at the familiar landscape with a wave of foreboding that had nothing to do with the emerald pastures or the sprinkling of sheep and cows that dotted them. Behind her hunkered the castle ruins, ahead and to her right the three standing stones with a flat tableau top that made the dolmen, which had stood sentry there for time unmeasured. At her side, Áedán stiffened and his tension traveled like a spell to every nerve in her body.

It no longer felt like a dream.

"Come," he said again, taking her hand in the heated warmth of his.

And she thought in that moment she would follow him wherever he would take her.

He pulled her to a path that twisted into the forest, and something caught at the corner of her vision. There, in the long shadows of the trees, she saw a woman dressed in white from head to toe. Her skin gleamed like ivory, her hair so light it looked silver. She blocked their path, watching them both with eyes fixed, intense and enraged.

Áedán made a strangled sound, and before Meaghan could grasp what was happening, before she could react, he was gone. Shocked, Meaghan stared down at the hand he'd been holding. His touch still lingered even as a gust chased his scent into the wind.

Filled with dread, Meaghan returned her gaze to the woman in white. She stared back, her lavender eyes shot with starlight streaks that made them seem unearthly. She didn't say a word but slowly pulled something from a fold in her robe, and Meaghan saw that it was a comb. A sterling silver comb embedded with endless spirals, like the Book of Fennore. She ran it through her long, flowing hair, and each stroke made the locks dance and glitter like silky tinsel.

Then she paused and held out the comb to Meaghan.

Meaghan's alarm spiked and her escalating fear paralyzed her for endless moments. There was danger here, though she couldn't see it, couldn't begin to guess what it might be. Terrified beyond reason, she stared at the comb the woman held out and realized that she *wanted* it. Badly.

She *yearned* to touch the comb even as the thought of how cold, how sinister it would feel filled her with horror. Her hand reached for it while a voice shouted in her head to run, get away from this woman with her pale eyes and glittering hair. But the pull of temptation burned in Meaghan's gut. She *needed* the comb. She craved it with every cell in her body, and the intensity of that desire terrified her all the more.

A surge of power seemed to rise up from the woman in white and wash over Meaghan. And then Meaghan's fingers closed over the sterling comb, and a million sensations bombarded her thoughts with images that rushed through the dyke she'd opened with just her touch. The spiral engravings burned hot against her skin, and the teeth cut into her flesh. She heard a whimpering sound she knew must be coming from her own lips but couldn't stop it any more than she could stop her knees from shaking and her stomach from churning with terror that went deeper than her bones.

Suddenly the woman tilted back her head, the silver hair spilling over her shoulders, and she keened, *keened* in a mournful, high-pitched wail that battered Meaghan in undulating waves of agony. The sound sliced and diced, eviscerating her will, exacerbating her fear.

Helplessly, she stared at the comb, where it hung suspended between them, one end in the woman's hand and the other in her own. It had cut them both, and drops of blood wove through the teeth, filled the spiral engravings. Aghast, Meaghan watched the inevitable with the inexplicable feeling she'd been running from it for her entire life. The blood pooled and then raced down the grooves to the middle of the comb where the droplets met.

Where they merged and became one.

Jerking her gaze up to stare into the other woman's starlit eyes with horror, Meaghan screamed.

The sound of her own shriek jolted her from sleep and slammed her bolt upright on the cot, her body hot, her mouth dry, her breath coming in raw gasps. Darkness veiled her in a suffocating shroud, making her thrash to get free of the twisted covers.

She sucked in a deep breath and tried to calm down, but it was so dark. The moon had masked itself in clouds, creating layered shadows that fingered her childhood fears hungrily. The black of night surged over her with unrelenting glee, mocking her attempt to deny it.

"It's only dark," she whispered. "There's nothing in it."

She raised a shaking hand to push back her hair, the dream still a cloying memory that clogged her throat and doused all rationality. The paleness of her skin made a gray dent in the gloom, and for a moment, she held her fingers in front of her face, trying to make out the familiar size and shape, reassuring herself that the dark had not changed her, that her blood mixing with the dream wraith's had not fused her to her nightmare and allowed it to follow her out into the real world. Yet the greedy shadows felt savage now, ordered and hostile. The clouds around the moon gathered as if by command and held captive the waning light.

Meaghan could see nothing beyond her own bleak dismay. She rubbed her fingers with her thumb, intending to ground herself with the sensation. But what she felt had the opposite effect. Something damp and sticky clung to her skin. She lifted her other hand and felt the same substance.

Fear spiked deep within her and rebounded endlessly off the parallel mirrors of disbelief and conviction. The reflection it created refracted into a million questions and a never-ending tunnel that led to an impossible conclusion. Blood. There was blood on her hands.

The need to see swelled with her horror and swallowed her whole. She shot from her cot out into the kitchen, turning on the light. Dark, tacky red covered her fingers and splattered her palms. That whimpering sound she'd heard in the dreams returned, and with it the burn of air moving through constricted passageways. Quickly she turned on the faucet and scrubbed her hands until they were raw. The blood washed away easily enough, but she still felt it, slick and clinging. . . .

She could see no cut, no wound, no puncture mark made by the sharp teeth of the comb. Nothing to explain the blood that had followed her from the dream. Still trembling, she went back to the storage room and checked her sheets. Her bedding was unmarred by stains. Her heart thudded painfully. Had she imagined it?

She tried to convince herself the answer was yes, but it took a long time for her heartbeat to slow and her lungs to give leave to normal breathing. After a few minutes, she reluctantly turned out the light and returned to her little room.

Just as she settled onto the cot, she heard a door open and slam shut. Cautiously, she moved to her knees and peered at the door to the storage room, seeing the gray shades delineating the opening. Her ears rang as she tried to separate the clumsy stumble of footsteps navigating an unlit room and see the source of the sound. At last, the clouds shifted and a lone beam of moonshine nipped through the windows and caught the man swaying in Colleen's kitchen.

Mickey. He'd come home. Áedán had promised to keep him away, but there he stood. Did that mean something had happened to Áedán? Or had he lied about protecting them? Heart plunging, Meaghan covered her mouth and tried to be silent.

Quickly she eased to her feet, hoping he didn't know where Colleen had put her to sleep. Her legs trembled and her stomach hurt.

She could feel the stab of adrenaline hitting her muscles, urging them to flee, but she fought the instinct, forcing herself to stand still and not draw attention. The wall behind her felt solid, and she leaned hard into it, reaching down to fumble under her pillow for the knife she'd stashed there earlier, not daring to take her eyes from the doorway. She felt the cold of metal, and without looking, slipped it into her pocket. Mickey wobbled on unsteady legs, then seemed to get his bearings and took a lurching step around the table. He came very near the doorway into the storage room. If he turned his head, if he looked inside . . .

Her fear took on a sour edge. What if he caught her in here alone? Would he finish what he started? Before he'd sauntered off with the others for the Pier House, she'd heard his voice return to normal, but the eyes had still glittered sharply.

As if he'd heard her thoughts, he took another step closer. Drunken, he could barely keep his feet beneath him. She sucked in a silent breath. With his senses so impaired, maybe she'd have a chance of fighting him off.

The moment seemed to freeze, with Meaghan a marble statue solidified by her fright and Mickey vibrating with his hostility. Slowly he turned his head and looked at her.

It was too late to hide, not that the storage room offered her any options.

Praying with equal fervor that the moon would continue to cast its glow on the room and that it would slip behind the clouds and shield her in darkness, Meaghan squared her shoulders and pulled the knife from her pocket.

But it wasn't a knife she held in her hand. It was a comb. A silver comb. For a moment, her mind locked up as it stuttered over the impossibility of the comb clenched between her fingers, and then she flung it away. It hit the bed and bounced in the tangle of covers.

Biting back the scream that wanted to emerge, she swung her gaze back to Mickey.

"What do you want, Mr. Ballagh?" she blustered, her voice firm and unwavering. She tried to sound tough and thought she did a fair job of it. He couldn't see her shaking hands and banging knees.

Mickey had crossed the threshold into the tiny room with a strange, jerking gait that stroked a note of alarm in the crashing discord of her fear. The oddness of his movements made Meaghan cringe against the wall, wishing she could punch through it and run.

"Stop right now, Mr. Ballagh. I'll scream if you don't. I mean it."

She might have been talking to herself for all the good it did. Just then, the clouds shifted once more and another bright shaft of moonlight slanted into the kitchen. Mickey's hovering mass in the doorway blocked it from the storage room, making her small space seem darker, more confining. She'd let him trap her—she'd let her own panic create a prison that he now filled with his looming presence. He took another step and she gauged her chances of lunging past him and through the door into the kitchen, then made a break for it. She expected him to try to stop her and nearly laughed with delirious relief when he didn't.

Mickey turned to watch her, his awkward pace unnatural and sedate. Grime streaked his pale face. His clothes looked black in the shadows and his hands strangely white. As if disconnected, they floated at his sides. The stench of him rushed at her like a swampy wave, rancid and repulsive. He smelled of something washed up ashore and decaying beneath the hot and ruthless sun. She could feel the intensity of his stare even if she couldn't see it.

She searched for signs of attack, tensing muscles, shifting weight, but Mickey showed nothing except that focus that felt like a laser beam following her every movement. Though the rest of him remained in shadow, his features suddenly snapped into focus, and Meaghan felt a gasp freeze in her chest. She'd thought it was grime that coated his face, but now she realized it was much worse.

It was blood. A lot of it.

He staggered from the storage room after her, stopping a few feet away. Now, the moon broke free entirely, bathing the room in a cold, bright light.

And as frightened of the dark as she was, Meaghan wished for it to return.

She could see everything now. The spotless kitchen, the pots and pans, spices and jars that lined the shelves. The table that she'd sat at just hours before.

And Mickey.

She could see Mickey as clearly as she'd seen him in the light of day. A deep wound above his eye spilled blood down his face, where it met another slashing cut that arched from ear to artery and sent a gusher over the front of him. As horrible as it appeared, that wasn't what made Meaghan clap her hands over her mouth to hold back the scream, though.

Colleen's butcher knife protruded from his chest.

It had been sunk deep to the hilt, where its blade would find his heart. His shirt had been gray and stained when he left that night. Now the front was soaked in blood from the collar to the sleeves, making it look thick and tacky and black. She watched with shock as blood dripped from the shirttail that hung untucked at his hips and plopped with a sickening sound to the floor.

He stared at her with eyes that did not gleam with that hard flat glitter that she'd seen before. There was no violence in them now. No fury waiting to erupt. They were endless pits, empty of thoughts, of feeling. Of life.

The blood should have told her, the knife in his heart should have confirmed it. But his mere presence—his *mobility* no matter how stilted—had contradicted what common sense might have shown. If he was walking, then he must be alive.

But Meaghan realized as she stared into those empty eyes that it wasn't so. The lights might be on, but there was nothing and no one home inside. It didn't matter that he stood in front of her, dripping blood on Colleen's kitchen floor.

Mickey Ballagh was dead.

Chapter Seventeen

FOR hours after the fight, Áedán had sat in a corner at the Pier House watching Mickey enjoy being the center of attention. He knew it was all an act. A sly contrivance that Cathán performed using Mickey as his puppet. Mickey drank and laughed, belched and railed with the others just like he had on any number of nights in his past. But the Mickey they'd all known no longer existed.

Áedán shifted in his seat, observing but shielded from the others by the shadows and his unobtrusive stillness. He'd mastered the art of obscuring himself in this way when he'd lived among his brother Druids but thought the skill lost. Somehow using the power he'd siphoned from the pendant had opened a doorway within him, and now he could reach those parts of himself that had been so long dormant. Deep inside, his own rare gifts began sparking to life.

It elated him, but it also worried him. He could feel the turn of history bearing down, preparing to repeat itself. Power had been at the crux of the events that culminated in his condemnation. He'd be a fool not to consider its role in things to come.

A war waged within him as he watched the merriment in the bar. Part of him wanted to race for the doors, find Meaghan, and leave this island and everything it represented behind, even if it meant swimming across the cold, hostile sea. Another part braced and prepared for a battle that had been eons in the making. He would need the pendant to do his part, and he had no delusions that Meaghan would willingly give it up.

He rubbed his gritty eyes and looked around him. Compact and stinking of old fish, grease, piss, and sweat, the Pier House looked ready to burst at the seams from the crowd it held. Behind Áedán, windows stretched nearly floor to ceiling and looked out on the small, Ballyfionúir port, with its man-made rock wall that kept the fierce tide subdued and the bobbing boats in its protective embrace. In the windows' reflections, he could see the men clamoring around the bar at his back, standing shoulder to shoulder, happy to be in the stinking place, breathing air so laced with the fumes of spirits that it was like drinking the brew with each breath. He had no trouble identifying Mickey in the thick of it.

Beneath the roar of laughter, Áedán heard the insidious drone that was the signature of the Book of Fennore. Even now it spoke to Áedán, coaxing him like a whore from a candlelit window, but it could not reach him. Not anymore. That, too, had changed.

He couldn't tell if the drone came from Mickey or from another source. A gut feeling told him that Cathán and the Book of Fennore worked through more than just Mickey, and he'd already taken his next victim. Perhaps that man stood in this room even now.

"To Áedán, the best worker the seas've e're seen," Mickey slurred, slopping his dark brew as he drank thirstily.

Whether a ruse or sheer intoxication, Mickey no longer seemed to remember the fight that he'd started and Áedán had finished. In fact, some time ago, he'd begun to speak of it as if it had been a skirmish over manners and not a battle of life and death.

"Then why was you out to kill him if he's so grand?" Hoyt O'Shea asked, projecting his voice to be heard over the din. Hoyt had sat watchful all night, fanning the hot embers of aggression into sparking fires that flared and hissed.

Mickey leveled a finger at Hoyt and said, "Didn't I tell you already? I wasn't out to kill him, was I? I meant Áedán no serious harm. 'Twas just a lesson in respect, you see."

Or a possession by the Book of Fennore, Áedán thought grimly.

"He can work for me if you don't like his attitude," Hoyt answered, making the words sound like a threat.

Mickey came out of his chair, his face darkening and his eyes wild. "The hell he will, you bleeding Welshman."

Hoyt jumped to his feet as well, but the men on either side of them urged the two back down. Mickey put up a show of resistance, but really he was too drunk to do more than fall into the chair. Hoyt sat with slow deliberation. Should they come to blows, Áedán had no doubt Hoyt would beat Mickey to a pulp. After a moment, the voices around him rose again in unnatural gaiety.

"And then comes Mickey, like fecking Ruairi of Fennore hisself, I tell ye," a fat and ruddy man said, punching the air and miming Áedán staggering back before crashing down like a felled tree. Mickey grinned at the story, which had somehow grown from a one-strike knockout to a fistfight that had spanned an hour and miles of the island. Both Áedán and Mickey had been compared to Ruairi of Fennore countless times in innumerable repetitions, but no one seemed to notice the reiteration. Like oversaturated sponges, the drunks could not retain the words that swilled around them.

He didn't understand what game Cathán played here, but he saw that it might go on all night. He should go, find Meaghan, and relieve her of the pendant. He could guard against Mickey's return from the back porch of the house as well as he could here.

Reluctance—not prudence—kept him in his seat. He didn't want the confrontation that would come if he simply tried to take the pendant away from Meaghan, and he knew that she would not allow him to beguile it from her. She'd leave him no choice but to overpower her—physically, mentally—perhaps both. And then she would hate him, as Elan had come to hate him.

The thought of it felt like a stone on his chest. He didn't want to hurt her.

Fool.

She'd been in his thoughts all night. In those moments when he'd pulled the power of the pendant to him, something of Meaghan had been in the mix. Something rich and sweet as wine, something intimate and yielding. It burned in his blood even now.

Earlier, on the cliffs above the lighthouse, she'd felt like a fantasy in his arms, her flesh hot against his own. He'd wanted to strip every barrier that kept him from the softness of her skin even as a part of him feared her, feared the way she made him feel. He'd wanted to bury himself inside her right then and there, against the looming rocks, and be damned the consequences. And she'd wanted it, too. Whatever lies her lips spoke, her body had told the truth.

But there lay the road to insanity.

When she'd stood strong against Mickey, brandishing the pendant and all its power, his last doubts about the fleeting glimpses of lavender in her eyes and what they might mean had vanished. In that moment, she'd looked so much like Elan, the White Fennore, that he'd nearly wrapped his hands about her throat and squeezed. But Meaghan seemed to have no awareness of Elan moving within her. Yet he knew Meaghan wouldn't have considered using the pendant like a weapon if Elan had not led her to do it.

Again he dwelled on Elan's promise to one day return and *judge* him. He wondered if she'd chosen Meaghan as a means to that end because Elan had known—in that way she'd always known things without being told—that he would not be able to resist Meaghan? Or had Meaghan's imprisonment in the Book of Fennore simply provided Elan with a convenient receptacle?

He couldn't guess. Elan had been a mystery to him from the start.

Either way, the die had been cast. The fact remained, however, that no matter what Elan planned, Áedán refused to return to the Book of Fennore. And he would never be safe in a world where both the Book and the pendant coexisted. If Elan had returned in the guise of Meaghan Ballagh, she'd made a fatal error. Now, with all the pieces reunited—the Book, the pendant, and the White Fennore—the sacrificial ceremony that had begun his own imprisonment could be repeated.

Only this time it would be Elan who was cursed for all of eternity.

He fought the scrabble of his conscience reminding him of the moment when he'd stood above the churning sea with Meaghan and confessed that he was Brandubh, the Druid. Her voice had been soft as she'd calmly answered.

I know something about people, too, she'd said. *And I don't think you're evil.*

He hadn't wanted to feel anything at those words, and yet it seemed that he was helpless when it came to Meaghan. His heart had clenched, and for a dark moment, he'd wanted to weep at the pure simplicity of her statement. She touched something deep within him that he'd thought long dead and eradicated.

She'd made him feel . . . *human*.

And in that painful moment, he'd hated and loved her for it. It had taken more than he'd thought possible to pull his armor tight and shield what he felt. She'd manipulated his corroded emotions with the skill of a *seanchai*, weaving words into invisible strings as she lured him down a twisted road.

What did she want of him? What was he willing to give?

And what, Áedán wondered, would he be willing to take? If the moment came, would he, *could* he condemn Elan when it would also condemn the woman who felt like salvation in his arms? Would he trust in fate, or would he finally, irrefutably carve his own destiny?

He would get no answers here and he might wait forever for Mickey to leave. Better to take himself to the Ballagh house and talk to Meaghan, learn what he could. If Mickey came home, Áedán would be there waiting.

He slipped from the bar, following the twisted path inland. No lights burned in the windows he passed along the way, and the Ballaghs' home crouched equally still and dark. He crept to the back door and quietly stepped inside the kitchen.

At first he didn't notice Meaghan standing against the wall with her hands clapped over her mouth. But then he looked again at the pale smear in the darkness and saw her. Her eyes looked huge and stared fixedly at a point between them. Her chest heaved as she sucked in air and she made a wheezing noise as it passed her lips. She trembled, quaking from head to toe. He could see it even in the dark.

"Meaghan?" he said softly.

Her fixed gaze did not waver, and she gave no indication she'd heard him. The expression of terror on her face had him glancing around, looking for signs that Mickey had been here. Had he left the bar after Áedán and managed to slip past him somehow? Was he upstairs? Had he gone for Colleen?

"Meaghan," he said again, keeping his voice low but adding urgency to it. He moved closer when she didn't respond, but it wasn't until he touched her arm that she saw him.

Her hands flew out to ward him off just as a strangled shriek tried to emerge. He clamped his own hand over her lips, trapping the sound before she woke the whole nosy village.

"It's me," he said, thinking that should hardly reassure her but hoping it did. The irony of his being there to ensure her safety had plagued him the whole way over.

"Meaghan, it's Áedán. Look at me."

She did, finally focusing on his face with those shock-widened eyes. Her pupils were so large that they swallowed the blue. Then she made a sound of such relief that it tickled a warning in him. She launched herself into his arms with a muffled cry.

Her body felt soft and yielding, her scent a drug to his senses. He couldn't help but hold her close, breathe her in.

"What happened?" he asked. "Did Mickey come back? Is Colleen all right?"

"Yes. I mean, no—yes."

He tried to pull away to see her face, but she held him too tightly. "Which is it? Yes or no?"

"No, he didn't come back. But I saw him."

"Where? Outside?"

She shook her head. "He was fecking dead," she said, and her voice defied him to doubt her even as it quavered. Tears streamed down her face and burned where they pooled against his throat. At last she eased back, her expression so filled with horror that it made every hair on his body stand on end.

Memory crashed down on him with a force that stole his breath.

She'd said dead.

She'd seen Mickey dead, and from her reaction, he had to assume seeing the dead had never happened before. She didn't understand the implication of it, but Áedán did. Doubts that he'd tried to fortify as he'd made his way here disintegrated in thick and muddied puddles like dust in a rainstorm.

Forcefully he pushed her back, holding her at arm's length, squeezing her shoulders until she looked into his eyes.

"You saw his spirit?" he asked.

She stared at him blankly, as if he'd spoken a foreign language she couldn't translate.

"Mickey," he repeated patiently. "You saw his specter?"

She nodded, shook her head, nodded again.

"I don't know what I saw. He looked so real. His throat had been cut and Colleen's knife was plunged in his heart. There was blood everywhere." Her voice rose in panic and fear. "There was blood on my hands."

He gave her a gentle shake, trying to keep her focus from spiraling back to what she'd seen.

"Did he speak to you?"

She made a high, squeaking sound, like air forced from a constricted opening. Her lips worked for a moment without managing to form words. She looked horrified, terrified, ready to split at the seams.

Something inside him twisted at her agony, fought to deflect her pain and carry it for her. He didn't understand the feeling but couldn't deny its strength or determination.

"No, he didn't speak," she breathed at last. "He just came after me."

"Like he meant to hurt you?"

Anger flared in the molten pool of distress—not directed at Meaghan, but at Cathán.

How dare he threaten Meaghan?

"I don't know if he meant me harm. I don't know."

She spoke of Mickey, but Áedán knew that Cathán pulled Mickey's strings, and by doing so, whether he meant it or not, Cathán succeeded in harming Meaghan. Áedán would see him punished for it. The violence beneath the fierce promise he silently made shook him, but he refused to stop and analyze it. He refused to hear that possessive voice inside him that claimed this woman as his own and vowed to protect her, to avenge her.

Refused the voice that reminded Áedán that his plans for Meaghan were equally cruel.

She stared at him with tear-drenched eyes, her expression so young and vulnerable that it tugged at the heart he swore he no longer had. He shouldn't offer her comfort. It was her way to entice him, to make him think she was defenseless when he knew better. But his arms seemed to be taking orders from another part of his brain.

Áedán pulled her close, letting her tears dampen his shirt as she cried. He'd forgotten. How, he didn't know, but he had forgotten. Elan's ability to see death had destroyed all hope for their future together.

Elan couldn't see the dead without wanting to save them. Would Meaghan be the same?

Was this part of her game? Make him watch her destroy everything again? Was Meaghan connected to Elan on a spiritual level, or was Elan simply pulling her strings, using *her* as Cathán had used Mickey?

He'd decided that Elan had come back in the form of this feisty Irish woman to judge him. Now he feared it would be much worse than that. She'd come to torment him, to make him the helpless spectator as once again the tragedy of their lives played out.

"Did you kill him?" Meaghan asked, her voice muffled by his chest.

It took a moment for him to understand what she asked. "No. Mickey was alive and well when I left him at the Pier House."

And Áedán knew with utter certainty that Mickey was still alive and well. Not dead. Not yet.

As if his thought had called the other man, he heard a voice singing discordantly and knew Mickey had come home at last. Áedán toyed with the idea of killing him here and now, but he couldn't, not in front of Meaghan. Not when she was so upset.

Besides, he'd have to be careful when he chose to do it. Times had changed; *Áedán* had changed. If he killed Mickey this night, he would find himself imprisoned once more—this time in a cage of another making. His freedom had been too short, too sweet to risk it.

He saw the door to a small storage room with a cot inside and assumed Meaghan had been sleeping there before the spirit had come to her. Pressing his hand over her mouth, he pulled her back into the room. She fought him, and when he closed the door, he remembered something else about her.

Elan had been afraid of the dark. Meaghan, it appeared, shared that deep-seated fear.

He knew why, of course.

Using his body to hold her still, Áedán pressed her tight against him, hand still clamped over her lips. "Calm yourself," he whispered. "It's Mickey coming home. He's not dead, Meaghan. He's alive."

"But I saw him," she said, her words muted by the barrier of his palm.

"Quiet," Áedán breathed. "You do not want him to find us here."

She stilled but it was too dark to see her face, to see if she understood. He could feel her heart pounding against his, feel the hot burst of breath against his chest as she exhaled in quick, jerky gusts. She was terrified and he could do little to comfort her, surprised himself with the realization that he wanted nothing more than to do just that. A deep need inside him yearned to assuage her fears and soothe her. He eased his hand away from her mouth and she took a breath. The soft curves of her body molded more completely to his, stirring that not-quite banked fire that had burned within him since he'd seen her in the cavern.

"Close your eyes. Think about light," he whispered against her ear, feeling the softness of her hair, inhaling the sweetness of her scent.

She made a small sound in her throat. Too proud to be a whimper, too wretched to be less. If possible, he pulled her closer, no longer trying to hide the fact that he was hard with need. She was too much a spitfire not to react in one way or another to his blatant arousal. Perhaps her anger would hold back her fear.

He knew he fooled himself into thinking that might be his goal, and his lips gently brushing the silk of her cheek only confirmed it. "I'll keep you safe," he murmured, damning himself further. "I won't leave you alone. I won't let anything happen to you."

The words flowed softly from a place inside him that had harbored such sentiments for an eternity. They were words he'd used before, words he'd spoken to Elan millennia ago. He remembered when he'd found Elan locked in the dark by the king's wife, whose jealousy and fear had driven her to cruelty and hatred. Elan had screamed until her voice no longer worked, sobbed until her tears no longer flowed. She'd been trembling, like this woman now. And when he'd touched her, she'd made a sound so broken he'd wanted to kill the one responsible for hurting her. He'd vowed to avenge her, wanted to charge off and do it that very moment. But all she'd wanted was to be held. To be comforted. And in the end, he'd avenged no one, not even himself.

Lost in the memory, he stroked Meaghan's back and arms, buried his face in the softness of her hair that spilled over her shoulder. Her fragrance was seduction itself, so soft, so feminine. Light as a summer breeze, sweet as honeysuckle. She pressed her face to his chest, and he felt her taking in his scent as well. She'd told him once he smelled of the forest—bright and fresh like juniper, rich and mysterious as the bark of blackthorn. He'd been enchanted with her words, entranced by the idea they were meant for him and only him.

Meaghan. Elan. The women seemed to tangle and merge in his mind, treachery and innocence tying him in knots.

Mickey turned on a light in the kitchen, and a sharp blade of luminescence found its way under the door. The glow eased the clench of terror he felt in Meaghan's body. They stood like two matched pillars of stone as Mickey fumbled at the icebox, and Áedán suspected he searched for the stew. While he listened to the man's clumsy movements, Áedán played scenarios in his mind. He would not allow Mickey to harm Meaghan, nor would he permit him to hurt Colleen or the baby, and if it meant dragging him off into the dark to kill him, Áedán would do it. Mickey settled at the table, spoon clanking pottery as he ate. The sound was monotonous, his grunts and slurps disgusting. Áedán shut him out, closing himself off to all but the feel of Meaghan's body.

She was more curved and supple than Elan had been. Her breasts felt full and heavy against his chest, her hips rounded and womanly against his thighs. The hard length of him found a soft haven in the hollow of her belly. She was short, so small that her head fit against his chest, and yet she seemed perfect for him.

Was he insane to think that somehow Elan had wedged her spirit beneath Meaghan's skin? Meaghan said she'd sensed no evil within him. Elan had known it existed from the start.

He found his fingers tunneling beneath her hair to cup her head in his palms. It seemed they moved without his thought or will. He tilted her face back so he could look at her. Her skin glowed like ivory, her eyes dark and drowned with emotion, her mouth soft and full. She'd bitten her lips in her anxiety, and now they were red, a vibrant splash of color in the gray world.

Her eyes widened as he lowered his mouth to hers, but she didn't turn away, nor did she push him away. He felt the pending rush of fate slam into him as his lips touched hers. Thoughts of the stolen moments on the cliffs that afternoon had all but consumed him. He'd craved the sensation of her arms clinging tight, the softness of her breasts crushed against the wall of his chest, her hips pressed to his. . . .

Now he felt like an anchored ship whipped by a storm that refused to let it idle securely at bay. He ripped free in a powerful surge, backing her to the wall, needing that solid surface to keep from hurling himself out to sea.

The eye of the storm was within him, the fury of it all around. It uprooted his convictions, his resentments, his foundation. For a thousand years, he'd loved Elan, despite her betrayal, despite her condemnation. For a thousand years, he'd hated her, bitterly tarnished every memory, purposefully corroded every recollection until what he felt was a mordant collage of distorted untruths.

Meaghan made a soft sound that was so heartbreakingly familiar, so longed for, so desired that it made his knees buckle. She kissed him back with desperation, begging him with her lips to make Mickey and all the terror he represented go away. Áedán tried, even though he feared it might be futile.

He realized then that she might have once been the woman of his past, the woman who had destroyed him, but she was something else now. She was more . . . and less. Better . . . and worse. Different. Excitingly fresh, startlingly distinctive. She might flash glimpses of Elan's eyes, but her scent, her lips . . . her kiss. Everything about Meaghan was unique.

Some distant part of his brain heard a soft knock at the back door, but who would be knocking at this hour? He had a moment to wonder if he'd imagined it, and then Mickey's chair scraped back and his footsteps thumped the floor. The door squeaked when it opened, and the glass panes in it rattled when he closed it behind him.

"Is he gone?" Meaghan asked.

"Yes," Áedán said, though he didn't know where or for how long.

Who had knocked? Where was Mickey off to now? A part of him worried over it, but another dismissed him with relief. Áedán didn't care where Mickey went as long as he stayed gone.

Meaghan's mouth grew hot and hungry, and he met each kiss with passion of his own. Her lips parted and the soft velvet of her tongue stroked his, bold and demanding. Elan had been an awakened virgin, needing his guidance, his teaching. Meaghan knew what she wanted and would settle for nothing less. Her hands moved from his shirt, where they'd clutched him in fear, and now her arms twined around his neck, pulling him closer.

He was flame, she an incendiary, and the need between them brushwood waiting to ignite. His hands roved down the slope of her back, fingers grazing the fine ridges of her spine before finding the soft round of her bottom. He molded her closer, lifting her up to her toes, then off the floor as he tried to fight the barriers of gravity, of nature, of all the damn clothes they both wore.

She hitched a thigh up and round his hips, anchoring the burning heat of her passion to his as she rocked her hips in an instinctive taunt that nearly pushed him over the edge. Elan had been goodness and light, but this woman was desire and heat. Meaghan whipped his blood into a boil until he knew nothing but the feel of her body, the need to make her his.

Muffling his frustrated groan against the silk of her throat, he turned so the wall braced his back instead of hers, letting it support him as he slid down to the floor. Meaghan stiffened for a moment, as if just realizing what she was doing. He felt the hesitation and it cut him like Mickey's knife. He kissed her, refusing to let her doubt the passion he felt raging beneath her skin. With one hand, he reached toward the cot, caught the edge of the dangling blanket, and pulled it onto the floor, rolling them both on top. Pinning Meaghan with his body, he eased his hips between her legs, his arms bracing his weight as he plundered her mouth, drugged by the taste of her, by the sensuous slide of her legs against his, by the small sounds she made in her throat.

Meaghan still wore the wool dress Colleen had given her, and he reached for the buttons, slipping each free and following the opening he made with his lips. Meaghan arched for him so he could drag the fabric down her shoulders, where it pooled at her hips. She wore that lacy undergarment that had entranced him in the cavern. It cupped her breasts, concealing and revealing with seductive skill designed to drive a man mad. It succeeded with Áedán. His blood blazing beneath his skin, he tongued her nipples through the lace, then blew softly over one, making it harden and strain against the wispy veil. The sheer fabric turned dark and translucent, but even that was too much. He worked the straps down, and Meaghan lifted again, reached behind her back, and unsnapped it. Freed, her breasts were more beautiful, lush and weighted in his palms. He thought he could spend the entire night holding them, kissing them, listening to the small sounds she made, and watching her body move with each sensation.

But Meaghan had other ideas. She reached for him, fumbling with his buttons, and he hurried to help her, suddenly wanting nothing more than to feel his skin against hers. She didn't stop with his shirt, and he almost died a death of pleasure when she stroked the length of him through the thick material of his cotton trousers. His hips bucked and he pushed to his knees, straddling her as he unfastened his belt. Meaghan followed him up, her hands roving down his back, over his buttocks, her mouth open and wet against his bared stomach. She tugged at his fly, and he winced as she eased the zipper over his swollen erection, and then he, too, was trapped with his clothes half on, half off. Meaghan didn't seem to care.

With his pants and drawers bunched at his bent knees, she gripped his hips and took him into her mouth in a long, wet kiss. Áedán groaned, bracing himself with one hand against the wall. The sensation of her tongue against him, circling, teasing, her lips soft and tight, her teeth a gentle rasp . . . He couldn't breathe, decided he needn't ever breathe again.

Cupping her face, he pulled away and pushed her back until she lay prone beneath him. He kicked free of his pants and then jerked her dress down and off. Another lacy wisp barely covered her hips. It was pale as a pearl and showed him glimpses of dark blonde hair and pink flesh. His skin felt too tight, his arousal so painful he thought he might not survive it, but he couldn't rush. He couldn't hurry even a moment of this incredible act. He kissed her stomach, feeling her suck in a shaking breath as he pressed his open mouth to her hip, to that small point just above the lace, moving down, where he tasted her for the first time. She was hot and exotic, her scent and taste like nothing he could have imagined. His skull burned with need for more, and the sharp cries she caught in her throat made the flames inside him flare and sear until there was nothing beyond this moment and this woman.

As much as he wanted to linger, his desire rode him fiercely. He slid the lace down the silky length of her legs and then pressed hard against her. Her mouth found his and she rocked her body into his, bringing her legs up and around him, pulling him closer until he found the place where he belonged. He entered her in a long, slow thrust of hot pleasure and near pain. She felt like a tight fist around him, hot and wet and burning. It was Áedán who trembled now. Áedán who feared. He'd forgotten the power a female could wield, never imagined he'd be such a willing victim to it ever again.

Her breath came in short, choppy bursts as he moved, pulling out and sliding back in with a rhythm older than his memory, more potent than anything served at the Pier House, more meaningful than he was able to acknowledge. He looked down at Meaghan's face and saw nothing of the woman from his past—only the woman of a future he dared not dream. And yet he knew that something of both women lived within her.

"Open your eyes," he said softly, surprised at the rasp of his voice.

Slowly those beautiful blue eyes opened, and Meaghan stared at him as he buried himself as deep as he could within her.

"You've come back to me," he said. "You belong to me."

The words shocked and elated him. They rode a fierce wave of possessive need and drowned him in their glory.

She was *his*. Would always be *his*.

She blinked, dragged from the sensation of his body into the emotion of his words. He kissed her deeply, pulling out, thrusting in, bringing her to the edge of a chasm that waited greedily to devour them both.

He felt the rush of liquid fire surround him, and she said his name, pressing her open mouth to his chest as the orgasm tore through her body, taking him over the edge with her. He felt his climax from his head down to the soles of his feet, pouring from him in a wash of joy and anguish and need that had driven him for time unending. She came a second time—as if the power of his release had driven her to it—and made another of those sounds that fired his blood. He lost himself completely in the paradise of her touch.

Only then did he notice that the light under the door had turned gray, letting him know the sky outside had brightened. Time barely existed for him, though. There was only now as he rolled to his side, tucking Meaghan to him.

Thoughts of the pendant and how he would take it from her had faded for a time, but as he lay beside her catching his breath, he felt them begin to crowd in again. No matter what he thought in the heat of the moment, reality still waited outside of this room. Somewhere Cathán still searched for a means of escape. The pendant might give Áedán a way to stop him. Or, in Elan's hands, it might lock him up alongside of Cathán.

Feck.

A baby's cry carried from upstairs. Beside him Meaghan stiffened, and with a reluctance that went down to his soul, he withdrew just enough to look at her. Her lips were swollen, her hair tousled, her skin pale as pearl in the muted light.

"You are so beautiful," he said.

She made a soft, self-deprecating sound and raised a hand self-consciously to smooth her hair. He caught it in his own, weaving her fingers with his. He pushed her arms up and trapped her wrists above her head, her body stretched like a sacrifice to him. Then he kissed her, a slow, enthralling kiss that made him both jailer and prisoner. Somewhere in his subconscious, he heard a lock click and a key clatter down a dark drain and acknowledged that any hope he'd harbored of salvation had died in her embrace.

"We are not finished, you and I," he murmured as he pulled away.

"No," she agreed, but he heard doubt in her tone. "But there's more between us than just this, isn't there, Áedán? I just don't understand what it is, what you want."

You, he thought. He almost said it but caught himself. He'd already learned that he couldn't depend on his body, his senses, hadn't he?

She'd reached for the brown dress and covered her naked flesh while his thoughts circled in his mind. He hooked his shirt with a finger and pulled it on.

Slowly he stood, intending to dress and prepare to face the world outside of this room. But as he turned, he caught sight of something silvery glinting in the muted light. Stunned, he stared at it as his troubled mind worked to place what he saw.

A comb. A silver comb lay against Meaghan's pillow.

He didn't want to recognize it or give it significance, but how could he not?

It had once belonged to Elan. He knew, because like the pendant, he'd made it with his own hands. And now it lay in Meaghan's bed. It felt like a confirmation of everything he'd feared, all he'd tried to deny.

The White Fennore and Meaghan Ballagh were connected, and though Meaghan pretended to know nothing of it, he could no longer believe it. Like Elan, Meaghan tried to trap him in a honeyed web that would lead to hell.

Chapter Eighteen

Meaghan followed Áedán's stare to the stripped cot pushed against the wall. She didn't understand the look of horror on his face until she saw what lay there on her pillow.

The silver comb from her *dream*.

She remembered pulling it from her pocket, thinking it the knife, and then flinging it onto the cot. She'd thought—*hoped*—she'd imagined it, like the walking corpse she thought she'd seen.

"That's not possible," she said, her voice a thin reed in a murky swamp. Áedán's gaze swung to her face, and he studied her with a coldness that went deep.

"What's not possible?" he asked softly.

"I dreamed about a woman last night, before you got here. She wore white and had silvery hair. She carried that comb. I thought it was my subconscious spitting out the conversation I'd had with Kyle—"

"What conversation with Kyle?" If possible his tone dropped in degrees and his words became hardened missiles. She realized her blunder too late.

"After you and Mickey left, Kyle came here to talk to me."

Even the room seemed chilly now, but she forced herself to go on. "He told me a little about the legend of the Book of Fennore and the woman—the White Fennore. I thought talking about her had caused the dream. But I cut myself on the comb in the dream, and then when I woke up, I could still feel the blood on my hands. But there was no blood on the sheets. I must have been still asleep and dreaming. I told myself I imagined it."

"And what did you tell Kyle in this little heart-to-heart the two of you had?"

Not a modicum of emotion tinted the words and not a trace of it danced on the air. Yet Meaghan felt his anger, his hurt, his sense of *betrayal.*

"I didn't tell him anything—anything important." She paused, knowing he wouldn't like what she said next but needing to be honest, to show him her sincerity. "I didn't tell him who you are, Áedán, only that no one could see you before."

A flare of fury darkened his eyes and then disappeared just as quickly.

"I had to," she continued. "They'd talked among themselves. They all agreed you weren't with us when we were prisoners. They thought you were lying."

"And did *Kyle* tell you who he is? *What* he is?"

"What do you mean?"

Again he studied her, examining every nuance of her expression, seeking something she didn't understand.

"He is a Keeper, Meaghan. His purpose, his *calling* is to find the Book of Fennore and keep it safe from humanity."

"Yes, he did tell me that," she said, trying to understand why this seemed to enrage him. "That means we want the same thing, right? We want it found. We want Cathán stopped."

"Do we?"

Meaghan stilled, frightened by the simple question and the frigid tone with which he'd delivered it.

"You can't want it back, Áedán. You can't want to return to it."

"No," he said. "That's not what I want."

But an unguarded look had flashed across his face, and in it, Meaghan read something ugly. Suddenly broken fragments of scattered memories began to fit together in her mind and form an image.

"Last night," she said low, sure, but praying she had it wrong. "You came here for the pendant, didn't you?"

"You're not safe carrying it around in your pocket."

"You mean *it's* not safe, don't you? You didn't come to protect me. You came to take it."

The truth glittered in the green and golden hues, so harsh, so vivid that it rocked her.

"Fecking Christ," she muttered. "I am such an *idiot*. What was all this?" She waved a hand at the love nest they'd made on the floor. "You fecking seduced me so you could steal it?"

Footsteps sounded on the stairs just as a polite knock rapped the front door and echoed through the quiet house. An instant later, they heard the door open.

I have found you. . . .

Meaghan froze. The voice came from inside her head and filled it to the point that she heard nothing else. Vaguely she was aware that Colleen had greeted someone, and male voices answered with a pitch of anger and a touch of panic.

But she heard only the voice within.

Did you think to escape? Did you think to leave me?

Her eyes locked with Áedán's, and she saw his face pale. He pushed away from her and backed into the corner, seeming unaware of what he did. She didn't need her empathic abilities to get what he felt. Terror—the kind that made animals flee blindly into danger—tightened his mouth and turned the skin white at the corners. His eyes widened, the pupils dilating until they swallowed the green and made him look sightless. He began to shake.

As much as the voice had terrified her, the sight of this big implacable man *trembling* snapped Meaghan from whatever spell had been cast.

"Áedán," she said, approaching him like she would a wild animal caught in a snare.

I will punish you! I will imprison YOU!

The voice rebounded inside her with triumph and malicious joy. It pressed against her ears from the inside out, threatening to rupture the fine membranes. Tears streamed down her face, blurring her vision. She swiped them away.

Áedán's eyes had become glassy and blood trickled from his nose. His entire body shuddered, as if he'd been plugged into a socket pumped with a thousand amps of electricity.

All the hurt and anger she'd felt still rattled within her. He'd come back for the pendant, not to see her. Not to be sure Cathán hadn't found a way to hurt her, but *for the pendant.* She couldn't let herself pretend otherwise. But she couldn't stop the hand that reached out for Áedán, the need to calm his fears.

"Áedán," she said in a soft, soft voice. She took his face between her palms. His skin felt cold and the quaking seemed to come from his very bones. "Sssshhhh," she crooned, pulling him into her arms, hearing the voice echoing all around them.

IwillhaveyouIwillpunishIwillimprisonPUNISHIMPRISONPUNISH.

Was it talking to Meaghan? Or did it speak to Áedán?

He shook his head, as if in answer to her silent question. His eyes were completely black now. No iris, no whites, no beautiful greens and golds. Shock swelled with superstitious fear and washed over her as she stared into them.

"Brio—I mean, Mr. MacGrath," Colleen said from the front door, surprise evident in her lilting tones.

Moving like his limbs were made of wood, Áedán pulled away from Meaghan. He used the wall as a brace to stand and move to the door.

As if called. As if *summoned.*

Meaghan scrambled after him, fumbling to button up her dress. She grabbed his arm and stopped him before he stepped out. What she saw marking his forearm almost chased every other thought away. Spirals, thin and shadowy, so faint they were almost invisible, seemed to be embedded just below the surface of his skin. Three spirals, stacked one on the other in an endless line. No beginning, no end, the marking began just below the heel of his hand and stretched across the blue veins of his wrist for several inches. She brushed a thumb over it, expecting to feel a ridge, but the skin was smooth.

Áedán tugged, still trying to get away.

"What are you doing? Where are you going?" she whispered harshly.

He looked at her with those midnight eyes, seeing nothing, hearing nothing.

"Áedán? What's wrong with you?" She took his face between her palms again, turned it away from the door, pulled him down until he was nose to nose with her. "Áedán, look at me. Hear me. Whatever that voice is, don't listen. Just listen to me."

She moved her lips to his ear. "I know you can hear me," she said. "Think about last night. Think about my touch, my mouth. Everywhere you felt it."

His hands went to her waist and gripped her convulsively.

"That's right," she said. "Hear me. Feel me."

She kissed the sensitive skin of his throat, nipped at his earlobe, found his mouth with hers. She kissed him like life and death depended on the touch of their lips, the brush of their tongues. His hands tightened, and then he pulled her against him, his grip painful. The shudders wracking his body eased, and she sighed into his mouth, giving him her breath, feeling him take it in and make it his own.

By degrees she knew the black wall of his terror faded to gray and then silver. It thinned until only a membrane held him by sticky threads.

"Look at me," she said, pulling back.

Slowly he opened his eyes. She could see green again, shifting with golden flecks and shadowed hues. She held his face until she was sure he saw her, until she was certain he heard her.

"Who am I?"

"Mine," he said thickly, as if speaking were something he'd not done in a million years.

Reluctantly a part of her admitted that might be true, but it was not the answer she wanted. "Try again. Who am I?"

She formed the syllables of her name with her lips as he spoke.

"Mine."

"Meagh-*an*," she sounded out for him.

"Meaghan," he said at last. But his eyes were hot and they still said *mine*.

"It's barely dawn," she heard Colleen say from the other room. "What are you doing here, Mr. MacGrath? And who's that with you?"

"Thank God," she heard the man who'd been there last night answer. "I feared. Christ in heaven, I feared—"

"Good morning to you, Mrs. Ballagh," a second man spoke. "'Tis Francis Murray, here. May we come in?"

Meaghan stepped away from Áedán, though he didn't let her go. Turning in the circle of his hands, she crept to the kitchen doorway with him following, still holding her. She peered out past the door frame. From this vantage, she could see a slice of the sitting room but nothing beyond. Áedán felt like a furnace at her back, and Meaghan struggled to focus on Colleen and her guests when he stood so close.

"Come in?" Colleen repeated as if the words were unknown to her. "You want to come in? Well, I suppose you can, but my Mickey isn't awake yet," she said.

"He's home then?" Brion MacGrath asked with a sharp edge to his voice.

Colleen said nothing. Meaghan remembered hearing Mickey in the house last night and then his leaving, which had filled her with relief.

"Is Mickey at home, Colleen?" Brion MacGrath asked again,

gentling his voice now, as if he asked something of the most delicate matter. Given the circumstances of Colleen's relationship with Mickey and the fight that the entire town had witnessed last night, Meaghan supposed the question could be construed as sensitive in nature.

"No, he's not home," Colleen confessed.

"Mrs. Ballagh," the other man said. "Perhaps you should have a seat."

"A seat?" Colleen said blankly. "Why? I've just gotten up. I need to feed young Niall before he puts on a fuss for us."

"It will just take a moment," Francis said.

Meaghan sensed Colleen's hesitation before she moved into sight. Dressed, she held Niall in her arms and her face was flushed, her eyes uncertain. Brion MacGrath—the big man who'd been there the night before—followed behind her. Next came a smaller, fussy-looking man with a thin, long face and sad, dark eyes. That had to be Francis. Meaghan thought he looked familiar, and then realized with a start that she knew—or would one day—his grandson, Frankie Murray.

Áedán leaned closer to look past her, keeping out of sight of the people in the front room. Colleen perched nervously on one of the straight-back chairs set before the worn sofa, her back to the kitchen. Brion and Francis sat awkwardly across from her.

"Do you know where Mickey is?" Brion asked, earning a surprised look from Francis.

Colleen shook her head. "I'm sure you heard we had a bit of a run-in last night, him and me. I'll wager the tongues are wagging even this early."

"I heard he and the man he's got working for him had a go at it, as well," Brion said in a careful tone.

The first alarm bell went off in Meaghan's head, but she couldn't see the danger that it warned of. Something wasn't right here, though. Of that much she was certain.

"Mr. Brady was defending me," Colleen said softly. "He wasn't having a go with Mickey, only trying to throw water on the fire."

Brion bristled at this, and Meaghan knew instinctively that he resented any man but himself defending Colleen. Would he rather that Mickey plunged his knife into Colleen than have Áedán come between her and her fecked-up husband?

"When was the last time you saw your husband, Colleen?" Brion asked.

The slur had been slight, and yet Meaghan heard the derision in his tone when he said *husband*. She knew what he thought of Mickey Ballagh as a husband, and she couldn't agree more. Grandfather or not, on his best day, he was a drunken sod. If what she'd seen last night was true, his best days were long gone, and the thing Mickey Ballagh had become defied description.

Colleen gave a quick glance over her shoulder, as if she sensed her granddaughter lurking in the shadows, watching and listening, and had heard the silent condemnation of the man who would one day be her grandfather. Meaghan didn't think they'd been seen, though. The sun had barely risen and the low slant of its rays streaming through the window in the front room cast the doorway where she stood in darkness.

Sighing, Colleen looked down at the baby in her arms. Meaghan saw shame hunching her shoulders and wanted to burst into the room and tell her she had nothing to be ashamed about.

"Mickey did not come home last night," she said at last. "He'd been at the bottle more than a bit."

"He was powerful drunk," Francis said. "I saw him at the pub. Didn't even recognize me he was so stinkin' full of it."

Brion cast the other man a disparaging glance.

"I'm just saying, he was sodden—"

"We understand," Brion said. "He'd a lot to drink."

"More than—"

"And he didn't come home," Brion said forcefully, at last shutting the skinny man's mouth.

"It's not uncommon," Colleen said in a small voice. "For him to sleep on *The Angel*, I mean. And not come home. He does it often."

This seemed to please Brion greatly, but he fought to keep the smug look off his face.

"We've some hard news for you, Mrs. Ballagh," Francis said with a nervous glance at Brion. "Brace yourself, ma'am."

Colleen's head snapped up. Meaghan couldn't see Colleen's eyes, but she knew her grandmother studied Francis's long face before shifting her attention to Brion's. Meaghan caught the glimpse of remorse and glee, shame and satisfaction, all muted by the mask Brion tried to hide behind.

"Mickey is dead, Colleen," Brion said softly.

For Meaghan, the words seemed to echo endlessly, a sonic bomb in a salt-laden lake, confirming things she didn't want confirmed. Thick and catastrophic, it rippled innocently across the surface while beneath, it wreaked devastation beyond belief.

Dead.

Just as she'd seen him in the kitchen. In her mind, Meaghan saw those sightless eyes staring at her, staring *through* her. She pictured the grisly gash across his throat, the handle of the knife protruding from his chest. Like the dream about the woman in white, Meaghan had denied what she'd seen. She'd assumed her overactive imagination had cast him from the shadows, and when the *real* Mickey had come home, calmly eaten supper, and then departed again, she'd convinced herself that the dead man had been a waking dream.

Áedán pulled her back against his chest, her spine fit to the hard muscle, her bottom cradled against his thighs. The feel of him gave her strength when her legs turned rubbery and her insides shuddered.

"Dead?" Colleen repeated in a toneless voice. "No, I'm sure you're wrong."

And Meaghan heard in those words the truth. She did not deny his death because she couldn't face it. On the contrary, Colleen could not imagine that life would allow something as final as death to save her from an eternity of suffering at Mickey's hand. Death was too easy an out from a marriage she'd expected to torment her forever. Colleen thought death too kind a fate for the likes of herself.

"He was found murdered, Mrs. Ballagh," Francis said, earning himself another cutting glance from the big man at his side.

Behind her, Áedán sucked in a soft breath, his hand moving across Meaghan's stomach as he anchored her more firmly to him.

"I heard someone last night," he whispered into her ear.

"Mickey coming home," she breathed back.

"But then he left. There was someone out in the back. I heard but . . . I didn't care who it was as long as he made Mickey go away."

He'd heard someone out back? Meaghan hadn't, but she wasn't surprised. The raw truth of his words echoed what she'd been feeling at the time as well. She hadn't cared for anything but Mickey's absence. At least she hadn't been alone in the consuming heat that had engulfed her—only in the motivation. That sobering thought brought her back to reality. Áedán had wanted Mickey gone for entirely different reasons than Meaghan. He'd wanted Mickey away from the pendant because Áedán wanted it for himself. Meaghan had been wrapped up in only the passion of the moment and the sweetness of his kiss.

She tried to put an inch between their bodies, quelling the desire to close the gap as soon as she'd made it.

Brion reached over and touched Colleen's hand. "I know this must be a shock for you," he said gently. "And I'm sorry, lass."

He looked sorry. Not that Mickey was dead, but that Colleen might be hurt by it. Meaghan had a moment to feel pity for Brion MacGrath's wife. She didn't stand a chance against the adoration in Brion's eyes as he gazed at Colleen.

Colleen nodded, the motion wooden and forced.

"We found him just before the sun came up. He'd been stabbed, Colleen."

By her kitchen butcher knife. He didn't say it, but Meaghan had no doubt it was true. How could it be that she'd seen him dead before it had happened?

Sick with uncertainty and fear, she watched Francis pull a bound object from the large pocket inside his jacket. He unwrapped the thick, stained canvas from around it and showed Colleen a knife. *Her* knife. The one Mickey had plucked from the counter and wielded against her at supper. Dried blood crusted the blade.

"Do you recognize it?" Francis asked.

Again, Colleen nodded. "Last night, Mickey became very angry with me," she said in a wavering tone. "I shouldn't have raised my voice to him, I know that. But I did and he threatened me with that knife. Mr. Brady stopped him before . . . before . . ."

"And that's when the two of them went at it outside?" Brion asked.

"Yes. I don't know when Mickey was killed, but I'll tell you now, Mr. Brady only defended himself. Mickey was as violent as a half-gelded bull. He wanted blood. My blood was what he was after, but Mickey was deadly drunk, and he would have drawn a pint from anyone in reach."

"So you believe Mr. Brady killed him, then?" Brion asked.

"No. I mean, well, who else would have done it?"

"'Twas my thought as well."

"But that makes no sense," Francis said, scowling. "I saw Mickey at the pub, and he wasn't gnashing over that bone anymore. In fact, he was puffed up like a rooster over what a fine worker he had aboard his boat."

Brion gave Francis another quelling look, but the thin man blustered on.

"Well, sure, and don't we all know Áedán could be earning a full wage if he was of a mind to insist. Any of us would take him on and pay him right, but Mickey, he got him for a meal and a bed. We said as much to him, too, and so Mickey decided that Áedán was like a son to him and the ties of loyalty kept them together to hear him tell it. There was no anger in him. I'd swear to it."

"And Mr. Brady? Where was he?" Brion asked.

"I don't know, but not standing at the bar with a knife in his hand," Francis answered indignantly.

"Perhaps not. But if Mr. Brady heard such talk, he would have felt powerfully wronged, I would think." Brion paused.

Meaghan had the distinct feeling that the conversation had become a train with Brion skillfully laying the track in front of it.

"Witnesses say that Mr. Brady was in that bar and that he sat in a corner saying not a word and drinking nothing," Brion went on. "And then what did he do but leave without saying good-bye? No one could say if he was in a temper or not. His leaving like that might have set Mickey off again."

Meaghan glanced over her shoulder. Behind her, Áedán listened with his head cocked to one side, as if analyzing a piece of modern art that made no sense to him. His pupils had returned to their normal size, and the greens of his irises glittered with the myriad forest colors that made them so unique. The whites were clear and bright. He caught her staring and captured her gaze for a hot moment.

"Why would Mickey be angry because Áedán left?" Colleen asked softly.

"Well," Brion answered, sounding suddenly discomfited. "What if your Mickey thought Mr. Brady had come back for *you*?"

The last was said in a harsh tone that brought Colleen's head up. "Who would tell such a lie? Mickey trusted Mr. Brady. He's a fine man."

Brion's jaw clenched. "Is he?" he said coldly. "And did you see him last night, after the fight with your husband?"

"No," she answered.

"Do not lie to me, Colleen."

"I am not lying, Mr. MacGrath," she said, lifting her chin higher.

If she could see them, Meaghan was certain Colleen's eyes would be sparking like striking flint. Brion MacGrath treaded dangerous waters, and Meaghan was not the only one who saw it. Francis shifted a bit away from the bigger man.

"You see," Francis began, his voice consoling. He glanced at Brion as if he expected aggression from him and didn't want to be caught in the backlash. Meaghan understood his concern. Brion looked like only a tenuous line held his control in place.

"Mrs. MacGrath told me yesterday she'd heard Mr. Brady begging Hoyt O'Shea to hire him."

"What business is that of hers?" Colleen asked coldly, looking at Brion.

It was the big man's turn to look uneasy.

Francis answered, "Just that she heard it and Hoyt turned him away. Said it wouldn't be right to steal another man's help."

"And you're about thinking that would be reason enough for Mr. Brady to murder my husband?" Colleen said with blatant disbelief.

Francis cleared his throat. "You see, Mrs. Harper told us—"

"Mrs. Harper?" Colleen demanded. The Harpers lived on the other side of Colleen, and Meaghan distinctly remembered them scurrying into the house when the commotion had begun. "What did she tell you? And shame on you both for believing it, whatever it was."

Meaghan agreed wholeheartedly. The Harpers were notorious snoops. Even fifty years from now, everyone knew them as nosy gossips that used exaggeration as a measuring stick. The Mrs. Harper who lived there now had died when Meaghan was a baby, but they said she liked to spin a story so much that she couldn't be counted on to tell the truth about the sky being blue and the sun yellow.

But that didn't explain Mrs. MacGrath's lie. Meaghan had been there when Hoyt O'Shea had all but begged Áedán to work for him. Even last night he'd repeated the bid. What possible motive would Mrs. MacGrath have for saying otherwise?

A chilling answer occurred to her. Perhaps Brion MacGrath's wife knew who *had* killed Mickey. Perhaps it had nothing to do with Áedán at all and the skirmish they'd witnessed. Perhaps it was Brion who was at the center of it. Brion who'd held the knife . . .

He hated the man who'd wed Colleen. Had he taken advantage of the explosive argument and used it to kill him, knowing blame would automatically be placed on Áedán? And was his wife now covering for him?

Meaghan closed her eyes, thinking back. What about the voice she'd heard? Twice it had spoken in her head. Twice Brion MacGrath had walked through the door shortly afterwards. Meaghan's skin raised in gooseflesh, remembering her conversation with Colleen the day before. She'd talked about Brion MacGrath and rumors over his luck. Meaghan had guessed then that Brion MacGrath was Cathán's dad. Could Cathán be so twisted that he would corrupt his own *father*?

She stared hard, trying to make out the glitter in Brion's eyes. Did they have that flat, unnatural look to them? She couldn't tell, not from where she stood. But when Colleen's visitor had come from the past to deliver a message, she'd specifically said that Cathán knew the future and would be trying to change it. Was this his first step to that end?

Had Cathán pushed his father to murder Mickey Ballagh? Meaghan knew her grandfather had died before she was born, but she had no idea when exactly, what had caused his death, or if history was playing out as it should. . . . Or if Cathán had already twisted its winding road. The Book was responsible for her presence here. That alone might be the only turn the past needed to skew it in a new direction. Perhaps all Cathán had to do next was sit back and wait for her to destroy her own future.

"Well, it wasn't only Mrs. Harper who told us," Francis was saying, bringing Meaghan back to the drama unfolding. "Mr. Harper concurred. They both saw Mr. Brady return here late last night and slip in through the back door."

Meaghan felt light-headed. She swayed and only Áedán's grip on her hip kept her from bumping into the wall and drawing the attention of the others in the front room. Áedán had been seen coming back. And she knew what the next words would be.

No one had seen him leave.

"It's true, Colleen," Brion said and now he looked like he had a better grip on himself. Perhaps he'd heard the outrage in Colleen's words and it had soothed the beast inside him.

"They both saw Mr. Brady sneak in through the back door. He didn't turn on the lights. Then not long after, Mickey came home."

"He did not," Colleen said emphatically. "I was upstairs the entire night through. He never came up."

Brion nodded and spoke as if she hadn't interrupted. "Then Mickey left again, along with Mr. Brady."

Meaghan shook her head. What were they talking about? Áedán hadn't gone anywhere.

"I don't believe it," Colleen said.

"We think Mr. Brady waited for him," Francis said nervously. "Then lured him down to the docks and killed him there."

The silence that followed was thunderous. Colleen shook her head, nervously bobbing the baby on her lap, who fussed and squirmed, preparing to throw the fit Meaghan knew he would if breakfast didn't appear soon.

In a muted voice, Colleen asked, "But why would he do such a thing?"

"Are you so blind, Colleen?" Brion said, his words soft and raw. "A man will do most anything for a woman."

Colleen stared at him blankly. "You mean for me?" she asked, incredulous.

A shudder went down Meaghan's spine, spreading across her flesh like a winter frost. She knew Áedán hadn't left the kitchen with Mickey. But if Áedán was right and he'd heard someone outside, then who had it been?

"Of course for you," Brion said angrily. "This Mr. Brady wants you. How can you not see it?"

Francis startled at the rage in Brion's outburst and eyed the other man with surprise.

Because she knew the truth, Meaghan had to wonder at Brion's warped reasoning. As far as she knew, there had never been any hint of scandal regarding Colleen and Áedán. No gossip. Nothing. She wondered if the same could be said about Brion and Colleen. Had people guessed at their relationship and condemned Colleen for it?

Was Brion trying so hard to pin this murder on Áedán because *he* was the one who killed Mickey?

"We don't want to jump to conclusions," Francis said quickly. "Not until we know what happened for sure, of course. We'll be needing to talk to Mr. Brady to sort it out."

Colleen nodded stiffly. "He usually comes up for breakfast. He should be here in a bit. Did you not see him on *The Angel*?"

"No," Francis said. "No one has seen him since last night."

"He's on the run," Brion said. "He murdered your husband and now he's hiding. Is he here, Colleen?"

"Here? Are you unhinged, Brion MacGrath? What in heaven's name would he be doing here before I'm even up and around? With Mickey gone at that?"

"We have to say something," Meaghan whispered to Áedán, seeing where the train was leading. Knowing the devastation that was sure to come. "Stay here."

Áedán reached out to stop her, but when he did, the marking on his arm caught his eye. He pulled back, turning his wrist so he could see the spiraling symbol that had manifested beneath his skin. A look of disgust and horror masked his face.

Meaghan thought the marking had darkened since she'd first seen it, but she kept her opinion to herself. While Áedán continued to stare at his arm in shock, Meaghan stepped out from the kitchen, drawing Brion's attention.

"Who in bloody hell is this?" he demanded, pushing to his feet.

Colleen spun around and saw Meaghan hovering in the shadows. "Meaghan," she said. Then, with a nervous glance at Brion, she repeated it. "Meaghan Ballagh. My cousin from Wexford."

"I didn't know you had relatives in Wexford," Brion said, drawing a frowning glance from Francis.

"And why would you know?" Colleen retorted with raised brows, sounding every bit like the spirited woman she would one day become. "But sure and I do have relatives there, and here is one of them."

Meaghan gave a hesitant smile and took another step into the room. "I'm sorry to have been eavesdropping, Colleen, but I couldn't help but hear. Is it true then? Is Mickey dead?"

"Yes," Francis said, watching her with rounded eyes.

The shock on his face made her wish she'd taken the time to brush her hair or check a mirror before she'd stepped out. What must she look like? A wild woman who'd been shagging her brains out on the floor all night? She hadn't taken the time to put on her bra or find her panties in the mess of blankets. Now she did the walk of shame into the front room.

Blushing, she perched on the chair next to Colleen's, careful to keep her hem down and knees tight together. Niall squealed with delight at seeing her, and she let him wrap his chubby fingers around her thumb.

"Have you seen the man who works for your cousin's husband?" Brion asked, sitting again, although he still looked very suspicious as he watched her.

This close she could see that his eyes were bright and no flat glitter gleamed from their depths. She bit back her sigh of relief. At least for now, Cathán and the Book had not corrupted him. But that didn't mean he had nothing to do with the murder.

"Have you seen this Áedán Brady?" Brion demanded when she still hadn't answered.

Meaghan wet her lips. "What do you want with Áedán?" she stalled, trying to think of the best way to avoid this train wreck.

"He's wanted for murder, and as the magistrate for Ballyfionúir, Francis intends to hold him until the authorities arrive."

Francis looked both surprised and resigned by this announcement.

"Áedán didn't murder anyone," she said. "Least of all Mickey. You don't believe them, do you, Colleen?"

"No," Colleen agreed. "I do not believe it."

"You seem quite certain," Brion said with a piercing look at Meaghan. "You also seem to know this man exceptionally well. Why is that?"

"Well, as it turns out, I do know him. We were friends before we came here."

"Were you now? And when did you arrive?"

"Just yesterday. But I was here when Mickey . . . when he tried to harm my cousin. Áedán saved her."

"Yes, we've established that," Brion said. "What is still unclear is where he went after that."

Meaghan glanced over her shoulder. From this angle, she could see Áedán watching her, and the stricken expression on his face silenced her for a moment. He looked like a man about to meet his death sentence. She realized in that instant that he expected her to condemn him. To shove him under the train as it raced ever closer. To betray him.

"He did come here," she said, pulling her gaze back to the men seated in front of her and Colleen, perched so stiffly at her side. "To see me."

All three of them gave an incredulous, "What?" at the same time. Under different circumstances, it might have been funny. But these weren't different circumstances. They were very dire ones.

"And we heard Mickey come home as well," she went on. "He ate something. His dishes are still in the kitchen where he left them."

"He came home?" Colleen repeated weakly.

"But then he left again after he'd eaten. We heard someone else, but we don't know who."

"What time was it?" Brion demanded, his face white with anger.

"I don't know. I couldn't see the clock, but I would guess after midnight."

"And where were you and Mr. Brady at the time? Did you speak to Mickey?"

"Well, no." Meaghan could feel her face growing hotter by the second.

She felt like a virgin confessing to her first tryst. She was a grown woman, entitled to a bit of a romp when she wanted. But this was 1950-something, and women of this era did not romp, even with their husbands. Sex was a sin unless performed for the purpose of procreation. Divorce wouldn't even be legal for decades to come.

Meaghan realized she'd gone from uncertain footing to perilous ground. To this generation's way of thinking, if there was passion between a man and a woman, it had better wait until they were married, and it certainly should not rage out of control in a storage room off the kitchen of the woman's grandmother's house. It seemed sordid now, regardless of how it had felt when it happened. And it had felt . . .

She gave herself a mental shake.

"Where. Were. You?" Brion repeated. His face tightened with fury and his blue eyes blazed.

"In the storage room?" she admitted, and even she heard the question mark at the end. Her face had grown so hot that sweat began to prickle at her scalp. She felt like the word *fornicator* had been etched on her forehead. Francis looked too stunned for reaction.

The silence that followed her words seemed insurmountable. Her entire body was on fire now, and not the way it had been last night. Not with passion. Not with desire.

"And when did you and Mr. Brady leave this *storage room*?" Brion demanded.

"Just a little while ago. There's no way Áedán could have killed Mickey. He was with me all night."

"You spent the night with Mr. Brady?" Colleen said. Her widened gaze skittered to Meaghan, then to the kitchen doorway. "Together? In me kitchen?" Her voice squeaked at the end.

Brion lunged from his chair and charged to the kitchen, Francis following close on his heels. Meaghan hurried after them, braced for Brion to shoot first and ask questions later. But when she rounded the corner, she didn't see Áedán anywhere.

Meaghan barely had time to register this before Brion jerked the storage door open. She let out a shaky breath. Áedán wasn't hiding there, either. While Brion, Francis, and Colleen stared into the tiny room, Meaghan tried to peer through the panes in the window for a sign of Áedán. He'd been quick—she didn't see a trace of him.

Reluctantly, she watched the others, who stood like statues arranged in an arc around the storage room's doorway. The cot had been stripped and the blankets were on the floor where she and Áedán had made their little love nest. The scent of sex wafted out on the crisp morning air. The bra she'd been looking for when she'd dressed poked out of the tangled mess. Brion stepped over the blankets and lifted the lacy scrap with one finger. The absolute silence shouted just how very scandalized every one of them was.

Thinking she might expire from embarrassment, Meaghan yanked the bra from Brion's hand and crammed it in her pocket.

"You'd have me believe he was with you in this small room *all night*," Brion sneered. "You lie."

"I don't lie," Meaghan answered, lifting her chin in a gesture Colleen often made. "I don't need to lie. Yes, he was here. With me. All night. And we didn't need a lot of room, if you get my meaning, Mr. MacGrath."

Behind her, Colleen made a strangled sound that was somewhere between a laugh and a gasp. Francis gulped loudly. Brion stood speechless, his mouth opening and closing soundlessly.

Colleen interrupted the painful silence that had fallen. She shifted the baby to her other hip and indicated her kitchen with a disgusted look. "This is Mickey's mess. The man was a pig."

As one they all turned from the long, narrow closetlike room and surveyed the kitchen. The stew pot sat on the counter, stew slopped over every inch of space, spilled on the floor, spattered on the table. It looked as if, in his drunkenness, he'd intentionally flung it everywhere he could. Meaghan was pretty sure he'd been too intoxicated for any deliberate action, though.

The bowl on the table held a dried crust of the stew's gravy and a fat fly buzzed lazily over the droppings. Bread crumbs covered the table and floor around it, and Meaghan saw that Mickey had foregone the knife to rip hunks from the loaf with disregard to anyone who might want a piece of bread when he was finished. The bottle Mickey had been drinking from last night sat opened beside an empty glass with a brown ring at the bottom. It had been three-quarters filled when they'd sat for dinner. Now it was nearly empty.

"Well, then," Francis said, blinking at the mess. "It appears Miss Ballagh has told us the truth about Mickey coming and"—he gave the storage room an embarrassed glance—"and about the other as well. I'd say Mr. Brady has a solid alibi. This changes a thing or two."

Brion made a growling sound but nodded. "Aye, that it does."

Chapter Nineteen

THE Irish were a superstitious lot. They feared death in ways that other cultures never considered, and at the same time, they loved it. Few would choose to miss an Irish wake—not even the deceased. The last funeral Meaghan attended had been Colleen's, and people had come from near and far to say good-bye.

Meaghan doubted Mickey Ballagh had inspired love from anyone and held equal skepticism that he'd even been particularly liked. But death was death and rituals had to be followed. Once the end came, it mattered little whether the dearly departed had been adored or hated, admired or despised.

Enid arrived first with a casserole and a warm, caring smile for Colleen. But others came soon after, interrupting Brion and Francis in order to express their sympathies, offer pearls of wisdom, or just appease their blatant curiosity. Ballyfionúir was a peaceful town, and the excitement of a good old-fashioned murder was not to be missed.

"'Tis sorry I am to hear of your loss, Mrs. Ballagh," they said, one after another. "A dastardly thing, stabbings. Sure and wouldn't there be a lot of blood. I heard his head was chopped clean off. Is it true?"

And in their faces, Meaghan saw the grisly hope that the rumors were true.

Most of them knew—or thought they knew—what kind of man Mickey was and what kind of marriage Colleen had with him. They suspected that Colleen secretly rejoiced his gruesome demise but no one said it—not to her anyway. But they didn't hesitate to discuss it in pseudowhispers behind her back.

Meaghan's sense of the surreal grew to mammoth proportions as the morning ticked on. People whose faces she'd known her entire life appeared now without wrinkles or recognition when they turned her way. She'd played with many of their grandchildren, dated some of their grandsons, and babysat their great-grandkids—but none of those people had yet to be born. In reality, *Meaghan* hadn't either. Occasionally someone would give her a peculiar look, as if something in her genetic build had sparked a memory, but then they'd turn away, certain they'd made a mistake.

She kept to the edges of the gathering, bobbing her father on her hip and smiling when addressed. But her thoughts stayed mainly with Áedán. The comb had meant something to him. It had linked facts and suspicions that Meaghan couldn't begin to guess at. When she'd mentioned the woman in white, his face had paled and the look in his eyes . . . She shivered. It had been such a bewildering mixture of joy, dread, and rage that it left her uneasy even now.

The woman had to be the White Fennore, the one Kyle claimed Áedán had betrayed, thus motivating her to curse him until the end of time. But according to Áedán, it was the White Fennore who had done both the betraying and the cursing. Elan, he'd called her, and he'd spoken the name with a soft lilt he couldn't disguise.

She looked down at her hands, thinking of the blood that had coated them. Could it have been real? As real as the comb she'd slipped in her pocket when no one was looking? She shifted the baby to her other side and reached down to touch the comb, feeling the grooves, the teeth. Assuming the dream had been more than *just a dream*, why had the White Fennore come to her? Why had she given Meaghan this comb? And what did it mean to Áedán?

She forced herself to focus on Colleen and what her poor grandmother was going through. Colleen stood straight and proud in her kitchen, greeting the newcomers, pretending to be unaware of the gossip raging in every corner or of the big man looming over her. But Meaghan could see the tiny cracks in her mask. Brion MacGrath was not someone to be ignored, and Colleen was perhaps more susceptible to him than anyone else.

"Mrs. Ballagh!" A plump woman with bulging eyes and bad teeth charged forward with a plate of pastries that looked like it might have been dropped on the way, and a meaty hug that could have broken Colleen in two. "I'm so sorry, I am. I come as soon as I heard."

Colleen looked surprised but quickly hid it behind a polite smile. Already there were too many people taking up the limited floor space in the kitchen, but the woman squeezed herself into the mix, never taking her gaze off Brion MacGrath.

She looked at him with such longing, Meaghan was half convinced she wished her own husband had been stabbed to death and she the widow who'd earned a visit from the handsome Mr. MacGrath. It seemed funny in a macabre sort of way. When at last the woman looked back at Colleen, she said in a sugary voice, "Mr. Ballagh was a sweet, kind man. We'll be feeling the loss of him for a long time to come."

The disbelief that comment generated barely had time to register before another female appeared at the back door. This one was as tall and thin as the other was short and round. She had wavy black hair, cut tight around her face and piled high on top. A bow that looked a bit girlish for her long, angular features held back the curls at her temple, and bright lipstick drew the eye to a wide mouth and full lips. Dark brows made perfect wings over brown eyes that had been outlined with a pencil, making them look bigger and more alluring. Bedroom eyes. She was beautiful in an interesting and intriguing way. The kind of woman who in certain lights and at certain angles would be breathtaking while at the same time, under others might appear harsh and rawboned.

This morning she was made up to perfection, shadows and blushes applied with a skilled hand to make the most of what she had. But for all her beauty, she lacked grace. With her narrow shoulders and long neck, Meaghan had the impression of an ungainly giraffe. It wasn't until the woman turned that Meaghan noted with surprise that she was pregnant—more pregnant, by the looks of it, than Colleen, but the baby bump was somehow lost in all the long angles.

"Marga," Brion exclaimed angrily. "What in bleeding hell are you doing here?"

"Well, I've come to pay my respects, of course," she said with a guileless smile that made Meaghan shiver. This woman was as ingenuous as a cobra, and there was nothing even close to sympathy in the emotions that wafted off her.

She moved smoothly to Brion's side, snubbing the plump woman who greeted her effusively. Wrapping a possessive arm around Brion's waist, she tilted her head back for a kiss. Face flushed with anger, he gave her a stingy peck on the cheek, but she slid a cold and triumphant look at Colleen after it was done. Suddenly Meaghan got the picture that had eluded her. This was Brion's wife.

"Poor Mrs. Ballagh," Marga said, facing Colleen. "My heart and prayers are with you."

But Meaghan got a whiff of her emotions, and what Marga felt was vindication. She thought Colleen deserved any tragedy that might come her way.

"Thank you," Colleen mumbled, not looking up.

Seeing the two women together, Meaghan had no trouble understanding what Brion had meant when he'd fervently whispered to Colleen as he'd pinned her body against the wall. His wife *was* cold as the fish in the depths of the sea. She looked like a spire of ice, all edges and towering height, her skin so white it had a tinge of blue, her eyes so dark they seemed cavernous in the chill of her face.

Her dispassionate gaze skimmed the occupants of the kitchen, widening when they reached Meaghan. "I don't think we've met," she said with a grimace that might have been a smile and might have been something else entirely.

"No, I don't think we have," Meaghan agreed with equal politeness but didn't offer to introduce herself either. She was no stranger to the superiority game and knew that it irked the other woman to go first.

"I'm Mrs. Brion MacGrath," she said in a tone that could have easily replaced the name *Brion* with the words *Your Highness.*

For a moment, the devil inside Meaghan spurred her to say, *And I am the Druid Brandubh's love slave,* but as soon as the thought formed, the humor left. Perhaps it was too close to the truth.

"Meaghan Ballagh," she muttered.

"Relative of Mickey?" Marga asked.

"Colleen," Meaghan answered.

Marga sniffed at that. Though Colleen and her husband came from very distant branches of the Ballagh tree, Meaghan all but heard the word *inbreds* forming in Marga's head.

"I heard about this one last night," the plump woman with the bad teeth offered about Meaghan while giving Marga a look that said, *And I don't like her either.*

Meaghan wondered just what she'd heard but couldn't ask and wouldn't even if she could.

Once again, Marga ignored the other woman. Feck, it was hard to decide who Meaghan liked the least in this crowd.

"I've brought some of my famous curry dumplings," Marga said. "I know you'll appreciate them."

They sounded disgusting to Meaghan, but she held her tongue. Marga waited pointedly, as if expecting a servant to rush forward and relieve her of the dish. When none appeared, she looked around for an inch of open counter space and then set the dish rudely on top of another, squashing the contents of the first without apology.

When she moved, she did so with exaggerated care, as if the

weight of the baby she carried in her womb were an overwhelming burden. Smiling, she rested her hand on her swollen belly and rubbed it fondly. And yet, once again the emotions did not match the action. Meaghan sensed no warmth directed to the life she carried. She might have been patting a basketball for all the feelings she put into the gesture.

"When are you due?" Meaghan asked.

"Three months," Marga said with a grating smile. "We are very excited for little Cathán to be born, are we not, Brion?"

Cathán.

The baby Marga MacGrath carried would grow to become the man who terrorized Meaghan's world. Meaghan had guessed that somewhere in this time an infant Cathán might be crawling around. She'd even surmised that Brion MacGrath was his father. But somehow that baby bump had not registered with Meaghan until she heard the name spoken.

Cathán.

"What if the baby's a girl?" she asked with numb lips.

Brion interrupted with a stony expression before Marga could respond. "It's time for you to go, Marga. We've still business with Mrs. Ballagh."

Marga's smug smile faltered. "Business? I should think the only business would be to arrest Mr. Brady. The whole town is talking about him this morning."

Just as they'd been talking about Meaghan yesterday, evidently.

"Talk should not determine a man's fate," Colleen said with a hint of steel in her voice.

"No?" Marga said, brows raised. "I suppose you're right. But where there's smoke, there's often fire."

A number of quick and cutting responses popped into Meaghan's head at that, but sparring with Marga would accomplish nothing. An awkward silence engulfed them, and the too-crowded kitchen grew uncomfortably hot.

"Why don't I make us all some tea?" Enid asked brightly.

Seeing that his wife had no intention of leaving, Brion angrily faced Colleen. "I'll be looking for Mr. Brady," he said. "And you will send word if he comes by."

Colleen stiffened. "Was that a question, Mr. MacGrath?" she asked.

Meaghan hid a smile. Mickey had bullied the spirit out of Colleen, but with Brion MacGrath, it sparkled fiercely in Colleen's eyes. Something sorrowful unfurled in Meaghan's heart. Why couldn't fate have dealt Colleen *this* man to love and cherish? For all the warts on his character—for all that he wasn't such a knight in shining armor—Meaghan sensed devotion and adoration coming from him when he looked at Colleen. If Mickey had made Colleen a different woman with his violence and disgust, then perhaps Colleen would have made Brion a man as true as his emotions said he wanted to be. He certainly brought out the facets of her personality that Meaghan most loved.

"I only mean to say, we'd *appreciate it*, Francis and me, if you'd send word when Mr. Brady shows up."

Colleen nodded, the stiffness draining from her. "Aye, I will do as you ask."

"Áedán didn't kill Mickey," Meaghan said. "You won't find blood leading back to him. I'm telling you the truth. He was with me all night."

Brion scowled. "And yet I still wouldn't call him innocent. Not by a long shot."

"To my way of seeing," Marga said sweetly, "your vouching for Mr. Brady doesn't make him less of a murderer, but it does say a thing or two about you."

"Shut up," Brion snapped at her and she recoiled, blinking her big, painted eyes with surprise.

He gave Francis a sharp nod. "Doesn't seem much else we can do here except be in the way. Let's take our investigation elsewhere."

"Aye. Good day to you, ladies." Francis doffed an imaginary hat at Colleen. "Mrs. Ballagh."

With a last, dark look at Colleen, Brion stormed out the back door, taking Francis with him like a leaf caught in a gust. As if by command, the others who'd crowded in the kitchen migrated to the door and said their farewells, too. Only Enid, Marga, and the plump woman with her buggy eyes and rotted teeth remained.

Marga made a great show of being amused by Brion's words, as if his telling her to *shut up* in front of others were an endearing antic and not a mortifying verbal slap. But Meaghan felt her emotions, and she was plenty pissed and humiliated. For a moment, Meaghan almost felt sorry for her.

"Well," Marga said with another superior sniff. "I should be going as well. Colleen, I'm sure we'll talk soon. My sympathies to you and your . . ."

Marga let the unsaid hang with such studied skill that Meaghan wanted to shout, *Feck off with your fecking sympathies.* She thought she deserved a medal for keeping it inside.

With all the pomp of royalty, Marga whisked herself out the back door and left the rest of them in relieved silence.

"Curling up to that woman on a winter's night must be like hugging a frozen shark," Enid muttered, and Meaghan burst out laughing.

"Or a snake," she said.

"Not enough teeth," Enid disagreed. "Although the scales and venom are right enough."

The bug-eyed woman gaped at them. "She's as kind as the good Mary herself."

"Why don't you run along and tell her so," Enid said. "I'm sure she'll invite you to the big house for tea."

With a huff, the other woman left, taking her downtrodden pastries with her. Even Colleen smiled at that. Alone at last, Enid said, "Our Niall looks ready for a lie down. So do you, Colleen. Sure and wouldn't I wager you got no sleep to speak of last night. Go upstairs with the wee one and close your eyes. I'll be putting my considerable talents to work here in the kitchen. When you come down, it will all be put to the right."

"You're a good friend, Enid," Meaghan said.

"Oh *pish*, I'm nothing special."

Colleen hugged her friend tightly and then did as she was told. With a huge yawn and a sad smile, she took the baby upstairs. Meaghan turned to Enid after Colleen left and began to help.

"I reckon you have things you should be doing as well," Enid said, nonchalantly. "Like hunting down that man of yours."

Meaghan almost said, "He's not my man," but stopped herself. She'd just confessed to spending the night with him, having sex in a storage room. It would hardly do to confess all of her uncertainties about Áedán Brady now.

"I would like to see if I can find him," she answered instead.

"Sure and don't I think that's a good idea. Fix up a bit first, if you don't mind me saying so. You'll want to look good for him."

Meaghan gave her a chagrined smile. "I'll do that."

With a quick hug that surprised but obviously delighted the other woman, Meaghan searched out her jeans and T-shirt, which were now clean and dry, and used the bathroom for a quick shower. After brushing her teeth and restraining the wild mess of her hair, she felt as ready to face Áedán as she ever would.

When she came out again, Enid eyed her clothes with a scandalized look but merely wished Meaghan luck. Borrowing the coat she'd used yesterday, Meaghan stuffed the silver comb in her pocket, donned her runners, and left in search of Áedán.

She intended to find him, ask him point-blank why he wanted the pendant, and hope her instincts about him ran true. With a cautious look around, she moved to the side of the house, retrieved the pendant, and put it in her other pocket, and then set out for the bay.

Chapter Twenty

ÁEDÁN moved about the deck of *The Angel* while around him others pretended to go about their business aboard their boats. They were late to cast off this morning—the sun had already breached the horizon and burned through the dawn mists. But with all the excitement of a murder, no one had wanted to answer the call of duty that their ships and the sea represented and miss a moment of the glorious drama unfolding on their shores.

He'd expected Brion MacGrath to appear by now to question him, but apparently Meaghan had convinced him that Áedán had nothing to do with Mickey's murder. That didn't mean the man didn't still have his suspicions, though. Áedán was certain he hadn't seen the last of him.

Áedán planned to take *The Angel* out to check the traps he and Mickey had set yesterday, but only because he needed something to do to keep his mind off everything else. Once he would have taken chisel and hammer to a piece of granite and worked the stone until his mind had cleared. People would have come to watch, keeping a respectful distance, admiring without interrupting.

But those days were gone.

That life was gone.

He rubbed his arm, staring at the spirals that had appeared under his skin, wondering when they'd begun to take shape. When he'd made love to Meaghan? Or when he'd heard that voice in his head? He didn't know why it mattered—the Book had marked him on the inside centuries ago. And yet this physical reminder disturbed him. The spirals had been so pale they'd looked like a shadow when he'd first seen them. But now they'd darkened and it seemed they'd moved closer to the surface. It distressed him more than he would admit.

He'd never been so uncertain. Each step made him feel like he stumbled through time, today merging with yesterday, overlaying history with the present, the present with a millennium past. Before he'd become a prisoner to the Book of Fennore, the people who'd revered him, pandered to his favor, *worshiped* him like a god, had turned against him. He'd been wounded and infuriated by their fickle loyalties. He'd wanted to punish them, felt the darkness that he'd ultimately instilled into the Book taunting him, demanding he acknowledge the rightness of the mayhem that his creation inflicted on the people.

Áedán let out a breath as he reached for the net he'd been working just yesterday when his world had turned upside down again with the arrival of Meaghan. Methodically he spread it on the deck of the small ship that had been the link between survival and starvation for the Ballaghs. The softly swaying ship had the effect of anchoring him in the here and now. This boat had been Mickey's family's livelihood. Now what would happen to sweet Colleen and her babies?

Not his problem, an angry voice spoke inside him. He had enough to concern himself over without worrying for her. He was in the fight of his life. Cathán had grown in power. Mickey's murder was proof of that. Áedán didn't know who exactly had done the killing, but he had no doubt that Cathán had manipulated whoever it was.

When he'd heard that voice in his head this morning, he'd felt like a wild animal driven to madness. He'd felt his own consciousness slipping. Like a thrall, he'd been compelled to answer.

Meaghan's touch had broken the trance, but he didn't like to think just how close he'd been to answering the voice and following it back to the Book of Fennore. Last night, after he'd tapped the power that flowed between the Book and the pendant, he'd thought himself immune to its call. He should have known better. Hadn't he switched tactics when he'd come across a particularly stubborn prey? Why should he be surprised that Cathán would do the same? But he had to stay strong. If he let that power reach him, he would be lost forever.

The Book of Fennore had taken on a life of its own so long ago that Áedán couldn't even say when it had happened. Áedán's goals had aligned with it at one time. But now the power that was in the Book aspired to things that did not agree with Áedán.

Blood. Death. Mayhem.

Things of his past. Things that filled Áedán with sharp remorse and bitter regret.

He exhaled, shaking his head, admitting, if only to himself, that the reason behind his transformation was Meaghan. The woman who'd slipped beneath his skin despite his efforts to bar her. A woman he wanted. A woman he needed.

A woman who could destroy him.

Again.

He scowled. How could he trust her when every internal compass he had pointed to the repeat of history? She had the key. She heard the voices. She saw death.

Feck. He felt like his mind had been twisted into a knot.

He looked out at the bay in despair. One by one, the other ships left their dock and arrowed to the harbor opening. As they passed, the men eyed Áedán with misgivings. The friendly waves that would have come just yesterday were no more. Once again he'd been accused and condemned without a chance to defend himself.

He turned away, wondering where Meaghan would be now? At Colleen's, caring for the baby?

Last night she'd been like liquid fire in his arms. She'd been a homecoming and a leave-taking all in one. She'd welcomed his heart and banished his fears, if only for a time. In some ways, she seemed innocent, and in others . . . How could he not suspect that she would bring disaster in her wake?

In the slip across the way, Hoyt O'Shea prepared his lines with studied precision, but Áedán felt the other man's gaze stray to him when he thought Áedán wouldn't notice.

Then, as the *High Tide* began to pull away, Hoyt called, "Mornin', Áedán. Glad to see the sorry business with Mickey didn't hurt you as well. It's a nasty thing, murder."

Surprised, Áedán straightened from the net, hating the grateful churn in his gut at the friendly greeting. He didn't need *friends.*

"It is a sad affair," Áedán said, the sun shining in his eyes as he looked at Hoyt. He mimicked the musical cadence of Hoyt's speech effortlessly, hiding his own turmoil beneath it. He'd spent eons studying people, seeking the best way to exploit them. It came as second nature to use those skills now when it felt like the world caved in around him.

"Me wife said Brion MacGrath is charging from one end of the valley to another looking for the culprit. Ask me, it'd be to shake his hand. Mickey Ballagh wasn't worth the salt in his body."

The air shifted and Áedán caught the scent of the Book. Like a rabbit emerging from a hole to find a circling hawk above, he fought the instinct to scuttle back into the dark and await its departure. The very idea of cowering infuriated him, though. He moved port side and squinted to see Hoyt more clearly.

"It's bad luck to speak ill of the dead," he said in a mild tone.

Hoyt's face remained in shadow, but that sense of the Book rose like the lapping waves. Then the *High Tide* turned toward the barrier opening at the mouth of the bay and the shadow of the cabin broke the sun's fierce rays. For one naked moment Áedán saw Hoyt's flat, dark eyes and the sharp gleam that revealed so much. It took all Áedán's composure not to stagger back as the full impact hit him.

Hoyt had been the presence he'd sensed in the pub last night. Hoyt had come in contact with the Book of Fennore.

The moment was quickly there and gone, but Áedán had no doubt that Hoyt had killed Mickey Ballagh. He would have to keep his guard up around the other man unless he wanted to find himself in similar dire straits.

"Áedán?"

The woman's voice calling to him spun Áedán as Hoyt motored away. Meaghan, dressed in her borrowed coat and the blue jeans she'd had on yesterday, made her way to him. She stepped onto the deck without asking his leave to come aboard.

"Has Brion MacGrath been here already?" she asked.

"No."

"I'm sure he will be soon. He seemed determined to blame you for Mickey's murder."

"Grand," he said in response.

They surveyed each other warily, and something inside him ached at the guardedness in her manner, at the stiffness in his own. Her eyes looked like rain and storm, more gray than blue this morning—but not, he noted with relief—a bit of amethyst. She was upset, though. Well, honestly, so was he.

How quickly *emotions* had become as natural as pulling air into his lungs.

She had the pendant with her. He felt it moving in the air particles, dancing on the breeze, and he realized that she must have stashed it somewhere last night because he hadn't felt it when he'd come to her.

The chug of the *High Tide*'s motor faded in the distance as it reached the harbor break. Relieved that Hoyt had moved too far away to take note of Meaghan, Áedán gathered up the net he'd just spread out and stuffed it in the bin anchored to the deck. Without a word, he went to work on the lines holding *The Angel* in her slip and cast them off.

"Where are we going?" Meaghan asked, gripping the rail.

"Out."

Away from Ballyfionúir and murder. Away from Brion MacGrath and his witch hunt. But not away from Meaghan. Meaghan he took with him.

The few days he'd spent at sea with Mickey had given Áedán a rudimentary education on how to get *The Angel* from dock to the mouth of the harbor. Hoyt's ship had become a dot in the distance by the time Áedán steered past the seawall where the waters turned harsh, buffeting the small boat and forcing his thoughts to focus. At last he cleared the breakwaters and motored toward the middle of the endless sea. Only then did he cut the engine and face the woman watching him with all-too-knowing eyes.

"We need to talk, Áedán," she said.

He gave her a curt nod of agreement. They did need to talk, but he wanted to lead the conversation this time. It was Meaghan's turn to writhe under a blistering spotlight.

"Where was the pendant last night?" he demanded.

"Why did you freak out when you saw this?" she countered, pulling the silver comb from her pocket. As it had before, the sight of it hit him like a blow to the solar plexus. For a moment, he could barely breathe.

"How big are those pockets? You seem to be forever pulling surprises out of them," he forced himself to say calmly.

She almost smiled. "Answer me, Áedán. I know seeing this upsets you."

"Do not presume to know me, Meaghan, just because we shared some kisses."

"We shared a lot more than that. Deny it if it makes you happy, but it's the truth."

It was, and as much as he wanted to hurl a rebuttal at her, he could not. "Happy," he said instead. "And what is happiness?"

She moved to the bench on the starboard side and sat, watching him with perceptive eyes. He kept his face impassive. At least he hoped he did. With Meaghan, he could be sure of nothing.

"I want to know about the White Fennore."

"And why would you want to know about her?"

"She meant something to you," Meaghan said simply. "She means something to me, too. I just haven't figured out what yet."

He digested that in silence, torn with indecision. What should he tell her? What should he hide?

"Elan," he murmured, almost to himself. "Her name. It means bringer of light."

And it had fit the woman he'd loved. She'd brought light into his life right up to the moment she'd banished him into the black world of Fennore, transforming him from a man with a heart and soul into an apathetic and cruel entity. She'd sealed him in darkness for eons, made him yearn for the brightness of her smile, the warmth of her glow. He'd mourned her loss and then he'd turned bitter. In the end, his rage, his need for vengeance had consumed him.

Meaghan watched him closely, and then said, "In your version of the story, she betrayed you."

"My version?" he asked sardonically. "You mean, in the true version."

"That's what I want to know. Kyle said—"

"Kyle," he snarled, feeling that alien flare of jealousy and hating himself for it.

"He said that people feared the Whi—Elan—because they were superstitious and she saw dead people. They wanted her sacrificed because what she saw frightened them."

Meaghan's voice wobbled over those words, and he knew she was remembering Mickey and the bleeding corpse that had visited her last night, but she kept her chin up and her gaze direct, revealing nothing of what went on behind her eyes. Áedán wished he could present such an implacable front.

"That part is true," he said. "People did fear her. But it was more than that. Elan was so beautiful that it hurt to behold her. She was perfection in flesh and blood. It seemed she shouldn't be real. No man was immune to her beauty."

"Not even you."

Especially not him.

"Our king—Conlaoch—had a very jealous wife. She hated Elan from the first. It was she who proclaimed Elan to be the White Fennore. We were forbidden to call her by her given name after that. We could only address her as the White Fennore—a thing, not a person. In one calculated stroke, the queen turned her into an object to be worshiped from afar. She isolated Elan and made her a slave."

"I'm hearing two things there. She was worshiped but she was a slave?"

"You do not befriend a god. You do not speak to a god. You pray—which means you ask it to give you everything you want, and in return, you ask it for more. They took all that made her who she was. They enslaved her with their needs, their demands."

"And then they wanted her to die when she couldn't deliver?"

"Yes."

Even now, he felt something clench inside him. Elan had been so young, so innocent, and so heartbreakingly beautiful, and they had destroyed her. Then she had destroyed him.

"And the Book?"

Wondering where his determination to make Meaghan the victim of this interrogation had fled, he said, "We never intended for it to become what it did. We cast it into existence as a way for her to relieve the pressure she felt. It was a time of sickness among our people, so everywhere she looked, she saw death. Her heart would not let her ignore it, but each time she tried to stop someone from dying, she merely brought misery and fear."

"And that's when the king said she had to die?"

"When she had a vision of his wife and child dead, yes. He had coveted Elan, as well, and it vexed him that his wife ruled with such iron control that he dared not take her as his lover. When Elan predicted the deaths, I think he meant to relieve himself of temptation at the same time he appeased his jealous wife."

"But didn't they know she was yours?" Meaghan asked softly.

The words washed over him with sudden heat. *His*. But Elan had never really been his, had she? And neither was Meaghan.

"No," he said, his voice rough. "Our love was forbidden."

She startled at that and repeated the word, "Forbidden."

"We met in secret. I planned for us to escape, to run away and start a new life together, but obviously, that never happened."

"Where was this secret place where you met?" Meaghan whispered.

"I think you know."

"The cavern beneath the castle ruins."

He nodded. "Though the ruins didn't come until centuries later."

Meaghan searched his face for a long moment, and then she said, "Why didn't it happen? Your plan for the two of you to escape?"

"What did your precious *Kyle* tell you?" he asked.

"That Elan saw her own spirit and knew that you meant to kill her. Because she was never able to change the deaths she saw—she thought it was inevitable."

Inevitable.

He scoured the stubble of whiskers on his face with his palms, struggling to find the words to explain just how *un*inevitable it all had been.

"I meant only to conjure her death—to fake it. I had planned it to the last detail and I was certain it would work. But I couldn't share it with Elan. I had to keep it secret from her."

"Why?" Meaghan asked, incredulous.

"Elan could not lie. She had no deceitfulness in her. She could not have gone to the sacrifice and played the part without revealing the truth."

"So you just didn't *tell* her?"

"No," he said angrily. "No, I didn't tell her. I thought she would trust me. I would have died for her. She knew that. She should have believed in me. She should have known that I would keep her safe."

Meaghan stared at him with frank disbelief, rekindling his anger.

Who was she to judge his actions? She hadn't been there. She couldn't know how desperate he'd been for a solution.

"It would have worked," he insisted. "Except I didn't take into account the Book. By then it had become a monster on its own, and it moved against me."

"How?"

He exhaled. It had been his own ego, his foolish pride that had turned the Book into the creation of darkness it became. In those days before his world had imploded and Elan had betrayed him, he'd felt his control over the Book vanish. And yet he'd refused to acknowledge the Book had taken a life of its own. Refused to ask for help from those who might have aided him. There'd been other Druids—men who had taken him in as a child and trained him. Men whose wisdom he'd greedily absorbed.

Yet the more powerful Áedán became, the less he'd cared for his mentors. He'd begun to think himself omnipotent. He'd believed that the knowledge he'd acquired had been within him all along—not learned, but innate. *His* by right. And he hadn't wanted to admit to his weakness. Rather than go to them for help, he'd kept the beast he'd created a secret, concealed the danger that he felt growing within it, and battled the unbeatable odds alone.

"Even now I cannot tell you how it transformed from what we'd meant it to be into what it became. A thing of power can never be trusted to act as it was intended. It is a fact of life."

She looked unsettled by this simple truth. For a moment, she sat quietly, absorbing all he'd said. He wanted to know what she thought, but he didn't ask. Instead he braced himself for her next question. Knowing her as he'd come to in the time they'd spent together, he assumed he wouldn't have to wait long for it.

"So you didn't trust Elan with the plan and then you blamed her for not knowing how it should play?" Meaghan said finally. "And then the Book of Fennore made an even bigger mess of things. Do I have that right?"

Yes, damn her. He scowled. "I didn't know it then, but the Book began to speak to her. It gave her a vision of me carrying her bloody corpse to the cliffs and hurling it over. Then it showed her another woman with me, together, in the cavern. It convinced Elan that I had created an elaborate ruse to murder her so I could be with someone new. I still cannot fathom how she believed it. No other woman existed in my eyes. If she'd come to me, I could have stopped it all, but she didn't."

"If she'd come to you . . . if you'd gone to her . . . It doesn't sound like either one of you had your heads on straight."

He wanted to growl at that. He wanted to call Meaghan's words ridiculous. But she spoke nothing less than the truth, and he could not pretend otherwise.

"I was arrogant. I believed that my word should have been indisputable."

"So what happened next?"

"The Book of Fennore had metamorphosed into something unrecognizable, and neither of us had guessed at the extent of its power. But I thought I'd found a way to destroy the monster we'd created. Of course, she never gave me the chance."

The old anger within him flared. He swallowed it and went on.

"I worked out a blood ritual that would seal the Book forever and essentially smother the power within it like a flame deprived of oxygen. It required three things: her blood and mine. And a sacrifice."

"A real one, you mean," Meaghan said. "A human one?"

"Yes. I planned to wait for Elan's next visit from the dead and then use that person for my purpose."

"Sacrifice someone you knew was going to die anyway," she murmured. Her eyes narrowed and she studied him. "I can see where you might have thought it a perfect plan, but didn't it feel like playing God? How did you get Elan to go along with it?"

He stared at her, struck speechless for a moment. *Playing God?* Leave it to Meaghan to call it exactly what it was.

"I didn't tell Elan about that, either," he said, looking away. "She never would have agreed. After failing time and again, she would not accept that the fates of the dead she saw were inescapable. She would have tried to save whoever it was, no matter the cost."

"Áedán," Meaghan said, standing and moving to his side. "How did you ever imagine your plan would work? Couldn't you see the disaster just waiting to happen?"

Frustrated, he glanced into her face and then away again. He couldn't explain how desperate he'd been. He couldn't make her see he'd done the only thing he could.

"If I did nothing, she would die. No matter how crazy, how demented and wrong my plan was, it gave her a chance."

"But—"

"Conlaoch did not simply demand that Elan be sacrificed, Meaghan. He demanded that *I* be the one to perform it. He wanted her blood on *my* hands."

"Wh—"

"I don't know why," he cut her off angrily. "Perhaps he knew of our love. Perhaps he meant to punish me. My choices were to kill her myself or do everything I could to save her."

His voice cracked and his eyes burned. Shamed by the depth of his feelings he turned his back and took a step away. Behind him, he heard Meaghan draw in a deep breath.

"Okay. Okay, I get it. I see how you felt like you were up against a wall. And maybe it wasn't such a stupid plan, trying to fake her death. But when you realized what she thought—that you meant to murder her . . . Why didn't you level with her?"

"I didn't realize it, Meaghan. Not until after she'd betrayed me did I learn what happened. Not until she'd cursed me and I became a part of the Book we'd created did I see the truth." When Meaghan frowned with confusion, he said, "The Book knew, you see. It knew what I planned. It knew that I'd found a way to destroy it."

"And it told Elan?"

"No." His smile felt bitter. "It made a deal with her. It promised her the things she wanted most in the world. It sweetened the pot and she grasped it with both hands and never looked back."

"What did it promise?" Meaghan asked, bewildered.

He refused to let Meaghan see how deep it cut, even now, to speak the words. "It promised to free her of her curse. Never again would she see the dead. It promised to save the ones whose names she'd already written in its pages. It promised her great power so that she would never be dependent on a man again. Even Conlaoch would bow to her. And it promised to punish me for the treachery it told her I intended."

Silent, Meaghan waited for him to go on.

"*I* had promised to love and cherish her until the day I died. *I* had sworn to protect her to my last, gasping breath. Perhaps, in time, I could have found a way to stop the dead from coming to her. I had powers of my own. But she had no faith in my word. She cared more for her dead than she did for me, who lived to please her. She saw only what the Book offered, not the man who would have cut out his own fecking heart to keep her safe. She gave me up like that." He snapped his fingers. "Once she'd imprisoned me, the Book took great pleasure in showing me the full extent of her betrayal."

Meaghan shook her head, moving so she could see his face. "I'm sorry."

He wanted to look away but found he could not. Meaghan had strung his emotions out to dry, and now she watched them flap in the wind.

"Do you think she realized?" Meaghan asked. "Do you think she saw her mistake in the end?"

"No. Her voice followed me into the darkness. She said one day she would return to judge me. If she found me worthy, she might release me from my prison."

"Has that day come, Áedán?"

He pinned her with a hostile look. "What do you mean?"

"I mean, her appearing in my dream and then leaving me this comb. Last night, with the pendant and that . . . surge of power. These are signs, aren't they?"

Heart pounding, he watched as she took the comb from her

pocket once more. Her fingers played over the teeth and he felt them strumming the heart he'd long thought dead.

"What is the significance of this comb, Áedán?" she asked. "Why would she leave it?"

He didn't want to answer her. He didn't want to talk about the gift he'd given with his love.

"In my time," he began thickly, and his throat clogged with the depth of his feelings. Appalled, he cleared it and tried again. "When I was a young man, we did not exchange rings to signify a marriage. We gave gifts of the heart. Something that came at a cost."

He took the comb from her, dismayed by the way his hand shook. Slowly he turned it, remembering how he'd toiled, how he'd worried over every carved groove and placed gem. Without a word, he moved behind Meaghan and pulled the rubber band from the tail of her braid.

"What are you—"

"Shhhh," he said and began running the teeth through the silk of her hair as he spoke. "Elan had hair that was like silvered moonlight."

"I know," Meaghan whispered, her voice making a funny hitch that seemed to hook his pulse and send it pounding. "I saw it in the dream."

Elan's hair had been baby soft and as fine as gossamer. Meaghan's was a heavy fall of satin, alive with hues and warmth.

"Your hair is a weave of the rainbow, so many colors all in one. Silken. Beautiful."

For a moment, he lost the train of his thoughts and indulged his senses in the heated weight of Meaghan's hair. He remembered burying his face in its softness, breathing in the scent.

He cleared his throat. "I made this comb for Elan. I smelted the silver, etched the runes. The teeth are whalebone, and it was not easy to come by, not easy to fashion. I can still see myself struggling to make this gift represent everything I felt. When I gave it to her, it was with my heart."

For a moment, Meaghan's silence filled the air. And then in a voice as soft as the locks he held, she said, "And she kept it. Even after she thought you'd betrayed her with another woman and plotted to *kill* her, she kept it. She must have loved you, Áedán."

Love. Did he even believe such a thing existed?

He lowered the comb, reluctantly letting the glossy strands slide through his fingers, wishing the convictions he'd armed himself with for an eternity would slither away with it. But he could not forgive what Elan had done to him.

He handed the comb back to Meaghan as she turned to face him. Her eyes had darkened to midnight pools and her color was high. Glints of pewter mixed in the storm of Meaghan's eyes and said things that were too deep for words. They tore at him, dicing his tattered composure into small, bloody chunks.

"What if she figured out that she was wrong? What if she's sorry, Áedán? Why else would she have given me this comb that symbolized your love?"

"You speak as if she lives."

"No, *you* speak as if she does. You speak to *me* as if I am connected to her. Why, Áedán?"

"You said it yourself. We have history between us."

"That's right. Between us. But *I* am not Elan."

"I know that."

"Do you? Do you, Áedán? Because that's not what I'm getting from you. You said you wouldn't allow me to betray you."

"And I meant it."

"Why would you even think I would? What are you basing that on, Áedán?"

Should he tell her what he'd seen in her eyes? If he trusted her with that information, what might she do with it? He'd be worse than a fool to give her the power to betray him again. But he couldn't explain to himself what he felt when he looked at her. How could he hope to explain it to her? The past, the future, the knotted weave where they twisted together. There was something in it, something he couldn't unravel. If only he could see the truth concealed in the frayed fibers.

Meaghan wanted to find the Book, and he would help her to that end. But Meaghan wanted the Book to go back to her own time. Seeing the comb in her bed this morning had convinced Áedán beyond a doubt that Elan had returned. That meant he had a chance at securing his freedom and exacting the revenge he'd spent millennia imagining.

A blood ritual, which would seal Elan inside the Book and then destroy its power.

It had to be done. As long as the Book still existed, as long as it could toy with the people of Ballyfionúir—or anywhere—Áedán would never be safe. As Cathán became more firmly entrenched in the Book, his power would grow. He would search, would manipulate, would control anyone and everyone until at last he got Áedán in his clutches. Then he would use Meaghan and the key to free himself and enslave Áedán once again. Cathán would find a way to do what every fool who searched for the Book longed for.

He would use it. He would become *all-powerful*. He would control the heavens and earth.

Áedán could not let that happen. He would not go back to that nightmare, even for Meaghan.

The only way to end the reign of Cathán was to end the Book of Fennore. To do that, they would need to recreate the ritual that had sealed Áedán between those hellish covers and then finish it with the final step—the sacrifice.

In every dream of revenge, Áedán had held Elan under his blade and taken not just her blood, but her life.

He'd have to trick Meaghan in order to force Elan to show herself. When Meaghan had held the pendant against Mickey, Elan had emerged. Could bringing the pendant and the Book together do the same thing? And if so, could he really bring himself to take those final steps? Could he spill Meaghan's blood in his quest for vengeance?

He hated the question. He hated the answer.

"What are you thinking, Áedán?" Meaghan asked, moving closer to him, touching his arm with her fingertips.

"I'm thinking of you, Meaghan," he said without meaning to.

Chapter Twenty-one

MEAGHAN stayed still and quiet as Áedán glanced away and then back. His eyes looked very green now, as green as the pastures that stretched out across the island hunkering in the distance. He was, without a doubt, the most beautiful man she'd ever seen. Even now she wanted to touch him. As if hearing her words, he caught her gaze with his and held it.

Meaghan took a deep breath. He said he thought of her, but what, exactly, filled those thoughts? The same mystifying blend of turmoil that constantly simmered within him spiced the air, offering no easy answers.

Taking a deep breath, she decided to change her line of questions and see what else she could learn. "Brion MacGrath, he is—or soon will be—Cathán's father."

Áedán nodded.

"When Brion came to Colleen's today and we heard the voice of the Book of Fennore, I wondered if Brion had come into contact with it. Do you think he has?"

Áedán looked away and a flush crept up his face. "I cannot say. I don't remember much of those moments. I was not myself."

"No. You weren't. I was afraid for you."

This obviously startled him, and for a moment he simply stared at her.

She went on, "If the Book has searched out Brion MacGrath, there has to be a reason."

"You think to apply the rules of logic to something that does not live within its borders. It wants. It takes. It matters not why."

"And yet, it has intelligence. We've seen it. So what does it want with Brion?"

He didn't answer and Meaghan waited, frustrated, caught between fear of pushing too hard and not pushing hard enough. She tried again.

"And you, Áedán? What does it want from you?"

Again, he remained silent, wary. Meaghan let out a pent breath and said, "It did something to you, Áedán—when it spoke to us. It made your eyes change and you . . . you seemed mindless. Like your response had been hardwired into you to answer that commanding voice. You didn't have a choice about it. There was no *you* in your eyes anymore. They looked like black pits. I feared I'd lost you."

He caught his lip with his teeth, avoiding her gaze. His emotions rose like a tempestuous wind, pulling at the debris on every surface until she could no longer discern what comprised its fury. Anger, she knew by its bite. The bitter burn of deceit joined with despair. Resignation. Fear. But she felt hope mingling through it all. Though besieged, it fought for survival.

What did a Druid hope for? What did he fear?

As if hearing the question, he frowned, and now those eyes looked guarded. He felt cornered, she could see it, sense it in the air. Meaghan knew instinctively that if she kept pressing him, he would close up completely.

Softly she said, "I know what it feels like to be so exposed."

He blinked and narrowed his eyes distrustfully. She caught the blast of his disbelief.

Meaghan supposed it was justified. He'd revealed so much of

himself, of who and what he'd been. But she'd shared very little with him. She didn't like talking about herself—not surprising. When people found out about her gift, they generally had two reactions. Either they treated her like a novelty and made her feel like a freak, or they became reserved, doubtful, reticent. She'd become so sensitive that even curiosity, like Kyle had shown, made her self-conscious.

She'd learned over the years to hide her empathic gift—especially from men who couldn't fecking stand the idea that she knew their feelings. But with Áedán, she needed to swallow her fears and show him something of who she was or he'd never trust her.

"Remember when you asked about . . . when Colleen called me odd," she began haltingly.

He nodded, watching her closely.

"Well, it's true. I got so defensive when you brought it up, because I'm not quite . . . normal, I guess you'd say."

"Normal?" he asked, brows lifting.

"I'm empathic, Áedán. I sense the emotions of others. Whether I want to or not." She gave a small laugh, feeling more exposed than she'd ever been in her life. "I wish I could control it, but I can't. For the most part, I consider myself lucky that I can at least discern which feelings are mine and which come from someone else. There are empaths who can't. They feel every emotion like it's their own."

"You've had this gift your entire life?"

She shook her head, surprised that he asked this first. She'd been braced for the usual question—*what do you feel from me?* Without fail, anyone she'd told had always asked that before anything else.

"No. It didn't develop until puberty."

"You don't consider it a gift," he said.

She shrugged. "People lie all the time. They are uncertain, angry, often rude. They look in your face and smile while they wish you'd go jump off a cliff or something. It's hard to feel their honesty and never be shielded from it."

"This is why you've never mated?"

She felt her face flame with embarrassment. She knew what he meant, but the word *mated* brought the memory of doing just that with Áedán too close to the surface.

"I suppose," she said. "I have trust issues."

He smiled then, a full, surprising smile that chased back the chill that had swept through her during her confession. He said, "Perhaps this is why we get on so well."

Did they? Get on well? She usually felt so confused around him she wouldn't have described it that way. But now that he'd spoken the words, she realized the truth in them.

She found herself grinning back. "Perhaps. Does knowing this about me make you . . . ?" *Like me less? Want to run away? Wish you'd never met me?*

"No," he said, as if he was the empath and he'd read her uncertain emotions. He gave a shake of his head and a short laugh that held irony.

"I am somewhat . . . reassured by this," he said softly.

Surprised, Meaghan asked, "How so?"

"You tell me you can sense what is at the heart of me, what I feel."

She nodded.

"And yet you insist that you don't believe me to be evil."

"That's right. I know you're not."

"I have done things—hurt innocent people without conscience. For all the eternity that I have acted like a monster myself, I never thought I'd have another chance to be human again. To be less and to be more. I've never thought I wanted that chance. I've never thought I deserved it."

Until you.

He didn't say it, but he didn't need to. Meaghan felt a weight, which had bowed her shoulders since the first time she'd revealed her empathic ability only to be shunned for it, ease and then lift.

It was crazy to feel so right when everything around them felt so wrong. But as she stared into Áedán's eyes, she realized that she did.

"Was it really *you* doing all those things, Áedán? I don't believe you acted alone. From everything I've learned, from what I saw today, you had no will of your own. That voice spoke and you answered without conscious decision."

He seemed to consider this and she waited for his response. "I would like to believe that is true, but I cannot shirk responsibility. I cannot pretend I am blameless."

"Fair enough," she said.

He hesitated before speaking again. "Cathán knows you have the key," he murmured.

Meaghan frowned, scrambling to shift gears and follow. "The pendant?"

He nodded.

"Does he know what it does? Do *you* know?"

He frowned, pensive, and then said, "Like the Book, the pendant has taken on a life of its own. I cannot say what powers it holds now."

"I know you didn't intend for the Book to become the monster it is, but I just can't figure out how—if you had all this *Druidness* going on—you couldn't have seen where it was headed. Why didn't you know what it was becoming?"

Áedán said, "Last night, you saw Mickey."

"Don't remind me."

"For Elan, visions like that came daily. People she knew and cared about. Strangers she'd never have the chance to meet. Their spirits bombarded her. Tormented her day and night. Elan wanted nothing more than to escape them, but her heart . . ." He swallowed thickly. "Her heart was too open to turn them away. They spoke to her and she listened."

And in his words, in the way those beautiful lips formed them, she glimpsed just how much he'd cared for Elan. How much he'd loved her.

"I wanted to protect her. Shelter her, *shield* her from them. I would have done anything to make them stop. And so, we created the Book. We didn't mean for it to become evil, but we knew at the start that it couldn't be a simple thing. It had to be more than a scroll.

It had to be bound and spelled because it would hold great secrets. It had to be powerful."

"Why? Why powerful?" she asked.

"Because we hoped it would do what Elan could not."

"What do you mean?"

"The Book of Fennore was meant to save the people she saw. What it offered her in the end, we'd created it to do. But the Book became sentient the moment of its birth, and it had other, darker goals. Even if I'd suspected what was in store, I was already too late to stop it. The ball was already in motion. But it was my arrogance that shaped the being inside the Book. *My pride* warped it, made it think it deserved to be more than a tool. My flaws became its strengths. You're right, Meaghan. I should have known. But I was too busy *playing God*. Too blinded by my own sense of greatness."

Warily, she moved closer, feeling the rage and hatred of his emotions, knowing they were directed inward.

"The pendant—the key—was for Elan to lock her secrets away once she'd shared them with this powerful Book we'd created. Only Elan could open the Book. Only Elan could lock it. But the Book did not want to be locked away. It began to incite that which we'd created it to prevent."

"What does that mean?"

"It brought death."

In her head, she heard Kyle speak. *They suspected that she called death to them. . . .*

"And they blamed her," Meaghan said. "You made it to protect her, but it became the reason your people wanted her sacrificed?"

"Yes. When we realized just how dangerous the Book had become, we tried to destroy it, but we could not. In vengeance, it sent out its powerful signal, and it drove the people of the village mad. Blood spilled between friends and family. Husbands turned on wives. Mothers murdered their children."

"And Elan saw it all."

No wonder she'd been desperate enough to grasp it when the

Book offered its deal. She'd sacrificed Áedán to save who knew how many others. What she'd done was unforgivable, and yet . . .

"You think she made the right choice," Áedán said.

Did she? If Meaghan saw everyone she knew the way she'd seen Mickey last night, would she be desperate enough to do anything to stop it?

"No," she said, surprised at the certainty she felt. "I would have sacrificed myself before I made that choice."

"Perhaps," he said softly. "And perhaps you'd choose exactly as she did."

Chapter Twenty-two

ÁEDÁN cursed himself silently. He should never have left the door open to Meaghan's curiosity, shouldn't have given in to his desire to exonerate himself in her eyes. With a plunging feeling, he looked down at the markings creeping up his forearms. They'd almost reached the crook of his elbow. He pictured them inside, shadowing his veins, tainting his blood, marking him as the monster he knew himself to be.

"I suppose it's human nature to doubt," she said. "But I am not Elan. I know my heart. I'll be true to it."

She believed it but he could not.

"It may be human nature, but I am not human."

Meaghan's lips quirked in a grin that mocked his blatant lie. For it seemed each moment on this island made him more human than the last. Each second in her presence transformed him into a man. Just a man, with wants and needs that ruled him.

"Let me know how that works out for you," she said wryly. "I guess I can count on you never making another mistake again."

"You can't count on me at all. Why can't you grasp that simple fact?"

"Because actions speak louder than words, Áedán. And your actions are screaming at me. They tell me you are a good person. They tell me you have a heart. They tell me you can be hurt. They tell me you care."

He gave a bitter laugh and shook his head. "And you believe them, beauty? Do you not see that we are trapped, you and I, in a repeat of a history we have no hope of escaping? Your blood is the only way out of this nightmare."

"My blood?" she repeated, paling.

"Yes."

She cocked her head, considering. But he saw no revulsion on her face when she should have been looking at him with fear and disgust.

"How much blood?" she asked after a moment.

Flummoxed, he said, "How much . . . Does it matter?"

"It might. A pint or two I could live without if it meant saving our fecking arses."

He stared at her, uncomprehending. He'd expected anger, outrage, hurt that he'd even voiced the horrible reality. Instead she wanted to calculate quantities. He could not bring himself to tell her that the amount of blood he'd need could not be spared.

"Cathán is a mindless beast of power, rage, and endless hunger," he said. "Combine that with the entity I gave breath to, and you have something that is malevolent beyond belief."

"I've heard the legends say the same thing about you."

He blanched but nodded. For centuries he'd preyed on the greedy, on the needy. He'd offered them exactly what they wanted but gave them nothing of what they needed. It didn't matter that the Book of Fennore and its wants played the leading role in his actions. He'd taken everything and repaid nothing. And he'd felt justified in it. He'd felt vindicated. He hadn't cared if they were innocent or not. He had been innocent once. He had known a love so strong it drove him to his destruction. Why should he worry about the mortals who heard his call and craved his touch?

But now he was mortal once more, and with each sweet breath he took in, the desire to stay that way consumed him and repelled him.

"I will not go back to what I was," he said.

"I don't want you to."

He turned on her, taking her shoulders between his hands. "You don't understand. For the ritual to work, someone must die. Unless you know a volunteer, that someone must be me. Or you."

She heard him. She even understood him. But he could see that she would not accept his words as truth.

"I won't believe those are my only choices. Áedán, you were once the most powerful Druid ever known. You still have power and not just because of the Book. I believe in you. I think you'll figure it out."

"Figure it out?" he said, and he'd meant it to sound derisive. But instead a note of longing crept in. *She believed. . . .*

As if hearing his thoughts, she repeated it. "I believe in *you*, Áedán. If you need to spill my blood to end it all, then so be it. I'll trust you to take care of me."

"Why?" he said as inside something burst in his heart.

She placed a hand over his chest, as if to capture the wounded organ in her hand. "I feel what's here. I can feel it now. Hope, fear, longing. But I don't feel deceit. You will do the right thing, Áedán. I know it. I have faith in you."

Humbled, astonished, *grateful*, he could only gaze at her. But he knew how futile her faith was.

"Your faith is misplaced, beauty," he said harshly, each word a razor that left him bloody and in pieces.

Chapter Twenty-three

MEAGHAN heard his words, but what she saw, what she felt spoke stronger. She stared into the swirling hope of green and the flickering strength of gold, tasted the emotions coating the space between them, thick and honeyed.

"Do not think me more than I am," he said.

But what she felt radiating off him was somehow purer, richer than anything she'd felt before. Like a flower to the sun, she turned to it, opened herself to him.

"I won't, then," she murmured. The tone of her voice made him stiffen, the contradiction of her meaning to his, made him scowl. She didn't need to spell out that it didn't matter what denials he made, she would believe in her heart. She would believe in his.

She didn't say it, though. Words had little importance when it came to communicating with this man. He didn't trust them. He didn't trust himself. But she could make him feel, and right now she wanted that more than anything.

Without stopping to question the wisdom of her actions, Meaghan took his hand and led him to the place below deck where he slept. The small cabin was spotlessly clean and smelled faintly of bleach. The bed tucked into the nose of the boat was big enough for Áedán and neatly made. The window above it opened to the fresh salt air.

A palace compared to the storage closet.

With a doomed sense that things were coming to a head, that the Book was churning Ballyfionúir into a crazed and violent beast, that this might be the only chance she had to be with this man who touched her heart, who seemed to have been hers for an eternity and, at the same time, for only a few hours, Meaghan pressed her body to his.

She felt Áedán stiffen, knew some part of him wanted to resist her, but she refused to allow it. The air swirled with his confusion, his desire, and his struggle. As usual, Áedán was in conflict with himself. He wanted her as much as she wanted him, but he didn't know how to let go of his fears and misgivings and succumb to his yearning.

"What do you want from me?" he groaned, his fingers clenching against her hips, his face dipping to the crook of her shoulder and neck.

"Everything," she said simply. She took his face in her hands and forced him to look into her eyes. "I want it all."

He made a sound in his throat, and then his strong arms circled her, pulling her against the hard lines of his body, making her feel every inch of his desperation to have her.

He kissed her, stealing her breath along with her desire to breathe. She kissed him back, showing him how completely she yielded. Áedán's hands trailed over her back, down to the curve of her hip. He held her tighter, moving against her body.

With care and attention, he worked his way from her lips to her cheek to the curve of her throat, the swell of her breasts. Each brush of his lips, each stroke of his tongue brought another wave of emotion, each stronger, surer, fiercer than the last. Meaghan felt adrift in the chaos and grounded in her certainty that this was where she belonged, in Áedán's arms.

Dropping to his knees in the swaying boat, Áedán spread his hands over her hips, pressed his face into the soft dip of her belly, then he tugged Meaghan down to kneel in front of him. He touched her face, turning it up to his. For a moment, the two gazed at one another, and Meaghan felt the love, the longing well up inside her own chest and caught her breath, overwhelmed by the power of it.

Love? Was that what she felt for this complex man?

"Damn you, beauty," he groaned. "You make me want to be a man once more." He searched her face with a look of such hurt and surprise that it wounded her. She didn't know what he saw in her eyes. Her feelings felt too new and raw to expose them. But after a long, still moment, he said, "I cannot believe I've been given another chance."

Whether he meant at life or at love, she couldn't guess, but now his eyes had grown hot and possessive, and she couldn't think past the moment.

Heat pooled low inside Meaghan, and it felt like a drug, towing her into a warm place that flowed with sensuality and promise. Áedán was big and powerful, his body itself an aphrodisiac she seemed all too susceptible to. His scent, his taste, every inch of him teased her senses and made her want to take until she could take no more. Give until she was empty inside.

Áedán's warm hands cupped her face, the pads of his long fingers gentle against her throat. The caress burned a trail down to her heart.

Meaghan's hand shook as she settled it against the rough stubble on Áedán's face, returning the fierce look that smoldered in them both, melting them together. She breathed in his intoxicating scent, stared into eyes like the forest, dark and enigmatic, beautiful and captivating. Her lips softened under his gaze, and her body ached for his touch. She might have some mysterious connection to Elan—admitted even to herself that it existed deep within her—but Elan did not define Meaghan.

This moment, however, might change her forever. She held nothing back.

She felt the brief burst of heat against her skin as Áedán exhaled a deep breath. And then he was leaning down and she moved forward, into his arms, into his kiss. His mouth found hers, parted her lips so he could taste her and she, him. The kiss was like a draught of dark wine, heady and sweet, embodied with mystery and redolent with the dregs of tragedy. The velvety softness of his tongue sent a shiver through her, made her want to wrap her entire body around him, hold him to her, within her. His kiss tasted like spice and wine, wild and male. Erotic, enticing and corporeal.

Their clothes suddenly felt too heavy, too hot. She pulled at his shirt and then fumbled with his pants, forcing him to break the kiss while he tugged them off and tossed them on the floor. Finally, his body was naked and gleaming, muscles hard and strong over long bones. His chest was the toasted brown of earth and sun, polished angles and hot skin. Hard, slabbed muscle that had been hewn by hours beneath the open sky, working with his hands aboard the ship, stretched taut over every inch of him. Last night it had been too dark to admire him, but now, in the light of day, he took her breath away.

He was beauty, covered with sun-kissed flesh.

She made a small sound in her throat and leaned forward again, pressing her open mouth to his skin, savoring the salty heat of him. His taste was an addiction she couldn't get enough of. His hands tugged at her clothes, and she let him pull them off and discard them next to his own. For a moment, he froze, staring at her naked body like it was sacred. In that breath of time, her heart seized within her chest and she wanted to cry out at the fates that had hurt him for so long. Then his hands were warm on her skin, the rough pads trailing her throat, gentling over the bones of her shoulders and chest, then down to her breasts, where he cupped the soft weight in his palms. The sound that came from his throat ignited a flame within her, and she arched into him, needing more. Needing everything she'd thought never to have.

His hands moved again, skimming over her ribs, around to the slope of her spine, his fingers playing a haunting melody of desire against the small bones they caressed. He followed the curve of her hip to her thighs and hefted her up so she straddled him as he knelt on the floor. The shock of his bare chest against hers traveled like wildfire through her, burning away any other thought.

He captured her mouth once more, pouring his heart into the kiss. She felt each sensation, the stroke of his tongue, the soft warmth of his lips, the heady seduction of his need. She let her hands stroke the smooth heat of his shoulders as she gripped him with her thighs, flexing against the rigid length of him. Inside she felt like melted wax. Fluid, pliable, molten.

His touch was so gentle, so reverent, and yet there was possessiveness in every stroke. Demand in each brush.

"Come here," he said, pulling them both to their feet and then to the bed. She lay on her back, watching as he covered her with his body. Each point of contact made her burn and shiver at once.

He murmured her name as he found the sensitive skin between her neck and shoulder, the crook of her elbow, the softness of her belly. She sank her fingers deep in his black hair, feeling the strands slip through her fingers. His large hands pushed her legs apart as he moved lower, tongue tracing the rounded bone of her hips, the long muscle of her thigh, then hot against her, pulling all of her senses down to that point where his tongue circled and rubbed, his lips nipped and tugged.

Her entire body became a bow pulled by his strength. She was a thing of sensation, tuned only to the flicking suction of his mouth, the brush of his long fingers as he circled and spread, baring her to his touch.

Nothing she'd shared in the few serious relationships she'd had in the past came close to the intimacy of this moment and the touch of this man. But her body responded, knowing what it wanted even as she reeled with the shock of the sensations he ignited. Áedán seemed to understand exactly what she desired, and now a coil of need twisted within her, nocking her like an arrow poised to fly. Áedán bit down, so softly, so gently—his teeth an abrasion that rocketed through her body—and then his tongue followed, pulling everything back to that point of origin until the waves of tension released like floodwaters and crashed around her.

She cried out as Áedán moved up, cloaking her with his body, bracing his arms on either side of her head as he cradled her skull with his hands. For a moment, he stared deeply into her eyes, and then he pressed his mouth to hers, and she tasted herself on his lips, tasted Áedán in the heady mixture, felt the heavy weight of his arousal against her belly.

She lost herself in the forest of his eyes as he moved, dropping his hips between her legs, easing himself into her with slow and deliberate strokes, his muscles bunched with tension, his skin puckered as he fought the desire that darkened his eyes and beaded his skin. She felt something within her give, pool like an underground well finding the surface. Inch by inch, he filled her until she felt there was room for nothing else, and still he pressed forward until at last his hips met hers.

"Meaghan." His voice was rough and husky. He said nothing but her name, yet she felt the question within it.

She could not find her own words, so she answered with her body, rocking against him, pulling his head down so she could press her mouth to his. With a sound that came deep from within him and reverberated through her body, he began to move, still slow, still gentle. But the tide inside them ebbed and flowed, rising higher and crashing fiercely around them. He became the earth and sun, the moon, the wind, the breath of life, and Meaghan knew only that she wanted more. She wanted everything.

Her body flexed instinctively, finding the rhythm he set and matching it. He buried his face against her shoulder, mouth hot as he murmured her name with words of love that washed through her. His breath quickened and the pulsing beat of his body against hers sped with her heart. He kissed her again, deep and intoxicating, and she felt the rush of pleasure and pain that came with release. An instant later, his arms clenched her tight as he careened over the same erotic edge.

In the quiet that followed, he pressed his lips to hers and murmured words she didn't understand in a language she thought more ancient than the soul she saw staring out from his eyes.

Love is often a violent and doomed thing, he'd told her once.

But she refused to believe that, no matter the soft wind of foreboding whispering across her skin.

Chapter Twenty-four

For a long while afterwards, they lay in silence, Meaghan tucked up against Áedán's side. The steady rise and fall of his chest beneath her cheek brought comfort, but at last Meaghan had to break it. The closer she got to this man, the more desperate for a future she became. She hadn't yet spoken those words, but she would not belittle it and call it less than love. He consumed her thoughts, he possessed her heart. Denying it would change nothing.

"Áedán, I've been thinking," she said.

"No good can come of that," he answered, his deep voice rumbling against her ear.

"We can't do this on our own," she went on, wishing she didn't have to bring the note of seriousness into this quiet, warm moment. But the cold light of reality would not be doused, and the sooner they found a way out of the maze that trapped them, the better. "I think we should go back to the lighthouse. We need help and they've offered it."

Áedán shifted so he could look into her face. What he saw there hardened the golden flecks in his eyes, turning them a dusky bronze. He pulled away and stood.

"Áedán," she said.

He shook his head, giving Meaghan a quick glance of absolute disbelief, as if she'd suggested they beseech Satan for assistance instead of the three men who'd come from the same nightmare they had. She felt as if she'd been pressed through Colleen's washbasin's wringer.

"You ask too much," Áedán grumbled as he pulled on his pants and fastened them.

Perhaps she did. But it was the only way she could see out of this mess. Allowing either one of them to be the sacrificial lamb to the Book of Fennore wasn't on her list of options.

"They know about the Book. Kyle knows the legends—"

"*Kyle.* I do not trust Kyle Mahon."

"I know, Áedán. But you don't really trust anyone, do you?"

He looked at her sharply, his eyes the color of fall, his gaze lingering on her bare breasts and becoming the heat of summer. "I trust you."

His words felt like rain on a parched desert. Despite their dire circumstances, they soothed and fortified.

After a moment, she said solemnly, "Then I need you to trust me on this, Áedán. You said that your arrogance kept you from seeking help once long ago when you needed it. It changed everything for you and the woman you loved. Don't make that mistake again."

His mouth tightened at that, but he gave her a grudging nod, and reluctantly he agreed to go with her to the lighthouse. Without another word, he moved above deck, brought *The Angel* around, and headed back to port. After she dressed, Meaghan came up to watch him, feeling like she'd never get tired of seeing the grace of his movements, the power of his body. He caught her staring and gave her a knowing look, the smile that quirked his lips smug, the heat in his eyes possessive. She'd always considered herself a modern woman, but she didn't mind the ownership she saw in his silent perusal. She didn't mind because she knew the same look glimmered in her own eyes.

Less than an hour later, they'd brought *The Angel* to port and once again had their feet on dry land. Another storm had trailed the sun across the sky and now hovered dark and tumultuous above them as they trekked across the rocky terrain toward the lighthouse. Rumbling warnings and sharp blades of lightning urged them to move faster. Áedán said nothing as he eyed the churning banks of clouds, but Meaghan could feel his misgivings moving in the damp, electric air.

At last they crested the rise over the cliffs of Fennore and stood looking down at the lighthouse braced like a lone sentry against a battalion of wind and sea.

They rang the seaman's bell and Jamie opened the door without a flicker of surprise, making her wonder if somehow he'd expected them. The idea of it made her shiver with that same menacing chill that had taunted her earlier. She hoped she was right in trusting these men.

Silently Jamie led the way upstairs to the round room where they'd met the first time. "I'm making sandwiches. Hungry?" he asked when they stood awkwardly beside the big wood table.

"Sandwiches?" Áedán repeated with a shocked expression. Meaghan felt the bite of his suspicion. Did he think Jamie intended to poison them?

"I'm starving and we'd love a sandwich, thank you," she said when Jamie paused and eyed Áedán with equal distrust.

The tense moment stretched for a beat, and then with a grunt, Jamie moved to the kitchen.

"Can I help?" Meaghan asked.

"Naw. Sit down. I'll be with you in a minute," he said gruffly.

Jamie went into the kitchen while Meaghan and Áedán took seats and waited. Áedán surveyed his surroundings as if he expected wraiths to materialize in the shadows of the lighthouse, but he said nothing.

"You know what I miss?" Jamie said awhile later as he approached the table with three plates in his hands. "Skippy Super Chunk peanut butter."

Meaghan smiled. Áedán did not.

"My mom used to make us a peanut butter sandwich every day.

We couldn't afford anything else. I got so I couldn't even stand the smell. And now that's all I want. Fucking Skippy peanut butter. I asked for it at the market, and they looked at me like I'd asked for minced baby pie."

"Where are the others?" Áedán interrupted, impatient with small talk.

Jamie seemed mildly amused by Áedán's agitation and answered without rancor. "Eamonn's lurking around with his Chihuahua looking for a squeak toy or some shit."

Jamie's joke was lost on Áedán, but Meaghan bit back a smirk.

He returned to the kitchen for a pitcher of iced tea and glasses. After he'd poured, he took a seat, gave Meaghan a wink, and started on his sandwich. Meaghan took a bite of hers, found she hadn't been lying about being starved, and ate with gusto. From the corner of her eyes, she watched Áedán sample his sandwich and chew with obvious—reluctant—enjoyment.

Jamie swallowed a huge bite and said, "I don't know where Kyle is," picking up on the conversation as if there hadn't been a pause. "He went somewhere last night and didn't get back until late, and then this morning, he was up and gone before the sun rose."

"Is that normal for him?" Áedán asked.

"He's an early riser. Likes to commune with nature and God in the quiet hours. I get that. I like to run before the world starts to stir. But he's got a bug up his ass about something. Didn't say more than three words yesterday and two of those were *fuck off*."

"Kyle?" Meaghan exclaimed with disbelief. She couldn't picture the soft-spoken man speaking that way. "Was something wrong?"

Jamie shrugged. "PMS maybe."

"What is it, PMS?" Áedán asked her.

"A joke. He means Kyle has been moody." To Jamie, she said, "Kyle came to see me last night. He wanted to talk about the Book."

"Kyle thinks your man here has more than a few secrets he's not sharing."

"Why?" Áedán asked, surprising him.

"None of us saw you before—in the world of Fennore. That's one. But there's more than that. There's something about you that the both of us feel. Can't put a label on it, but it's there. Kyle thinks you're the Druid."

Jamie said it casually, but his eyes were laser sharp as they watched Áedán's reaction.

Áedán looked at Meaghan for a long, considering moment, and then before she could anticipate what he was about to do, he pushed back his sleeve and showed Jamie the marking on his arm.

"I am the Druid."

Meaghan nearly choked on her sandwich. She'd talked Áedán into coming, but she hadn't expected that he would give up his secrets so easily and so completely.

"Thought as much. Mind telling me what you're doing here?" Jamie answered calmly.

"I believe I am here for Meaghan."

This caught both Jamie and Meaghan by surprise. Meaghan had begun to believe it herself, but she'd never thought Áedán would confess such a thing, especially to Jamie. And what did it mean, his being there for her? To exact his revenge? Or to finally right the wrongs of the past?

Jamie said, "There was a prophecy that I was told before we got out of the Book's twisted world. It said that one day the Druid would walk the earth and bring havoc to all who lived here."

"And did this prophecy mention Cathán?" Áedán asked softly.

"Not that I know of."

At that moment, Eamonn came in the room with his wolf at his side and stopped at the sight of Áedán and Meaghan sitting at the table, eating sandwiches with Jamie.

"There's ham in the kitchen," Jamie offered, as if this were a casual conversation that didn't concern Druids and unspeakable consequences.

Eamonn moved to the bench where he'd sat the day before, muttering, "Not hungry," under his breath.

Áedán gave Eamonn a long, considering glance and then turned back to the fierce black man who watched him with equal attention. "I believe the prophecy you speak of has come to pass, but like any prophecy, it only tells of one possible outcome. No one could have predicted the twist of fate that has brought us to this point. Even I could not have guessed the chaos Cathán would bring. He is here, now. He is moving among us."

"I've felt the bastard," Jamie said with a wary nod.

"I have felt him as well. He is stronger than I ever was. He is more powerful than I had ever dreamed. And he is not satisfied with jumping from victim to victim. He wants total control."

"Over?"

"Everything. Everyone."

"Can he get it?"

Jamie hid his fear well, but Meaghan saw the telltale signs that revealed his agitation. His fingers drummed the table, his jaw clenched and unclenched.

"I believe so," Áedán answered darkly. "This morning at the Ballaghs' house, I felt him in my head. It was like a homing signal. I couldn't do anything but respond. When I came to myself again, I saw this on my arm. Each moment since, it has grown in size and darkened. Eventually it might cover my entire being. I cannot know what will happen to me then. All I do know is that Cathán did this to *me.* What he could do to someone . . . *normal* is inconceivable."

Jamie cursed under his breath. Eamonn made a noise in his throat that sounded suspiciously like a growl.

"I heard his voice, too," Meaghan said. "It came from a place so deep inside my brain that it was hard to distinguish it from my own thoughts. When he called Áedán—it was terrifying."

"If Meaghan had not been there with me, I would have followed his bidding. She kept me from going to him."

Jamie eyed her. "That true?"

"Yes."

"What about this business with Mickey Ballagh? Folks are saying Áedán killed him."

"It was not me. It was Hoyt O'Shea."

"Hoyt?" Meaghan exclaimed. "How do you know? Why didn't you say anything?"

"I didn't know until I saw him this morning. Last night I followed Mickey to the Pier House, and I sensed the power of the Book in the room, but I could not pinpoint the source. I felt that it had found a new victim, but I couldn't be certain. Then today I saw Hoyt. I saw *it*."

"In his eyes," Jamie said. "He had Cathán's eyes."

Áedán gave one nod.

"But why kill Mickey?" Eamonn asked, speaking for the first time. "What has he to do with this mess?"

"Hoyt never liked Mickey," Áedán answered. "I suspect he was jealous of what he felt was the good fortune that Mickey had. Mickey's wife is lovely and sweet while Hoyt's is a slovenly shrew. Mickey stumbled over me like a gift from the fairies and got me to work for him for nothing. Hoyt struggles each day to fill his nets."

Áedán paused and they waited in silence for him to continue.

"When a man—or woman—comes to the Book of Fennore, they come pleading their case. My guess is that Hoyt asked for power over Mickey. Cathán gave it."

"To what end?" Jamie demanded.

"To eliminate me. If I am rotting in prison for the crime of murder, Cathán will find me and . . ."

"And?" Meaghan breathed.

"And I would be at his mercy—you saw what he did when he summoned me this morning. Without you there, I would be his slave."

"Fuck," Jamie muttered.

Áedán went on. "The prophecy did not tell you that the Book is a being as well as a vessel. When I was imprisoned by it, our power worked in tandem. Each time I took from my victims, we shared the spoils. The entity is in some ways the soul of the Book, and it wants what I wanted, what Cathán wants—to be free of its bindings. But the entity of the Book cannot simply leave it. If it could, it would have done so eons ago. The Book must take a prisoner and work through him. Once I was that prisoner. I was its hostage. For millennia I was alone there. I ceased to think of myself as separate from the Book. I began to consider its strength, my strength. I thought myself indivisible and invincible."

"Godlike," Jamie said.

"In every way," Áedán admitted and Meaghan saw a dark flush creep up his neck. "I forgot what it meant to be human, to be a man."

With these words, his gaze lingered on Meaghan, and she felt the heat of it warming the cold places that tried to settle inside her.

"When Cathán was sucked into the Book of Fennore with me, he became a disease that wiped out everything that was mine. His presence released me from my chains and then . . . then I was . . . ejected."

"By Cathán," Jamie said slowly, as if processing everything Áedán said in small, digestible chunks.

"No." Áedán looked at Meaghan. "By you," he said softly. "You did not leave me there when you escaped."

Jamie mumbled something under his breath, as if he were remembering the world of Fennore and understood Áedán's words. Meaghan thought back. Áedán had been unconscious in the chaos of those final moments. She hadn't known at the time who or what he was. She'd known only that he had helped her and she had to help him. She couldn't leave him in that nightmare. And so when she'd felt herself being pried free and thrown out of it—ejected, as he said—she'd gathered his unconscious form to her and . . . taken him with her.

Now, she stared into his eyes and felt a swirl of gratitude mixed with a surge of fear coming from him—not fear of her, but fear *for* her. He was worried that in saving him, she had condemned herself.

"You said you got here a week before her," Eamonn accused.

"And that's true. But when speaking of the Book of Fennore and all it encompasses, time is rarely linear. Your presence here is statement to that."

Jamie made a sound that managed to convey anger, confusion, and frustration all at once. It spoke more clearly than words.

Áedán went on. "The point is that I could not have escaped—aided or otherwise—if Cathán had not been there to take my place. Make no mistake about it: The Book of Fennore is not an object. It lives and breathes and it *wants*. It requires its slave. It demands total submission. Cathán did not realize this, I think, until it was too late. Now he knows. During the time we shared that world, he and I . . . brushed against each other's consciousness. He learned from me and I learned from him. I saw the black pit of his soulless being, and he saw the pit of mine. He believes I have the knowledge he needs to escape."

"Do you?" Jamie demanded.

"No."

A weighted pause followed and each of them absorbed that response and what it meant.

"So we're screwed?" Jamie asked.

Now the wash of Áedán's emotions tasted bitter and anguished. They hit Meaghan with the force of the tide and pulled her into his despair.

"I wish I had killed the bastard the first day I saw him," Eamonn interrupted in a voice so deep and harsh it sounded kin to the low growl of his wolf. "Because of him, I lost everything. My mother. My father. My brothers and sister. My *life*. He came to us from the future, and every single day I go out and search for him, thinking I might find the man he was before . . . before the Book. Before the bloodshed. I will keep looking until I hold him beneath my blade. And then I will slaughter him like he slaughtered so many of my own. I will prevent him from ever finding the Book."

"You can't change the past," Jamie said angrily.

"Yes, you can. We do it now without even trying," Áedán answered. "However, it is a dangerous game."

"I don't care," Eamonn said. "I *will* find him."

"Well, you'll have a long wait, Eamonn," Meaghan said calmly. "Cathán hasn't even been born yet."

All eyes turned to her, and Meaghan felt the crash of shock raining down on her.

"How do you know that?" Jamie asked.

"Brion MacGrath is his father," Áedán answered softly.

"And Marga is his wife," Meaghan finished. "His *pregnant* wife. She's due in a few months."

Eamonn stood so suddenly his wolf startled and turned on him with a snarl. When the beast realized only his master stood behind him, the lips uncurled and the fur smoothed, but the animal still looked wild and vicious. Like Meaghan, the animal felt his fury.

Eamonn said something in a language Meaghan did not understand, and Áedán answered him in the same tongue. The words sounded urgent. Angry. Then, without explanation, Eamonn and his wolf stalked from the room. They heard his footsteps on the stairs, and then the front door slammed shut.

"What was that about?" Jamie asked.

"Eamonn has never known peace," Áedán said. "Not from within or from without."

Meaghan narrowed her eyes. It was a nonanswer, a talent Áedán wielded with great skill. She'd grown used to the avoidance tactics, but Jamie wasn't having any of it.

"What did you say to him?"

"I told him trying to change history could bring disasters worse than those we have endured. He did not agree."

Before Jamie could question Áedán further, the door slammed once more and rapid steps flew up the stairway. Kyle burst into the room out of breath and red-faced.

"Get away from her," he said in a low, angry voice.

Áedán, Jamie, and Meaghan all stared at Kyle in surprise. His rage gave him a wild-eyed appearance that reminded her of the flat glitter she'd seen in Cathán's cold gaze. But there was nothing cold about Kyle. He looked like an inferno ready to incinerate anything in its path.

"Kyle, what—"

"Get away from him, Meaghan. He's not who he says."

"I know who he is."

"Do you know *what* he is?"

"He said he's the Druid, Kyle," Jamie answered, obviously taken aback by the passion and wrath he read in his friend. "I think we need him if we're going—"

"Need him?" Kyle repeated, spinning to face Jamie. "*Need* him? Did he tell you he killed Mickey Ballagh last night? In cold blood?"

"No, you're wrong—" Meaghan said, but once more, Kyle cut her off.

"I *saw* him do it. I saw him stab Mickey to death. Without provocation. Without remorse. And then he came after me."

Stunned, Meaghan tried to grasp what he said. He was wrong. Of course he was wrong.

She said, "Áedán was with me last night."

"I saw him leave the Pier House," Kyle went on. "I was worried for you, Meaghan, so I followed him. He waited for Mickey in the shadows and then he killed him. He stabbed him until he was nothing more than a bloody hunk of flesh."

"No," Meaghan insisted. "He was with me."

"After he killed Mickey, Meaghan," Kyle insisted. "He came to you after."

She shook her head, but Kyle looked so certain. So intense.

"I followed him to your door," he finished in a low, certain voice.

Áedán was watching her, and when she jerked her gaze from the space between them to meet his eyes, he saw the doubt that she didn't want to feel but couldn't seem to hold back. It crowded in for a fleeting second, but that's all it took. She felt his awareness of it in the wash of cold that iced his emotions. Suddenly he stood and took a step away from her.

"You thought you could get away with it," Kyle said. "But I see what you are. You were evil when you were trapped in the Book, and you are evil now. Evil to the core. She's too good to see it in you, but I see. I know what you are."

"Son of a bitch," Jamie said under his breath. He stood as well and moved to box in Áedán between them.

"You're wrong," Meaghan said, but Áedán took another step back.

She felt she stood at the epicenter of a giant quake that had yet to do more than rumble beneath the surface. Soon it would begin to rattle the foundations of everything she knew, everything she loved.

Áedán's eyes looked like a glacial pond, filled with pale greens and frozen gold beneath a layer of grime. Jamie reached out and Áedán spun around, backing to the stairs as Kyle and Jamie closed in. Kyle lunged and grabbed at the same time that Jamie charged and struck. Meaghan felt a pull of energy swirl through the room, knew it was Áedán gathering power from the air, from the rumbling storm that hovered around the lighthouse, from her. And then he fired it back with a string of words that sounded more ancient than the pyramids and more lethal than gunfire.

Jamie and Kyle both flew across the room, knocked off their feet by the blast. Meaghan felt a hot wind whisk against her skin. It lifted her hair and blew it away from her face. Dry and blistering, it singed her eyes and made her close them in defense.

When she opened them again, Áedán was gone.

Chapter Twenty-five

KYLE didn't want Meaghan to leave the lighthouse after Áedán vanished, but she refused to stay hidden like some cursed fairy-tale princess in a round tower. Kyle's impassioned accusations had shaken her, had made her doubt for just an instant, but almost at once, she'd realized how foolish her misgivings about Áedán had been. She didn't know what Kyle had seen or thought he'd seen, but she did know she trusted Áedán. She needed to find him.

Even if Kyle had told the truth and Áedán *had* killed Mickey, he hadn't done it in cold blood no matter how it had appeared to Kyle. Meaghan knew this in her soul, and she berated herself for letting Kyle's accusation spin her into doubt. Whether Hoyt or Áedán had ended Mickey's life, the fundamental fact remained that she *knew* Áedán, and he was not evil.

And if Áedán had lied about the killing . . . well, look where the truth had gotten him so far in his life. He was the Druid Brandubh. He had enough baggage for ten people. Her uncertainties had only confirmed his fears that history was repeating itself. His fear that Meaghan, like Elan, would have too little faith in him to see them through.

Dejected, Meaghan left the lighthouse as Jamie and Kyle argued over what they should do next. She hurried to the docks, thinking Áedán would return to *The Angel.* The storm overhead churned with a gusting wind that bit to the bone.

As she crested the last rise that led down to the docks, Meaghan paused. The harbor below swarmed with people moving to and fro. The Pier House doors stood open and overflowing. She knew the murder of Mickey Ballagh had stirred up the small town, but it looked like every soul who lived there had ventured out beneath the brooding storm. Slowly she approached, feeling like an alien in a world that no longer made sense. People turned and watched her with hard eyes that glittered flatly. *Cathán's eyes,* she thought with panic, but it seemed that everyone had them, and the sheer impossibility of that made her certain she must be wrong.

She veered away from the masses to the dock where *The Angel* berthed.

"Áedán," she called, climbing aboard. But the ship was still, the door to the cabin shut. She peered in, seeing the rumpled sheets, remembering how it had felt to lie there in his arms. Frustrated she turned back and almost ran smack into Jamie. The black man stood in shadow, the storm above giving his skin a greenish tint. He must have followed her when she left the lighthouse without her realizing.

"Jamie, you startled me. I didn't hear—"

Before she could finish, the boat swayed, the shadows shifted, and a glimpse of his face silenced her.

A long, bloody gash extended from his forehead to his brow, gaping and oozing as if his skull had been pounded until it cracked open. His right eye was shot with blood, sightless. The other shifted wildly back and forth. Deep cuts and bloody abrasions covered the skin of his face and throat. One arm hung at an awkward angle from his shoulder to flop uselessly at his side. She could see bone shards poking from the ripped and ghastly skin of the other. He tried to take a step forward, but his legs gave and he crumpled in front of her.

Meaghan screamed as his body hit the deck with a sickly splattering sound, and she fell back against the cabin door, trying to think past the terror and panic that shot through her blood.

In the next instant, he disappeared.

For a moment, she could only stare at the spot on the floor where he'd fallen, hiccupping with hysterics and an insane need to laugh and cry at the same time. Then she stumbled forward, foolishly taking a wide step over his nonexistent form before she raced across the deck and off the boat. Once her feet hit solid ground, she turned, backing away, still expecting Jamie to lurch over the railing like a zombie in a movie.

A man disembarked from a small fishing boat a few slips down and caught her eye. She didn't know his name, but it didn't matter because as she turned to face him, she saw the front of his shirt dripped red, and a blackened stain spread from a fist-sized hole in his chest. He reached a bloody hand out to her. Stifling her scream, she turned and saw that beyond him, others staggered toward her, reaching out, beseeching with glazed eyes.

She struggled to catch her breath, heard a wheezing sound and knew it came from her constricted chest and overinflated lungs. In another moment, she'd be hyperventilating or simply suffocating as her fear tightened like a noose around her throat. It took extreme effort to move her head and scan the bustle she'd mistaken for busy, gossiping people.

Now she saw the truth. They were dead. Every last one of them.

She heard Áedán's voice, dark and smoky. *It began to incite that which we'd created it to prevent.*

"God no," she breathed.

Meaghan ran.

Her feet flew over the uneven terrain as she raced away from the docks toward her grandmother's house. Her heart beat so fast it hurt, and her lungs burned, but she didn't slow. She could feel *them* behind her, following, begging for something she couldn't give. She stumbled but managed to stay on her feet as her terror closed tight around her. She wanted to look over her shoulder but was too afraid until at last Colleen's house was in sight. Only then did she glance back.

The dirt road behind her was empty. No one chased her; no corpses lurked in the gray green dusk. Nothing but the sour tang of her own fear hung in the air.

"Feck," she breathed, bending over and bracing her hands on her knees. She pulled in deep, painful breaths as she tried to slow her racing pulse. What the hell had just happened? It had seemed like the whole town had been stumbling after her with that disjointed gait of the dead.

Overhead a great clap of thunder reverberated, and with it came the echoing memory of Áedán's words.

It drove the people of the village mad. Blood spilled between friends and family. Husbands turned on wives. Mothers murdered their children.

Was the Book doing that now? And was Meaghan, like Elan before her, destined to be the witness who could not change it?

Shaking, Meaghan went to Colleen's, stopping before she entered to put the pendant in her hiding place to keep it safe until they needed to use it. By the time she opened the back door, her breathing had returned to normal, but her heart still pounded with fear and the need to *do* something. Where was Áedán? How would she cope if the next specter she saw belonged to him?

She refused to consider it.

The house was still and quiet when Meaghan moved through the kitchen, and only the uncanny silence and the lingering scent of despair waited in the air of the front room. Worried about her grandmother and the baby, she hurried upstairs, praying she'd find them sleeping peacefully. When she opened the bedroom door, she saw that both the crib and Colleen's bed were empty.

The apprehension that had settled around her bones now sliced into the heart of her with the speed of a lightning strike.

"Colleen?" she called out, knowing it was pointless. No one was home. But she couldn't help herself. "Nana?"

She didn't hear an answer. The shadows seemed to crowd in with glee at her anxiety while the thunder added a dramatic boom that shook the windows. For a moment, Meaghan didn't know what to do. She hurried back to the kitchen, looking for a note and finding none. Trying to quell her unease, she went out the front door and hesitated on the porch, unsure which way to turn. Where would Colleen go?

And where was Áedán? She felt his absence in the very heart of her. Since she'd opened her eyes here, Áedán had been with her, helping her navigate the treacherous waters of their new reality. Now he'd abandoned her, and she could blame only herself. She needed him. She'd come to rely on his calm strength, on his quiet wisdom. On the way he made her feel alive just by standing near.

The afternoon had taken on a sickly glow as the sun hid behind thick gray clouds and the storm swirled overhead without erupting. A wind blew with a forbidding howl that promised mayhem and disaster.

She went to Enid's and knocked on the front door. Enid answered with a look of surprise.

"Meaghan, what is it?"

"Do you know where Colleen is?"

"You mean she's not home?"

Meaghan shook her head, feeling her stomach plummet.

Enid hurried to reassure her. "I don't know where she would have gone. Perhaps she needed some time alone, away from the house. People kept stopping by. . . ."

It was as good a reason as any, and yet Meaghan couldn't quite believe it. "Thank you, Enid. I'll let you know if I see her."

With a worried nod, Enid closed her door and Meaghan returned to Colleen's, but she didn't go inside. She felt too keyed up and worried about her grandmother to simply wait for her return.

Even if Colleen had wanted to be alone, Meaghan couldn't believe she would have left the house without at least scribbling a note. There was something not right about her being gone—something much deeper than just her absence, and no amount of rationalizing could convince Meaghan's gut otherwise. She knew Colleen would not have headed into the small market where, at this time of day, people would be gathered, talking about the murder. Gossiping about the new widow. But where else would she have gone?

To Brion, perhaps? Maybe to plead Áedán's case?

Pulling her borrowed coat around her, Meaghan headed toward the castle ruins and the house where Brion MacGrath lived, taking the path she'd walked just yesterday with Colleen and Áedán. The road seemed as desolate and barren as it had been the day before, and though no visions of Ballyfionúir's dead residents visited her, she wished for Áedán's company. She needed him. And she knew he needed her.

Where do you go, little witch?

The question boomed in her head and made her stumble. It was not Áedán who spoke, but the voice used the same seductive tone, murmuring *little witch* in a way that made it sound alluring and sexual. The way Áedán said it.

Come to me and I will answer your prayers.

"Go to hell," she shouted at the wind.

She'd barely calmed down from the scare of seeing Jamie and then everyone else . . . now her adrenaline spiked, and Meaghan hurried toward the castle ruins. She was shaking when she reached the place where the path split, one side snaking past the ruins and down to the cliffs that loomed above the cavern. The other trailed lazily to the front door of the house that crouched in the shadow of the desecrated turrets and walls.

She hesitated, unsure which way to go. Logic turned her to the front door of the big house, but instinct urged her toward the ruins. The instinct won, and before she knew it, she was running down the path. She opened her mouth to call Colleen's name as she rounded a blind turn and plowed straight into Marga MacGrath. Knocked breathless, Meaghan staggered back, dazed and confused. Marga let out a shriek and fell on her butt at Meaghan's feet. The billowing maternity top she wore flew up, and Meaghan stared with disbelief at what she saw beneath.

A strange, flesh-colored girdle bulged over Marga MacGrath's torso, listing off to the side where the baby should be. But there wasn't a baby inside it—no, Meaghan could see the stitched fabric, the sphere-shaped object that had been slipped into the pocket of the girdle to make it look like she was pregnant.

Marga yanked her maternity top down to cover the fake belly and glared at Meaghan with a combination of rage and horror. Even after it was hidden again, Meaghan found she couldn't tear her gaze from the swollen abdomen as her brain struggled to understand what she'd just seen. Then slowly Meaghan raised her eyes and stared at Brion MacGrath's wife. In her head, she heard Brion's desperate voice whispering to Colleen, *The child cannot be mine. . . .*

A burst of air escaped her in a strangled laugh. Well, he had that right. The child was not his or anyone else's for that matter. Marga wasn't even pregnant. But what had she hoped to gain by faking it? Sooner or later, she'd be expected to give birth, and the ball of stuffing under the blouse wouldn't pass muster. She couldn't even pretend to have a miscarriage when she was so far along—even in this day and age, she'd be expected to produce a fetus, wouldn't she?

Emotions poured off the other woman as Meaghan stared in disbelief. Desperation was the strongest and it hit Meaghan with a sickly sweet blow, bringing with it the perfect picture of the woman's intentions. She'd known Brion was in love with Colleen and had contrived this pregnancy to bind him to her. A part of Meaghan almost understood the actions of the hopeless woman, but how could she be so deceitful? If it was love Marga felt for Brion, Meaghan might have even sympathized. But that wasn't the emotion oozing from her now. There was no love inside her for Brion—quite the opposite. She *hated* him. Meaghan's intuition told her that her hatred stemmed from Marga's inability to make her husband love her. She'd gotten him to the altar, but he'd never cared for her. He'd never heeled to her commands or fallen prey to her manipulations.

Until now. Only her pregnancy had pulled him from a brink she'd seen in the distance. Marga must have known how he felt about Colleen, and she'd acted in desperation to keep him.

All of it, Meaghan got in a rush of vivid and rank emotion.

"But what did you think would happen when it was time to give birth?" Meaghan blurted without meaning to, unable to move past the simple logistics of the matter.

Marga opened her mouth, closed it. Opened it again. And then she covered her face with her hands and began to sob.

"You don't know what it's like," she moaned into her palms. "To love someone so much that you'd do anything for him. To know he will never be yours."

"You don't love him, though. You hate him," Meaghan said. Again, she hadn't meant to speak, but the force of Marga's emotions acted like a trigger, and she couldn't keep her tongue silent.

"I did. Once," Marga spat, lifting her burning gaze and staring at Meaghan with outrage that contorted her features.

Meaghan said nothing to that. What could she say? Cry me a river? Try falling in love with an evil Druid if you want to see how much love sucks?

The word *love* stuck in her mind, and for a moment, it blotted out the sobs of the prone woman at her feet. It was the second time she'd found it hovering there. Was that what she felt for Áedán? Was it love?

Had it ever been anything less?

The feelings deep within her were rich and fertile, consuming and obsessive. She felt him in every step she took. Every move she made. And even as she doubted him, she knew she would stand by him. To the end.

"You don't know what it's like to love a man like Brion MacGrath," Marga went on bitterly.

"I know what it is to love," Meaghan said softly. "It's a doomed and violent thing."

Marga laughed shrilly as tears continued to stream down her face, turning her black liner into inky rivers. "Yes," she said pitifully.

The silence that fell between them became weighted.

"What will you do now?" Marga demanded. "Run and tell?"

"I don't know. It's not my business, but . . . well, what do you imagine is going to happen in the end, Marga? You can't pull this off. You've taken it too far to say you had a miscarriage. You know that? At this stage, there would be a baby—stillborn yes, but a baby all the same."

"Do not concern yourself with what I will do," Marga said, rising to her feet and donning her haughty expression. She looked like a hideous clown, with black streaked over her face and red rimming her eyes. But she leveled a deadly gaze at Meaghan.

"It is not your business, as you said. And don't you dare tell a soul what you saw. You cannot imagine the troubles you will bring on yourself and your cousin if you do."

"Are you threatening me?" Meaghan asked, pissed.

"Take it as you will. Stay out of my business."

Meaghan raised her hands, palms up, and shrugged. "Don't worry. I wouldn't put my foot in that pile for anything."

Chapter Twenty-six

MEAGHAN only waited a moment before she continued through the ruins. She could feel the emotions of her grandmother, and she honed in on them like a signal. She felt a driving need to see Colleen and reassure herself that her grandmother was safe and *real.* Not one of the walking dead she'd seen earlier.

She'd send Colleen home, tell her to lock the doors and windows. And then Meaghan would search for Áedán. Each moment away from him escalated the fear inside her that a time bomb ticked away someplace close. She needed to reach it and defuse it before it exploded.

She'd given her heart to Áedán, but she hadn't told him what she felt. He'd left thinking she distrusted him, and she worried that he might act out of his anger and do something. . . . She stopped herself, refusing to go any further. She would find him before he did anything rash.

She loved him. She would show him just how important he was to her.

She heard the soft weeping before she came upon her grandmother perched on a flat boulder with Niall in her arms. Silently Meaghan moved to her side and sat next to her.

If Colleen was surprised to see Meaghan, she gave no indication of it. She said nothing. Just cried in deep, wrenching sobs that made Meaghan's eyes water in shared pain. The tears were too raw to be credited to Mickey, and so Meaghan put the few facts she knew together and came up with a different answer. Brion. Marga must have followed Colleen to this desolate point and confronted her about Brion's continued obsession with her.

"I saw Marga," Meaghan said at last.

Colleen remained silent for a moment and then said, "So did I."

"Whatever she said to you, Nana, put it out of your mind. She's jealous and she has reason to be. But it is not your fault that Brion loves you. I heard you last night. You told him to go home. You turned him away."

Colleen made a choked sound that was a cross between laughter and crying. There was shame in her and heartbreak that made Meaghan's eyes sting.

"Is that what you saw, granddaughter? You saw me turn him away? Because isn't that the opposite of what I wanted to do? I wanted to beg him to hold me. To keep me forever. I wanted to fall on my knees and plead with him to take me away."

Hurt and longing hung heavy around Colleen. The teeth of Colleen's regrets bit deep and tore at her heart.

"I love him," Colleen whispered. "More than air. More than life. But I am trapped in a web of my own weaving." Colleen sighed. "You tell me when I grow old I will be a woman who's admired and loved. But if you knew the truth about me, you'd feel differently."

"No, I wouldn't."

Colleen shook her head sadly and adjusted her hold on Niall, who lay curled against her, sleeping peacefully. His lips moved compulsively and he made soft cooing sounds as he snuggled, safe in her arms.

"I've loved this child since I first held him," she said.

"I can tell. He loves you back."

This made Colleen's lips tilt in a too brief smile.

"When I first came to Ballyfionúir, I was a desperate girl. I came because I have family here—an aunt and uncle. But I'd heard of Brion MacGrath and how he treated the people of his island."

Meaghan listened without interrupting. Nana had rarely talked about her past.

"From the moment Brion set eyes on me, he began his pursuit. I knew he was married. Who doesn't know about Marga MacGrath? Some say she's got royal blood in her and that's why he wed her, but who knows the truth about the choices a man makes but the man himself? Even then, I wonder if they know themselves."

Meaghan thought of the tortured look in Áedán's eyes as he'd made his confessions that morning and had to agree. Men might pretend to rule the world, but inside they were no more sure of themselves than the little boys that often looked out of their eyes.

"Brion would not take no for an answer," Colleen went on in that sad and resigned voice. She looked so very young and lost. "He said it was love at first sight, and fool that I am, I wanted it to be true. I'd never been loved before, not like that. He was forbidden, but I wanted him like a bird wants to fly. I could not have denied him, even though I tried. I could not conceive *no* when it came to Brion MacGrath. He was like a fairy tale come true, and I yearned to be his princess so badly that I pretended what we felt was the real world and the other life, his wife . . . that was the make-believe."

Her shame blew with the wind, sharp and abrasive. It cut to the bone. Overhead the sky rumbled and quaked, and the air grew damp and cold, making Meaghan shiver.

"Brion treated me to love and kindness. The first I'd felt in far too long."

Colleen's drenched eyes begged her to understand, begged her to forgive. Meaghan didn't need to forgive her, and she understood all too well.

Love is a doomed and violent thing.

"Perhaps it was meant to be, you and Brion," she offered gently. "There doesn't seem to be any love lost between him and his wife."

"No. There is none of that. They married young and hastily, and they've had years to regret it. He has anyway. But it was something both of their families wanted. Now their parents are dead and they are still locked in marriage."

"Was she ever a good wife to him?"

"No, and he was never a good husband to her. Don't misunderstand me. I'm not about condoning what I've done or what they've done to each other, but two people less suited would be hard to find. She is as cold and conniving as a . . ."

"Snake?" Meaghan offered helpfully.

"Aye. And he's a big child who needs a woman with a firm hand." Said in a tone that could not hide her love.

"Oh, Nana. I'm so sorry."

"Ach. Don't be. I deserve the lot I've been given."

"Why?"

"I coveted another woman's husband," she said, head hung with disgrace. "I took him to my bed."

"How . . . I mean, Mickey . . . how did you get away with it?"

"It was before Mickey."

"Oh." That made sense at least. There was no way the vicious and domineering man she'd married would have given her enough freedom to carry on an affair. He'd have killed her if he'd ever caught her.

Meaghan said, "It takes two, Colleen. You didn't do it on your own."

"That is true." She took a deep breath and slowly let it out. The press of Colleen's agitation rasped against Meaghan's overwrought senses. Whatever weighed on her grandmother's mind was heavy.

At last, she said, "There's more. I can scarce tell you the rest."

"I'm not here to judge you, Colleen. My love for you is unconditional. You've been an anchor in my life, and you've given me your support when I've needed it the most. I'll do no less for you."

Colleen blinked her eyes, looking overwhelmed by the loyalty she saw in her granddaughter's face. Meaghan felt every bit of her emotions and shared the gratitude she felt.

"It's Brion's child I carry," she whispered.

For a moment, Meaghan couldn't process that. And then suddenly the words made sense. "It's Brion's baby?"

Miserable, Colleen nodded.

"And he doesn't know?"

She shook her head. "He thinks it's Mickey's. I married Mickey as soon as I learned the truth."

"Did Mickey know you were already pregnant?"

She nodded. "It was Marga who arranged the marriage."

Meaghan's mouth opened and closed for a moment before she managed to sputter, *"What?"*

And then Colleen told her the most impossible truth she'd ever heard.

"You know that sometimes I see things."

Meaghan nodded. "Like a granddaughter who comes from the future?"

Colleen almost smiled. "Aye. It's a gift—or a curse, depending on the day and the message it gives. Sometimes I can glimpse what is to come. Not always, not even always accurately. But I can see some things looming in the future. I think I must have seen Brion in my dreams long before I saw him in the flesh. I was already half in love with him by the time we came face-to-face."

Watching her, Meaghan said, "When you're older, you'll be better at discerning fact from fiction. You always seemed to know what was to come."

"Lucky me," Colleen answered bitterly. "When I discovered I was with child, I had a vision of my future. I saw myself with Brion, wedded to him. And then my vision turned dark, and I realized that the only way for me to be his wife was for Marga to be gone."

"Gone?" Meaghan repeated.

Colleen nodded. "He might have gotten an annulment. She'd never conceived and any number of people could testify that she is colder than a winter's wind. But that's not what I saw. I saw death and I knew that my Brion had killed her."

"You didn't see him do it, though?"

"No, and for that I'll be forever grateful. I saw only the deed, done. She was dead and I was the new Mrs. MacGrath. He killed her for me. I knew this in my vision, and I could not suffer it. I'd sinned by lying with him. I'd sinned against God and against myself by being his mistress. I'd acted the filthy whore that Mickey always accused me of being."

"That's fecking bullshit, Colleen. You live in a backward time. It'll be a long time before divorce is legal again, but it will be because it *should* be. Because sometimes people marry the wrong one, and they should be able to walk away without violence. I'm not saying marriage vows shouldn't be sacred, but sometimes people make mistakes."

"The time you come from sounds so different from now. It's hard for me to picture it."

Meaghan sighed. "How did Marga end up playing your matchmaker?"

"She knew I was pregnant. Or at least she knew that I stood the chance of becoming so. She came to me with a deal. She'd tried time and again to have a child. Had faked pregnancy and miscarriage twice. And she saw me as a means to an end. I'd only just learned that I was pregnant, only just realized what my future held when she approached me. 'Are you with child yet?' she asked me, and she knew the answer by the expression on my face. And so she arranged for me to wed Mickey, whose wife had died and left him with wee Niall to care for. He couldn't do it on his own, as you saw for yourself. He needed a wife and . . . and . . ."

Meaghan clapped a hand over her mouth. "And she's going to *steal your baby* and pretend it's *hers*."

Colleen nodded miserably. "'Tis why Mickey hated me so. Before we . . . before me, he was a good man. An honest, hardworking man who loved his wife. He never stopped mourning her."

Meaghan didn't know what to say. She couldn't think of the violent Mickey Ballagh as a *good* man. But she could hear the sincerity in Colleen's voice.

"Marga has a midwife who will lie for her. She will deliver my baby and pretend it was born dead. We've been telling everyone that I'm only a few months along when I'm near due, so the miscarriage won't cause such a stir. They won't even expect a funeral at that stage. And on the same night I 'lose' my baby, Marga will give birth to a healthy child, binding Brion to her forever."

"Oh my God," Meaghan breathed. "The *bitch*."

"She is the wronged party in all of this, Meaghan. It was I who dared to make her husband mine. You cannot pretend that it's otherwise."

"Yes . . . and no. You slept with her husband. It was wrong. I'll admit that. But what she did . . . what she plans. Jesus in heaven, Colleen. It's trafficking babies is what it is."

Colleen gave her a perplexed look.

"You need to tell Brion the truth. He deserves to know."

"I cannot," she said. "If I dare speak against her, she'll bring charges of adultery and robbery against me. She'll say I came into her house and stole from her. She'll see to it that I go to prison and I will lose my baby anyway. At least now he'll be raised with his father."

"Who doesn't believe the child is his. I heard what he said, Colleen."

"Aye, but the babe will resemble Brion. He is the true father."

"Or maybe it will resemble your great-uncle Fred."

"Who?"

"I'm saying, the baby might look like any one of *your* relatives and none of his own. Did you ever consider that?"

Colleen shook her head. "He will not. He'll have eyes as blue as the sky and he'll be named for Brion's great-great-grandfather. You heard Marga yesterday. His name will be—"

"Cathán," they both said together.

Cathán MacGrath. Wife beater, murderer, monster.

"Yeah," Meaghan said. "I know exactly who he'll be."

Chapter Twenty-seven

ÁEDÁN had the net out again, but his mind was locked so tight in the knot of impossibilities that he'd only been staring at it. He'd wandered in frustrated anger for the past hour. He'd been trying to clear his head, to banish the scent of Meaghan from his senses.

He'd failed on all accounts.

He didn't notice the man approach until he had one foot on the deck, the other still firmly anchored on the dock. The man leaned his arms on his bent knee and stared at Áedán in silence. Cathán MacGrath's father could have been a mirror image of the man Cathán would grow to be.

"What do you want?" Áedán asked.

"I want to know what game you think you're playing," Brion said. "I know who you are."

"I doubt that."

"Oh yes, I know. It told me."

"It?" Áedán asked with raised brows. "And what is this *it* that speaks to you?"

"The Book of Fennore," he said without hesitation.

Áedán winced. He didn't like to even hear the name. It had taken all his control not to clamp a hand over her sweet mouth when Meaghan had spoken it. He swallowed hard, anger and hurt rushing at him from opposing sides as he thought of Meaghan. The look in her eyes as she'd listened to Kyle's accusations still felt like a thousand blades flaying the flesh from his bones.

He'd never meant to let her get so close. Never dreamed she would become so important.

"It told me you have power over it," Brion said.

Surprised, Áedán just managed to keep his voice level, but inside churned fear and anger. "I have no power," he said coldly. "I'm just a fisherman."

"My arse. You're no fisherman, Áedán Brady."

He didn't bother to argue the point. Obviously he wasn't fooling Brion MacGrath. Instead he eyed the other man, noting his pallor, the tension in his shoulders. Áedán didn't sense the Book hovering about him, but he noted that flat glitter that marked its victim's eyes. He didn't think Brion had been near the Book yet. He hadn't touched it. But if it spoke to him, it was only a matter of time.

"It promises you things, doesn't it?" Áedán said softly. "It tells you whatever you want to hear. It promises to make you so powerful that no woman could say no to you. Not even another man's wife."

For a moment, confusion clouded Brion's face, and he swayed. Then he scowled at Áedán, and once more those eyes were as hard as the seawater slapping against the boat.

"How would you know what it does and doesn't promise?" Brion asked.

"Because it promised me things, too. That's what it does. Do you know the story of the genie in the bottle, Brion MacGrath?"

Brion swallowed thickly. "What does that have to do with anything?"

"The legends say that you rub the bottle and the genie appears for your wishes. That's what the Book wants you to believe. That it's there for your command. It tells you, *Come closer, make your wish*."

Brion said nothing, but he was listening.

"But the genie always warns you to be careful what you wish for. The genie cautions you to choose wisely and think first. Think long and hard. Do you know why?"

Brion narrowed his eyes. "Get to the point."

Áedán smiled grimly. "It warns you because what you ask for is exactly what you get. It doesn't listen to the nuance of your request and deliver what you want. It gives only what you ask for. Ask for happiness, and you will get it along with poverty and helplessness. Ask for wealth, and you will abound with it, but you will be alone and desolate. There is no way to outsmart it, to trick it, to be more astute than it is. In the end, you will trade away the very things about yourself that make you who you are. You will barter your soul to get the love of a woman only to discover that she no longer loves you because you have changed too much. In the end, you will take your life because your life is worth nothing. That is what the Book of Fennore does."

"How do you know so much?"

"How is unimportant. I know." He watched Brion digest this. After a moment, he asked in a deceptively soft voice, "Did you kill Mickey Ballagh?"

"No."

Áedán raised his brows doubtfully even though he'd already decided that Hoyt had committed that crime. "But you considered it, didn't you? You thought about it. It made you weigh the pros and cons. Tell me it didn't. It made you think it was your idea to hunt him down, to kill him. It made you think it was the right thing to do."

"I didn't kill anyone."

"Maybe. Or maybe if Hoyt O'Shea hadn't killed him first, you would have done it."

"Hoyt O'Shea?"

Something in the tone of his voice made Áedán pause. He'd expected surprise, but what he heard ran deeper. Disbelief based on something stronger than simple denial.

Brion said, "Mickey Ballagh was killed sometime after two in the morning. Hoyt O'Shea was at home with his wife."

"So she says."

"Not just her. One of their boys was sick and had them up taking care of him. About one o'clock in the morning, Hoyt's wife sent him to get Dr. Fitzgerald to come see to him. He was there until after dawn."

"Then who killed Mickey?" Áedán muttered, not meaning to ask the question aloud but too stunned to keep it in.

"I thought it was you. I would've bet the bank on it. But if Colleen's cousin says you were there, and Colleen believes her, then so do I."

Áedán was only half listening. He'd been certain Hoyt had murdered Mickey. But now . . . "It has to be you."

Brion's head snapped back, as if he couldn't decide if he'd been insulted or commended.

"I did not kill Mickey Ballagh."

Áedán heard the truth in his voice, though it made no sense. He shook his head, assessing Brion MacGrath. Áedán suspected that Brion had been close to answering the call of the Book. But his instincts told him that he had not yet caved in, and it had not pulled him into its spell. A grudging respect formed for the other man.

"What's inside the Book, Brion . . . it doesn't care about you. It should, though. It's the epitome of arrogance that it doesn't."

"Why should it care about me?"

"Tell me, does it sound familiar, the voice you hear?"

"From the bleeding Book? Why should it?"

"Because it's your son's voice, Brion MacGrath."

Brion scowled. "I have no son."

"Yet. But your wife is heavy with child, is she not?"

Brion licked his lips and nodded.

"And until this voice began talking to you, you were willing to be the husband you should be. Weren't you?"

"Perhaps." He gave a disgusted shake of his head and muttered, "But the child isn't mine."

"You know that's not true."

"Who are you to say what I do and don't know as truth? Who are you to tell me what is and isn't mine?"

"The child is yours. He will be named Cathán, and he will look just like you."

Brion pulled his foot from the deck of *The Angel* and took a step back. "How would you be knowing that?"

"There was a time when I knew much. I have met your son, Brion. He is not worth any of what you do now."

Brion was shaking his head. "You don't know—"

"I know that he will lead you to do things that blacken your soul. And then when you've made such a mess you can't see the way out, he will offer you one. But the price. The price is everything you hold dear."

"It told me you would try trickery."

"Did it?" Áedán stared at him with clear eyes. "What power do you want that you do not already have?"

Brion swallowed again and looked out over the sea. "I am married to the wrong woman. God help me, I pray that I will lose her somehow."

"Lose her?"

He looked down. "In childbirth perhaps. Disease. I don't even care."

"You want her dead?"

Shamed, he nodded. "I don't even care if she gives me the child first."

The callousness of his statement hung between them, and there was nothing that could unsay the words. But the look on Brion MacGrath's face was tortured. At his core, he might have weaknesses. A wandering eye, roving hands. But he was not a murderer, and he was not the kind of man who wished death on his own.

"The child will be evil?" he said.

"No. He will be made into evil," Áedán answered. "Or not."

"What riddles do you speak?"

"You have choices laid out in front of you, Brion. They are your choices. I can see that you still have them to make. But soon they will vanish like the tide retreating. Listen to the voice you hear, obey it, and there will be nothing left of yourself that you recognize. You may end up with Colleen in your bed, but you will have condemned her to a man who does not even know himself. A man who hates what has become of him."

"Then what do I do?"

Ah, wasn't that the question. And Áedán didn't have the answer. He remembered others, many others who'd chosen to take their own lives rather than face what they'd brought on themselves. Now they haunted him, voices pleading in the darkness of his prison, coming to him for help. Oma, begging for her children. Saraid, willing to give anything to save her precious Ruairi. And so many more. Even the entreaties of Cathán, desperate and alone, pinged against his conscience now. Their pain felt like tiny barbs ripping at his flesh. He'd given each of them what they'd asked for and taken more than they could bear in exchange.

"Do you know where the Book is?" he asked Brion.

"No. It talks to me, but I've yet to find it."

"It waits until it owns you. It sends out its signal, always searching for someone who can hear it. Then it draws them in, promising what they want. Do not touch it, should you be unfortunate enough to find it."

"It said you were the one I should fear."

"And yet it sent you to spill my blood. If it had the power to give you what you ask for, would it not be able to slay its own enemy?"

Brion considered this with narrowed eyes. "Is it true, though? Were you once a part of the Book?"

Áedán thought about it before he answered. It was risky, telling this man so much. He was in contact with the Book of Fennore. Might even be an open channel to Cathán, twined with the sentience of the Book. But Áedán needed to speak of the horrors. Something deep within urged him to confide in Brion, to help this man navigate the dangerous waters he treaded.

"I was a prisoner. And now I am free. But it was not I who controlled what happened. I am as much a puppet as you are."

"What do you want, then? What do you hope to gain now that you are free?"

The question, asked in a soft and earnest voice, lashed out at him like a whip. What *did* he want?

"I want to be a man again," he said, and his voice grew husky with the words. "Just a man. Nothing more."

Disconcerted, Brion said, "You are a man."

"But it can easily be taken from me. Perhaps you will choose to put that knife through my heart, and then my chance is gone."

"I'm not going to kill you," Brion said.

And perhaps he wouldn't. But the truth of what Áedán had said resonated through his entire being, making his mouth dry, his veins shrivel, his skin shrink. He didn't want it to be so, but his existence felt precarious. And what of Meaghan? He'd begun to think of her as a future he'd dared not dream. Was he as big a fool as any of the victims he'd preyed upon in the past?

"What does the Book want from you?" Brion asked.

Ah, what did it want? Vengeance? Power? Everything?

Somberly, Áedán said, "To be trapped in the world of Fennore is to be part of a void. Empty, but for your rage and appetite. Hungry, but you cannot eat unless your call is answered. The only way to fill the emptiness is to beckon others to come and then take from them all that makes them worthy. But it's never enough, because no matter how powerful you become, you are still trapped. Still the treacherous genie, caged in a bottle. There is no escape, and you are enslaved to those you seek to master."

"And yet you escaped," Brion said, and his voice held something that sounded suspiciously like compassion.

It stunned Áedán, threw him off balance. In millennia, no one had ever felt compassionate about Áedán.

No, a voice corrected. That wasn't true. Meaghan had. And she'd opened a floodgate of emotions with her act of caring, emotions he wished he could deny.

"It remains to be seen whether or not I have escaped. Perhaps it's just an illusion. Perhaps the power that is the Book of Fennore merely taunts me with what I will never truly have. Perhaps it will be you who recaptures me. Perhaps I will be foolish and take a wrong turn once more. How many chances does a man deserve? I do not know how or why I've come to be free so how can I contemplate the permanence of it?"

He knew Meaghan Ballagh had freed him—and if she'd opened the door of his cage, did it not make sense that she could also close it up again? If she found the Book of Fennore, if she used it to return to her time, she would be forced to give something up, and Áedán knew that Cathán, manning the helm, would want her to sacrifice not herself, but Áedán.

How could he trust her not to betray him?

"I believe a man is measured by his actions," Brion said softly, as if reading Áedán's mind. "I have been unwise in my choices. I married a woman I knew I didn't love—married her because of her bloodline. Because of her wealth. I've taken every shilling she brought with her and turned it into twenty. I am a rich man, but I'd gladly give it all to undo my vows."

"Does she know this?"

"Yes."

"And what of the child?"

"I tell you, Áedán, the child is not mine. I've lain with my wife only once since the year began and then . . ." He looked uncomfortably away. "It's awkward, between us. It always has been. Like we are a lion and a gazelle trying to mate. We do not fit."

Áedán frowned. "But you are the same species, and you do fit."

"Not in the way we should. I don't know how I can make you understand, but know this. My seed has not been in her body. Not for over a year."

"But the child will be yours, Brion. I have seen him. I know him. He could be your reflection."

"It makes no sense," Brion muttered.

Áedán agreed. No sense at all. The child that would grow to be Cathán could be none other than Brion's son.

Brion shook his head, and then, suddenly, he paled. "Bleeding Jesus, what am I thinking?"

Áedán had no clue what thoughts filled Brion's head, but whatever they were, they made his eyes widen and his mouth thin to a hard line. Áedán was bewildered, a state he'd become far too accustomed to.

Brion's chin came up and he looked around, as if he'd heard his name called.

"What is it?" Áedán asked.

"The voice . . ."

"The Book is speaking to you?"

Brion's nod looked unnatural, as if control of his mind had been taken over.

"Resist it," Áedán urged, but Brion had already turned and walked quickly away.

Áedán jumped from the deck of *The Angel* and followed. "Brion, where are you going?"

"The ruins," he shot over his shoulder and broke into a run.

Áedán quickened his pace until he raced toward the ruined castle just behind the other man. If that was where Cathán wanted Brion, then Áedán would be there, too.

Chapter Twenty-eight

MEAGHAN heard the scream at the same moment as a wave of terror slammed into her. Looking at Colleen with shock, she turned to the sound.

"Did you hear that?"

"Aye," Colleen said.

As the sky overhead roared with thunder and flashed with lightning, Meaghan spun and warily made her way through the ruins, Colleen with Niall in her arms following behind her at a slower pace. As soon as she rounded the jagged remains of what had been a turret in its day, she saw a man dragging a woman across the path that led from the MacGraths' house to the cliffs. He had a hand clamped over her mouth and now the screams came muffled.

She recognized Marga instantly, but the man's face was turned away. The shadows and gloom worked against her until a huge furry shape moved from behind the cover of a toppled stone and bared its teeth in a silent growl.

Eamonn's wolf.

Eamonn held Marga captive. For a moment, she could only watch him pull the resistant woman into concealment behind the crumbling walls and scattered stones. Once far enough in that they couldn't be seen by anyone approaching from the house, he pinned Marga against his massive chest with one arm and used the other to press something against her throat. He'd had to remove the hand at her mouth, but he gave her a sharp warning.

"Scream again and I'll be done with you now."

Marga nodded her understanding. "Don't hurt me. Please. Please don't hurt me."

The other woman's fear smelled sour and sharp, her panic whipped in the wind and singed Meaghan's raw senses. Meaghan hadn't moved since she'd seen them. In truth, she didn't know what to do. She couldn't just stand by while Eamonn murdered the other woman, but she couldn't believe that was his intention, despite the knife and his aggression. Granted she didn't know this man, not really. But she'd never have thought him capable of killing an innocent woman.

"I don't want to hurt you," Eamonn said, and Meaghan felt the blast of his distress. He seemed conflicted by his determination to do what he'd come for and the horror he felt at being there, at the steps he planned to take.

Why would he want to hurt Marga?

And then she heard her own voice in her head, *You'll have a long wait, Eamonn. Cathán hasn't even been born yet.* Eamonn thought Marga carried Cathán MacGrath in her womb, and he planned to kill her for it. He'd said Cathán had destroyed everything he loved, and now he intended to right the wrong before it happened.

Behind her, she heard Colleen's footsteps. Quickly Meaghan stepped out of the shadows, drawing Eamonn's attention. She held out her hands in the universal *take it easy* sign as she stepped closer.

"Eamonn, no," she said. "You're wrong. What I told you was wrong."

Eamonn looked at her in shock. He pressed the blade of his long, wicked knife to Marga's throat.

Meaghan licked her lips. She wanted to tell him Marga wasn't even pregnant, but she feared Marga would blurt that Colleen carried the child. Meaghan couldn't—*wouldn't*—endanger her grandmother that way.

"Eamonn, look at her. She's innocent. Even the baby is innocent. You cannot mean to do this."

There were tears in Eamonn's eyes as he stared at Meaghan and so much pain that it cut and tore at her. "I had a family once," he said in a broken voice. "A family who loved me. Cathán destroyed them. Cathán destroyed *me.* He made me a traitor. An exile. I am a man without a home. Without a life."

"Eamonn, if you hurt her, you will hate yourself."

"I already hate myself."

His voice cracked and his shoulders slumped. With relief, she saw in his face that the moment when he might have plunged his blade into Marga had come and gone, and now he was simply trapped by actions he couldn't undo. Disgust and shame filled the dusky air between them.

"I cannot kill a woman. The one thing that might change it all, and I am too much the coward even for that. I know she carries the spawn of all evil, but I cannot destroy it."

Self-loathing rolled off him in waves. Meaghan felt sickened by the power of it, saddened by the intensity. Eamonn carried so much remorse and guilt that it had turned the man inside into a shadowy being that knew only disgrace.

Marga sobbed in his arms, but his words seemed to penetrate her terror. "Spawn of—no, I'm not carrying anything. I'm not even pregnant. There's no baby," she babbled.

From the corner of her eye, Meaghan saw two men running toward them, but the ruined castle stood between them and Eamonn, and he went on unaware of their approach.

"What do you mean there's no baby?" he demanded.

"I'm faking it!" Marga exclaimed wildly. "Let me show you."

Brion MacGrath had drawn closer but he paused to catch his breath, still shielded from Eamonn and Marga by the decimated turret. But from the point where Brion stopped, Meaghan suspected he could see his wife as she stumbled headfirst into the throes of hysterics.

Áedán came to a halt at Brion's shoulder, watching the unfolding scene with those enigmatic eyes. Meaghan felt his name on her lips, released it in a silent breath, and his gaze swung to where she hovered in shadow as if he'd heard her. Those eyes heated at the same time they grew more distant. She wanted to run to him, to throw her arms around him and tell him that she was sorry to have doubted him even for an instant. But there wasn't time.

"I'm not pregnant," Marga shrieked again. "I just pretended so my husband would give up his whore."

Too surprised to keep ahold of her, Eamonn dropped his arms and stepped away. Marga grabbed the hem of her shirt and lifted it to show him her faked pregnancy just as Brion stepped from behind the ruins. For a moment, a look of alarm crossed Brion's face as he saw the strange man with his wife. But then he caught sight of the stuffing she wore beneath her top, and like Eamonn, he stared in disbelief. Realizing that Brion had joined them, Eamonn shifted his shocked gaze to the other man, then took a hasty step back, his hands held out at his sides. The knife clattered to the stones at his feet.

Meaghan wanted to ask Brion how he'd known to come. She had the disturbing sense that somehow they'd all been gathered there . . . herded without them being aware. . . .

Marga continued her crazed admission, unaware of her audience.

"My blasted whoring husband would have left me if I hadn't . . ."

At last some inner sense of self-preservation seemed to alert Marga, and she hesitated, head cocked as if scenting danger. Then slowly she turned and faced Brion's thunderous expression. She still held the hem of her blouse in her fingers, and Brion glared at her with revulsion.

"Brion," she gasped. Tears streaked her blotchy face, her swollen eyes. Despite what Meaghan knew of this woman and her treachery, she felt sorry for her as she watched her scramble to do damage control. It was a pointless endeavor, but Marga didn't seem to realize that.

"She got pregnant to trap you, love, but I knew she'd only hurt you. I had to do something to stop her." Marga paused, her hands held out beseechingly. "She was willing to *sell* your child, Brion. *Sell it.* I couldn't let her raise our baby, not when I know how much—"

"Shut up," he said so softly that Meaghan thought she'd imagined it. He might have shouted it for the effect it had on his sobbing wife. She hiccupped, shook her head, and then tried again. "I love you," she cried. "I did it because I love you."

Just then Colleen finally made it to the spot where they'd all gathered. She rounded the bend from the far side of the ruins with her chin up but fear and anguish in her dark eyes. It was obvious she'd heard every word that had been spoken. Brion's eyes widened as he spotted her. Shaking his head in confusion, he cut his gaze back and forth between his wife and the woman he claimed to love.

"She was willing to *sell* it," Marga wailed, pointing an accusing finger at Colleen. "What kind of mother would do such a thing? Can't you see her for what she is?"

The silence that followed raged thick and harsh. A nerve ticked in Brion's jaw as he turned his icy blue eyes back to Colleen. "Is this true?" he asked, the hurt in his voice as poignant as the emotions rolling off him.

"No," she said. "Not all of it. She forgot the part where she threatened to have me arrested for crimes I didn't commit. She forgot the part where she blackmailed me." Colleen held her head high, but her shame thickened the air, her despair turning it into a fog that obscured all else.

"She was trying to protect you," Meaghan blurted to Brion. Only after she'd spoken did she realize that Marga had used almost the same reasoning.

"Protect me from what?" Brion demanded, his jaw tight, his eyes hard.

"From yourself." Áedán spoke softly, but Brion heard him and startled as if the words had been shouted in his ear. For a moment, the two men stared at one another, and Meaghan felt the silent connection, the message that they shared without a word.

Colleen had told her that she'd glimpsed a future in which Brion had murdered his wife. From the guilty expression on Brion's face, Meaghan surmised that he'd given the idea more than a passing thought—he'd actively contemplated ending Marga's life.

"I saw you," Colleen whispered. "I saw what you did—what you were willing to do. I couldn't let you."

Brion's throat worked for a moment before he cleared it, glanced at his wife and then back to Colleen. The anger in his gaze turned to misery as he searched the eyes of the proud woman he loved and realized the sacrifice she'd been prepared to make for him.

Meaghan looked away and caught sight of Jamie, standing beside her.

Once again blood covered him from his split skull to his unsteady legs. Once more he reached out, silently pleading with her, looking so real, though she knew he wasn't. Behind him stood Hoyt O'Shea and Enid Sullivan, both gruesomely dead yet moving, reaching . . . Someone new moved behind them. Too horrified to speak, to scream, to run, Meaghan focused on the animated corpse of Brion MacGrath who stepped in front of the others. It stood in the shadow of the living man, wavering in and out of focus. One side of his head had been blown away, as if by a gun discharged at his temple. The word *suicide* formed in Meaghan's head.

She stumbled back only to see another shape appear. This time it was Colleen.

"No," she whimpered as more people joined the mass of death. Like stars appearing in the midnight sky, they were everywhere, moving closer, crowding her. She tried to inch away, but they pushed and shoved until she was trapped in the middle. Frantically she searched for Áedán, praying she wouldn't find him among the deathly array.

Alive, Áedán still stood beside the real Brion, the one who lived and breathed as well. He watched her with troubled eyes, and in his emotions, she felt a blast of understanding. He knew what was happening. He didn't see the death surrounding her, but he knew that she did.

"Make them go away," she breathed. Áedán's eyes filled with frustration as he shook his head. He'd tried to make them go away for Elan and failed, that look said.

"Eamonn!"

The shouting voice startled them all. It cut across the tension and turned them in the direction the shout had come from. Jamie—not the ghostly one, but the real man—swayed at the edge of the cliffs, leaning heavily against a boulder before pushing off and stumbling toward them. Even from the short distance, Meaghan could see the blood. Certain her eyes played tricks on her, she turned to the specter and met dead eyes that beseeched. Her heart seized as she realized that Jamie's death was about to become reality. She didn't know how or why, but she knew it without doubt.

"Jamie!" Eamonn exclaimed, rushing to where the other man wobbled on unsteady legs, with his wolf in hot pursuit. "What's happened to you?"

Eamonn's words snapped her gaze back to the wounded man who looked so weak and battered that he might careen over the edge at any moment. Thunder boomed like an explosion, and finally the rain began to fall.

Chapter Twenty-nine

FOR a moment, Áedán didn't know what to make of the drama unfolding in front of him. First Meaghan looking at him like he was the answer to her prayers. Her blue eyes had been the color of a summer sky, clear and warm. She'd taken a step, as if she intended to fling herself into his arms. And he'd wanted nothing more than to open them and welcome her. But then he saw Eamonn with Brion MacGrath's wife held captive.

Now he looked back at Meaghan to find her eyes had grown wide and fearful. She darted her gaze around her, seeing things the rest of them could not. Her expression mirrored the terror she felt, and Áedán knew she saw the dead. From the look of her, there were many.

She spoke softly, but Áedán heard her plea to make it go away. Then Jamie's shout spun everything in a different direction once more.

He'd been beaten—stabbed, by the look of him—and he stood perilously close to the sheer drop of Fennore's cliffs. Was his one of the deaths Meaghan saw?

They were not friends, he and Jamie, and yet the sight of the powerful warrior wounded and staggering across the rocky shale filled Áedán with rage. He knew in that moment that whoever had killed Mickey Ballagh had turned his attention to Jamie—a man who'd been ripped from his proper time, wrenched from his life, and plopped down in one hell after another.

The scent of the Book of Fennore mingled with the smell of rain an instant before the sky opened and cold fat drops pelted them relentlessly. Brion and Meaghan had followed Eamonn and his wolf, and Áedán felt danger clench the air around them. He shouted for Meaghan to wait, but thunder drowned out his words.

Eamonn reached Jamie first, gripping the other man's shoulders and trying to pull him from the edge. Whatever Jamie said stiffened Eamonn's back. The wolf circled at their feet, growling and snarling as if something prodded it with a sharp, hot poker.

Áedán heard only a few words as he raced after Meaghan. He caught her arm and held her back as she reached the others.

"Kyle—" Jamie said.

"He's not here."

Brion demanded, "Who in Christ's name did this to you, man?"

Jamie's eyes rolled and he swayed alarmingly. Eamonn tried to steady him, but the storm worked against them all. Áedán felt the brush of the Book of Fennore like steel wool scouring his skin. He braced for the voice, but it didn't come.

"Where . . . Kyle?" Jamie asked, his voice weak.

Eamonn suddenly took a step back, his movements unnatural, as if a rod had been shoved down his spine. He opened his mouth to speak, but no sound came out. At his feet, the big wolf growled low in its throat and then began to bark and snarl ferociously.

"What's wrong with it?" Meaghan asked, moving closer to Áedán as the wolf bared its teeth. The growls grew louder, foam gathered at the black gums, and saliva hung in rivulets from its fangs.

It looked like the wolves that had run wild in the world of Fennore. The animal had been so tamed by Eamonn that Áedán had almost forgotten that it had come from the black world of its brethren.

The thought had only begun to form when the wolf attacked, charging Jamie with fury that stunned them all. Already weak, Jamie stood no chance of fighting off the beast. Eamonn cursed and commanded the wolf to heel, but the frenzied animal didn't obey. Determined, Eamonn tried to get between Jamie and the wolf, but he succeeded only in becoming the focus of the attack. Áedán and Brion both lobbed stones at the rabid canine, but it continued with its assault, ignoring the blows and focusing with singled-minded attention on the two men that had become its prey. All the while, the Book of Fennore rasped its power over the gathering, as electric as the bolts that cracked the sky above.

The wolf herded them to the edge of the cliff, biting and tearing at them, leaving no chance for anyone to help. Jamie and Eamonn teetered for a split second, and then the wolf charged, sending them all over the side to plummet down to the rock and shale below.

It happened so quickly. No one could have stopped it. None of them could comprehend what they'd just seen.

"Oh my God," Meaghan breathed in horror, stepping away from Áedán as she covered her mouth with her hands.

Brion rushed to the edge and looked down before wincing and shaking his head.

Áedán wanted to see for himself, still unwilling to believe that his old enemies, his new adversaries, had died so quickly and irrevocably. He felt like a part of him had been wrenched out and trampled. Neither Jamie nor Eamonn had ever shown him kindness. He cared nothing for them. And yet inside he mourned. Because of Áedán, both had been torn from their lives and delivered to this place and time where neither had belonged. Because of Áedán, they'd died.

So many had died.

Before moving to the edge and looking down on the carnage, he grabbed Meaghan's arm with one hand and turned her back to the ruins. "Wait for me there," he said. With a sorrowful nod, she trudged away.

With a sadness that nearly overwhelmed him, Áedán gazed down at the broken bodies for a long moment. When he moved away to join the others, he felt as if he'd left some part of himself behind. "Feck," Brion said, stunned, moving quickly to follow. Marga had remained in the ruins, huddled beneath the dangling arm of a parapet walk. She didn't look up when they joined her under the overhang.

Brion shook his head, looking at his wife with a combination of sympathy and disgust. "Has the whole bleeding island gone insane, then?"

Áedán thought so, and he turned to bring Meaghan close to him, to keep her as safe from the insanity as he could.

"Where is Meaghan?" he demanded, scanning the clustered group for her face.

"She was just here," Colleen said, alarmed. "Where could she have gotten to?"

Quickly he moved from the deteriorated half walls and overhangs so he could see clearly. The rain came down in droves of cold. He whisked it from his face, looking for her, calling her name.

"Where did she go?" he repeated angrily.

"It has her," Brion shouted over the storm.

He wanted to round on the other man and shout that it couldn't be true, but he knew it was. He could still feel the scrape of the Book's power in the air. Cathán wanted the pendant, the key to his escape, and he'd used one of his victims to snatch Meaghan who'd had it last. But where had he taken her? And did she still have it with her?

Áedán raced across the clearing, searching in every direction. On the hillside beyond the ruins, he saw the huge dolmen. The hulking formation loomed tall and gray in the stormy twilight, looking every bit the portal into the world of the *Others* that the ancients had thought it was. As he watched, a shape emerged.

Dressed in white from head to toe, the woman stood proudly before him. Her hair gleamed as if caught by moonlight and danced in a silvery veil around her shoulders, unaffected by the pouring rain.

Her skin had a translucent glow that made her appear to be lit from the inside.

Elan, bringer of light.

Elan, the White Fennore.

She lifted her hand and motioned him forward with an imperial flick of her fingers. And then she began to keen. Inside, Áedán's emotions churned. Just a few days ago, he would have raced across the distance that separated them and wrapped his fingers around Elan's throat. Now he didn't know if he should still do that or if he should crawl on his hands and knees and beg for her forgiveness.

He did neither.

Elan was his past. Meaghan was the only thing he cared about now.

Without looking back at the others, he slipped and slid in the mud as he struggled to reach Elan, praying she'd come to him now, after all these years, to guide him. To help him find and save Meaghan from the fate neither he nor Elan had been able to evade an eternity ago. With each slippery step, he felt his heart growing larger, filling with purpose that crowded out the old rage and bitterness. It felt as if his chest would not be able to contain so much feeling.

When he stood a few feet away, he paused, unsure what to say. She watched him in silence, her pale eyes—blue with a hint of lavender that had always reminded him of twilight skies—remained steady.

"You are here to judge me," he said, remembering her words when she'd condemned him. "But I beg you to help me first. Please, help me find Meaghan."

She did not answer, and he feared that perhaps her judgment, her revenge would be in her silence when he needed her to speak. The wind and rain battered him, filling his eyes, making it difficult to breathe. He wanted to shout, to rail, but instead he waited. When she finally answered, he heard her voice in his head as sweet and clear as a memory.

It is you who will judge me, Brandubh.

Her words shocked him. "I have no judgment to pass over you." And then, realizing only in that moment just how much he meant it, he said, "In your place, I would not have trusted me either."

She smiled, sadly, regretfully. *For too long I have been a blade pressed to your throat, a weight around your ankle, and you have been the same to me.*

He nodded, and didn't even try to staunch the tears he felt burning his eyes.

You must release me and I must release you.

He wasn't sure how he'd held her and, therefore, could not grasp what he must do to set her free. Before he could ask, she said, *The woman has placed the key in a hiding place outside of her grandmother's home. You must find it and you must perform the ceremony.*

The ceremony? He grappled with the word, trying to frame it in a new meaning, one that did not equal . . .

"Sacrifice?" he said. "You want me to sacrifice Meaghan? I won't do it."

You would not have sacrificed me either. I was too weak to trust you, and for my sins, I have walked without rest in the Otherworld, neither dead nor alive. I cursed myself as much as I cursed you. The woman brings us both hope. Her bloodline is strong. She is more than either of us ever could be. She will break our curse and free us.

"How?" he asked.

She feels the hearts and souls of those around her. She hurts when they hurt, she weeps when they weep. She is humanity.

Áedán still didn't understand, but his understanding didn't matter. Meaghan did. What he felt for her was too big to label with words or titles. She was air. She was food. She was life.

Yes, Elan said, as if he'd spoken aloud. *She is life, and the monster we created fears her. It will try to own her. It will do anything to have her. It will release Cathán, it will release you, if only it can keep her.*

"I will not let it."

I know. Trust in yourself, Áedán.

Her words echoed through him long after she'd faded from sight.

Chapter Thirty

ÁEDÁN left the others without bothering to stop and explain. Desperate, he raced over the rutted pathway to the house where Meaghan's grandmother lived. Fighting the storm, Áedán found the junk heap at the side of the Ballaghs' house. Even if Elan had not guided him, he would have known where it was. It felt as if the pendant had called him there, in fact. An accomplice in the war against evil. From there he knew exactly where he would go.

The cavern beneath the castle ruins.

The place where so many of his life's crucial moments had played out. He had no illusions about what would happen when he reached it. He knew that his journey into freedom would come to an end in this confrontation. Fate would once again try to condemn him to the Book of Fennore.

The very idea of it filled him with such remorse that he wanted to hurl himself off the cliffs and die as quickly and finally as Jamie and Eamonn had done. But he would not abandon Meaghan. He would not betray her.

And he would not lose faith. Meaghan had reminded him that

once he was the most powerful Druid to walk the earth. He'd let that knowledge corrupt him once. Now he would use it to defy any fate that meant to make him a slave.

He would be fighting both Cathán and the Book on their terms, but neither the sentient being inside the Book or Cathán knew that Áedán had powers of his own. Cathán must have worked through someone in Ballyfionúir to have captured Meaghan. The only way to ensure that she escaped was to go in after her. If her captor had impelled Meaghan to touch the Book, if that twisted evil had seeped beneath her skin, Áedán would fight to the last breath to bring her back.

He plucked the velvet pouch from the canister where Meaghan had hidden it. In his hand, the amulet blazed hot and cold. The markings on his arm burned as if in response, the black turning red before his eyes. He forced himself to look away from the terrifying sight. He needed to focus on one thing—Meaghan. It did not matter what happened to him if he could save her.

As he moved away, he heard the low voices of Brion MacGrath and Colleen as they approached from the ruins.

"Did you find her?" Colleen asked.

"I will," he answered.

"What can I do?" Brion asked. "Where should we look?"

"Stay here in case she returns." He swallowed, knowing that if he succeeded, Meaghan would be returning alone.

"I've sent word to Francis Murray about the bodies at the bottom of the cliff."

Áedán shook his head angrily. "Keep him away from the ruins. You don't want him involved in what is about to happen there."

"What—"

Áedán cut him off. "Don't ask. Just keep away."

Brion gave a sharp nod of acknowledgment and Áedán noted that his eyes still sparkled, but not with evil. He paused, studying the other man for a moment. His features appeared suddenly softer and when he glanced at Colleen, his heart was there in the look. . . .

“I’m going to be a father,” Brion said.

Father to Cathán MacGrath. Suddenly Áedán imagined the future stretching out in front of him. He saw how the fabric of it waffled and then distorted. He’d watched the future change before just as he’d witnessed the past warping and reshaping into something new. Brion was not the first MacGrath to tinker with what was and change what might have been. But this . . .

Icy fear coated Áedán’s insides with a new kind of dread.

If Brion raised his son, that son might not become the lonely, desperate man who sought the Book of Fennore. But what did that mean for his children? Would they still be born? Would Meaghan’s mother find Niall Ballagh and marry him? Would Meaghan ever be conceived?

Without a word, Áedán fled the kitchen for the cavern. He would need to do much more than simply dictate the destiny of the Book of Fennore. He would need to refashion fate itself.

Chapter Thirty-one

MEAGHAN struggled against the ropes that bound her, but they held tight and she couldn't get free. Kyle sat nearby, watching her with cold flat eyes that glittered darkly. The taint of the Book of Fennore peppered the air and made breathing a frightening and terrifying endeavor.

When he'd lunged from behind the crumbling ruins and captured her, muffling her screams so that they couldn't be heard over the storm and dragging her away without anyone noticing, she'd fought, using every trick she knew. She'd managed to slam her head back into his nose and almost got his knee with a hard thrust of her heel. But the creature sweet Kyle Mahon had become seemed impervious to pain. He'd only held on tighter as he dragged her away. She'd watched helplessly as the White Fennore had appeared and sent Áedán off in the wrong direction. She'd felt betrayed to her soul. And when the others left, Kyle had tied her up and brought her down, past the still and bloody bodies of Eamonn, Jamie, and the wolf, into the cavern beneath the castle ruins.

Once they'd entered the dark cavern, she'd fought back her fear of the looming shadows and blackened recesses. She'd tried to calm her panic and think of a way to reason with Kyle. She'd reminded him that he'd once been a man of God. A man who'd had a good heart. But that man had been devoured by the Book of Fennore, and her words couldn't reach him. His eyes had the hard flat glitter she'd seen in Cathán's, and his voice had warped until it no longer sounded like his own. Calmly he'd told her how he'd murdered Mickey in cold blood. And he'd enjoyed it.

The shell still resembled Kyle Mahon, but the man inside existed no more.

"Áedán won't come," Meaghan said again. "I'm telling you, he thinks I'm like the woman who betrayed him before. He thinks I will do the same."

"He'll come," Kyle said.

Meaghan clenched her eyes and prayed it would not be so, but a short time later, they heard movements at the rocky entrance into the cavern. And then he was there.

Áedán, so tall and strong. Áedán, with his green eyes and tender touch. She felt the blast of his emotions, hot and possessive, infuriated to have had her stolen from him. There was rage, but it didn't slice at her. He directed his fury at Kyle and only Kyle.

He'd brought a torch, and now he lit it and chased back the dark for her. He stepped into the shadowed cavern without a word, but in his quick glance, she saw his concern, his dread that he might have been too late.

"Let us begin," he said simply, moving forward like a man with a mission. He betrayed none of the fear she felt in his emotions.

"Begin?" Kyle said in a voice that echoed deeply. It wasn't his own, but a voice of ancient power. "You think to trick me, but I caution you to think again. I know the ritual."

"How do you know it?" Áedán asked, and though he tried, he could not hide his surprise.

Humor twisted the voice now. "My friend Kyle helped with that.

You see, he used to be a Keeper of the Book of Fennore. A scholar who studied all of the old ways."

Áedán knew that already, but Meaghan sensed his distress at having that strange voice speaking it, talking about Kyle in third person. It unraveled what little façade of calm she'd managed to maintain. If this entity inhabiting Kyle knew the ritual, how, then, would Áedán succeed in tricking it? For she had to believe that was his intention.

"Kyle knows the ritual and now, of course, so do I," the voice coming from Kyle went on.

Only the tick at the corner of Áedán's eye gave away his feelings, but Meaghan didn't need outward signs. She felt them.

"Good," Áedán said, calmly. "I won't have to explain things to you, then."

The response caught Kyle—or what had become of him—off guard. For the first time, his confidence slipped and he looked uneasy. "You intend to cooperate?"

"I do. I tire of humanity. For too long I existed without it. I find that humans sicken me now."

The disquiet on Kyle's face vanished, and he smiled coldly. "I do not believe you."

"I don't care."

Áedán strode to where Meaghan lay sprawled on the floor of the cavern and roughly hauled her up. Kyle hadn't expected this either, but he quickly recovered and moved to stop Áedán.

"What are you doing?" he demanded, grabbing Meaghan's other arm tightly.

"Start a fire," Áedán ordered.

And then he pulled from his pocket the pouch with the pendant inside. Meaghan felt its power surge around them. When Kyle hesitated, Áedán repeated the command, and his voice seemed louder, more commanding than the softly spoken words had been. It held that ancient echo she'd heard from the entity, and it frightened her.

A trace of doubt crept through her. What if Áedán was telling the truth? What if all of his protestations about becoming human again had been real? What if—

She cut her thoughts off. She would not doubt. Not now. Not ever.

Kyle took a jerky step back and then moved to the wood he'd already stacked. Silently he lit the fire.

"Where is the Book?" Áedán asked, gently settling Meaghan near the crackling warmth. In his emotions, she felt his frustration. His need for vengeance. His fear. But in his face, she saw only calm and calculation.

Again, Kyle hesitated, unsure of what to do.

"Cathán," Áedán said, addressing the power behind Kyle's glittering eyes. "Bring the Book."

With unstable movements, Kyle went to the back of the cavern and shifted a few large stones aside until he unearthed a canvas bundled around something large and bulky. He brought it to where Áedán waited, each step seeming to cost him a great deal. Meaghan had the sense that a battle raged behind those glittering eyes, and it gave her hope that maybe somewhere inside, Kyle still existed. Carefully he laid the massive bundle on the ground and then opened the canvas cover.

The Book of Fennore lay inside. Even if Meaghan had not seen it once before, she would have known exactly what it was. Kyle stumbled back as soon as he'd revealed it.

Primeval, the Book had weathered centuries, and looked it. Shaped irregularly—not square, not rectangle—its corners met at awkward angles, as if they'd been cut by hand without the help of a ruler or straight edge. It was as enormous as the Holy Bible that Father Lawlor kept on the pulpit at their little church, but there was nothing holy about this Book. The cover gleamed like oil. Shiny, black, and somehow sickly. Beveled in the surface were jewels that glittered sharp and bright, and a hundred—maybe a thousand—concentric spirals that had no beginning, no ending. The same spirals covered the ceiling, walls, and floors of this very cavern.

The Book began to drone in a discordant tone that raised all the fine hairs on her body. In the past few days, Meaghan had known fear that defied comprehension. But the sound the Book of Fennore made . . . it filled her with terror that surpassed all else. The malignant emotions inside it made her stomach churn. The high-pitched grinding sound went on, seeping beneath her skin until her bones rattled with the noise. The hollow cave gave it the perfect amphitheater, and the drone grew until even the crashing tide hammering against the cliffs outside and the thunderous storm wailing over Ballyfionúir waned.

Áedán shifted until he stood behind her and laid his gentle palm against her back, sending reassurance and strength through his touch. He was terrified, too, and yet he didn't give it away. Only Meaghan felt his fear.

"Cut her loose," he ordered.

When Kyle looked like he might argue, Áedán said it again, more quietly and yet with a power that compelled.

Without waiting to see that Kyle obeyed, Áedán moved to the Book of Fennore, and with utmost care, lifted it, keeping the canvas between his hands and the cover.

Kyle cut the bindings around her wrists but left her ankles tied. Áedán did not argue. She felt steely determination in him, tempered by the weight of his choices and something else that piqued her already rampant fear.

Regret. Mourning. Good-bye.

And in that instant, she knew what he planned to do.

"No," she whispered.

Áedán set the Book on a large, flat stone and began to speak. His voice flowed from some place deep within him, melodic, mesmerizing. He spoke in a language that sounded as ancient as the Book of Fennore, in words she didn't understand. But she didn't need to understand to feel the darkness behind them.

The ritual had begun and Meaghan felt the beginning of the end binding her as tightly as the straps that held her ankles secure.

"No," she tried to say again, but her throat had constricted, and she couldn't utter a sound.

Chapter Thirty-two

THE ancient words flowed like hot oil, searing Áedán's throat, burning his lips, incinerating the man he'd hoped—if only for a while—to be. Where she sat propped against the stones, he saw Meaghan's head fall back and her body go lax. Only her eyes moved as paralysis overtook her.

He closed his own eyes to the terror he saw there. Soon this would be finished for her, and if he didn't focus on the intricacies of what he did, her life would end before it even began. He had to be sure that the spell he wove around the Book of Fennore was tight. He had to be certain the beast that lived within it would die when Áedán returned to his prison.

The creature that Cathán had made of Kyle watched him with suspicion as he lifted his hands over the Book, and yet somewhere inside the man, he felt a piece of Kyle Mahon screaming for salvation. Slowly Áedán opened the pouch that held the pendant and dumped it into his palm. The twisted silver and gold felt hot to the touch, and it burned him, but he didn't let go. The symbols on his arms heated like coils of copper until he thought his skin might go up in flames. Still he held tight.

The cover of the Book of Fennore sprang open, eager. Greedy. *Ready.* It enjoyed his pain, relished his anguish. The pages began to fan with gleeful viciousness, and a foul odor rose from those pages, something that spoke of locked vats and decay, of murderous intentions and vile longings.

Shadow figures rose from the pages, memories that danced like wisps of smoke. He was aware of Meaghan watching them with terrified eyes, but he couldn't reassure her. He couldn't pull his attention from the task at hand. Kyle stood entranced as spiraling shapes wove around him, pulling him closer. The part of Áedán that had yearned to be human wanted to push the other man back, but sacrifices had to be made, and his only goal was to kill the beast and save Meaghan. Right now that beast controlled Kyle.

His chant rose as he cast his spell like a fisherman's net. The entity he and Elan had created rose like a writhing dragon. It waited, breathless. Within its eyes, Áedán saw Cathán. He saw evil. He saw utter darkness that stretched beyond eternity. The entity and Cathán were coiled so tightly that there was no way to distinguish where one ended and the other began. This was good, because it meant that he need only slay one monster. This was bad because their united force would be impossible to defeat.

Kyle said they knew the ritual, so Áedán had to be very careful. The steps were clear. Once the beast was roused, he must feed it blood, then use the pendant to enthrall it while speaking the words that would pledge his soul and free Cathán's. Like any deity, the entity wanted blood given in sacrifice.

Still streaming the words of power out into the sea of darkness and corruption that lurked between the Book's covers, Áedán took Meaghan's unresisting hand in his own. It looked so small and pale that it broke his heart. He pressed her palm to his lips, murmured, "I'm sorry," and then, "Good-bye," against the skin.

Meaghan pleaded with her eyes, but she couldn't move or speak, and Áedán couldn't stop the wheel he'd started spinning. Pulling his knife from its sheath, he slashed a line across her palm and turned her hand so that her blood would spill into the open Book. Then he took the knife to his own hand and let his blood join with hers.

A sound rose from the fanning pages, a keening that made his brain hot and his skin cold. He wanted to jerk back. He wanted to flee.

Instead he held tight to Meaghan's bleeding hand, placed the pendant in the scarlet pool in her palm, and then sealed it with his own open wound. The dragon beast made a sound of sheer pleasure. Sexual and perverted, it echoed through the cavern. Meaghan made a sound as well, one of violation and rage. The feeling of desecration found root inside Áedán, as well, and slammed home the memory of what it was to be part of the Book. He'd told Meaghan he was a prisoner, a hostage. Now total recall of the twisted and sadistic relationship burst forth, reminding him of its dominance, of how it had made him submit to its will.

It demanded submission now, but Áedán forced himself not to weaken. He spoke his words, compelling the dragon to fixate on the pendant soaking in their spilled blood. He watched the viscous red leak from between their fingers and slide down their arms.

Something within him seemed to rise up, and he knew it was his soul—his essence. Kyle's empty shell collapsed and Áedán felt his own knees wavering as his spirit joined the other shadow figures hovering over the Book of Fennore. He sensed his body still standing, hand clasped tight to Meaghan's, but the center that made Áedán who he was had been cored.

The force of the beast sucked him in like a great tornado and spun him around, slamming his consciousness against Cathán's. He felt the life draining from his body, his will to live as a human being evaporating like condensation in a hot wind.

His voice was no longer his own. The beast had taken control, and now it chanted a different spell—one of its own making. The very spell that Áedán had heard on that fated night millennia ago when he'd been sucked into the world of Fennore like krill into the whale's gaping mouth. He tried to reach out with what remained of himself, pulling at the emotions that would have no home within his prison.

As if sensing the rush of feeling he grappled with, Meaghan's eyes blinked open, and then she looked at him. Not at the body he'd left behind, but at the spirit he'd become. He forced the love he felt for her to travel the short distance that separated them. Urged her to follow the trail, to *feel* what he needed her to do.

She blinked again and then focused on something beyond him. From the corner of his eye, he saw a blinding light and then a pulsing glow.

Elan. Elan, moving closer. He felt the instant that Cathán and the beast saw her, too. A howl rose from one, a whimper from the other. It seemed they knew more than Áedán about her purpose, because for the first time, he felt fear in them both.

She bent and picked up the knife Áedán had dropped. Holding her arm out, she drew the blade over her wrist, opening the veins that held her lifeblood.

"No," he shouted, but he had no voice of his own.

She held her wrist over their still-clasped hands and let her sacrifice cover them in a hot spill. Though his connection to his body had been severed, Áedán felt it and it grounded him, drew him closer to the corporeal existence that had once been his.

Her light began to dim in moments, but Áedán felt stronger with each fading pulse. Meaghan sat straighter and then she rolled to her knees. Elan pried open their two hands and plucked the pendant from Áedán's paralyzed fingers. Their blood dripped from the dangling amulet. Elan placed the pendant around Meaghan's neck and settled it against her bare skin.

As soon as the pendant made contact, Meaghan gasped, and Áedán felt its power shooting through him like a flaming lance.

Elan moved to Áedán's side, her light nearly extinguished as the blood poured from her open wound. It looked brilliant against the paleness of her skin and the white of her robe.

"I free you," she said, and she flattened her palm on the spread pages of the Book of Fennore, smearing it with her blood and pouring her last bit of light into the depths of darkness. "I make myself your sacrifice."

As if ripped, the ties around Meaghan's ankles fell away and Meaghan stumbled to her feet, gaze fixed on the extinguished glow of the White Fennore.

The pages of the Book fanned violently, Elan's substance so depleted that they moved through her hand and wrist as if they didn't exist. Meaghan stepped past her and pulled Áedán's inert body into her arms. She pressed her mouth to his unfeeling lips, murmuring words that he couldn't hear, couldn't understand. But he felt them, a hot vibration against the ice of his skin. A sleek memory in the turmoil of his thoughts.

And then, she gave him her breath.

The sweet purity of it filled his collapsed lungs and traveled through his sluggish bloodstream. Emotions infused the gift, hot and electric, rich and nourishing. He felt love and compassion, forgiveness and hope, joy and goodwill. Twisting through them was loss and grief, but even those had a sweetness that blossomed in his chest. The feelings mixed with the darkness, becoming every color ever conceived. In light, white is the presence of all colors. Inside Áedán, it was the same.

The brightness exploded, chasing back the shadows, incinerating each tendril of gloom. The beast within the Book howled and fought to keep Áedán captive as the light and Meaghan's love wrenched him free.

Chapter Thirty-three

WITHIN the writhing vapors above the Book of Fennore, Meaghan found Áedán—not in flesh but in soul. She saw the clear brilliance of his essence, the muddied chaos of his emotions. Surrounding him were other shapes, sliding in and out of focus. A creature that took the shape of every nightmare monster she'd ever dreamed. Dragon, devil, *beast.* And linked by chains as thick as her arm was Cathán with his hard blue eyes. Pain and terror contorted his striking features as he fought a battle she couldn't see.

On one side of her stood Áedán's corporeal form, on the other, the barely flickering light that was the White Fennore. Meaghan made the link between them, connected to one by touch and the other by some indefinable bond. The pendant burned against Meaghan's skin, but she felt it fortifying her. She could sense how thin Áedán was stretched between the Book and the world that was real.

She stared into his eyes, willing the man behind them to return, to blink, to react. The deep forest within them shifted and shivered with the effort, but Áedán didn't return. She felt danger all around her, threatening to spill out and take him over. She was afraid—only a fool wouldn't be. But Meaghan would not retreat. She took his face between her palms and let him see that she would love him no matter what.

"I feel what's in your heart," she said. "And it's good."

She stretched up until her lips met his, breathed into his mouth the words that filled her own heart. "I love you, Áedán. Trust me. Trust *yourself*."

And at last his arms went around her, convulsed until he had her in a grip that was painful, but she didn't complain. He buried his face in the crook between her neck and shoulder, and she felt him breathing her in, anchoring himself in her scent and feel. Her arms circled him, her fingers plunging into the silk of his hair as she held him, murmured senseless words, let him unravel the gnarled braid of his turmoil. He was not a man who trusted. She'd known that from the start, and yet she felt him trying, felt him reaching through his matted issues and trying.

She'd won a small battle. She'd restored a part of him. But she could still see the swirling essence that made up his heart and soul trapped in the mists of the Book. She would not stop fighting until she held all of him again.

The horrible sound of the Book had receded, but she was not so foolish as to believe it had gone away.

Moving with instinct that had no reason other than its burning pressure, she placed her sliced hand against Áedán's once more, feeling the heat of their blood mixing together, feeling a surge of energy coil in the tight hollow where their palms met.

Áedán's voice rose again, speaking that strange tongue that she couldn't understand, and yet she knew that he cast a spell upon the beast and upon Cathán, who writhed in agony in the vapors. She felt Cathán reaching out to her, his voice more powerful than Áedán's, his will so irresistible that it coaxed her to release this man who she loved and join him instead.

It tempted. It lured.

Áedán's fingers tightened around hers, and she felt his spell taking hold. The drops of their blood binding them to the Book, binding the Book to the spell. Trusting Áedán to keep her safe, Meaghan did what she'd been afraid to do for her entire life. She opened herself, spread her thoughts and senses to the wind, and let them guide her.

The feeling that hit her was like a million volts of electricity. The beast within the Book roared with power. Even as she took up her weapons and faced it, she felt it seducing her, offering her everything she ever wanted, all of the power in the heavens and earth. She would be a goddess if she joined it. And in that promise were images, bright and crisp. There was her family and everyone she loved with her, living a blessed life filled with every advantage possible.

It was the stuff of dreams, of fantasies. But what the clever beast inside the Book of Fennore had not taken into account was that Meaghan, unlike Elan, had no doubts about Áedán. She knew that his word was the truth, and she would stay the course.

She fought back her panic and stepped forward, mentally entering the churning world of the Book, feeling the decrepit touch of the beast, the hungry grope of the thing that had once been Cathán and then, trapped in the center of the malaise, was Áedán's soul. In the real world, she held his hand in hers. In this world, she took him in her arms, lifting him with strength that came from within. She would seal the Book, but she would not leave Áedán behind.

The beast screamed in rage, cringing back from the light she shed in the darkness. Still Áedán's voice went on, and she could feel the tendrils of the spell hardening, tightening, *working*. At last Meaghan pulled Áedán free. As his soul slipped back into his being, Áedán's voice grew stronger, louder. Their blood pooled over the pages of the Book, and the symbols dissolved beneath the onslaught. Áedán spoke three sharp sounds, and the Book slammed shut. He released her clasped hand and turned their opened palms to the beveled cover, smeared it with blood, over the sides, into the creases of the pages. Every place it touched, it clung and thickened. Meaghan yanked the pendant from around her neck, pressed it to the lock and twisted it. The click came like an explosion, and the bloody Book went quiet.

Áedán blinked his eyes, gasped, and stared at her in stunned disbelief.

"I knew you could do it," Meaghan breathed into the sudden silence.

Áedán's expression held no joy, though. His eyes desperate, he shook his head. "No," he said. "What we did, what happened today, it will change everything. It will change *you*. I thought I could fix it, but I failed." He fell to his knees. "I failed."

At first she didn't understand—not his words, not the tears in his eyes. He tried to lower his face, to hide them from her, but they'd come too far for that. One spilled over his lashes. Meaghan knelt beside him and pressed her lips to the salty trail it left on his cheek.

But in the emotions that he felt, Meaghan saw the clear picture. In the past that stretched behind them and wrapped into a future yet to be realized, they'd changed too many critical elements. Cathán's birth would no longer be shaded by Brion's suspicion that another man had fathered him. He would not grow up in a loveless household. He would not turn to the Book of Fennore to fill the gaping lack in his life. He wouldn't vanish from this very cavern, leaving Meaghan's mother free to marry Niall Ballagh.

From this point on, the Book of Fennore would be sealed, the power within it forever snuffed.

Panic threatened to overwhelm her. Had they changed things so drastically that she would not be conceived? Would Meaghan, like Elan, merely fade into nothing?

As if in answer, Meaghan sensed a glow coming toward her. It spread outward and a voice began to speak—not the dark and insidious tones of the Book of Fennore, but a sweet melody that she knew came from the spirit, from Elan. She no longer keened for all she lost. She wove a song of tomorrow and brought the notes as a guide to lead Meaghan now.

Ask for what you want. . . .

Meaghan had to believe that nothing they'd changed would impact the future that was meant to be. Her brother traveling into the past hadn't altered the circumstances of his birth. He was meant to be part of their family just as he was meant to be Ruairi of Fennore. He'd been able to be *both*.

Ask for what you want. . . .

Meaghan closed her eyes, and she put her trust in the woman who'd sacrificed herself to right a wrong as ancient as the Book of Fennore. Meaghan asked for what she wanted.

She wanted what was meant to be, to be.

Chapter Thirty-four

MEAGHAN opened her eyes in a room she did not recognize. She blinked, looking around with confusion. It was a large room with pale, sunny walls and bright white curtains. A fresh breeze redolent of sea and salt wafted through their gauzy lace, and a rising sun shot speckled patterns on the walls.

She was alone.

Memory hit her at once, a solid wall that flattened her as she slammed into it. The cavern . . . the Book . . . Áedán.

Where was Áedán?

She sat up suddenly, light-headed and anguished. She had failed. She hadn't asked for the right thing—or she hadn't asked in the right way. If she had, Áedán would be here. *He was meant to be with her.*

Her heart felt heavy as she moved from beneath the covers. She wore a shimmery camisole of emerald green with matching lace-trimmed pants. A satin robe lay on the end of the bed. She grabbed it and shrugged it on before stepping out into the hall.

It took a moment for her to recognize where she was.

The castle . . .

Her sister's husband had rebuilt it from the ground up with all the modern amenities available. Meaghan lived there with her mother, father, Danni, Sean, and their children. She'd slept here just a few nights ago, before she'd gone in search of her brother and been lost in the world of Fennore, before traveling through time. It was all the same . . . and yet it was all *different*.

The runner in the hall was no longer red—now it was a deep, velvet blue. The chandelier hanging in the stairwell hadn't been there the last time she'd walked this way and new tapestries hung on the walls.

She hurried through the hall, tilting her head back to view the mosaic on the ceiling as she went down the stairs. The last time she'd looked, it had been a pattern of tiles that mimicked the spirals on the cover and pages of the Book of Fennore.

Now . . . She froze, standing against the balustrade and staring in shock.

The mosaic stretching across the domed ceiling showed an epic scene of Ruairi of Fennore with the most beautiful woman Meaghan had ever seen. One hand rested on the curve of her waist. His eyes laughed as he clasped his forearm to the forearm of another man—someone Meaghan recognized from the world of Fennore. Tiarnan. And beside him stood the woman who'd been with him and the others she'd seen when they'd been trapped. Liam—his younger brother. And the little girl with her distant eyes . . .

Unsteady, Meaghan moved down the last few steps and entered the familiar great room. Once again she had that sense of things being the same and yet totally different. The furniture, the knick-knacks, the lamps . . . She stood staring, taking it all in while goose bumps rose on her flesh.

She heard footsteps and turned to see her sister, Danni, enter the room.

They stared at one another in silence, and Meaghan had the feeling that Danni knew what she was thinking, but Meaghan couldn't decipher the emotions she felt in the air between them. Danni smiled at her, though, and nodded to something behind Meaghan.

"Someone's been waiting for you to wake up," she said.

Spinning around, Meaghan found Áedán standing behind her. Tall and sculpted, strong and gentle. His eyes darkened with every color of the forest. His lips quirked in a small smile.

"How are you feeling, beauty?" he asked as if nothing were out of the ordinary.

Meaghan found she couldn't speak. Mutely she stared at the man she'd come to love, the man she'd feared she'd lost forever.

"You hit your head pretty hard," Danni said. "We found you passed out in the cavern."

Surprised, Meaghan turned her gaze back to her sister.

"Well, Áedán found you."

Feeling as if an earthquake had somehow shaken reality and then settled it in this new shape, she asked, "How do you know Áedán?"

Danni smiled. "Oh, I've seen him around." Her eyes sparkled knowingly. Meaghan wondered just what her sister knew, but before she could ask, Danni went on, "You two have a lot to talk about, I think. I'm off to find Sean and see what he's up to. Can't turn my back on that man. Who knows what he'll want to restore next."

And with that, Danni left Meaghan alone with the man she loved. His gaze traveled over her, taking in her rumpled hair and the emerald silk of her attire with interest.

"How did we get here?" she asked.

"A miracle. A leap of faith. Magic. Take your pick."

"And the Book . . . Did we do it? Did we seal it?"

Áedán nodded and shrugged at the same time. "We did, and yet . . . We wouldn't be here if it had stayed sealed. I think Elan must have seen that, and she . . . *changed* the outcome. I don't know what the Book of Fennore has become, but I sense it's still out there, somewhere . . . and yet I no longer feel the threat of it."

"Could she have destroyed the evil but not the Book?"

He lifted his arms and showed her the stretch of skin above his wrist. The symbols that had burned into his flesh were gone. "I don't know what she did. I only know that I am free of it. That *we* are free of it. Elan released us."

Elan. Meaghan could still hear her voice telling her to ask for what she wanted. Meaghan's answer had been to make what was meant to be, *be*. Meaghan could only hope that Elan had found a way to do that without unleashing the Book's monster.

"I'm so confused. I don't understand what we did, Áedán. I don't understand *how* we did it."

"Elan said she made herself my sacrifice," Áedán said. "The Book required one, and I meant it to be me."

"But she took your place," Meaghan murmured, gratitude swelling inside her. "I felt her emotions as her light faded. So much sorrow. So much regret. She wanted to right all the wrongs."

Silent, Áedán nodded.

"What about Cathán?" Meaghan went on. "And Kyle? I hope she found a way to save Kyle."

"Do you remember what you asked for in the end?" Áedán said.

Slowly, Meaghan nodded. "Yes. But when I woke up alone, I was so afraid I'd asked for the wrong thing."

"No, beauty, you asked for exactly the right thing. And Elan, in her final act, delivered it. When I opened my eyes and saw you beside me so still, I thought I'd lost you. I got you out of that cavern as fast as I could. That's when your sister, Danni, found me. She said she'd been waiting."

Not surprising. Her sister had inherited Colleen's uncanny ability to look into the future.

"She brought me here and when I saw the mosaic of Ruairi . . ." He paused, seeming to choose his words with extreme care. "I asked your sister about Cathán. She told me he'd disappeared over twenty years ago from the cavern beneath the ruins."

"Because he found the Book of Fennore?" Meaghan breathed.

"She wouldn't say. She only smiled—somewhat enigmatically, if you ask me—and told me that there were rumors to that effect, but who really knew? She said he'd always been a troubled man, something to do with a scandal over his birth that never quite died down."

Meaghan thought of Brion's first wife and the twisted plan she'd had to steal Colleen's baby. The people of Ballyfionúir would have been talking about it for years to come. Had it been their gossip that had warped Cathán into a desperate man?

She recalled those last moments when she'd realized that they had changed the past so much that she might never be born. A future that included Meaghan had no room for Cathán MacGrath. Had Elan seen that and corrected the disaster Meaghan had brought onto herself?

The Book of Fennore had been entwined in the lives of her family members for so long that Elan could not simply amputate it like an infected limb. Evidently she'd been forced to make allowances in order to grant Meaghan's wish that she make whatever should be, *be* . . .

Meaghan gazed at the mosaic on the ceiling above her, seeing her brother's sparkling blue eyes and the love that shone from them for the beautiful woman beside him. Without the Book of Fennore, he wouldn't have traveled through time to find her.

Just then, Colleen Ballagh entered the room with a smile. Aged and wrinkled, she still managed to look regal and lovely. She wore blue polyester pants and an American brand of runners with bright symbols on the side. She looked around her at the home Danni's husband had made of the castle that had once stood in ruins. The Book of Fennore had brought disaster, but it had also brought them together in ways Meaghan knew she'd never fully understand.

And it had brought *her* Áedán.

Meaghan stared in joyous surprise. Alive, not buried in the family cemetery as her grandmother had been when Meaghan went to the cavern that fateful day that she'd traveled into their past.

"Welcome back, granddaughter. It's good to see you up and about."

An instant later, Brion MacGrath came through the outer door, older than the last time she'd seen him—as gray and as handsome as

Anthony Hopkins. He'd aged with grace and he looked at Colleen like she'd hung the moon. If Cathán had still grown into a man bitter enough to seek the Book of Fennore, Meaghan knew this couple had not had an easy or idyllic life, but the love that they'd felt for one another had endured, and she didn't need to be empathic to feel it cementing them together even now.

"Niall and I are going to take the young ones out for some fishing," he said happily. As he passed her by, he gave Meaghan a hug. "Good to see you up, sweetheart. It would be better if you'd put on a bit more clothes before you make young Áedán here swoon. Colleen, could I talk you into a few sandwiches for the road . . . ?"

Meaghan watched their departing backs without saying a word. When the house fell silent again, Meaghan turned back to Áedán.

"I can hardly believe any of this," she said.

Áedán's eyes were very serious as he pulled her into his embrace. "I almost lost you, Meaghan, and I realized then that I would rather die than live without you. You've given me more reason to live than anything or anyone I've ever known. You've given me back my humanity and my heart, and even when it aches, I am grateful to have it."

Meaghan had tears in her eyes as she held him tight against her. "I love you, Áedán, and I can't believe I am here with you. You are the future I always wanted but never thought I'd have."

The look he gave her was hot and possessive, filled with emotions that swirled around her and filled her heart.

"I love you, Meaghan Ballagh. I want to tell you that every morning and every night for the rest of our lives." He kissed her then, letting her feel the truth in his words. "I want to do that very human thing with you."

She gave him a wide-eyed look. "You want to have sex?"

"Well, that, too. But it's marriage I'm speaking of. I want the world to know you're mine." He paused, looking suddenly unsure, an expression she never thought she'd see on this arrogant man's face. "If you'll have me, that is."

Meaghan laughed. "I'm thinking . . . yes." And then she tightened her arms around him and held on. "Definitely, yes. I thought I'd lost you, too, Áedán, and I don't ever want to feel so wretched again."

"Ach," he said. "It'll take a wee bit more than that to shake the likes of me. I'm practically a god, you know."

"Or a very good human."

"Aye, I'd rather be that. You saved me. When I thought there was nothing good in me to be saved, you found me and you brought me home."

"I plan to keep you."

"Forever, I hope."

"Or longer."

"Ah, now doesn't that sound like a slice of heaven. I love you, Meaghan. So much that forever doesn't sound like half long enough. But I'm hoping it will give me plenty of time to get a look at those underthings you've got on beneath all that silk. You do have such interesting trimmings. . . ."